Yi Ch'ŏngjun

Your Paradise

Translated by Jennifer M. Lee
and Timothy R. Tangherlini

MASTERWORKS OF FICTION 1976

GREEN INTEGER
KØBENHAVN & LOS ANGELES
2004

GREEN INTEGER
Edited by Per Bregne
København / Los Angeles

Distributed in the United States and Canada by Consortium Book
Sales and Distribution, 1045 Westgate Drive, Suite 90
Saint Paul, Minnesota 55114-1065
Distributed in the United Kingdom and throughout Europe
by Turnaround Publisher Services
Unit 3, Olympia Trading Estate, Coburg Road
London N22 6TZ United Kingdom
020 8829 3000

(323) 857-1115 / www.greeninteger.com

First Green Integer edition 2004

This book was first published in The Republic of Korea
Published by agreement with Yi Ch'ŏngjun
Publication of this book was supported by a matching
grant from The Daesan Foundation (Korea)
for which the publisher and translators wish to express their thanks.

Design: Per Bregne
Typography: Kim Silva
Photograph of Yi Ch'ŏngjun

LIBRARY OF CONGRESS CATALOGING IN PUBLICATION DATA
Yi Ch'ŏngjun
Your Paradise
ISBN: 1-931243-69-7
p. cm - Green Integer: 118
I. Title II. Series III. Translators

Green Integer books are published for Douglas Messerli.
Printed in the United States of America on acid-free paper.

THE ISLAND OF THE DEAD

1

The night the new director came, two people escaped from the island. The escape wasn't really a coincidence. It was sort of a welcoming present for this new director. So he didn't hold his inaugural address but instead began to investigate the particulars of the incident.

The newly appointed director arrived at the hospital. After the earlier coup d'état, the hospital had been run without a director for a while. Kim Chŏngil, the chief of medical services, had been acting director for nearly two months. One August evening, after the hot muggy weather had been cooled by the fresh ocean breezes, a military officer on active duty suddenly arrived at the island hospital as its newly appointed director.

Colonel Cho Paeghŏn.

His complexion was quite dark but not from the sun. Rather, it looked as if he had been like that from the very beginning. His green military uniform suited both his tall physique and his exceptionally dark skin. From the moment he set foot on the island that evening along with his aide, one could clearly see that he was different from all of his predecessors.

"Who are all these people? Why did you bring the car?" he asked the hospital staff members waiting on the pier and, looking at the car, shook his head with displeasure. Ignoring both the car and the hospital staff members' welcoming greetings and guided by the chief of medical services, he walked briskly up to the hospital. His purposeful stride was as curt and abrupt as his speech which, on occasion, was tinged with P'yŏngan dialect. The first impression he made was formidable.

The new director spent a night at the hospital's official residence and came to work the following morning. But he didn't hold his inaugural speech. Of course, the reason for this was the escape the night before. According to standard hospital procedure, the incident had nothing to do with the new director whatsoever and so he shouldn't have concerned himself with it. Indeed, there was no reason for him to feel either responsible for the incident or to try to resolve it since it had happened before he had held his inaugural address and thereby officially taken over his new position. Either the chief of medical services or the manager could have taken care of the appropriate paperwork; briefing the director on the report afterwards would then have been sufficient.

But Director Cho was different. Perhaps it was a mistake on the part of the staff to have reported the incident to him even before his speech. But it was inevitable that it would turn out this way. The day before his arrival, the incident had been reported to the main hospital office by the police (the old patrol in charge of keeping the peace in the buffer zone). Yi Sanguk, head of the Hygiene Division, had received the report from the patrol office in Sinsaeng village. Two single male patients from Sinsaeng village had escaped during the night and had crossed the sea. It wasn't an unusual occurrence.

The chief of medical services and the other staff

members who came to the hospital later suggested that they postpone reporting the incident to the director until after he had held his inaugural address.

"Let's take care of this incident first and then report it to the director."

Sanguk disagreed however. In the past, the patients had without fail welcomed the new director with an escape. It wasn't something that could be hushed up. But more than anything else, Sanguk wanted to see how the director would react to this "welcoming present."

"There's no reason to cover it up," Sanguk said.

"I didn't say we should cover it up," said the chief of medical services, "but since we need to gather the patients for the inaugural speech and so forth, I thought that after that...."

"Let him see things the way they are."

"I know this matter is under your jurisdiction, but I say we should think about it carefully." The chief of medical services—a short, extremely fastidious man and a specialist in dermatology—disliked any kind of trouble. During the several months when there had been no director and he had been the acting director, he had been more enthusiastic than anyone about treating the patients and furthering the hospital's welfare work, but he couldn't stand any kind of trouble or conflict.

Sanguk remained silent and waited for the arrival of the director. Along with the two hundred or so staff members at the main hospital, he sat waiting in the conference room. He had no intention of taking the chief of medical services' advice.

At around ten to eight the director finally entered the office guided by the head of personnel. Actually, it looked as if the pudgy head of personnel was running to keep up with him. The new director came up the stairs to the second floor taking long strides. In the mean time, the chief of medical services along with several members of the executive staff had gone to the private meeting room adjacent to the new director's office in order to greet him on this, his first day at work.

"Did anything happen last night?"

The director's first words pleased Sanguk immensely.

As a first greeting to his staff, these ordinary words sounded absurd. Even though the director's military uniform was crisply ironed for his first day on the job and he was wearing a gun strapped to his belt, his greeting was as banal as if he had known the hospital staff for a long time. His surprisingly flat and apparently impatient first words flustered the people who had been waiting for him in the meeting room.

In this moment of confusion, the chief of medical services looked over at Sanguk. Sanguk, however, didn't care about his attempt at eye contact.

"I have something to report..."

Sanguk's words made the director, who had already turned his back to his staff so he could enter his office, stop.

"I've summoned the staff of the main hospital to the conference room."

When the director turned around, the chief of medical services quickly interrupted Sanguk, stepping in front of him. The director didn't pay much attention to him, but turned instead to Sanguk.

"What is it that you want to report?"

He must have sensed the urgency in Sanguk's look. As if pressing Sanguk to speak, the director stood in front of him, staring at him.

Suddenly, Sanguk felt his heart sink. Everyone

in the room turned his eyes to him. But Sanguk had an odd trait. For as long as he could remember, going all the way back to childhood, he hated being stared at. In fact he feared it. When confronted by someone's gaze, even before he knew it, his heart would sink. Once he became aware of those eyes, he would be troubled for days by hallucinations so distressing that he could not bear them. Even when he was alone in a room, he couldn't shake off the feeling of a distant eye staring fixedly and breathlessly at a point somewhere on his back.

He broke out in a cold sweat, but there was nothing he could do at this point.

"Tell me now. There's no point in reporting it separately." The director pressured him once again.

"There was an escape last night."

"What?"

Even before Sanguk had finished speaking, the director had raised both his eyebrows.

"An escape? Someone has escaped from this island?"

"Yes, apparently. It happens occasionally...."

The chief of medical services interrupted again, stopping Sanguk with a sharp glance, as if to say "I told you so." But again the director didn't seem pleased with the chief doctor's response.

"What do you mean by 'yes, apparently?' Either they escaped or not. So, where on earth did it happen? Where did they escape from?"

"From Sinsaeng village."

"I'm not asking what village. I'm asking which route they took and how they escaped."

"Ah! There's a little projection on the shore behind Sinsaeng village—they call it Tolburi, and it's often used as a point of escape."

"Let's go there and see."

"Do you mean now?"

"You have a habit of making people repeat themselves, don't you?"

"But the hospital staff is waiting to greet you in the conference hall."

"It's not important. I'll see them after I come back."

"You also need to gather the patients together today."

"That's not important. I'll see them when I want to and I'll let you know, so you don't need to worry about that either."

"But..."

Without realizing it, the chief of medical services was standing at attention. The other staff members in the office were also frozen in immobile postures as if they were following the chief doctor's lead. The director had not yet entered his office. Not wanting to look at the staff members who were now standing at attention, the director turned around but then, as if he remembered something, he turned his head and picked out Sanguk.

"It seems that the chief of medical services doesn't approve of what I'm doing so why don't you be my guide?"

The director, using the escape as an excuse, spent the first day at the hospital avoiding his inaugural address. That was unusual.

2

For whatever reason, it was quite unusual at the island hospital for a new director not to hold his inaugural address on his very first day. Every time a new director came, there was always hope. So when this new director didn't hold his inaugural speech they thought that he might be the first one who didn't have the cherished bronze statue in mind.

A new director would always give two inaugural speeches. The first one would be delivered in the early morning to the two hundred or so staff members at the main hospital with proclamations of new plans and proposals for a better hospital and improved personnel management. These decrees would be followed by a severe criticism of the staff's indolence and their "peace at any price principle" (it was not clear how the new directors came to such conclusions on their first day). The new director would then always make an impassioned speech about his innovative new policies for hospital management and would emphasize again and again his commitment, his devotion and his philanthropic mindset.

This was the usual speech to the staff. But the real speech was the second one, the one that took place in the presence of the patients. Every time a new director came, five thousand patients from seven villages, excluding those who were unable to walk, gathered at the park plaza in the patients' area in Chungang village, across the one hundred and fifty meter buffer zone that separated them from where the staff lived. Usually, after an introduction and a preliminary conference with the staff in the personnel area, the new director would go by car down to the park plaza in Chungang village and meet the patients. Of course, the new director would again declare his ambitious plans for improved hospital management and would promise to promote the building of new facilities to secure the interest of the patients. He would also promise to protect the rights and interests of the patients and the villagers living in the buffer zone and would commit himself to working toward achieving those plans. During the forty years or so since the founding of the hospital, approximately ten directors had done this. Therefore, it was natural to expect that this director would do so as well; this was simply customary practice.

However, this director seemed to have no interest in holding his inaugural address.

"Perhaps this one doesn't have a statue in mind," Sanguk thought to himself as he followed along behind the director as if were being dragged. In any case, the director was impatient. He also showed an extraordinary amount of engagement.

The director's car was ready, waiting in front of the hospital entrance.

Before getting in the car, he turned to the chief of medical services who had followed him to the front entrance and said, "While we're gone, make sure to finish the hospital operation's report." Sanguk followed the director and got into the car. Since the director had already taken the front seat next to the driver, Sanguk, who was supposed to be his guide, ended up sitting in back.

"Have a good tour. Manager Yi, I'd like you to explain things thoroughly."

The chief of medical services bowed politely and glanced over at Sanguk as if he was worried about something. Again, the director didn't pay much attention to him.

"Let's go," the director urged the driver and then, reminded of the escapees, he fell into a foul mood and started to curse them.

"Damn it! What kind of a sonofabitch would run away without even getting a look at my face!" Because he was mad and swearing, his speech was tinged with his harsh dialect. As the car came down a small hill and entered the buffer zone between the personnel zone and the patients' zone, the director, as if suddenly remembering the presence of Sanguk, turned around and asked, "You, what are you in this hospital? What's your position?"

"Me sir? I'm Yi Sanguk, in charge of the Hygiene Division." After the director asked the question, he turned toward the front again and Sanguk replied to his back rather curtly. Then the director asked another question. "Hygiene Division? What do you do in that division?" Unlike the previous directors who pretended to know everything about the hospital—especially in the beginning—this director asked questions without any reservations.

"It's a part of the Medical Services Division. Mainly we're in charge of the patients' bacteriological examinations and their recuperation training. However, we're also in charge of handling the corpses and cremation as well."

"Compared to others you must know quite a lot about the patients' situations. Today I expect you to fill in all the gaps for me."

"I'll explain whatever I can."

The car entered Changan village, passing through the buffer zone, and then traveled along the barbed wire fence that surrounded the area. On the right side, the director could see the refreshing deep blue sea. The road that stretched out along the shore was thick with bright earth-toned pine trees. Only a few sailboats crossing Tŏknyang bay dotted the clear blue sea that was so still it looked like a lake. The archipelago was known for its beautiful scenery, but the views on this island both summer and winter were incomparable.

"Beautiful…the scenery is wonderful."

Like others, the director seemed enchanted by the island's beautiful landscape. He was absorbed in looking out the car window, watching the scenery pass by. It seemed that the foul mood brought on by the escape had subsided. A little later, he turned around again and asked Sanguk,

"How big is this island?"

"I believe it's a little more than twelve hundred acres. One third of it is the official residence, and the rest of the island is divided into the seven villages for the patients. We're passing through Changan village right now. According to them, they call the personnel area the island's Seoul and I've heard that this village is called Changan because it's the one closest to this Seoul."

Was it due to the beautiful landscape? Sanguk also felt the oppressive tension he'd experienced in the office ease little by little. As the director lost himself more and more in the landscape of the island, Sanguk started to feel a greater and greater generosity toward him. Even though the director didn't ask, Sanguk started to give detailed explanations.

"The whole island looks like a huge park," the director murmured as if he were talking to himself, not showing much interest in how the name of the village came to be. For the first time, Sanguk realized that the director was sinking into an immense misconception of the island. However, he had no intention of exposing this delusion just yet. He understood that as a new director, this false impression was perhaps legitimate.

"Before long, he'll come to the realization that he's been operating under an illusion," Sanguk thought to himself.

"As you know, the name of the island means 'little deer.' They say it was named 'Sorok Island' not so much because it's shaped like a deer, but because of the beautiful scenery. But speaking of parks, there really is a park. The next village is called Chungang village. When we stop by later you'll see. But the park there was made for all of the patients on this island and..."

The director remained quiet and sank deep into his own thoughts.

After entering Changan village, the car would pass a patient on the street from time to time. Most of the women wore white *ch'imajŏgori* while the men wore pants and summer shirts. They didn't look any different from people off the island. An old woman with tired legs carrying a basket on her head coming back from market, a young woman scurrying home from the fields to nurse her baby, a young man with a straw hat who had just woken up from a nap walking lazily to the fields. These were people one could see anywhere, the old woman, the young woman, the young man. Women worked peacefully in the furrows of the radish fields, squatting with folded towels on their heads to block out the late summer sun. The only difference was that, on closer inspection, almost all of them were wearing sunglasses. At one point, a middle-aged man came by on a bicycle. When he got closer, they could see that he was biking along skillfully with only one leg. He biked by whistling as he adroitly dodged the director's car. It should have been an unusual sight for a newcomer, but the director didn't seem to be impressed.

"Beside last night's escape, have you had many others?" The director asked the question suddenly, his eyes fixed on the scenery outside the window. His tone of voice indicated that he simply couldn't understand why people would want to escape from this place. Yet another illusion. At last, a faint smile appeared on Sanguk's lips.

A long time ago, a beautiful woman artist had visited the island. She came to the island and met a poor girl. The girl's mother had been infected and had come to the island, forgetting all about the outside world. However, the girl couldn't forget her mother. Later she became a nurse and came to the island so that she could live near her mother and she stayed on the island for a very long time to be with her. The artist left the island soon after she had met the girl. However, she couldn't forget her and, over the next twenty years, she thought of her from time to time. Then, one summer after those twenty years had passed, the artist began to paint the girl's face. She painted countless faces of the girl. Sometimes she painted her with a flower crown in her hair and other times she painted her with a shining veil as if she were a bride getting ready for her wedding. She painted her in profile and she painted her from the front. Most of the paintings were infused with a soft orange glow or pervaded with the light violet of wisteria. In every painting, the girl had beautiful lips, like two flower petals coming together, but those lips didn't utter a word. The girl's story was told through her eyes. Her eyes told many stories of the island. They were sad but beautiful stories. When the artist's private exhibit opened, many people said that they read the beautiful island stories in the girl's eyes. And they said that they began to love the girl and the island. The beautiful girl! The lovely girl! And the girl's island! To them the island was beautiful like a dream. And to them, this was the girl's island.

"Well, I can't say that it happens too often, but it

does happen once in a while," Sanguk answered ambiguously.

"It happens once in a while..." The director cocked his head.

"Especially when a new director comes..."

"Why do they choose to escape when a new director comes of all times?"

"It could be mere coincidence. But I don't remember a single time when there wasn't an escape when a new director came."

"Is there any special reason?"

"Well, there isn't any particular reason, but...."

"But what?"

"Well, if a coincidence happens time and again, you can't really call it a coincidence, I don't think. I'm sorry to say this, but you should think of this as your welcoming present and let it pass..."

"Welcoming present...? I don't really like it as a welcoming present. How am I supposed to take this?"

"Well..."

"Tell me. If there's a hidden meaning to this welcoming present, don't you think I should know exactly what it is?"

"I'm not confident enough to tell you." Sanguk tried to get out of the situation. As if a thought had suddenly occurred to him, the director said,

"Not confident...You're sounding very lofty. So you mean to say you couldn't tell me even if you did know? Is that what you're trying to say?"

After he reproached Sanguk for a little while, he said, "All right, if you don't want to tell me, I'll find out myself."

He had a resolute expression on his face and turned away. A faint smile crossed Sanguk's face again.

In the meantime, the car had passed Changan village and was passing through the streets of Chungang village where the main clinic and the Catholic church were located. Sanguk asked him if he wanted to stop and look around, but the director wanted to stop there on their way back and urged the driver to continue on to Tolburi shore, the place where the escape had occurred.

Finally, the car reached Sinsaeng village's Tolburi shore and the two of them got out of the car. It was desolate since people rarely went there. The summer ocean waves crashed at their feet. Noktong harbor across the strait looked close enough to touch. To get there by motor launch would take about ten minutes. A six hundred meter wide strait separated the island from the harbor. But, even though the strait was less than a kilometer wide, it was filled with bitterness, since once the patients crossed from Noktong to the island, they could never return alive.

"How could they possibly get across from here?" The director, who had been staring silently at Noktong harbor, turned to Sanguk as if he couldn't imagine them escaping.

"They either hail a passing fishing boat or, using a piece of wood, they swim across."

"The current seems strong though, doesn't it?"

"That's why those who swim end up getting caught in the current."

"What about those who escaped last night?"

"Perhaps they hailed a boat. If they tried to swim across, they might have met the same fate."

"...."

"We've been working on various strategies to prevent escapes. The outer block road we were just driving on was originally built for the shore patrol to prevent escapes, but it doesn't work."

"What kind of deterrent would that be anyway? These are people who risk their lives even though they know that they might die if they get caught in the current, right?"

"They're desperate."

". . . ."

The director kept silent. With nothing more to see, he trudged off to the car. There was nothing more for him to learn there at the Tolburi shore devoid as it was of all traces of people.

The director made the driver go back. He wanted to go back to the patients' zone at Sinsaeng village and asked Sanguk to arrange for him to meet some patients. Of course he didn't particularly need Sanguk's help to do this. As soon as the car entered the village, he easily met some male patients who were passing by. He hurriedly got out of the car.

If the "welcoming present" escape was the first frustration he had met, he met his second in Sinsaeng village. He got out of the car and approached the men who'd apparently thought that the car was just passing by. When they realized that the director was walking toward them, they oddly enough began to stagger away backwards.

"Hey you. What do you know about the escape of two men from this village last night?" Not knowing what was going on, the director asked his question while approaching the two men who were backing hastily away. They continued their retreat as he advanced toward them. And they stared at him blankly, showing no sign of intending to answer his question.

"I'm the new director. Please answer my question. Didn't two of your villagers escape last night?"

They continued to act the same. Did his appearance—a military uniform with a gun—make them more fearful? They looked as if they were fearful, apparently ready to run away. A strange, unpleasant silence—one that was both intense and precarious—hung in the air between them, neither side able to determine who was more afraid of the other. The late summer afternoon's heat silently melted the space between the director and the men.

Finally Sanguk intervened.

"This is the new director. You know about last night's incident, don't you?"

The men stepped five or six paces back from

Sanguk, keeping their distance. But they answered his question by nodding reluctantly.

"Why did they escape? Do you know the reason? Why would you want to escape from the island?" Again, the director interrupted rashly. And again the men kept silent. Unable to endure their silence any longer, he screamed, "Talk to me! Why won't you talk to me?!"

The men kept silent.

"Tell us what you know. Now." Sanguk pleaded. Finally one of the men slowly brought his hand toward his mouth. With his head half turned, and his hand still covering his mouth, he spit out contemptuously, "If you don't know the reason, then neither do we."

The man's fearful eyes were suddenly ablaze with hatred. As soon as he finished speaking, he turned around. The other man, who had stared at the director with the same look, turned his back on him at the same time.

"Tell me! Talk! You must know! Tell me!"

For a moment, the director's right hand trembled near the butt of his gun. He screamed at them as if he was insane. But once they'd turned their backs, the men looked as if even lightning wouldn't stir them, and they continued without hurry up the road. Once he'd lost his temper, the director couldn't calm down. When the men finally disappeared from the road, the director, giving up on the men, suddenly rushed to the nearest house in the ward and, entering the front yard, shouted for someone to come out. Surprised at the commotion, an old man emerged from a room. Again he met with frustration since the man didn't speak to him. Stubbornly stepping back to keep enough distance from him, the old man just stared coldly at this man in a uniform as if he were watching a fierce beast in a cage.

"Why are they doing this to me?" The director, still fuming, asked in the car on the way back. Even though he was the director, it was obvious that he didn't know what was going on. He felt completely humiliated not knowing the reasons behind these people's actions. His fury wouldn't subside easily. Sanguk didn't have any clear explanation to give him. It wasn't something that one could understand with just a few words of explanation.

If you don't know why, neither do we—this was another way of saying that they both actually knew the reason. Especially if he had come to the island as the director, he should already have known the reason. If he didn't already know, no explanations could make him understand. Not only about the escape, but also why the men had stubbornly kept their silence. The reasons were, in fact, the same.

—Why don't you find out for yourself why those people wanted to escape from the island, why those people wanted to avoid talking with you, why they fear you and why they fear providing you with the correct answer? Even though it may take time, you should unravel the answer yourself! Perhaps that's what you need to do first on this island. Sanguk thought that if the director didn't have a statue in mind, if he had no intention of giving his inaugural address, then there was a possibility that he could learn. However, he wasn't in a position to answer the director's question with silence, so he started to say absurd things.

"Uh, you mean why those men kept stepping back from you? That's the regulation here. When a patient talks to a healthy person, he's supposed to keep a distance of five paces and, when talking, he's supposed to turn his face forty-five degrees sideways and cover his mouth with his hand...Since these are the regulations, they were just following rules."

The director must have known that Sanguk was trying to skirt the issue. He paid no attention to his preposterous reply.

On their way back, Sanguk took the director to some noteworthy facilities on the island. Because of the unpleasant encounter he'd had with the men, he wasn't interested in looking around, but Sanguk purposefully guided him to the various facilities. He wanted him to understand the island better. As with the many other new directors, this one could easily misunderstand the island from the very start. His misconceptions of the island had begun when he'd compared the island to a park. At least in his eyes, the island wasn't sad like for those who'd heard about it either from the artist or from the stories they'd seen reflected in the eyes of the girl in the paintings. And that was why he couldn't fathom the reasons for the escape.

But Sanguk knew. He knew that the landscape the director so admired was not actually the island. The beauty of the landscape was the outside world since, from the island, one was looking at the beauty of the outside world. Likewise, the story of the girl the artist painted wasn't beautiful when it was told on the island. It was beautiful only after it left the island. Off the island it was transformed into a beautiful story. Sanguk wanted the director to see the real island. Rather than simply hearing about it by visiting the people and hearing business-related reports from his subordinates, Sanguk wanted to give him a chance to see the island and feel it himself.

The first place they stopped was Mallyŏng hall, located on the slope of a mountain near Sinsaeng village. The cylinder-shaped concrete building with its hat-like roof held the ashes of the five thousand odd souls who had died on the island over the past forty years. Sooner or later, it would also be the final destination for the remaining five thousand or so people still alive on the island. They'd be put to rest here when their turn came. Every time people who lived on the island looked at the building, regardless of their hopes for leaving the island after being cured, it reminded them of their sad fate. The place was also known as "Napkol hall" or "Napkol pagoda."

"How many people's remains are enshrined here?"

As if he couldn't bear to look directly at the atrocious face of the guard—whose appearance was more ghostlike than human—the director questioned Sanguk while staring up at the tower.

"As far as I know, there are five thousand of them."

"Have there been any cases where their ashes were taken back?"

"If there are any living relatives at all, we send them a letter after the cremation notifying them of the death. But usually nobody comes."

Apart from not wanting to come to take back the ashes, relatives rarely allowed patients to write to them for fear that others would learn of the existence of a leper in the family. Customarily the patients kept their names and hometowns a secret and so, as a result, no one cared about such things. This was inconvenient for the hospital administration, but they could do nothing about patients who steadfastly concealed their identities. There weren't many families who came to collect remains. But even leaving aside the question of remains, the many patients who kept their names and hometowns a secret made it difficult enough to locate a relative to whom notification of the death could be sent. The new director couldn't possibly understand this situation yet. He listened silently and carefully to Sanguk's explanation.

The next place Sanguk took the director was the pier on the shore of Tongsaeng village. This was the gateway to the patient area and it had taken many years to complete. The hospital's fourth director, the Japanese Shū Masahide, mobilized the patients to build this gateway. It was considered the lifeline of the island since all supplies to the patient area from outside and all products from the island traveled through here. Together with the construction of the road that stretched along the ocean and the construction of a brick factory building that stood at the heart of the island, the construction of the pier had cost the lives of many innocent patients. Accordingly, many people harbored a deep resentment toward this place.

"This pier was built by the fourth director, Shū Masahide, in order to bring boats straight up here without going through the personnel zone." Sanguk explained its history even before the director asked. The director had kept quiet until now, but he knew that much about the island and so he got ahead of Sanguk, saying,

"Wasn't the fourth director, Shū Masahide, the one who made the island what it is today?"

"Yes. He's the one who accepted the statue of himself as a present for his contributions to the island—building this pier and the road along the coast."

"What do you mean he accepted the statue as a present?" The director threw the question back, as if the tone of Sanguk's voice was uncertain.

"The statue was presented to him with the wages collected by the patients who had been mobilized to construct the pier and the road."

"Is the statue still standing?"

The director seemed to have understood what Sanguk was getting at. He wanted to see the statue. The car was on the road again. This time the car returned to Chungang village and stopped in front of the Kura tower which had been built in the park plaza to commemorate the hospital's fortieth anniversary.

"Where the tower is now is where Director Shū's statue once stood." Sanguk continued with his explanations. "Director Shū stood here, looking down at the island until the end of the colonial period. Even after he was stabbed to death in front of his own statue."

"How was the statue removed?" The director

looked as if his curiosity had been stirred.

"Thanks to the copper delivery quota. When resources were scarce at the end of the colonial period, the statue became subject to the copper delivery quota and disappeared from the island. This tower was built in its place several years ago to commemorate the fortieth anniversary of the opening of the hospital."

Sanguk had a purpose in mind when he mentioned the connection between the principal actor of the pier construction and the history of the Kura tower. And the director seemed to have read his mind, too. He nodded, keeping silent for a while, but he turned to Sanguk again and looked as if he expected to be guided to another place.

Sanguk sensed in the director a somewhat importunate disposition coupled to an intense fighting spirit. He had already sensed this intense fighting spirit from the very beginning given the director's curt speech and his dark complexion. In fact, it was clear from his appearance, his proud military uniform, as well as in his hasty temper, and his willingness to postpone the inaugural address to investigate the escape. Following Sanguk around the island, the director hadn't looked tired or bored, not even for a moment. He was eager and willing to see places, and he had followed Sanguk around, enthusiastically asking questions and thinking. This was related to his strong sense of duty. What Sanguk feared the most was the director's strong sense of duty. If he no longer saw the island as an idyllic landscape that was fortunate. But if from there, a new fighting spirit and sense of duty were kindled, then that would be something to fear. Sanguk felt it necessary to wear him down a bit more and continued with his explanations.

"You may not be interested in this, but I have one more thing to tell you. This big granite platform you're standing on right now has its own extraordinary history. Director Shū set one day a month aside as a "thanksgiving day" when all the patients would gather here before him and his statue to offer a silent tribute of gratitude. After that he would stand on this dignified platform to lecture on moral principles to the patients. This kind of stone was not available on the island so it was brought from somewhere near Wan island by boat to the pier. And from the pier the patients carried it here on shoulder poles."

As the final stop on the tour, after the Kura tower, Sanguk took the director to the island prison located in the corner of Chungang village.

"As you may know, a director could sentence patients to detention for up to thirty days. But what made this place particularly beastly for the patients was the regulation that, after they were released from detention, they would be forcibly castrated. In the past, not only directors but even chief nurses or patrol officers could throw patients into this prison, forcing them to be castrated." Sanguk then launched into a long explanation while the director stood in front of the prison with a somewhat puzzled expression on his face. At last, he began to look tired.

"I guess there isn't a single place on this island that has a cheerful history. Every sight we've looked at is filled with bitterness and resentment." He had finally begun to express his discontent to Sanguk. He sounded tired. Sanguk swallowed his smile.

"Actually, the entire island is bitterness itself. It starts in the area of oblivion right after they cross the barb wired buffer zone from where neither patients nor healthy people ever return…"

"I understand. Please stop now." Clearly, the director wanted to return to the hospital. "Right, there's no need to torture this man all at once," Sanguk thought. When Sanguk saw his tired look, he felt a strange sense of relief. He thought of ending it right here.

"Shall we go back to the hospital?"

"Yes, let's go back."

"Would you be interested in seeing the chapel and the medical treatment area?

"Why don't we come back next time?"

They turned the car around and left the patients' zone. The director was silent. Perhaps everything that had happened today was utterly unexpected. It was clear that even the report was completely unexpected. The director kept his eyes closed and fell deep into thought. He looked as if he had lost all confidence. As Sanguk looked stealthily at him in the rearview mirror, a faint smile—perhaps of relief—again appeared on his lips.

The director was an impatient person. But, as if all his new discoveries hadn't been enough to explain why the people had escaped the night before, when the car entered the personnel zone, he suddenly asked,

"How is the outcome of the patients' treatment?"

"Ever since we began using DDS, the outcome

is quite satisfactory. The recovery process is fast and there are quite a few patients who have been completely cured."

Since Sanguk had clearly misunderstood his point, the director asked once again, "How are the patients' attitudes toward fighting their illness? Do they have a firm belief that, if they get proper treatment, they can be completely cured?"

"Since they see it with their own eyes and since we educate them, they know it to a certain degree. However, they still tend to believe that, if they leave the island and go to the mainland, they can get better treatment with better quality medicine and get cured quicker."

"Isn't that the reason for the escapes then?" The director again changed the topic of the conversation to figure out the reason for the escapes. Even after he'd looked around almost the entire island, he still needed a definitive reason for the escapes.

"Well, some of them escape because of the rumors." Sanguk partially admitted to the director's charge, but soon he contradicted everything that the director had said.

"But one can't believe that's the main reason behind this escape."

"Why's that?"

"The hospital recently stopped detaining patients who are cured. Instead, we try to persuade them to leave the island. Even those patients who aren't completely cured but wish to leave the island can get permission and visit their families for a certain period of time. But in cases like this, they'd usually rather stay here."

"Then who are the ones who risk their lives swimming across the ocean to escape?"

"Well, they're the same people."

"What kind of nonsense is that? How can you say that the ones who're allowed to leave the island, those who can leave whenever they want, and those who risk their lives to leave the island are the same people? Why would they do a crazy thing like that if no one stops them from leaving the island?" The director, turning sharply, suddenly raised his voice, seeming unable to understand what Sanguk was saying. However, far from talking nonsense, Sanguk was getting clearer.

"Of course, they wouldn't attempt such a dangerous thing for fun. But as I said, they're the same people, and it's the truth."

"I still don't understand. First of all, I can't really

follow what you're saying."

"Actually, it's a simple story."

"Okay, let me hear that simple story."

"This is how I understand it. Those who don't leave the island even when they're allowed to are the patients. When they became ill, they were chased from the outside world and forced to come to the island. Therefore the patients have continuously harbored both fear and resentment toward the outside world. But those who risk their lives to escape the island are no longer those patients. Before they're patients, they're human beings. They're tired of separating their existence as patients and their ordinary lives. Therefore they want to throw off their 'special' existence as patients and follow this strong impulse to live as human beings. These are the ones who risk their lives to leave the island. But the ones who are patients and the ones who aren't are in fact the same people. Everyone who is living on this island lives a different life as a patient and as a human being, so in that way they lead dual lives. I think their contradictory behavior—a behavior that we can't easily understand—stems from that."

Without realizing it, Sanguk had grown more

and more excited. Still the director was shaking his head.

"As I said before, you're a difficult person. Your words are too intelligent sounding. You said it's a simple story, but you sound as though you're toying with me."

Of course, what the director meant was that he didn't understand what Sanguk was saying. But he had already come to a full understanding.

"Then, even if what you've said is true, why do they have to choose such a dangerous route to escape the island, not as patients but as human beings? You said that, if they chose to, they could walk out in a dignified manner whenever they wanted to."

Again the director pressed Sanguk hard. Sanguk kept silent. But the director continued to press him.

"And something else. If they wish to escape the island to exist as human beings, doesn't it mean that they can't exist as human beings on this island? Is this island truly such a place? Is it such an atrocious hell that, in order to live as a human being, one has to escape?"

Sanguk couldn't keep quiet any longer.

"I just wanted to point out that we should not assume that the escapes are motivated simply by dissatisfaction with the treatment here or to seek better medicine on the mainland."

Sanguk gave an answer appropriate to the question and looked out the car window, avoiding eye contact with the director. The director's answer was so close at hand. However, he reigned himself in. He thought it would be better to wait a little longer. The car stopped in front of the main hospital.

3

That the new director didn't harbor a secret desire for a statue was becoming more and more apparent. Even after he returned from his tour around the island, he still gave no indication of wanting to hold his inaugural speech. He was trying hard not to reach any hasty conclusions regarding either the motives behind the escape or the various things he had seen and heard while touring the island. However, after he returned to the hospital, he issued an ominous decree, instructing the staff to place suggestion boxes in the patient areas of each village before the day was over. He also ordered all staff to go to the villages and encourage the patients to write down their requests for improvements, their honest opinions concerning hospital policy and any other suggestions they might have. He then ordered the suggestion boxes to be brought directly to him the following day at noon so that he could look at them right then and there. In order to protect the writers' anonymity and to encourage the patients to write down their opinions and suggestions freely, he insisted that the suggestion boxes be brought directly to him. His instructions seemed to indicate a desire to eliminate any possibility of the staff tampering with the anonymous suggestions.

Even after he ordered the suggestion boxes installed, he didn't hold any separate formal meetings. Instead, he shut himself in his office, deeply engrossed in his thoughts. Occasionally, he called in members of the executive staff both to greet them in his capacity as the newly appointed director as well as to listen to matters concerning their jurisdiction. He seemed to be more interested in waiting for time to pass than in his work. He had high expectations for the suggestion boxes.

The staff were on their toes, watching the director's every move with a tense look in their eyes. Without realizing it, they had been overpowered unbelievably fast by this man whose actions were a little unrefined and unpredictable. After the order had been given, the staff went down to the villages with the suggestion boxes. The entire island was enshrouded by an oppressive nervous tension.

Sanguk too felt tense, although it was a different kind of tension. Since he could predict the outcome of the director's new measure, a strange curiosity was surfacing inside him. That evening Sŏ Miyŏn, one of the teachers at the preschool, came to visit him again using the director's new order as an excuse. After Sanguk had returned to his quarters to rest, Miyŏn showed up immediately and knocked on his door. There was no need for a preschool teacher to concern herself with whether the new director's hospital management policies were right or wrong. Since she had come to the island as a volunteer, it was even more unnecessary for her to be concerned with it.

Miyŏn had come to the island about a month

before. She worked both as a nurse and as a teacher at the branch school looking after the uninfected children. From time to time women would come to the island to help out with the children for a short while and then leave. They would come to the island vowing to help look after the children and would beg and plead to be allowed to stay and work. Their requests couldn't be readily accepted from the hospital's side. The hospital staff would explain the situation on the island, ask the women to rethink their decision and then have them return home. At this point, most of them would abandon their plans and they would leave the island saying either that they would reconsider their decision or that they would discuss the matter with their parents. And they would never return to the island. But there were a rare few who wouldn't give in and insisted on staying on the island to work. In the case of those who, despite repeated attempts at persuasion, wouldn't give in—their intentions were understood to be sincere—the hospital respected their wishes to stay on. And a few of the women who came to the island like that remained. Among the preschool and branch school teachers as well as among the nurses, there were one or two people who came to stay like that.

Miyŏn had come to the island a month ago and like all of the other women who had come and gone, she vowed to work hard and to sacrifice herself. Then she began working. She was a small but stubborn woman who had studied at a school of theology in Seoul but, after much deliberation, had decided to come to the island. There was a custom on the island that once someone came to work voluntarily, and was determined to stay, no one pried into his or her personal history. It was quite possible that everyone, both the healthy people and the patients who were in some way related to the island, had hidden secrets they couldn't reveal. Of course, Miyŏn was the same to the island people. After it was clear to them that she was going to stay, they showed no interest whatsoever in the story behind her unknown devotion. She'd been thought of as someone who had given up on theology school and, after having contemplated what she should do, had come to the island. A strange woman from Seoul. Accordingly the people were a little thankful but, as a healthy person, she also had to endure jealous glares from some of the patients.

There was no reason for her to feel fearful of the director. Of course, this wasn't the first time Miyŏn had visited Sanguk. Perhaps her frequent contact with him was because he was the head of the hygiene division and thus in charge of the children's health. For some unknown reason, after she had come to the island, she went to him whenever she needed to discuss things. She depended on him and discussed trivial matters such as the living situation, kitchen duty and matters pertaining to her work in the preschool as well as general hospital formalities.

Among all the hospital staff, she felt most comfortable with him and so she approached him unreservedly. She had a male colleague at the preschool named Yun Haewŏn. Whenever he saw healthy women, he would drive them off the island by humiliating them or insulting them in one way or another. Once Miyŏn had figured out what he was up to, she came to see Sanguk. After she had come to visit Sanguk—who lived alone—under the pretense of needing to discuss that matter with him, she began visiting him in the late hours as well. Sanguk strongly believed that she had something else she wanted to confess. Every time she came with one or another thing she wanted to discuss, Sanguk realized that it was really something else she had on her mind. Even though she talked about the things she had come to talk about, her eyes said there was something else she wanted to talk about. She wanted to tell him, but she couldn't. Eventually, she would sadly get up to leave. Sanguk often wondered what the hidden story was. Perhaps it was related to her background and her past experiences. It didn't matter to him what it was. The fact that Miyŏn wanted to talk to him about it meant that she trusted him and he was thankful for that. Sanguk didn't know when it had started, but deep inside he was secretly waiting for her to speak.

Perhaps tonight was to be no different from any other night. What she wanted to reveal, perhaps, had no connection whatsoever to the new measures the director had implemented. It was not clear whether Miyŏn felt strongly about the new measures. No matter what the motive was for her visit, and whatever her hidden story was, Sanguk couldn't welcome her this evening with the ease he showed on any of the other nights. He couldn't be attentive to her story.

"I'm sure he did it unknowingly but he certainly

knows how to make things happen. I'm certain something interesting will happen tomorrow..." said Sanguk.

It was because of the director. No matter what Miyŏn wanted to talk about, Sanguk was completely preoccupied with the director's order. The entire island was the same. With his one order, the entire island had fallen utterly quiet, enveloped by this strange tension.

Finally morning came.

Since the early morning hours the director had seemed nervous. He got to the office before eight and waited for noon to roll around, the time he had designated to open the boxes. He paced back and forth in his office like a caged animal, as if he couldn't concentrate on anything else. As the time pass-ed, his nervousness intensified. The staff couldn't hide their agitation either.

Finally the clock struck noon. As planned, the seven suggestion boxes that had been placed in the patient areas the night before were delivered to the room adjacent to the director's office. With the arrival of the boxes, every single member of the executive staff gathered in the room. Of course, the director had ordered them to do so earlier.

Soon he entered the room and, without speaking, checked the suggestion boxes for any evidence of tampering. The atmosphere of the room was electric with an intensity one would expect at the office charged with administering the general election. This silence of hitherto unknown proportions—like that before the opening of ballot boxes—smothered the room.

"Now, let's open them one by one," the director said solemnly as if he was the chief administrator of an election. At last, the first box was opened. It was from Changan village, the one closest to the personnel area. Strange. There was nothing in it. The box, which had caused this strange mixture of tension and nervousness mingled with expectation and doubt, was empty. There wasn't a single suggestion slip from the patients in Changan village. Not even a piece of trash.

How could this be?

The staff were as surprised as the director. Everyone was at a loss for words and silently traded glances with each other. An even heavier tension than before filled the room.

"Open the next one!" the director ordered. One could hear the strong P'yŏngan accent in his voice.

The next one was from Kubuk village. But it was the same. Not even a scrap of paper could be found inside the box. Suddenly his dark face started turning red. The staff encircling the boxes held their breath. Although his face was turning red it didn't seem as though there was anything particular he wanted to say. With lips tightly closed he waited for the next box to be opened. As if it was too distressing to watch, Kim Chŏngil, the chief doctor, quickly jumped in and started opening all the boxes. It was the same. Every box was empty. Chungang, Sinsaeng, Tongsaeng, Kubuk, and Namsaeng villages. The boxes were opened in this order but they were all empty. While the chief doctor opened the boxes, his fingers trembled slightly with fear. Unexpectedly the director's reddened face had returned to normal as the boxes had been opened one by one.

"How can this be...." After the chief doctor had opened all seven boxes, he raised his head, stretching his back slowly in a rather uncomfortable manner. He was pale with fear and looked around with spite in his eyes, seemingly on behalf of the director.

"What does this mean?"

There could be no answer. With blank looks on all their faces, none of the executive staff bothered to avoid the chief doctor's gaze, save for one person. A faint smile passed across Sanguk's lips.

"Say something! Are you doing your work properly?" At that moment, the director, who alone nodded his head, suddenly reproached the chief doctor.

"Stop it. What more do you want? Isn't everything pretty much clear at this point?"

4

It was quite strange. But if you really thought about it, perhaps it wasn't that strange after all—the director who nodded his head and reproached the chief doctor in the end and Sanguk who stood in the last row, smiling faintly—at least, for these two people, it wasn't that strange.

That afternoon was the day of the meeting between the uninfected children and their parents. The preschool children's visit with their parents was arranged once a month on a designated day. This meeting was handled by the General Affairs section and the Hygiene Division. After lunch, Sanguk went down to the uninfected children's preschool with an employee from each one of the divisions. The preschool was located inside the barbed wire fence of the personnel zone, before the transition to the buffer zone. It functioned as a "branch" of the elementary school and it was almost like a half-buffer zone. Among the three hundred uninfected children on the island, those who had reached the age of matriculation would be sent to an elementary school over the hills for healthy people. After all the paperwork was completed, they would study at that branch separately while the rest of the younger children who didn't show any particular signs of infection would be isolated in this branch until they matriculated.

The parents had already come into the buffer zone. Standing in a line behind the barbed wire fence separating the healthy from the infected, they waited for their children. The meeting soon began. Using the fence as a dividing line, the parents in the patients' zone approached first but stood back six feet. Staff placed around the area at regular intervals supervised the meeting. The children approached the fence looking for their parents. Each of the children also stood back from it, stopping on the line that had been drawn six feet from the fence.

The meeting lasted five minutes. During those five minutes, unlike any other place or time on the island, countless stories were exchanged. First, the parents from behind the barbed wire fence would confirm that their children were healthy, and then they would ask about their school and about other things that had happened since the last meeting. After that, the parents would tell their children about family members in the patients' area and those who couldn't make it to the meeting and relay their messages. Then they would tell them what to do until the next meeting. While the supervisors weren't watching them, the parents would secretly give their children food or money that they had brought hidden under their clothes. This was one of the meeting customs that couldn't be skipped.

Of course, Sanguk didn't interfere with these small things between the parents and the children. He didn't really like this kind of meeting. He came out to the meeting place only because he was in charge of the affair, but he didn't like to observe the happenings up close or eavesdrop on the conversations. He usually stood quite a distance from the fence and would wait for it to end. However, today the new director had come down to observe the meeting between the parents and the children.

"Hmmm, it's quite a sight." The director suddenly drew close to Sanguk as if the incident regarding the suggestion box had been forgotten and as if nothing had happened. Sanguk had no choice but to help out with the director's "sight-seeing."

"They don't seem to know how leprosy is transmitted." He spat out the words as if he had nothing to do with them.

"All this business with the barbed wire, why are they standing so far apart?"

Sanguk understood what the director wanted to say. The director was quite direct and frank. At the same time, Sanguk knew well that this kind of person could easily betray one in a frightening way. He watched the director's face carefully.

"The reason why they separate them with the barbed wire is due to sudden emotional outbursts from the children. Often they rush to their parents to hug them."

"Of course. Diseased or not, they are their parents." The director nodded.

"As you said before, on this island there is a big discrepancy between what is said and what is actually done. Well, this is considered the norm."

"Tell me in more concrete terms." The director kept his eyes on the people standing in their rows but he didn't let any of Sanguk's words pass by.

"We always teach them that leprosy is not hereditary. Because unlike other diseases leprosy is among the least contagious so they aren't any different from the healthy children. But look at them. They are unable to attend schools with the children of personnel, the school over the mountain pass. Not only that, healthy teachers rarely come to this branch school to teach. The teachers here are all former patients."

"Perhaps this is a fundamental problem. It's a matter of perception."

"Of course, I agree. But go to the clinic. If you go there, you'll find how deep the problem is."

"What's going on at the clinic?"

"I'll use the nurses who dispense medicine as an example. They wear sanitary gowns, masks and gloves. And as if that isn't enough, they use tweezers to place the pills hesitantly in the palms of the patients."

The director didn't respond. With his lips tightly closed, he stared at what had been going on for a while at the meeting place down the hill. One of the staff members who had been standing with the others supervising the meeting stealthily slipped out of line and started coming up the hill to where Sanguk was standing. It was Yun Haewŏn, one of the preschool teachers.

"Ah, Manager Yi! I'm glad you're here. I've been meaning to see you."

Haewŏn. Whenever he saw healthy women, he would create mishaps and try to drive them off the island. He'd already shown signs of wanting to drive out his co-teacher, Miyŏn. Haewŏn had reddish marks around his eyes and was one of the worst troublemakers on the island. No one knew how he had been infected and how he had been healed. He had spent several years at the preschool and, because of his eccentric conduct, the island people treated him as if he were insane. At times he would take the islanders' disease so lightly, he could be easily dealt with.

Haewŏn didn't care about the new director who was standing next to Sanguk.

"Is the meeting over?" said Sanguk. For some odd reason, Sanguk wasn't comfortable with the sudden appearance of Haewŏn.

The director's expression suggested that he didn't seem to mind Haewŏn being there. But Sanguk felt that Haewŏn was the kind of person who should be properly introduced first. Then again there was no reason for Sanguk to introduce him to the director, since he would learn all about Haewŏn after hearing a few exchanges between them.

"What is he up to now?" thought Sanguk. Remembering Miyŏn's visit the previous night, Sanguk had asked him the question sarcastically. But his reaction was what he would have predicted.

"Over or not, what's the point of watching them wailing and sobbing. Anyway, I have another favor to ask of you." He was ready to get on with business.

"A favor? What is it?"

"Do you remember the kid named Cho I spoke

to you about? I'd like to take him over to you for an exam again."

"If it's the Cho kid, it's been less than a week since I examined him."

Sanguk understood what Haewŏn wanted to talk to him about. He realized he didn't need to worry. It was a few days ago. Haewŏn brought a preschooler named Cho to the clinic for a bacteriological exam. The child looked perfectly normal, but Haewŏn had insisted on the exam. He said he had some doubts. The results were negative. Sanguk could still remember vividly that Haewŏn had had a strangely disappointed look when he saw the negative results.

"I know it's only been a few days, but I still think…"

"Are you saying you don't trust the results of my exam?"

"No, not that…"

"Aren't you thinking a little too much about the cherry blossoms when it's not even spring yet?"

"Perhaps I miss the pink color of cherry blossoms all the more because it's not yet spring. In any case, it's about time that the cherry blossoms bloomed on a few kids..."

The expression "cherry blossoms" originated with the pinkish color of the first symptom of leprosy that would appear on a person's face. Pink or burgundy was the typical color of leprosy that settled around a patient's eyes and remained there even after they were cured. All the patients on the island had had the hopeless experience of seeing the pink on their face and until now they cursed it. Because of some unknown fate, there were many people affected with the reddish color. Every spring pink clouds of cherry blossoms hung all over the villages and people came in groups from the mainland to see this pink island. They came to see the yellowish brown road, the cherry blossoms, and the people with the pink dapples that looked like shadows of the cherry blossoms on their faces. For the islanders, pink was the color of abysmal hopelessness. Everyone cursed the color pink.

But there was one person on the island who didn't curse it. Far from cursing it, he cherished it, as if it were a precious trace of flowers. In fact, he longed for it. In spring, when the cherry blossoms entirely covered the island roads, he would go about writing poems and painting as if he were completely absorbed in pink. He would talk thoughtlessly about the pink and the pink island. To put it simply, he was a pink maniac. He waited for the pink himself and in the end, he had experienced the same hopelessness just like any other islander. When he first came to the island as a volunteer teacher at the preschool, he was obviously a healthy person. But since then—and for several years after—he had developed this strange attachment. He had desperately longed for the pink to appear on his own face. Finally he experienced the hopelessness of the pink himself.

When the symptoms began to appear, he blissfully crossed beyond the barbed wire to enter the patients' zone. He was the first perfectly healthy hospital staff member in the forty-year island history to have contracted the disease. Until then nobody knew that his sister was in the patients' zone. He spent almost three years in the patients' zone with his sister. After three years, due to early detection and treatment, and without many scars, he was completely cured and regained his health. However, even after he had received all the treatment, he had no intention of leaving the island. His sister's symptoms were severe. She continued to suffer from the disease and, without leaving the island, he crossed over to the personnel zone to teach at the preschool. He was able to continue to work at the preschool since the school was always short staffed. By that time, his attachment to the pink had grown as deep as his affection for his sister. Although it was rare, when a child showed the initial pink symptom, he was never frustrated or depressed. Far from it. Whenever a child showed symptoms, his face would brighten strangely.

"It's about time there's some news of pink..."

In response to Sanguk's joke, Haewŏn didn't try to deny it. Haewŏn himself answered in a joking tone then smiled foolishly. However, a lonely trace of sadness tinged his smile.

"You don't seem to get along well with Teacher Sŏ." Sanguk brought up the subject as if he knew well what was going on between the two. After seeing Haewŏn, he couldn't get rid of the image of Miyŏn. As for Haewŏn, it wasn't absurd speculation. Of all the women who came to the island to volunteer at the hospital, only a few could endure the demands and finally decide to stay on. Often, even before a month had passed, they would leave. It was because of Haewŏn. He was the one who made it difficult for these young women to stay. He tormented them in a strange way and, in the end, he made them leave.

He was the same toward Miyŏn. After Miyŏn had decided to stay on, Haewŏn's eyes glittered with a new scheme and this time, he showed a slight change in his tactics. A few days later, he brought the Cho boy from the preschool to Sanguk to have him examined.

"Please examine him carefully," Haewŏn implored. His tone indicated he was hoping that the boy would start to show symptoms. Sanguk knew what kind of person he was, so without giving it much thought, he examined the boy. However, he found out later that the boy was particularly favored by the new teacher, Miyŏn. Sanguk soon had a strange premonition. There seemed to have been an ulterior motive for having the boy examined. Sanguk could guess what was going on in Haewŏn's mind. Haewŏn always thought that the young women's affection for the children was no more than the pity a healthy person feels toward a poor leper's kid, and that that pity was a disguised form of arrogance. He felt a certain contempt for Miyŏn's affection toward the boy. Obviously, he wanted to see Miyŏn betray the boy. He wanted to prove that Miyŏn's affection for the boy was no more than pity. If he could prove that, he wouldn't have to do anything more and Miyŏn would have no choice but to leave the island. To reach that end, Haewŏn became subconsciously engrossed in wanting to make the boy a leper.

Sanguk's speculations weren't far off from Haewŏn's plan. He immediately understood what Sanguk was getting at.

"Well, you know I've never gotten along well with any of the women who came here," he said sorrowfully. But the next moment he smiled coyly, as if he had been caught stealing. Sanguk himself felt uncomfortable as if he was hiding something from Haewŏn.

"I know. They usually don't last a fortnight but hasn't it been more than a month since Teacher Sŏ came?" asked Sanguk.

"You seem to think of me as a woman-hating

leper ghost or something. I'd be in trouble if you talked to her about me like that. But anyway, she likes those rascals too much, without giving it enough thought, especially that Cho kid. It's dangerous." Haewŏn chatted away with jealousy in his eyes. "Leper! Leper!" It was an unspoken word on the island which no one liked to say or hear, except in self-torture. Haewŏn was one of the few who used it casually.

"Why don't you wait and see? She'll leave the island on her own when she gets tired. I don't see any harm to the boy, either."

"I know it's no harm to the boy, but…" he retorted.

"I didn't know you were so concerned about Teacher Sŏ."

"Anyway, I wish you would re-examine the boy."

At the bottom of the hill, the meeting seemed to be ending. People began to move slowly away from the fence that separated them. Haewŏn, swaying gently, started to walk down the hill to the meeting place where people had already begun moving apart.

"I understand that uninfected children in the

preschool sometimes develop symptoms," the director murmured. Talking to himself, he went over to Sanguk after Haewŏn had walked down the hill. Just as Sanguk expected, the director had paid attention to their conversation.

"It's not that there aren't instances of that happening. One or two children a year develop symptoms and are sent back to the patients' zone." Sanguk spoke frankly and added, "But it becomes clear later that the contagion is either due to a failure to isolate them early enough or to carelessness. Anyway, it has a bad effect on the children. They think it will happen to them sooner or later, so they hope for sooner so that they can go back to their parents."

"I guess they don't believe what you tell them."

"It's quite difficult to make them believe what you tell them."

"I understand. What about that boy? He asked you to examine the boy."

"Oh, there's nothing wrong with the boy. He was just being…"

"If there's nothing wrong with him, why does he want you to examine him twice? He sounds like he's waiting for the kid to have symptoms." The director understood it like that, too.

"You're right. It appears that way. He acts as if he feels neither loathing for, nor caution toward leprosy. He doesn't take leprosy any more seriously than a cold. Many people on the island think he's crazy. But when you get to know him, there is something extraordinary about him. He shows an unusual attachment to this disease. Instead of trying to avoid it or defeat it, it seems as if he's clinging to it. In that respect, I think he's one of the patients who has the worst problem."

"Is he a preschool teacher?" The director already knew the answer but he asked the question anyway, implying dismay over how a person as dangerous as Haewŏn could be a teacher.

"His name is Yun Haewŏn. He's been teaching at the preschool for ten years and has never harmed the children in any way. Outwardly he is generous and easy-going so the children like him unabashedly. He took time off from teaching for about three years when he himself got infected."

"You mean he contracted the disease after he came to the island?" The director's tone changed. He was ready to bombard him with an endless flurry of questions.

"Yes, it was the first time that had happened at

the island hospital. We found out later that his sister was in the patients' zone. Anyway, he came to the island as a healthy person, but was infected. After he was cured, he came to the preschool again to teach."

"He must be quite a character."

"There are lots of stories about him, but hardly anything has been proven."

There was no one at the meeting place at the bottom of the hill. Sanguk began to walk slowly toward the main hospital. However, the director's curiosity, once aroused, was not easily satisfied. The director, who had already walked a few paces, all of a sudden turned to Sanguk again as if remembering something.

"Then who is this Teacher Sŏ? She seems to be somehow connected to that Haewŏn?"

This time it was about Miyŏn.

"It's really nothing..." Sanguk equivocated intentionally.

"If it's nothing...are you trying to tell me they're dating or something?" The director became impatient with Sanguk's evasive answers.

"You can hardly call it that. As usual, whenever he sees a healthy woman, he pesters her to leave the island and that's his way of driving them out."

"He purposefully pesters women, eh?"

"Whenever a woman arrives on the island, he confesses his love to her only a few days later."

"I suppose he has never been successful."

"That's why I told you before that it's his way of driving the women off the island. Whenever he confesses his love for them, they get scared and leave in a hurry."

"The reason he pesters healthy women is a peculiar characteristic of an unhealthy person's jealousy of healthy people, I suppose..."

"Yes, certainly. But perhaps the women are the ones who kindle jealousy in him. Those who come to the island always avow a deep understanding of the disease and plan to devote their lives to it. Teacher Yun doesn't believe them and through his failure to win their love, is able to prove their deception. The women have succeeded in convincing him again and again that he can't be the same as healthy men."

"Yes, it's jealousy. That's why he can't bear seeing Teacher Sŏ favoring that boy, to the point of turning him into a leper in his mind."

Before Sanguk explained in detail how the boy

was involved in the relationship between Haewŏn and Miyŏn, the director had already sensed it. He seemed to be confident in his conclusions. Sanguk felt it was safe to continue.

"But it's not at all necessary for the boy to be a leper. Teacher Yun will confess his love to Teacher Sŏ regardless of the boy and, in the end, she'll end up leaving the island."

Still Sanguk wondered whether Miyŏn might be different after all and wished that she wouldn't end up leaving the island. However, he suppressed his secret wish and spoke with a steady voice.

"It'll be an interesting thing to see." The director understood what Sanguk was getting at. He responded almost mischievously, agreeing with what Sanguk said. Then he kept silent. He walked for a while without saying anything. Then, as if unable to endure it any longer, he muttered to himself despondently, "Everybody is suffering from a serious disease…there's no way to prevent escapes this way. They're suffering from a far more dangerous disease than the physical one…I can't blame them for wanting to leave the island."

5

It was fortunate that Director Cho was slowly coming to realize the reasons behind the escapes. He seemed to understand now that the island was not an idyllic paradise for the patients and he began to display his new understanding of the reasons for the escapes. But his understanding of the situation seemed to be heading off in a strange direction, and his strong sense of duty and his fighting spirit had been roused. On the morning of the third day, he finally decided to deliver his inaugural speech.

That morning he was late to work. There were a lot of things about him people couldn't quite figure out. There was a rumor that at night he would go to the patients' zone alone and spend the night there. No one saw him at night either at his office or at the official residence. But at dawn a patrol officer who made the rounds in the patients' zone, while passing through Chungang village, had seen him staggering out of the Cathedral. It wasn't clear whether he had spent the night in the Cathedral or had been seen just when he was coming out. In any case, he was late to work.

Although he came in late, he started rushing to hold his inaugural speech.

"Let me meet with the patients today," he requested quietly and humbly. As the new director, he couldn't continue to work without holding an inaugural address. In contrast to his low-key approach toward the speech, it turned out to be a rather big event.

His command was carried out without delay. Except for those who couldn't walk, all five thousand patients from the seven villages in the patients' zone were asked to gather in the Chungang park plaza at ten in the morning. For the first time since his arrival, the director asked for a morning meeting. Perhaps this was because as of yet there had not been an occasion for an official meeting, but certainly he must have had things to say to the staff before he stood in front of the patients. He also called for a special meeting of all the staff at which he gave a rather unusual speech.

"I don't have anything special to say. I'm going to meet the patients today, but I'm not meeting them alone, but with all of you. Today you need to meet the patients again with me. I want you to remember both what I ask of them and promise to them today. All of you should promise the same…"

His was completely different from all the other directors' speeches and was a prelude to what he would say to the patients. He didn't explain in concrete terms what he would promise to or ask of the patients, but from his short speech, his intentions were clear. Whatever he did, what he would ask of the patients, it would be done in the name of "we," the entire staff. Simply put, it was a demand for unquestioning trust and obedience from them.

Sanguk started to get nervous. "Perhaps this man has a statue hidden in his mind after all. What is he going to promise them and what is he going to demand from them?"

As he made his way to the patients' area along with the rest of the staff at the appointed time for the patients' gathering, Sanguk entertained endless doubts about the director's sudden change in attitude. It was natural for a person to think at one time or another of having a statue.

Perhaps it is natural to have a statue hidden deep inside one's head. Then it becomes a matter of how well one hides it. It's a matter of how one resists the fantasy of a statue. More difficult is how one would go about tearing down this desire for a statue. The director couldn't wait to deliver his inaugural speech but one couldn't blame him for that. It didn't matter what kind of promises he offered them. What was important was how closely his statue was related to what he intended to promise them and how wisely he would suppress his own impulses to reveal his wish to stand victoriously in front of the patients. What he wanted to promise should come after he was aware of his own ambitions. But Sanguk couldn't trust him.

The five thousand patients had already gathered in the Chungang central park plaza. In an orderly manner, they formed themselves into columns arranged by village and quietly waited for the director. It was a frighteningly quiet group of people. There was not even the sound of throats being cleared.

The staff was standing in a line facing the patients. The chief doctor, Kim Chŏngil, stepped onto the platform first, the very same platform in front of Kura tower that was built to celebrate the fortieth anniversary of the hospital. Director Shū had brought the platform there from the outside world twenty years ago. He had placed it where his statue eventually was erected, before the tower was built. It was a momentous place and Director Shū had stood in front of his own statue and had offered a prayer of thanksgiving once a month.

"Uh…The reason why I asked you to gather today was…" The chief doctor began to explain the reason for the meeting but there wasn't much response from the patients. They stood stiffly, not moving even a finger, gazing at the platform. However, the chief doctor was already used to that kind of reception.

"…as you know already, we have a new director. Today, I am greatly honored to introduce our new director. Colonel Cho Paeghŏn has devoted himself to hygienic and military medicine in the past, but now our merciful God has sent him to us. In the past couple of months, due to the absence of a director, this hospital's ability to provide medical services as well as carry out other administrative matters has suffered significantly. But now we are honored to have the great and respectable Colonel Cho as our new director. Let's welcome him and celebrate his inauguration. Now, here's our new director, Colonel Cho Paeghŏn."

The chief doctor descended the platform after a rather lengthy introduction. Still there was no response from the patients. No one even squirmed to avoid the scorching summer heat that burned their necks. Miyŏn and Haewŏn who led the preschool children stood in the front row and they too endured the summer heat. The whole crowd stood like a large, heavy lump of silence sunk beneath the ocean.

The chief doctor guided Director Cho into the middle of that silence. The director stood in front of the platform.

At once, ten thousand eyes were riveted on him. Even after he received a military salute from the patients' representatives, he just stood there for a while without uttering a word. He wasn't about to reproach the patients who stood there quietly without clapping their hands to welcome him despite the chief doctor's lengthy introduction and plea for a warm welcome. He felt as if all those quiet eyes riveted on him were drawing closer and closer. He turned pale as if he were being suffocated. His tall stature and the military uniform that had been so becoming now hung on him awkwardly. His military hat and those silvery badges on both shoulders looked strangely unimposing and devoid of dignity.

"I'm Colonel Cho Paeghŏn," he finally introduced himself. He raised his voice as if trying to break the dismal and mysterious silence.

"Since it's hot, I'll make it short by sharing my impressions of the island since my arrival."

He began to talk in a frank manner about what he had seen over the past few days and his impressions of the island.

"To be honest, I didn't know much about this island before I came here. Of course, I had some general knowledge. I knew both the number of regular patients and the number of former patients waiting to return to a normal life. And I knew the amount of government aid given to the hospital. Above all, I was quite impressed when I heard that this island was no longer beleaguered by prejudice and riddled with humiliation, but had become a patients' paradise, a hometown to be proud of. I was told that the scars of the cursed disease were healing. I was told that the social welfare system and the facilities were expanding, and human rights—which had formerly been trampled on—were gradually being protected. I was told that this island was slowly but surely becoming your paradise. I too had that image of the island when I first arrived and, after coming here, I concluded that this was not simply a groundless rumor. You're receiving good treatment and recovering fast. No other place could provide a better environment for convalescence than this beautiful island. All kinds of welfare facilities and conveniences are being expanded for you. Unlike in the past, there are no people who interfere with or persecute you. To my eyes this island seemed to be both your hometown and your paradise."

"But I misunderstood. A couple of days ago—the night I first came here—two people escaped. This 'welcoming gift' was meaningful. What I mean is that the incident taught me that you don't consider this island to be your paradise. The incident made me realize that. I couldn't understand why. But soon after I looked around the island, I understood the reason. I had misunderstood. You're still suffering from a terrible disease. Of course, you're recovering unbelievably fast from the physical disease, but I've learned that you're still suffering from the psychological side of the disease that is far more debilitating than the physical side. This island is afflicted by distrust and betrayal. You and this island have been infected by this disease of betrayal and distrust down to your very bones."

"It doesn't matter what I think. If you don't think this is your paradise, it will never really become your paradise. That's what's important to me. I now know what I need to do here."

The director's voice was passionate, but there was no response from the patients. There was no way of telling whether they were listening to him or not. He raised his voice all the more trying to elicit some kind of response from the silence that was so heavy it seemed to come from the bottom of the ocean.

"We have to rebuild this island."

There it was. At last the promise the director was going to make began to reveal itself. What the islanders feared most came out of the director's mouth. He declared that he would rebuild the island. He said he would make certain that this time the island would become a true paradise for all the people living there. He would make it the home they would want to return to even after they left. He also promised to set up a self-supporting system where anyone who lived on the island could make his own living while improving the environment as well.

"The whole country is embarking on a reconstruction plan so we should rebuild this island too. Rebuilding would mean more than anything else. However, before we can accomplish this, there is one important precondition." He began to spell out to the patients his requests.

"I need your cooperation to set an example for others. The entire staff who stand here before you and I will try our best to achieve this goal. We will work with you. But you mustn't forget that this is also your work. This is only possible when your self-determination and dedication are firmly grounded and directed toward accomplishing this task. But look at yourselves right now." The director stopped for a moment and looked down at the patients as if he were reproaching them. Suddenly, with an excited tone of voice, he made a conclusive remark and continued.

"You have no confidence and, since you've lost trust, that old and ugly sense of betrayal haunts you. To be frank, you are still pathetic slaves to this sentiment. Even now, you live deep inside the husk of your own private worlds, keeping quiet. You're suspicious of me and dream of a ridiculous betrayal. I'm trying to understand. I'm sure you have your reasons. You haven't been able to live your lives in a dignified manner, and I know people haven't tried to understand you. And so you've lost your trust. There has been nothing but distrust and betrayal in your lives. But there is nothing for which to forgive you. Who can possibly forgive you? In order to rebuild this island, you yourselves have to be dignified. Throw away your distrust and betrayal. Cooperate and unite. The prouder you become of yourselves, the easier it will be. In order to accomplish this, you must first reconstruct yourselves."

"Before I go, let me sum up my points in a few words. First, we must rebuild this island. And to achieve this, I'm imploring you to be open, to unite, and to cooperate. You need to use these three points as a guide. This is what I ask of you. Of course what I mean by 'open' applies to you, to your neighbors, to the staff, and everyone on the outside. Unity and cooperation are the same as well. This applies to your friends and the staff. All of the staff here and I will do the same. You must reconstruct yourselves. In order to create your paradise, I will devote myself completely to it and help you to build it. I will even force you to take part in this reconstruction."

As the speech went on, the director seemed to gain more confidence and he raised his voice. His forceful and passionate speech ended there.

His face was flushed as if he was moved by his own speech. There was still no response from the audience. Even after the speech ended, there was no stirring whatsoever and they quietly watched for his next move. The colossal lump of silence endured the scorching midday summer sun.

"They didn't even pay attention to my speech."

That evening the director invited some of the managerial staff to his residence for a drinking party. He obviously wanted to get some feedback from them. It was clear that he not only wanted to get their reactions but also wanted to get a sense of the mood on the island. The chief doctor, Kim Chŏngil, was present and Sanguk had been invited, too, shortly before work ended.

Nobody mentioned the speech for a while after the party started. There was no point in talking about it. Even the director didn't feel right in bringing it up. He gave no hint of wanting to mention it first. They kept emptying their glasses while talking about banal matters. Quickly everyone got drunk. Their faces began to turn crimson and started to glow. The director and Sanguk were the only two whose expressions didn't change. Although the director was busy returning toasts from one person or another, he still seemed to be sober. When Sanguk noticed that the director was trying to stay sober, he, too, tried to do the same despite the alcohol that was coursing through his veins. The director hadn't noticed that there was another person, Sanguk, who was staying on guard. When the room began to sway with drunkenness, he finally brought up the subject he had had in mind all along.

"Today I didn't feel that I was speaking to living people. Were they listening to me at all?"

The drunken atmosphere suddenly became somber again. There was no one who wanted to answer him.

"Say something. Either they were listening carefully to what I said, or they were completely ignoring my speech. Which was it? What do you think?"

"I believe they were all ears," the chief doctor answered with no confidence whatsoever, seemingly unable to endure the director's pressure. He couldn't answer otherwise.

Then Sanguk, who was quietly looking at his glass, twisting the chief doctor's answer, said abruptly, "But it could also be that they weren't listening to you at all."

Everyone fell silent.

"What do you mean by they may or may not have been listening?"

Holding his glass in the air, the director stared angrily at Sanguk. After he had arrived on the island, he had come to see Sanguk's the most often. He was the one who observed him and his surroundings. At times he was impudent and at times he couldn't hide his apparent anxiety.

"I felt it several times but I really don't care for your twisted responses. Tell me simply what you mean." There was an impatient note in his voice. Now that it was out, Sanguk wasn't about to hold back.

"It doesn't matter how simply I put it, because it really doesn't matter whether they were listening to you or not in the first place."

"You lost me," the director said.

"Well..." the chief doctor, flustered, was trying to interrupt, but Sanguk said it first. "To be frank, those people were not listening to your voice, but a voice of someone whom they had buried deep in their minds. Through your voice, they heard that person's voice once again."

"To whom did I lend my voice?" The director seemed to have finally caught on. There was no need for Sanguk to hesitate.

"Please forgive me for sounding rude. Perhaps it was the voices of the previous directors. I think it was their voices. To give you an easy example, they thought they were listening to the fourth director, Shū Masahide." Sanguk paused for a moment but the director didn't say anything.

"...."

Sanguk went on,

"Thirty years ago, they were standing there in columns to meet a new director, just like today. There they listened to the new director's powerful and moving speech, a speech like they'd never heard before. They were encouraged, they gained a new hope and strength from this new director's speech." Sanguk's voice began to get excited.

"So I was repeating the same promises thirty years later." The director's eyes clearly showed disappointment. But he was a man of placidity. He wasn't about to interrupt Sanguk who was getting more and more wound up. Although disappointed, he had some room to smile mischievously. Sanguk didn't seem to care about the director's expression.

"He promised he would build a paradise for the lepers on the island. He persuaded them to help him make this island their home where they could live comfortably, supporting each other, without having to wander aimlessly after being mistreated and driven out of society. He encouraged them to have pride, dignity, and to be productive individuals. He promised he would build more wards and medical facilities and improve the other social support systems. In order to do this, he advised the patients that they themselves had to be reborn, rise out of their despair and shake off their habit of wandering. He urged them to be proud of building their own paradise. The patients applauded him wholeheartedly."

"He did keep his promise, didn't he?"

"Yes, but instead of keeping his promise, he built his own statue here."

The smile disappeared from the director's face.

"I think you're suffering from some sort of neurosis. This is the second time I'm hearing the statue story. What exactly is it that you want to say about the statue?" The director certainly was confused but he wasn't about to interrupt Sanguk. The invisible tension between the two completely silenced the room. Sanguk's impassioned voice wasn't about to cool down either.

"I think you know very well what the statue stands for. The reason why I mentioned the statue twice already is the people who were standing before you have seen too many of those statues. Even after Director Shū, every time a new director came, they saw their statue. Actually, they saw an image of Director Shū's statue. Those people who stood before you today saw ten times the hidden image of a statue in their new director. Every director who has come here has wanted to have a statue of himself.

Some have been successful and some have failed. Either way, what was left on the island was distrust. To be frank, those directors who were successful were the worst off."

"...."

"And so they always end up listening to Director Shū's speech and seeing the statue in the new director. They've experienced it more than ten times! You said in your speech that this entire island is filled with a sense of distrust and experiences of betrayal, but their sense of distrust and betrayal originates from the numerous statues of Shū Masahide. I'm sorry to say this but they can't help but think the same about you. I'm trying to say I have no doubt that while they were listening to your speech they were searching for Shū's statue."

As the party turned into a quarrel over the statue, people began to leave the room one by one, pretending to go out to take walks. But Sanguk and the director continued.

"How strange!" the director muttered to himself. "Only the dead speak on this island. Living people don't speak at all. The non-existent statue speaks now, the ghosts of those who died trying to escape speak, the numerous spirits in the Mallyŏng hall speak…Those are the only ones who speak. The dead come alive and speak about themselves here on this island. What's going on?"

"Yes, you're right. Like you said, it's only the dead who speak on this island. The living don't need to speak, because the dead have already spoken. And the dead are the only ones who speak honestly. This island is the island of the dead, but I'm sure there will be times when the living will speak about themselves." Sanguk agreed with the director for the first time. Their conversation was reaching its conclusion.

"The island of the dead. The island of the dead…That seems quite fitting." The director nodded as if everything had become clear.

"But when do you think the living will speak?" the director asked. Sanguk solved his curiosity with a simple answer.

"When they're dead. They'll begin speaking after they breathe their last breath. On the island of the dead, only the dead can speak."

6

Director Cho's speech must not have made much of an impression on the patients. It wasn't clear that Sanguk's comments about the shadow of Director Shū were true, but it was clear that the speech didn't awaken the hope and trust that the director had hoped for. The next morning, the director was betrayed yet again. In the singles residence in Chungang village, someone committed suicide.

The suicide became the director's second welcoming present. By the time Sanguk entered the office, the director and the chief doctor had already left for the scene in Chungang village.

"The director asked for you before he left," the chief of personnel said, looking at Sanguk out of the corner of his eye. "I'm afraid you went too far last night. He asked me about your background."

"My background?"

"Yes, about your past. He said you're like a mole that digs to the core of the island and wondered whether there was any particular reason for this. Well, he soon laughed it off, but don't you think you went too far?"

What he said was full of foreboding and suddenly Sanguk felt frightened. There was nothing wrong with the director asking for the head of the hygiene division before he left to investigate a suicide, but asking about his past wasn't welcome. Even if it was a joke. If he wanted to know about his past, he couldn't expect to find anything out simply by asking the chief of personnel, other than what was on his resume: he was a first year medical school dropout and an army medic during the Korean War. Beyond that, nobody on the island knew anything about his past, even the chief of personnel. If a person says he has secrets, he has secrets. For thirty years, there was one secret he'd kept hidden deep inside his heart. And for almost ten years after he had come to the island, he had kept the story to himself. It was not that he had tried too hard to keep it a secret. It was the same with other people on the island—no one asked about each other's past nor was there any need to talk about it openly. It's natural to keep a personal matter or two hidden. Even Sanguk himself hadn't paid much attention to it. If the director really wanted to know about it, he had no intention of hiding it from him.

However, the problem was the timing. It wasn't quite the time to talk about his past. There was a danger of instilling an unnecessary prejudice in him. There were already signs of trouble from the previous day's speech. The director promised to build a true paradise for them. But for now, it was only that—a promise. He better not try to erect a statue of himself in this imagined paradise. It was necessary to disappoint him gently. It was necessary to have him stop thinking about building a statue for himself, a desire which was hidden right now. Sanguk didn't want his attitude to bias him in any way. But how had the director become interested in his past?

Sanguk felt invisible eyes gazing intently at his back and he shuddered. He went to Chungang village with a heavy sense of foreboding. When he went down to the village, he was alarmed once again. The suicide was just as had been reported that morning to the main hospital. Han Min, who had lived in the facility for single men, had taken cyanide. Sanguk arrived in the village after the corpse, which had turned blackish red as if burnt, had been taken to the clinic.

Sanguk was surprised. He had known Min personally. He was no longer a patient. After being on the island for six years, he had been cured. Although he had slight scars on his fingers and face, after three bacteriological exams the results had remained negative. He was full of hope. However, like other former patients, even after they were completely cured, they couldn't easily leave the island. He never gave up though. He clung tenaciously to his dream of leaving the island, and he wrote endlessly about his experiences. He was writing about the joys and sorrows of life, living on the island and his experiences of fighting the disease. After writing these stories, he would send them to the mainland—in place of himself. He sent one after another to newspapers and magazines.

Each time he sent a story to a nonfiction contest he never failed to add a note:

> I'm not sure if my stories are worth publishing in your esteemed paper, but I'm sending this to get your opinion.
> If you could read the manuscript, I would be grateful. I look forward to hearing from you.

With that note inside the manuscript, he never gave up hope. But just because he wrote the note didn't mean that he got good news. In fact, there was never any news from the mainland. He never got any feedback on his manuscripts. Either the manuscript came back with no comment or never came back at all. But Min never got tired.

I look forward to hearing from you. Hearing good news…

"I think my stories are too somber. I guess my writing style is lacking, too, but I don't understand why my stories get rejected every single time. Today, only the manuscript came back. I don't think they even bothered to open it," Min had said to Sanguk only a couple of days before he died, venting his frustration. But Sanguk had failed to notice the dim shadow of frustration in his wry smile. Min had committed suicide.

Sanguk felt parched. However, as usual, he didn't try hard to repress his emotions or keep them to himself for very long. At the clinic, the director and some of the other managerial executives were discussing the circumstances of the suicide. The director seemed extremely annoyed with yet another incident since his arrival.

"Damn it! He didn't even bother to leave a suicide note!"

". . ."

"All right. Didn't anybody notice anything suspicious in the way he spoke or acted?" Nobody answered. The director sounded irritated as if he had been humiliated by the suicide. In any case, with this kind of incident, there wouldn't be any special circumstances. It was one of the many suicides that occurred on the island. The circumstances leading up to the suicide were usually the same—either similar reasons were given or similar suicide notes were left. It was a custom not to investigate if no suicide note was left. There was no point investigating. Even without an investigation, the dead had already begun speaking. It was simple to take care of matters after the person's death. After they issued a death certificate, the corpse would be taken to the crematory, and then to Mallyŏng hall. The paper work added an extra bit of trouble. The same procedure was used for Min since it was the established protocol for suicides. Sanguk as the head of the hygiene division had to follow these preset procedures. No one cared about the suicide. Nobody except the director showed any interest in figuring out the reasons behind the act. It was obvious that the director couldn't understand.

As they were leaving the clinic, the director turned to Sanguk and, as if criticizing him, said "Mr. Yi, I know you haven't trusted me from the beginning. I guess that man couldn't trust my promises either." He was talking about the paradise which he had mentioned in his inaugural speech and was saying that, just as Sanguk wasn't pleased with his promises, Min too didn't believe them and, therefore, had committed suicide. Indirectly, he was saying that Sanguk had to be pleased to have found such a strong and courageous supporter who so flatly rejected his promises. The director couldn't hide the anger in his eyes watching Sanguk approach this unexpected incident without even flinching. Perhaps it was natural that he felt that way.

Turning to him, Sanguk smiled warmly because he realized that the director had begun to see things more objectively.

"It's not a matter of me trusting you or not. It does appear to be true that Han Min didn't think of this island as a paradise," Sanguk carefully reaffirmed the director's words. The director once again stepped forward.

"Not only didn't that bastard believe this island was a paradise, but he didn't even believe in a future paradise. If one thinks that way, there's no room for hope."

Before he got in the car, which was parked on the front lawn, he muttered as if making a promise to himself, "It can't be done this way. Not this way..."

It couldn't be done. Not this way.

After parting with the director, Sanguk absent-mindedly repeated what he had said and walked toward Min's quarters, feeling utterly lost. The dead man had left nothing. People who ended their own lives on the island usually didn't leave anything behind, not even a note. Not leaving a suicide note was almost a tradition. However, Sanguk didn't feel at ease. This time, he wanted to see with his own eyes how much Min wanted to leave the island and how his wish had been mercilessly ruined by betrayal. He wanted to see the hollow emptiness that Min's desperate longing had left behind in this world. There was something else he also had to make sure of. He wanted to make sure there really was nothing left behind. Sanguk had once told Min—who had become something of a collector of island tales—about a boy who had left the island a long time ago. Min's eyes gleamed while listening to the story and afterwards he'd been writing stories about it. "Just wait. I'll have a surprise for you. The story of the boy will be a really good one," Min had said to Sanguk.

But Sanguk never saw the story about the boy. In fact, he didn't even know if Min had ever written about the boy. After this conversation, Min hardly talked about the boy or his writing or how it was going. Then this thing happened. Sanguk felt a need to find out what might have happened to the boy's story. It didn't really matter to Sanguk whether the story had been written or not, but he did want to make sure that the story had disappeared together with Min.

Min's room had already been cleaned and sterilized, and it sat there open and empty. Although it was called a single room, two men shared it, so it was a little different than the standard meaning of a single room. However, since Min's roommate had not returned from a holiday trip to the mainland, he had had a single room the last couple of months. The room had been sterilized and cleaned by volunteers and coworkers from the hygienic department. Things left by the deceased not delivered to the main hospital should not be in the room. As expected, there was nothing in the room. His room had always been cluttered with crumpled manuscript pages but not even a single scrap of paper remained. The people who cleaned the room wouldn't have removed any manuscripts from there without permission. Min must have gotten rid of them himself since the cleaning people would not have touched anything without permission.

Sanguk went to the kitchen and found traces of burnt paper still lying near the furnace. It looked as though Min had burned quite a few of his manuscripts and then doused the fire with water. There were traces of sodden ashes on the kitchen floor. The boy's story must have gone into the fire with the others. He needn't worry about it anymore. After making certain that there was no trace of the story, Sanguk felt both relieved and empty.

"It shouldn't be this way. Really..." He came out

of the kitchen and sat down on the wooden platform beside Min's room and muttered once again what the director had said.

As he had said, it really shouldn't be this way! Sanguk was aware of it from the beginning, but his meaning of "it shouldn't be this way" was quite different from the director's. Even though they used those same words, they meant the exact opposite of each other. For the director, Min's suicide was another escape, not any different from the ones that had occurred on his first night. Min didn't trust his promise of a paradise, and he didn't try to trust it. Therefore it was a betrayal. It was an escape both from the island and from the dream of creating a paradise. The director thought the two incidents were identical. That was why he bitterly kept repeating how it shouldn't be this way. It was natural.

But Sanguk thought differently. He couldn't let go of the director's thinking. He knew that the two incidents were exact opposites. If one regarded the first as a true escape from the island, then this second was the complete failure of a persistent will to escape. In that sense, the suicide was an eternal return to the island. For Min, it wasn't an escape, but a sad and eternal return to it.

It was true that at one time death had been the islanders' last means of escape from their accursed fate. That was at the time the disease was regarded as incurable, hereditary, and a humiliating curse from heaven. They were forced to this forgotten island in the South Sea and were cruelly exploited for their labor up until the last moments of their lives. They had two choices for escape—swimming to the mainland and risking their lives, or accepting their fate and quietly waiting for the day that God had promised would bring comfort and happiness. Some courageous young people repeatedly tried to escape by swimming, while most others waited for the blessed day promised by God. The churches and chapels scattered around the island were symbols of the islanders' deep and sorrowful prayers. Then there were the people who had grown too weary to wait for the blessed and promised day and forced it to come a bit sooner. In those days, suicide was a way to end a miserable and wretched life. So it was natural for the director to think of Min's death as a kind of escape.

But that was then. It had happened that way when there had been no hope of being cured and the island was nothing more than a huge slave camp where unendurable labor was forced upon the patients. There was no other future than a wretched end to a miserable life. But it was completely different now. The disease had proved to be curable and not hereditary. There was no more forced labor like in the past and the living conditions were improving day by day. Anybody could leave the island if they so wished and there was no need to end one's life in order to leave.

Suicide was a form of eternal return to the island. It was even more so in Min's case. He had persistently wanted to leave the island. He had been cured and it seemed as if he could leave the island whenever he wanted. But he couldn't quite leave the island. There was another huge obstacle. He had wanted to leave the island, but not as a patient. He had wished to return to the world where he could mingle with others, not as a former patient, but as a human being who had started having all kinds of humanly desires. He wanted to leave the island and coexist with people on the outside. Perhaps he was more desperate than other cured patients who simply wanted to leave their diseased nest. For him a paradise created for an isolated group was no longer a paradise. It was no longer a problem for Min who had heard the threats from the hospital staff that a leper couldn't live peacefully even after he left the island. Even with his resolute attempts to shake off his deep-seated fear and go back to the world, he couldn't get a response, he couldn't break through the stone wall that surrounded the outside world. In the end, like many people on the island, he collapsed in front of the wall and chose to have his bones buried in a corner of Mallyŏng hall. It was not an escape but an eternal return to the destiny of a leper. His corpse—burnt like coal from thc cyanide—proved it even more.

The director couldn't possibly have understood all that. He was the one who tried creating a paradise for Min. He couldn't understand that those who were asked to leave the island but couldn't and those who risked their lives swimming across the ocean to escape were the same. He couldn't understand when and where this betrayal had begun. He only understood that no one considered this island to be their paradise, and that's why he promised them a new paradise. By keeping his promise the island's contradiction would be corrected. It was natural for the director to see Min's suicide as another attempt at escape.

But it had nothing to do with it.

Mumbling, Sanguk leaned his head on the wall, watching the sky flowing sideways from the western mountaintop. Over Sipcha peak, there was a blue summer sky with a thin whisp of black smoke spiraling upwards. They must be releasing Min's soul from his flesh in the crematory behind the hill. He watched the gray smoke curling up into the sky for a while as it slowly disappeared. He stood up abruptly.

"Now he'll start speaking. No, he has already started to speak." Sanguk was mumbling to himself as he slowly walked toward the clinic,

"I wonder if the director can hear their words...when will the director understand the words of the dead..."

7

A few days later, Director Cho decided to create a council of elders. It was an ominous sign.

Everyone around the director watched him with great curiosity wondering what kind of effect these incidents would have on him. Sanguk, who was interested in the director's every move, was also curious for no other reason than the strength he had displayed during his speech. There wasn't anything visible. Promises had been made by each of the directors who had come to the island and had been heard again and again. For a while, the director attentively asked questions, carefully observed things and, in all earnestness, collected his thoughts. He looked as if he lacked all confidence and Sanguk was relieved to see him like this. These consecutive incidents could have driven him into a corner of more serious disappointment and greater hesitation, but the result was just the opposite. Something ominous was beginning to surface. The incidents didn't have the effect Sanguk had hoped. A few days after

Han Min's suicide, the director suddenly made his move. Perhaps it was a sign when he began to ask questions and quietly to collect his thoughts. A decision that came after much hesitation and serious reflection could only be more systematic and rigid.

One morning, the director instituted a new organizational structure for the hospital. First, he took down the slogans of the previous directors that hung on the center wall of the clinic and in the main office and replaced them with his own: "Openness," "Solidarity," "Cooperation," and "Reconstruction." These four new slogans were a simplification of what he had said during his speech. They intimated that, no matter what, his original intent would not be changed. But that wasn't all. What he wanted to instill in the patients went even further: "Leprosy can be cured. Leprosy is not hereditary." Within a few days, large signs sprung up all over the island. Next he implemented a plan to improve the treatment of the patients by hospital staff.

"The more you fear a disease, the more fearful it becomes. It's the same with the patients. The more distance you keep, the more miserable and vengeful they become. You know about this disease now, right? You have to change your attitude first." He advised the nurses and pharmacists not to keep such distance from the patients. He asked them not to wear surgical masks and hygienic gloves and not to use tweezers when they dispensed pills except in very special cases. The director ordered all of the doctors, nurses, and the rest of the staff to follow this new directive. He also abolished the rule that required patients to keep a distance of four to five steps, to turn their heads halfway, and to cover their mouths when they talked to healthy people.

In order to improve the morale in the patients' zone, and because it was considered to be a symbol of the brutal forced labor and persecution of Shū's days, he ordered that the chimney of the brick factory in the middle of Chungang village be destroyed. In so doing, he eliminated an object of the patients' long-standing hatred. He also ordered that the wards and the parks be kept nice and clean to prevent them from sinking into gloom. He had the barbed wire fence between the personnel zone and patients' zone removed, and the format of the once-a-month supervised meetings between the parents and uninfected children was changed. The meetings were now to be arranged at individually convenient times and places. As he shuttled back and forth between the clinic in the patients' zone and the main personnel office, he conceived one new measure after another and immediately implemented them.

The most astonishing measure among the ones he proposed was the mixing of the students from the personnel zone with the uninfected students from the buffer zone. One day he closed the branch of the elementary school that was located in the buffer zone. Of course this had been discussed and arranged with the principal of the main school, Principal Song. The director ordered the students in the branch school to go to the main school and had them receive the same instruction in the same classrooms. It was a hasty decision. People in the hospital were speechless. Most of the people in the personnel zone were hospital staff and their families and he thought that they would understand and support this new measure. But they immediately opposed it.

"Well, he had mentioned it before, but I'd said that it's not a simple matter so I'd seriously consider it and give it more thought. It wasn't decided at all. But the next day, his order came...." Even the principal was baffled and couldn't continue.

However, the director stayed firm in his decision. He wasn't going to pay any heed to opposition from the staff. Once it was decided, there was nothing left to do but implement the decision. Starting the following day, the children from the branch school were forced to attend the main school. Some parents expressed their discontent by not sending their children to school, but the director, underscoring that the decision was final, did not want to talk about it.

"He certainly is a man of action. If you want to make a drastic change, it should be done like that...I should be thankful that he didn't order the teachers from the leper preschool to teach at the main school. I would be out of job if he'd done that..." said Haewŏn. It was clear that he didn't really mean it, so this "man of action" talk was just nonsense. The real problem was the reaction from the patients' zone regarding the director's rash and unprecedented measures.

The signs with the new slogans that had been

placed in nearly every nook and cranny of the island proclaimed a promise of new hope for the patients. But they showed no interest and carried on as usual even after they had heard about the new management measures. When the director requested to have the park road rebuilt or decided to demolish the brick factory chimney, the patients quietly followed the orders but they remained uninterested. They kept absolutely quiet regarding both his decisions and his orders. Even after the nurses and the doctors began handing out medicine with their bare hands, the patients looked unimpressed. When they heard that their own children had started commuting to the main school to study with the children of the personnel zone, they had blank expressions on their faces. Their hearts remained tightly closed. In their abysmal dark silence, they quietly followed the director's moves. No one knew how long they were going to keep silent and what they were thinking.

At last, the director became frustrated. Perhaps their silence was more threatening to his new measures than any open opposition. He could not help but be surprised at the colossal, empty silence. For a while he looked as if he was trying hard to break through that mysterious and silent wall. Because of this, he decided to organize a council of elders to find out what the patients were thinking. He came up with this idea after much deliberation to break through the silent wall of anxiety. As far as Sanguk was concerned, it wasn't a good sign.

Again, things didn't turn out the way he thought they would. Once again, the patients showed no interest—neither good nor bad—in his proposals. When his order that they select the seven most influential elderly people from each village came down, the seven elders who had already been acting as representatives from their villages simply gathered at the assembly hall office in Chungang village on the designated day. But they had no reaction to the director's new suggestions.

"Based on recommendations from this council's meetings, I plan to institute various measures that will affect hospital management. This elder's council is expected to act as an advisory committee. Furthermore, the council will function as an official decision-making body regarding problems that each village's local government must adjudicate." Even though the director revealed his plan with passion, the seven representatives watched him disinterestedly, indifferent expressions on their faces. They maintained their heavy silence.

"Each of you came here as a representative of the patients from the seven villages. From now on, I plan to give each village as much autonomy as possible as long as it doesn't interfere with basic policies of hospital administration. For the benefit of each of your villages, for the patients as a whole and to make this island truly your paradise, I would appreciate any suggestions you may have as well as your frank opinions," the director continued. Although his voice was sincere and earnest, there was no sign from the elders that they accepted or welcomed his decisions. Instead of showing interest, they quietly followed his movements as if their lips were frozen and they were gripped by fear. But the director wasn't about to step back from his decision once he had spat it out. The morning after he had revealed his new plan, Sanguk went to his office to give him the hospital report and the director seemed quite confident.

"By the way Manager Yi, since you've mentioned Shū Masahide many times, I looked into his background. He was quite a man, unreserved and frank, wasn't he?" As soon as Sanguk finished his report, the director abruptly brought up Director Shū as if he had been waiting anxiously for this chance.

"Yes. He did accomplish many things swiftly and efficiently. As you mentioned before, he was the one who rebuilt this island," Sanguk answered, not knowing what was going on. He waited for the director to continue.

"Not only did he carry out many of his plans but, in the beginning, the way he executed them was commendable," the director continued.

"Yes, at least in the beginning there weren't any problems. I heard that the entire island was greatly moved when they first heard his plans and they volunteered their labor."

"I think that was a tremendous success, Director Shū moving the patients to the point that they volunteered their labor to work on a construction site. But in order for things to happen that way, he needed a mechanism that would make the patients themselves want to volunteer."

"That's why Director Shū selected ten representatives among the patients from each village and created a council. He consulted them during the decision-making process regarding the new hospital management and, as the patients' representatives, they listened intently and reflected on these various suggestions. It functioned as sort of a half self-governing body and half-consultative body. Actually, it's not very different from the council of elders you recently came up with," said Sanguk. Ultimately that was it. Now Sanguk realized why the director had brought up Shū Masahide. By going one step farther than the director, Sanguk had revealed his point. Now that Sanguk had started it, the director began to talk openly and without reservation about what was on his mind.

"You certainly catch on quickly, Manager Yi. In any case, there are some things I've been wanting to find out from you."

"…"

"How long are they going to be like that?" He suddenly raised his voice, as if the elders' silence had something to do with Sanguk.

"You know, the elders' council. They treat me as if they're looking at someone completely insignificant. Why are they like that? There must be a reason why they keep their mouths shut so tightly."

"..."

"Don't tell me it's because this is 'the island of the dead' again! Don't you think there's a limit to leaving the island to the dead? I was talking to living people. I don't mean to harm them, do I? I told them to relay officially any suggestions or complaints the patients might have regarding hospital management or its policies through these council meetings. I also asked them—on behalf of the five thousand patients—to request any changes whatsoever concerning things they dislike or are dissatisfied with among the things I'm doing. What is it that they don't like about my suggestions? Why did they turn into mutes?"

"It's not that they disliked your suggestions. They were afraid that there might be a betrayal lurking there." Sanguk finally started speaking. In contrast to the director's coarse tone, Sanguk was reserved and calm.

"A betrayal? Who'll be betraying whom? So, they're afraid I'll betray them and that's why they're consumed with fear this far in advance?" The director attacked Sanguk with glaring eyes. From the director's reaction to his word "betrayal," Sanguk gathered that he understood the word much more lightly. Sanguk continued calmly.

"Allow me to use Director Shū as an example again. In the end, they witnessed Director Shū building his own statue. You could say that he began to build his statue when he selected the patients' representatives and set up the advisory council. As long as this island exists, Director Shū's statue will remain eternally emblazoned on their psyches..."

"..."

"What they fear is not being betrayed by you, but being betrayed by themselves."

"Explain this to me. What do you mean by being betrayed by themselves?" The director at last seemed to have calmed down.

"To be precise, the building of the statue was not initiated by Director Shū. It was first brought up by the advisory council. The members of the council—representing the patients—built the statue themselves and dedicated it to him. You probably doubt that that could've happened. But it actually happened here. To be more frank, I think this could happen, not only in Director Shū's time, but any time."

There were a few more things Sanguk wanted to explain to the director concerning the advisory council. Despite what the director said, the advisory council's jurisdiction—and their ability to agitate for the welfare of the patients—would always be limited to what he would allow. The director's position on the island was that of an absolute ruler who held all the authority and all the power to govern both the hospital and the rest of the island. Perhaps the term "govern" was not the most appropriate one. He was in charge not only of hospital management but also of running the everyday matters that pertained to the lives of all the islanders. He could set basic rules and regulations to maintain order and could also have them enforced. He was also in a position to mete out the necessary punishments for those who broke the rules. It was natural that the advisory council representing the welfare of the patients had limited powers. It was the director who ruled and the patients who were ruled, and so it was obvious from the very beginning who would have to yield when disagreement arose. In those cases, the granting of a wish would depend entirely on the director. No matter how much the director tried to betray the patients, the advisory council couldn't impeach him. Perhaps that was the most fundamental problem. The basis of the patients' ability to maintain their rights and to look after their own welfare vis-à-vis the director would be the power to choose. It was meaningless if the patients were not allowed to have the final say. In any extreme situation, the advisory council did not have the power to choose the director. From the very beginning, that was not possible.

It was natural then that the advisory council had no choice but to avoid extreme confrontation. It was also the law of the power relationship to avoid any kind of conflict with the director within the domain of his generosity. After a while the members of the advisory council slowly learned the extremely selfish philosophy of power: it was beneficial for them to be near the ruler rather than being ruled. The diseased had the same desires as the healthy. As the pain of those who are ruled intensifies, their wish to escape becomes greater and greater. Therefore they readily succumb to their own weak human desires that are buried deep within them and move toward the side of the ruled.

Of course Director Shū hadn't figured that out from the start. He couldn't deny that the deadly labor got steadily worse with each passing day and the various measures imposed on the patients made the council react that way in the end. They began to move away from the ruled to the ruler and, finally, they built the statue for their ruler. The ultimate betrayal was carried out by the advisory council. Sanguk carefully explained the details of the betrayal. After he finished explaining, he looked at the director with a tinge of excitement in his eyes.

"Although the problem lay in the advisory council, they couldn't choose or not choose their director." Sanguk was a little concerned that he might have been too harsh. But the director didn't seem too bothered with what he had said. He looked nonchalant, as if he didn't care too much about Sanguk's opinions. But he was attentive enough to Sanguk's words that he forgot about the ash that was dangling from the end of his cigarette.

"Instead of saying that they betrayed themselves, isn't it possible that they truly wanted to thank the director for what he had done?" The director finally showed some reaction. From the grin on the director's face, Sanguk knew immediately that what he had said wasn't what he really wanted to say. But now there was no emotional room for him to smile.

"You're right. The betrayal developed slowly. At the time, they didn't even realize it themselves. There is a thing called a traitor's truth. A traitor is more faithful to a new ruler. Perhaps they were truly thankful, at least when they were looking at the living Shū Masahide standing in front of the statue that they had dedicated to him; and again once a month, when they gathered in front of the statue to offer prayers of thanksgiving and sang until they grew hoarse. However, the truth soon surfaced. One day one of the council members was stabbed to death by a patient. In the end, the owner of the statue met the same fate. He collapsed one morning, spilling blood all over the front of his own statue, during the thanksgiving prayer. Finally, they saw their own betrayal clearly." Sanguk's face turned pale.

"But didn't that happen several decades ago?"

"These people have repeatedly suffered from the

nightmare of the statue during those several decades."

"So you're telling me that once again I've stirred their nightmare? But isn't it about time that they wake from that nightmare? I don't plan to build a statue." A hint of a joke was mixed in with what the director said. However Sanguk's pale face didn't change.

"Whether you want the statue or not comes later."

"But you can't just wait around forever."

"There's no other way now."

"'No other way now.' What do you mean? I told you there isn't going to be any more betrayal on this island." The director said this firmly and suddenly stood up. As if to reassure him, he nodded firmly several times toward Sanguk and asked him a rather strange favor.

"By the way, I need you to meet with the council separately. I think you're the most appropriate person. I've already explained to them fully, but I think it would help if you could see them and explain once again and try to persuade them."

"..."

"Well, I don't mean you need to do this today or tomorrow. Do it at your earliest convenience..."

"I didn't know you asked for favors."

"Well, this isn't a favor really. It's more of a direct order." The director smiled again.

"I understand." Sanguk left the office.

8

The car had already departed for the clinic. In front of the entrance, only the director's jeep waited for its owner. But it wasn't certain when he would be heading back. Sanguk had no choice but to walk down to the clinic alone.

"This isn't a favor really. It's more of a direct order."

After stopping by the clinic, Sanguk thought of going to see Elder Hwang Hŭibaek. If he were going to talk to anyone on the elders' council, it would have to be Elder Hwang who was in his late sixties and came from Chungang village. It wasn't exaggeration to say that each of the five thousand islanders had a bitter history of his own. The number of tragedies on the island equaled the number of those who had passed away added to the number of those who were still living on the island. Among all of them, Elder Hwang had the most amazing story. From the time he had come to the island after contracting the disease until now, he had suffered the most dreadful things. He had many tales. He was the symbol of the island's tragic history. He was a living legend but he always kept silent. He silently closed his eyes and endured the problems, waiting for the ordeals to pass. Everyone on the island kept the image of Elder Hwang in their hearts and quietly followed him. When Elder Hwang prayed, they prayed too; when Elder Hwang cursed God, they cursed God too. Meeting Elder Hwang was like meeting all of the islanders.

Sanguk walked slowly down the hill, staring into the distance at the patients' zone that once had been encircled by barbed wire. The sea in the bow-shaped bay that curved in past Chungang village was especially blue today. If he saw Elder Hwang, what could he possibly say to him? What could he say in the face of his intimidating, suffocating silence?

Isn't it about time that they wake from that nightmare? I don't plan to build a statue.

Suddenly the director's confident words echoed in his ears. Sanguk stopped abruptly as if he had finally found a thread in his thoughts. But soon he took a step and shook his head.

"Can he really promise that?"

Of course, he couldn't find a clear and definite answer in the director's words. Even if the director was confident, he was not reliable yet. There was nothing for him to do but wait. But Sanguk couldn't wait peacefully for him. He thought of Shū Masahide. The answer lay with him. As long as the director's spirit was still alive, the answer to a part of the question lay with Shū.

In the beginning, Shū had given no indication that he wanted his statue built. He really had a naïve passion for turning the island into a paradise for those who had been driven here. Shū's plans had instilled great hope and excitement in the one thousand patients or so on the island at the time of his arrival. Even now, there were many who remembered the day of his inauguration speech.

One early spring morning that year, as was the

customary practice, nearly one thousand patients gathered in front of the assembly hall to listen to the new director's inaugural speech. When the time came, the director, who rode in a car from the personnel zone, stood in front of the patients for the first time. Everyone fell silent. The director who stepped up to the podium had immediately silenced the patients standing there in formation. The first impression he made was a formidable one. His tall stature was impressive and he stood silently looking down on the patients for a while. He had a dark complexion and an oddly hooked-nose. Compared to his tall stature and powerful physique, his eyes were unusually small.

"Hello everyone!"

He began to speak. His voice was high-pitched like that of a woman and it grated like metal on metal. He had both the voice and the look of the ambitious type, those who crave both glory and fame. The patients standing in the lines soon began comforting themselves. They shouldn't judge him because he had beady eyes and a piercing voice. There was a rumor that he had volunteered to become the director to help the patients. He had graduated from a prestigious medical school in Japan and started as a hygienist at the Government-General department. His past official posts promised him a bright future. If he had abandoned the guarantee of a bright future and volunteered to come to this remote island, he must have had a deep concern for the welfare of the patients. Even before he arrived on the island, there was a rumor that he had used the fund from the Kura Association and bought infertile land on the island. It was improper to judge a person by appearances alone.

That morning, the patients tried hard to rid themselves of their bias toward the new director, which was formed on the basis of outward appearances. Shū continued his impassioned speech in his piercing voice.

"I promise you…"

He promised the patients that he would turn the island into their paradise. He declared that the primary aim would be new measures to improve the hospital facilities, to expand the rooms for the patients in the patients' zone, and to improve the convalescence areas. He proudly said that by doing that, he would make this island Asia's best, the world's best leper sanitarium, making it a true and new home for those who had been expelled from society.

"You've been held in contempt and persecuted by your own neighbors. How many hundreds and thousands of miles did you have to walk with these memories of contempt and persecution? You are all tired from wandering. Now all of you have gathered here as neighbors. Let's create a new home with your other pitiable neighbors. Let's create a home and live harmoniously and welcome those who are still being held in contempt and being persecuted by their neighbors and family."

Shū's moving speech was enough to dispel their doubts and apprehension. After he finished, there were some who sobbed quietly. In their memory Shū's speech was inspirational. He got serious about the work but he wouldn't start it immediately simply because of that reaction. Instead, he made sure that things were ready before he actually launched his plans for the island paradise. First he selected ten representatives from among the patients and established a consultative body called a "patients' advisory council." The advisory council functioned as a mediator between the patients and the director. Then, he continued to emphasize the need for constructing a paradise on the island by conducting a meeting with the council members every Saturday. He continued to persuade them until the patients themselves were eager, filled with expectations for this new paradise. Finally, the patients volunteered their labor for the construction. Then and only then did Shū fully launch his plan.

In order to rebuild the island, they needed bricks first. Therefore he thought it necessary to build a brick factory. With the help of the ten council members, the director selected a site for the brick factory and soon held a groundbreaking ceremony. One cool autumn morning, a month after he arrived, the brick factory was built. Then they brought in a Chinese brick maker. For a while, he had the people learn how to make bricks from him, but after they had learned how to make the bricks themselves and had become accustomed to it, they suggested that they no longer needed his help. They made the bricks themselves and used them as a key material for building the new residences.

All the patients worked diligently. At the time,

there were three villages in the patients' zone. People from those villages who were capable of working went to the brick factory or to the construction sites every day. Even though they continued to do hard labor, no one got tired of working. They were happy that they were getting paid for their work for the first time and, most of all, they found comfort in the fact that they were making bricks themselves to build houses with their own hands that they were going to live in themselves. They were proud that they were creating their own paradise and so they found it rewarding.

The construction went smoothly. After having made enough bricks, the construction started the following spring and continued for three years. It was a success. After the construction, two new villages, Tongsaeng and Chungang, were added to the original three villages. As a result, the patients' facilities were expanded to accommodate four thousand patients. In the patients' zone, separate facilities such as a public kitchen, a laundry, an assembly hall and a rice mill were constructed for the handicapped patients' daily convenience.

The patients were pleased with everything.

There was no one who cursed the director. During the construction period, the rations were sufficient and the doctors weren't negligent. The patients began to praise the director's virtuous deeds and, after the construction was completed, they performed the classical opera "Changhwa Hongnyŏn" in a newly built assembly hall to celebrate. Shū was pleased too. He was happy for the patients and was satisfied simply by looking at the patients being happy.

But then the problems started. Shū's plan for the paradise was more perfect than what they had built. Moreover after their first successful construction project, he was full of confidence. So he rushed to get on with the second construction project. From that point on, the seeds of the tragic fate that would slowly end his life had been sown.

"No one should promise that. It's not something that anyone can promise."

Sanguk reached the clinic and stopped in front of it. He was very confused. A shudder of horror ran through his body from his head down to his toes. He lifted his eyes toward the sky for a while as if trying to collect his thoughts. At last, he walked hurriedly toward the front entrance of the clinic.

9

Even after Sanguk finished his work at the clinic for the day, he didn't go see Elder Hwang. He didn't think he had much to say to him at this point. Instead, after he left the clinic, he ended up heading for Kubuk village and the Tolburi shore. He frequented Tolburi to refresh himself whenever he had too many things on his mind. There was nothing special to do at the beach. He just sat on a rock looking at Noktong harbor across the waves, thinking of the boy's story that was long forgotten. Through the boy's ears, he listened to a fisherman's song from a boat passing slowly by. That was the only way he spent time at the beach.

The beach at Kubuk village was notorious since long ago as a place to launch an escape. Unable to endure the constant betrayals and oppression of island life, escapees plotted and then carried out their own betrayals at the beach. There was the story of a boy who had successfully escaped from the Tolburi shore. It was the story that Sanguk had once told Han Min for his novel. Sanguk began listening to the song of the fisherman through the boy and the boy's story came to him like a strange hallucination. It was a curious story and it wasn't only about the fisherman's song. The boy had been subjected to numerous unexpected and dangerous ordeals, and there were many stories about the boy from the time he was born until the time he left the island.

The boy's first memories were of the room he grew up in. The room was always tightly locked and the boy stayed there day and night, never so much as sticking a finger outside the door. Afraid that he'd be heard, his parents did not allow him to cry out loud even when he was very young. When the boy's mother heard any sound from outside, she would quickly hide him under the covers. She would turn deathly pale when the boy happened to talk loudly. The boy was always locked up in a pitch-dark room and he was covered with a blanket to avoid the prying eyes of strangers. When his mother left for work during the day, she tied his hands behind his back so that he couldn't open the door by himself and go outside. Even when she returned home from work, he wasn't allowed out from under the blanket since she was afraid that other people might notice him.

It was because of the mother. From the beginning, she was afraid of people, and so was the boy, just like his mother. He never saw a soul. His heart pounded when he heard somebody pass outside the door. He would be so scared he would pull the covers over his head and hold his breath. But even under the covers he couldn't feel safe. Many times he felt eyes staring fixedly at him from somewhere. No matter how much he covered himself with the blanket, those eyes appeared inside the blanket and he shuddered with fear.

Besides his mother, the boy felt safe with only one other person. Sometimes in the middle of the night, there was a man who would secretly visit his mother. He would enter the room late at night and would always leave at dawn as quietly as possible. The boy was not afraid of him because he knew that the man, like his mother and himself, was afraid of people too. The man was more afraid of people. Whenever he entered the room, he would put his two remaining fingers to his lips, gesturing to the boy to keep quiet. His pale forehead would always be covered with beads of sweat, and he would stand a while with his ears to the door to make sure nobody had noticed him come in, seemingly unable to relax. His eyes reflected his fear.

It was his harsh breathing even more than his eyes that revealed how frightened he was. Yet, when he finally sat down beside the boy's mother, he attempted to conceal his fear. He always tried to suppress his heavy breathing in front of her. No matter how hard he tried, he couldn't breathe normally. That was the one thing he couldn't hide from the boy's mother. He became more fearful when he sat with her and the more he tried to suppress his fear, the more it intensified.

Whenever the man would come visit the boy's mother, he would try to restrain his breathing like that until the dawn broke in that pitch-dark room. Then he would leave. Sometimes when the boy woke up in the middle of the night, the man, who had come in quietly while he was sleeping, would endure the heavy rasping sound together with the mother. There was no need to be afraid of the man. Nor did his mother try to hide the boy from the man. But it was strange. Did the boy misunderstand? He ended up leaving his mother and the island later because of the man.

One early autumn when the late rainy season

had begun, the man, who before had visited the boy's mother only once every ten days or so, came several days in a row. He would come and mutter something to the boy's mother and leave. Instead of his controlled but heavy breathing, the boy listened to his mother's sighs all night long. Sometimes the man and his mother quarreled in low voices and sometimes his mother would sob softly.

One day, the boy's mother skipped work and wept the whole day, holding the boy in her arms. That night the man came again and took the boy from his mother, whose eyes were swollen from crying. He carried the boy on his back, running through the darkness in the rain and put the boy down near the bushes at the edge of the beach.

"See if you can hear the song of a passing fishing boat."

The man shoved the boy into the bush. He hid himself too and lay on his stomach straining to hear the fisherman's song. But they had no luck that night. Since it was pitch-dark and pouring, there was no trace of the fisherman's song. They were surrounded by the sound of heavy raindrops beating on the leaves and ocean waves lapping at the shore.

The man carried the boy back to the village. The following night, the man carried the boy again on his back and lay in the bushes just like the previous night, waiting for the song from a passing fishing boat. For three nights they waited and for those three nights it rained continuously. Finally on the third night they heard the fisherman's song. The boat slowly crept around the corner of the shoreline. The man signaled toward it by lighting and relighting matches inside his jacket. The song stopped and soon the boat drifted close to the shore. The man and the fisherman hurriedly exchanged a few words, then the boy was carried quickly onto the boat. The man covered the boy with his jacket to protect him from the rain. And while the fisherman hurriedly rowed into the dark sea, the man stood on the shore watching the boat disappear into the darkness.

That night, however, the boy returned home. Once on the boat, the boy couldn't control himself and he cried out loud. He thought of his mother, biting her lips to keep herself from crying. And he was afraid of the boatman. He was also afraid of the black billows of the sea and the mournful sound of the rain. Sitting with the man's jacket over his body, the boy couldn't stop crying. Not knowing what to do, the fisherman brought the boy back to the shore. From there the boy walked home alone in the rain. For the first time, he saw the man's dreadfully scary look that night. The man had already returned to the village and was with the boy's mother. Before the man's face had always been pale and frightened of something, but when he saw the boy who had unexpectedly returned, his face became dreadfully distorted.

"Dirty damn leper!"

The man trembled with fury as if he was about to kill the boy. The boy had never seen him look so frightening. He had never imagined it, not even in his dreams. It was the first and last time. Ultimately the man didn't forgive the boy. The following night the man took the boy to the beach again and waited impatiently for the fisherman's song in the rain. And the boy left the island for good, never to return, on a boat that passed the dark island at dawn.

This happened on the Tolburi shore at the time when Shŭ's paradise project was at its peak. Whenever Sanguk came to Tolburi, he could hear through the boy's ears the fisherman's song mixed in with the sound of the rain. After he listened to the song quietly for a while, his heart would throb with excitement. In fact, he had come to the island because of this hallucinatory song. Was it because he had known about the song for a long time? He didn't know when it had started but even before he had come to the island, he often heard the song. He thought of the small island in the South Sea sometimes at school, on the refugee road during the Korean War, and even when he was in the strict military camp. Then he would hear the night fishing boat passing by and would hear the long and plaintive melody. One cold wintry afternoon he landed on the island of the forgotten people. He smiled bitterly recalling the fisherman's song even though he didn't know himself why he had decided to come to the island.

But unlike on the mainland, he couldn't hear the hallucinatory song he'd been hearing for so long. The fishing boats still passed the island. Was it because day and night are different? But there was no more fisherman's song. The boats passed by quietly, as if they had forgotten about the island. Sanguk was disappointed. The island with no fisherman's song was not the same island he had treasured for so long in his mind. He tried hard to hear the song. Whenever he remembered, he would go sit on the beach at Tolburi and would listen for the passing fishing boats. Finally he began to hear the fisherman's song. It was through the boy.

Today, as usual, Sanguk sat on a rock following the sad, slow melody of the fisherman's song and his heart trembled slightly with excitement. He didn't leave until dusk. For some odd reason, he felt strangely shaken. When he walked out of the patients' zone, heading toward his quarters, it suddenly occurred to him that he wanted to see Miyŏn and talk to her. Instead of heading toward his quarters, he walked toward the preschool and called Miyŏn out. It was the first time that Sanguk had asked to see her. Even after she came out to meet him, he didn't feel at ease. Miyŏn seemed to have already read his mind. Sanguk was always calm and composed, careful not to convey his feelings; therefore she felt somewhat relieved seeing him in this vulnerable state. Instead of easing his anxiety, she ended up adding to his stress.

Sitting on the front lawn of the preschool surrounded by withering orange canna flowers, Miyŏn started telling her story, which she had been hesitant to talk about before. Just as Sanguk had guessed, what she had been reluctant to tell him was the story of her past—how she had been adopted into a benevolent minister's family, how she had entered the seminary school, and how she had chosen to come to the island. She told him about important decisions and choices she had made before coming to the island and the reasons behind them. Her decision to come to the island and voluntarily devote herself was not strange at all considering her background. She quietly confessed her story without pausing, as if it was a form of self-torment or perhaps even rebellion against Sanguk. Then, as if she had revealed her inner most secrets, she waited quietly for him to return the favor.

Sanguk felt more and more uneasy. It wasn't something that he hadn't expected. He guessed it right from the time when he'd sensed that she had something she wanted to tell him. Of course, he hadn't wished for that. He had hoped that what she wanted to tell him all along wasn't about her past.

But his suspicions turned out to be true. By revealing her past, Miyŏn told Sanguk precisely what she had wanted to tell him. He wasn't completely shocked but it certainly wasn't a pleasant thing to hear either. He didn't know how to take the story or how to react. He had no impulse to tell her the boy's story. He thought that it might be of some comfort to her but he gave up on the idea. A hitherto unknown hatred toward Miyŏn welled up inside him. This feeling had more to do with self-hatred for being disappointed and confused, than his inability to console her or sympathize with her. The boy's story would be a vulgar means to comfort her because it could well be offensive. He needed to wait on the boy's story a little longer. It was another personal failure having sought out Miyŏn.

10

Director Cho knew that Sanguk had not yet talked to the elders' council. Perhaps he hadn't counted on Sanguk from the beginning. He didn't ask Sanguk about it and didn't seem irritated, either.

However, it was clear that he hadn't given up on his plan. He carried it out alone quietly. There had been several meetings in the church at Chungang village. The elders' council, whose function was abstract, was vested with some concrete authority. For example, he would first need to obtain the approval from the council to recruit the patients for labor. Also, the punishment for patient misconduct—such as thirty days incarceration in Kura tower—a punishment that had been decided by the director alone in the past, would now be entrusted to the council for discussion. There had been no way in the past to prevent personal attacks since the patients had been punished by the director on the basis of the personnel officers' complaints. It was impossible to protect the patients against the bias of these officers. Their misconduct in regards to the death penalty was notorious during the colonial period. The director now vested the elders' council with the power to discuss and assess appropriate punishments. The council was also given the power to audit the accounts of the commercial division. The commercial division received, managed, and distributed all shipments to the island and was vital to the patients' well-being. Among the many hospital divisions, the commercial division alone had a separate office in Chungang village in the patients' zone and the operation was entrusted to patients who were competent in finance. From the beginning, the division had been capable of self-governance. Because of the large number of shipments, the village elders supervised the entire division, from consultation to management. The director publicly put this under the jurisdiction of the elders' council. This meant that the commercial division would become an important body in accounting for and managing the quantity of shipments.

The elders didn't object to these new proposals but they didn't show any sign that they welcomed them either. They simply accepted the director's orders. However, the director's intentions were clear: he was ready to create a stir. He wasn't about to be satisfied with a few changes or improvements since he had promised to make the island a paradise. He had devised other plans as well. In order to carry out his plans, he needed a firm foundation, and sought the patients' moral support. It was exactly what Shū had done in the past, before he launched his plan.

As anticipated, the director announced his first major plan for the island. It was utterly different from what Sanguk had expected. It was such an odd thing. His plan was not to build a brick factory or build some new houses like Shū. Nor did his plan include constructing new roads or a park.

He suggested starting a soccer team. Later, at a council meeting, he suggested the same. He argued passionately before the elders' council that in order to create a soccer team, their understanding and cooperation would be needed. Of course, he didn't mean to include the patients who were undergoing treatment. But it was ridiculous. It wasn't just absurd, it was malicious—the idea that a soccer team would be used as a vehicle for creating an island paradise. Yet he was completely sincere.

"As you are already aware, this place is not an island for the living. There is not a single living person walking around. Everyone is a ghost. They wander around the island like ghosts, talking only to the dead and waiting their turn to become ghosts themselves. Well, I can understand those who are still struggling to recover from their illness, but those who are completely cured act just the same. Let's put a soccer team together. Let's give these footless ghosts a chance to walk on the ground themselves. I'm certain there are many among the cured who can kick a ball. They should kick the ball, not just for themselves but for those who are still bedridden. You have to prove to them and to yourselves that this island is not for the dead but for the living. This has to be done. I am confident and want to encourage you…" The director's persuasion went something like that.

He wanted to give life to this dead island by having partially cured patients kick a soccer ball. But it wasn't a good idea. It wasn't easy even for those who were completely cured to kick; their limbs weren't strong enough. Losing one or two toes was common for these people. Kicking a ball with a toeless foot was absurd. It was clear that he had a hidden motive for so strongly promoting this. But he wouldn't discuss it any further. No one could guess what was on his mind. For several days, his persuasive entreaties continued and the council members were as silent as stones.

One morning the director called Sanguk into his office. When Sanguk entered the room, the director was already sitting on the couch, waiting for him.

"Good to see you. I've something to discuss with you today," he said. Sanguk sensed something was up from his greeting.

"Something to discuss? Do you mean a scolding?" He tried to hedge with an apology since he hadn't done what the director had asked him to do.

"What scolding?" he asked nonchalantly as if he had completely forgotten the favor.

"Well, you asked me to talk to the council members separately but I haven't done it. I'm sorry."

"Ah, that? It's okay. It's not necessary now. But something else..." With a cigarette dangling from the corner of his mouth, the director's mischievous smile wouldn't fade.

"If it's not that...."

"You know how I'm trying to make them play soccer..."

"That hasn't been resolved yet?"

"No, that's why I wanted to ask you a favor."

"Well, I don't know what you're going to ask me, but don't you think it's impossible?" Sanguk cut him short, assuming it was about that. But the director didn't think it was impossible at all.

"Impossible? Why would it be impossible?"

"Most people know that lepers don't have fingers and toes. Isn't it ridiculous to have them kick a ball? I mean, it's cruel."

"What's wrong with them? They aren't the lepers the outsiders know. Plus, why are they lepers? They're cured. They're no different from you or me. You're the cruel one, regarding them as lepers who can't even kick a ball. It's not cruel to have them play soccer, and I don't see any reason why they shouldn't be able to."

"..."

"But they have absolutely no confidence! They refuse to listen to what I have to say. They're just full of jealousy. Look into their eyes. They're burning with envy toward healthy people because they have no confidence. They're turning into ugly monsters as their envy and distrust grow stronger and stronger. It's of utmost importance to instill confidence in them."

"Is there anything I can do to help?" Sanguk asked.

"Yes, there is." That started it. The director turned the conversation in a different direction.

"Before I tell you what you can do to help, there is something I want to ask you first. In Shū's days…" He brought up Shū unexpectedly. Judging from the director's mischievous smile, Sanguk could guess he wasn't going to find out what the favor was immediately. For some unknown reason, the director had already dug up detailed information regarding the days when Shū was in charge of the hospital.

"I looked through the records and found an interesting figure named Satō, the chief nurse. I'm sure you know about him already, don't you?"

"Yes, I do. But…" Sanguk was curious. Sanguk knew about Satō from early on. Anyone who had ever lived on the island would certainly know about him. Satō was one of the strange figures who had lived in the memories of the islanders for more than thirty years.

Satō's days began and ended with Shū. He stood behind Shū from the very first day when he gave that passionate and moving speech. After the speech, Satō was introduced and stood on the same platform with Shū, however briefly. At the time, the patients who were standing below the platform didn't pay much attention to this short, thin, and unpleasant man with beady eyes. Satō's existence was soon forgotten. The islanders went about their lives without having to worry about Satō. But the days were drawing close when the patients would have Satō, who was inherently malicious, etched onto their memories.

It was around the time when the second construction project got underway, immediately after the great success of the first project. Several facilities had already been completed, before this second project was launched. Besides the brick factory, important facilities such as the Mallyŏng hall mausoleum to enshrine the dead, the bell pavilion, and the lighthouse to guide the passing ships had been built.

Mallyŏng hall was built behind the hills in Sinsaeng village. It was a cylindrical building topped with a roof that looked like a hat. The lighthouse ceremony was held by the south shore of Namsaeng village. The bell tower was built behind the hills of that village in the shape of the main hall of a Buddhist temple, poking out above three-meter high stone walls. Blue and golden dragons drifting in the midst of lotus flowers were carved on the columns and cross beams of the buildings, and a big bell that weighed over three tons hung in the middle. The Buddhist followers watched after the tower and rang the bell. The sound of the bell not only echoed over the island but it resonated far into the distance across the ocean.

While these buildings were being completed one by one, the nature of the work slowly began to change. The construction budgets increasingly depended on the patients' volunteer labor. Around the same time, one day each month was designated as an "appreciation day." On that day, the patients would silently pray or honor those who contributed money to the hospital facilities. It was strongly urged that the patients donate their entire wages for the upcoming construction. So they donated their wages without any complaint. Some accepted this arrangement readily and others only grudgingly. Since the decision had been made by the council who represented them, the patients donated all of their wages regardless of whether they agreed or not. The work slowed down. Their enthusiasm waned and the projects didn't progress as expected. The patients were apprehensive about the fact that the hospital's financial situation was bad enough to use their wages to continue the construction.

The morale at the work site was utterly different from the first project. But Shū's conviction didn't change. His paradise became grander and more spectacular. He had to be the director who wouldn't be forgotten by the myriad islanders. So he soon started in on the second construction project. It was irrational. The willingness and enthusiasm the patients showed during the first project couldn't be duplicated. They took every chance they got to avoid work, at times barely making it to the work site at all. They werc uneducated people who had long been accustomed to the habit of wandering and begging. They became easily depressed and rebelled for no reason, revealing their exceptionally intense jealousies and deep hatreds.

Shū Masahide began to realize that the patients would not work continuously to meet his expectations. If the project was to progress, he couldn't depend solely on their volunteer labor. He needed to devise an efficient and systematic mechanism to control them. He needed to take decisive action before it was too late.

He soon came up with a new strategy. In addition to better treatment of the council members, who had performed their services since the first project well, Shū also increased the power of the council. He tried to win over the patients through the council members and appealed for more enthusiastic cooperation. The more efficient step was the establishment of the "senior officer council." In order to supervise efficiently the patients' medical treatment and the progress of the construction work, he appointed a few healthy people in each village and organized what he called the "senior officer council." Management of the village affairs was carried out according to an agreement reached between the senior officer council and the elders' council. The senior officer council was comprised of a chief nurse as supervisor, one head nurse, two attendants, an agriculture supervisor, an equipment and supply supervisor, and an assistant secretary. In addition to the council members, there was also one village representative, an equipment assistant, three to four operations assistants, and two foremen. The chief nurses assigned to each village as heads of the "senior officer council" were Japanese and were mostly former detectives, policemen, or military police.

Shū was still not content so he established a patrol office between the personnel zone and the patients' zone. He stationed one head patrol officer and ten officers there and had them constantly patrolling the patients' zone. They were also in charge of the detention room and matters pertaining to meetings. This rigid administrative organization resembled closely that of a forced labor camp. The patients became even more despondent. They reluctantly worked and openly began to complain. During this time, the Sino-Japanese War broke out, and the rations of daily necessities fell to inadequate levels. Even the food rations were reduced and medicine was scarce. The patients' wages were hardly paid at all and the senior officer council's control grew tighter.

The temperament of the chief nurses grew violent. The council members who represented the welfare of the patients didn't dare confront the senior officer council's ruthlessness. They were like mutes. Some of the council members and Korean patrol officers were busy looking out for their own interests rather than trying to help their fellow patients who were suffering. In order to maintain their positions, they were eager to prove their loyalty to the senior officer council at the expense of betraying their fellow patients and friends.

That's when the "deer hunting" incident occurred. At the time, there wasn't even enough fuel to heat the quarters and so it was forbidden to make fires during the day. Cooking was limited to morning and evening, and during the day even warming patients' porridge was not allowed. Then one afternoon, a female patient in Kubuk village secretly made a fire to prepare her bedridden roommate's porridge. Because the patrol officers were so vigilant, she had intended to put the fire out quickly. But she was unlucky. A passing patrol officer saw the smoke rising from her house. When he saw the smoke, he became enraged and burst into her house. He stomped on the pot filled with porridge and brutally beat the woman. The patrol officer was a Korean named Yi so and so who was infamous for torturing patients even worse than the Japanese officers. He was indebted to his fellow patients and neighbors for keeping his secret. He had a child and had secretly raised him until he could send him off the island safely. Suddenly his attitude changed as if he was repaying the debt in some perverse manner.

The young men no longer could suppress their anger after hearing the news of the beating. Rather than disclosing Yi's secret—the child he had raised and then sent off to the mainland—they chose to take the matter into their own hands. They waited for the right moment. Finally the opportunity came. They chose a day when Yi was assigned to patrol the outer block of the island and waited for him, hiding in the bushes. Caught by the young men, Yi was beaten almost to death on the spot. He would have died if he had stayed like that. He barely escaped their beating and headed toward the shore, nearly rolling down the hill. The enraged young men chased after him, yelling and screaming. One of the chief nurses asked about the noise, and the people in the village simply answered it might be a deer hunt. They really thought that a deer hunt was going on in the mountains. Yi was barely saved by other patrol officers who came running thinking that there really was a deer hunt. The young men who were involved in the incident were arrested and incarcerated in the island prison for three to six months. Following regulations, they had to be castrated before they were released.

...What am I to do?
Even an old shoe has its mate,
Because I'm a diseased criminal I need no
  children?
How can a man cut off a man's balls!
Oh god, what am I to do?
Tell me what I need to do?

This pitiful verse was the famous so-called "leper poem" and had been composed by a young man who had been forcibly castrated. It was recited by the people on the island from time to time.

The deer-hunting incident was the seed of a terrible betrayal that was about to take place on the island. However, it wasn't a problem for Shū. The paradise he had planned in his head had to be realized at any cost. The construction needed to continue. He feigned ignorance of the cruelty of the chief and head nurses. He paid absolutely no attention to the patients' complaints. Regarding the deer hunting incident, he didn't press Yi at all for what he'd done wrong. He had said one thing, "Rebellion is unforgivable," and this was the extent of his reaction toward the incident. When the young men were released from the prison after the three to six months, they found that Yi had been promoted to the Kubuk village council.

Under the guise of self-determination, new restrictions and measures were implemented each day and the tyranny of the senior officer council grew worse. Among the members of the senior officer council, there was one particularly vicious and malicious person. People began to remember his name and his savage-looking face. People became fearful of his words and actions and so they avoided him. It was Satō, the head of the senior officer council and in charge of supervising all of the chief nurses. Orphaned at an early age, Shū had adopted him and sent him to a veterinary school. Whenever Shū was transferred to a different post, he would always arrange a position for Satō to have him nearby, like his shadow. When Shū first came to the island, he even asked Satō to come up to the podium after he finished his inauguration speech so he could introduce him to the patients. Shū favored Satō, his loyal subject. Satō was known for wearing long leather boots and for carrying a whip at all times. His true nature surfaced during the pier construction and the improvement of the outer block road following the expansion of the patients' quarters.

The year after the second project had been launched, Shū began construction of another pier on the southern part of the island. There was already a pier in the personnel zone that was used for transporting materials to and fro. However, it was inconvenient to transport materials from the existing pier. First of all, it was far from the patients' zone. In order to get the materials moved to the patients' zone, they would have to go through the personnel zone where the staff lived and the staff would knit their brows. It was necessary to build a new pier in the patients' zone. Soon they built a stone pillar to inaugurate the construction of the pier on the grief-stricken shore of Tonsaeng village. This time the director didn't even try to persuade the patients or explain the project in order to recruit them to join. An order was simply delivered that every single able-bodied patient would be expected to work at the construction site. The working conditions were as cruel as if the site was a forced labor camp. Since there weren't enough tools, the patients had to work with their bare hands. Large stones and the like were carried on shoulder poles. Due to the tides, the work had to continue night and day. Even during the early evening, they had to endure the harsh ocean wind. This labor continued for four months. Every single day for four months, Satō was at the construction site whipping and tormenting the laborers. Owing to his cruel supervision and the snapping of his whip, the work was finally completed.

"You dirty lepers. What's the point of saving your decayed bodies, hunh?"

"Don't even think about slacking off! This whip won't leave the slackers alone. Those who want to die early, come on out. I'll kill them off right now. I'll be glad to do the deed."

Satō didn't just threaten them. His face was horse-shaped with a half-moon knife mark on his forehead. When his long nose twitched and he smirked, that meant that his whip was already on the way toward someone's back, dancing and snapping. If the patient had collapsed due to a lack of strength, he would spring up unable to endure the whipping. The head nurse and the other officers who followed Satō to observe the construction shuddered at the sight of him whipping patients while the patients shuddered whenever they saw Satō's shadow. He wasn't satisfied with his cruel actions at the construction site. His leather whip became more useful. Every chance he got, even while he was supervising construction at the site, he would go down to the villages and thoroughly search the patients' zone. He was looking for those who didn't show up to work. Even if a person was utterly exhausted, weakened and unable to work, it was extremely difficult to get exempted. He even accused the injured of purposely injuring themselves to avoid working. But no one could openly complain or rebel against Satō. If he sensed that, he would beat the person nearly to death and throw him in prison. Before their release, they would be castrated. Satō was that kind of person.

The pier was completed under Satō's whip. As soon as it was finished, another project was launched under the snapping of his whip, right in the midst of a harsh cold winter. Shū's paradise was still far from being realized. Escapes became frequent. It was an explicit way of betraying Shū's grand promise to turn the island into their paradise. Shū's promise had already lost its luster. It slowly became a target of all of the patients' resentment. The facilities for the patients increased in number: a new pier was built; a bell tower and Mallyŏng hall had been built—but all those things had nothing to do with the patients' paradise. The paradise existed only inside Shū's head and the meaning he had given to each project could only be realized within the scheme of his grand plan. From the patients' point of view, everything was torturous. With the addition of each new facility, their resentment increased a hundred-fold. Their memory of the torments of labor grew while the responsibility for maintaining the work pace without suffering losses increased. Because of the senior officer council's excessive interference, the new facilities were nicely kept and utterly unused. As the war intensified, materials became scarce. Not only did the patients not receive their wages on time but they were left virtually untreated for their illness. Serious injuries suffered on the construction sites, not to mention a lack of medical supplies, had lowered the patients' level of resistance to fight the disease. Contrary to Shū's plan, with each addition of a new facility, the island was turning more and more into a hell. People continued to escape. Those who were caught trying were punished severely. The number of patrol officers was increased several fold in the outer block of the island but the escapes didn't stop. In fact, the numbers increased day by day.

After several investigations, it was discovered that their route to the mainland started from Tolburi shore under Sipcha peak. Sipcha peak had many deer and was densely covered with trees. The escapees usually hid themselves on the mountain slope and bribed passing fishing boats to help them escape. But more and more, there were patients who staked their lives on a single piece of wood and swam across. Some succeeded and some were swept off by the waves and drowned. From Shū's point of view, the escapees were unpardonable traitors. They met their pathetic end, throwing away the paradise that had been created for them. Shū decided to put an end to such thankless betrayal.

He decided to construct a new outer block road following the base of Sipcha peak. During this time, timber thefts by mainland people occurred frequently. By building the road, he intended to prevent not only the escapes but also these thefts. The outer block road would also be a well-balanced improvement of the island infrastructure. Since it was a harsh winter, it would be difficult to do the work smoothly, but there wasn't enough time to wait. He started the project using forced labor once again. Satō's leather whip was busier than ever, as if it had met its perfect partner. Sipcha peak was on an extremely rugged cape. The base was a solid boulder. They started work only with hoes and A-frame carriers, without any proper tools. Countless people lost fingers and toes during the construction. They brought their severed fingers and toes home, wrapped them in their worn out clothes and cried all night long. The cruel whip of Satō succeeded in completing the four-kilometer road, piercing through the boulder in less than a month.

Satō was an unforgettable evil spirit and the instigator of an unforgettable betrayal. He was the main character of the tragedy, betraying the island as well as forcing the islanders into betrayal. He also made the director betray the island and in the end, he cruelly betrayed his own benefactor, ending his own life with the death of Shū.

Sanguk didn't know why the director was asking about him all of sudden. His mouth was parched.

"Yes, I know Satō well. There isn't a single person who came and left the island without having to learn about him." He repeated his answer tensely while looking at the director who lit a new cigarette.

"How do you understand him? What do you think of him in terms of his relationship to Shū?" the director asked, smiling mischievously. He already seemed to have an answer in mind and, by playing this riddling game, he wanted to tease it out of Sanguk.

"What do I think of him? I think he completely destroyed Shū while acting as his right hand man." Sanguk doubted whether the director knew the story up to that part. The director understood what he meant. He knew.

"Yes, you're right. He's the one who completely ruined Shū." The director whole-heartedly agreed. As Sanguk had expected, that was what he had ultimately wanted to say. But why does he need reaffirmation? What does this have to do with the favor he wanted to ask? Although Sanguk was suspicious of him, he had to agree with what he said.

"Perhaps it's not incorrect to say that Director Shū's failure was caused by Satō. But..." Even before Sanguk finished, the director interrupted.

"Then, isn't it possible to say that Shū wasn't really responsible? He meant well but if it was Satō who ruined his plan, blame Satō not Shū. Isn't it possible to praise Shū, instead of criticizing him?"

"Well, there were some who thought so, but Satō..."

"Ah, I know Satō was brought in by Shū. Even if their relationship had been different, the director would still have been responsible for Satō's actions. Shū was Satō's superior. Therefore Satō's flaws were in fact Shū's responsibility since he was the head of the hospital. But putting the hierarchy aside, if we talk strictly about Shū and Satō, don't you think Satō's flaws were greater than Shū's? Wasn't it Satō who eventually made Shū betray the island?"

"The reason why Satō was able to do so was because of Shū's ambition. He already saw in Shū that there was a possibility of betrayal. It's true that Shū pretended not to know of Satō's actions."

"You should remember that Shū was not a god but a human being. He had many shortcomings. Rather than criticizing his shortcomings, I think it was worse that Satō used it to his advantage. He was evil. If it weren't for Satō, Shū wouldn't have met such a tragic end."

"But it is also true that anyone in Satō's position might have done the same thing."

"Not if he knew the consequences, he wouldn't have done it."

"What do you mean?"

"I don't want to be like Shū."

"..."

"Manager Yi, you know very well that Satō's position had great potential for betrayal." The director finally brought up what he really wanted to talk about. The mischievous smile lingering on his lips disappeared all of sudden. His eyes were glowing. Sanguk kept silent as his face turned pale. Finally, the director revealed the favor he wanted to ask.

"I don't want to become another Shū. One Shū was enough on this island and one Satō was enough, too. You needn't worry about me becoming another Shū as long as you don't become a Satō."

"Do you know what kind of person I am?"

"A little...I know you don't trust me. I know that you always keep me on guard."

"I never said I don't trust you or have my defenses up."

"I know I've never heard you say it, but I can feel it."

"I don't distrust you to that extent."

"Perhaps it's more appropriate to say that it's Shū that you don't trust. But you always try to find Shū's ghost in me..."

"Don't you think you're jumping ahead?"

"Don't be so sure. I may know a lot more about you than you think." The director looked at Sanguk with that inscrutable, mischievous smile. Suddenly Sanguk became scared of him.

"What is it that you want from me?"

"Don't just watch, try at least to be interested in what I'm doing and help me."

"You mean forming a soccer team? You really want to have those cripples kick a ball?"

"Yes. For awhile I want to keep them occupied with kicking a ball."

"What I'm afraid of is your conviction," said Sanguk.

11

When Sanguk came back from lunch that afternoon, there was a parcel on his desk. Someone must have put it there while he was out. The parcel was not addressed to him but to Han Min. The addressee was a magazine publisher in Seoul. Sanguk could guess what it was. It was one of Min's stories that he had submitted to a contest and was now being belatedly returned. Since the parcel was opened, somebody had apparently read it before leaving it on his desk. "What kind of story did he write?" Sanguk wondered. Unconsciously he took the manuscript out and flipped to the first page. It was a manuscript approximately one hundred pages long, entitled "Homecoming." Silently, he started reading it.

An autumn evening in the early 1930s. A corner of a night train bound for the south, more like a freight car. A young man in his mid-twenties squats pathetically in a corner of the train like a potato sack away from the other passengers, hiding his face deep in his jacket as if trying to avoid the chilly air.

A woman, whose face is also wrapped in the collar of her jacket, sits opposite him under the dim light. She has been watching him carefully. She concentrates her gaze on him as if trying to find out more about him. After a while she suddenly seems to gain confidence. She moves stealthily closer to him and quickly whispers in his ear,

"You're going to the island, aren't you?" The man glances at her through his collar.

"I've been watching you for a while. I'm sure of it. You're fearful of people and trying to avoid them. But don't worry about it so much now. You can come with me. I'm going to the island too." The woman continued to whisper softly in his ear.

"I'm on my way back from home after a fortnight's vacation. My mother passed away. But I couldn't even enter the village. I had no choice but to turn back after seeing her funeral procession from afar."

As the woman speaks, his expression brightens with delight. But the man keeps silent. He gazes at the woman's eyes. The woman, too, stops talking. In the rattling night train the man and woman quietly exchange glances. They still wear fearful looks on their faces but they exchange warm glances. It is unclear who is consoling whom.

The novel opened this way. Sanguk's expressionless face suddenly started to change as he read. He continued reading with an intensity that suggested he was absorbed by his own ominous thoughts.

The man was Yi Sungu, around twenty-six years old. The woman looked three or four years younger than the man and was Chi Yŏngsuk. They silently accompanied one another, arrived in Sunch'ŏn and then left the station together early the next morning. They walked for a day and a half on unpaved roads and by the evening of the second day, had reached Noktong village where one could cross over to the island.

"I'm glad you left home. I'm sure it required great courage. But you have to be strong from now on."

"You can get treatment and be cured. Occasionally there are some who leave the island after getting cured." While they walked, it was the woman who spoke occasionally, encouraging him. The man simply listened. That evening they took the boat, crossing Noktong harbor and arriving at the island together. The man came to the island with only one thing, an old trumpet that held for him both treasured memories of his life on the mainland and his dreams.

Yi Sungu—it was the story of that man. The name of the patrol officer in the deer-hunting incident was Yi Sungu. There was no question about it now. Sanguk's nervous, tense expression intensified as he continued reading. If it was the story of Yi Sungu, the deer-hunting incident wasn't the end of it. There was the story of the boy who left the island. It was the story Sanguk had told Min. It was clear that Min had to trace the story back to Yi Sungu in order to talk about the boy.

After their arrival, Sungu went to the dormitory for single males and Yŏngsuk went to the female dormitory. From that day on, their isolated lives began. Since they had come to the island together, they developed a special relationship before long. One night, Yŏngsuk secretly visited Sungu in his room and pleaded with him to become her guardian brother. Sungu treated the people around him to a small ceremonial feast in keeping with the island's customs, and became her guardian brother. This wasn't at all unusual. Romantic relationships among patients weren't prohibited entirely. They were allowed as long as the man submitted to being castrated. Unless a patient had completely given up on the idea of being cured and being able to leave the island some day, he wouldn't acquiesce easily to the surgery. However, island life was hard and lonely. Patients would become brothers and sisters and seek comfort secretly. Sungu and Yŏngsuk became brother and sister too, but their relationship didn't stop there.

After Sungu came to the island, the melancholy sound of a trumpet would echo along the shore near the village and vanish into the darkness. It was Sungu's trumpet. On the mainland, when he played his trumpet, it was always a celebration of his youth. But now he began to express despair and sadness. He would often go out to the beach at night and play melancholy songs like "My hometown of spring" and "An old capital ground." One night,

Sungu was alone on a desolate stretch of the beach, listening to his own music disappear into the empty sky. Out of nowhere he heard a woman gently weeping. The sound came from the bushes near the sandy beach. A woman was secretly listening to his trumpet playing and had broken down. Sungu thought of going back but discovered that unless the sobbing stopped he couldn't move a step. Finally he started approaching the bushes where the sound had come from. When the woman heard footsteps, she tried to run. Sungu caught her and it was Yŏngsuk. That night Sungu and Yŏngsuk abandoned their relationship as guardian brother and sister.

The first chapter ended there and Sanguk began reading the second chapter. It was about her conceiving a new life. Even under the most intrusive surveillance and severe restrictions, youth finds a place for love. For Sungu and Yŏngsuk a place for love was the dark beach. They secretly stole off to the beach almost every night, despite the hard labor and tight surveillance. Every night they met each other secretly in the bushes and shared their love until dawn, forgetting the early winter cold that pierced their skin. Then they sat quietly with their foreheads touching as if each day was their last. Then they reluctantly returned to their quarters.

By this time a new life was growing inside the woman. The night she told him this unexpected news, they forgot even about their passionate lovemaking. Their eyes were filled with tears but it was unclear whether this was due to happiness or sadness. They gently rubbed their foreheads together all night long until the sun came up. A few days later, they were gripped by a new fear. They knew what lay ahead of them when they were found out. Castration wasn't their biggest worry at the moment. Their concerns were how they would endure the severe punishment they would receive from the hospital for violating regulations. They couldn't confess now and couldn't abort the baby either. As the days went by, their neighbors began to notice. From that point on, an inexplicable series of events took place. Their secret now became the secret of all the islanders. Everyone nurtured the baby, avoiding the hospital staff, as if the entire island had conceived this new life.

No one spoke of their secret. They kept silent, protecting the couple, as if their secret was their own. They quietly expressed their congratulations through their fear-filled eyes. Yŏngsuk's pregnancy held a hope riddled with fear for all the patients. After nine months of living in fear, she went into a labor painful for her, Sungu, and all the islanders. After ten hours of labor, the baby was born in the dark single's quarters. He was immediately wrapped in a blanket, not allowed to cry out loud. The next morning, news of the baby's birth quietly spread among the islanders. All the patients sighed with relief. The women blessed the baby with their teary eyes and the men looked up at the vast sky and worried about the boy's future. Surrounded by their silent gaze, the boy paradoxically grew up avoiding their glances. The boy was raised not by his father and mother alone, but by all of the islanders.

Sungu and Yŏngsuk were nervous. Someone might let the secret slip and the hospital might take the boy away. The hospital's surveillance of the patients grew more intense. The islanders lived in fear that a patrol officer might burst into the room after hearing the baby cry. They hid the baby under a blanket and were constantly on guard for the passing patrol officers.

Sungu was far more fearful than Yŏngsuk and,

because he was anxious, he needed to win favor at the hospital. He worked noticeably harder at the construction site and was the first to volunteer to help out in the village. His enthusiasm for working for the village and his work record finally won him the position of patrol officer. Even after he secured this position and had earned the patients' trust and confidence, he was still on edge. The more he was trusted, the more fearful he became. He worked even harder to compensate for his fear.

Five years passed and the secret was miraculously kept hidden. But Sungu could endure it no longer. The boy could not be kept hidden under the blanket in Yŏngsuk's room forever. At last one rainy autumn night, he stealthily left his quarters, carrying the boy on his back. Then he flagged down a passing boat to the shore and sent the boy off.

The second chapter ended here. Sanguk continued on to the third chapter which described Sungu's betrayal after he sent the boy away. Even after Sungu had sent the boy off, he still couldn't feel at ease. It was around this time that Satō's notorious lashing grew even more severe. The working conditions were getting worse and worse but his secret remained hidden. He wasn't sure when his secret would be exposed and he would be stripped of his insignificant position as patrol officer. Since the working conditions had become intolerable, there were people who were jealous of the minor privileges that came with being a patrol officer. He even became suspicious of his own neighbors. He was attached more than ever to his job and wanted to keep it at any cost. But as he gained favor from the senior officers council, he became more and more nervous. And he became suspicious of everyone around him as he tried harder to keep things under control.

Finally Sungu lost his sense of reason. He became abusive to his neighbors and other patients and acted as if someone wanted to reveal his secret. "Go ahead and try." But the patients didn't want to reveal his secret under any circumstances. It had long since become everyone's sacred secret, not just Sungu's alone. Knowing this, Sungu's arrogance and conceit intensified. He became the hospital staff's loyal subject and deliberately ignored his fellow patients' situation.

Here Min began to tell the infamous "deer hunting" incident. But Sanguk stopped reading and put the manuscript down. He was afraid to continue. It was strange. Sanguk only told Min about the boy escaping the island. He never mentioned that the perpetrator of the "deer hunting" incident was the boy's father. But Min already knew. What surprised Sanguk the most about the story was the boy's "homecoming." At first Sanguk couldn't understand the meaning of the title of the novel. Now he wanted to know how the story ended. He picked up the manuscript again and turned to the last chapter. The story ended with the boy's return to the island as an adult, devoting his time working for the patients. That's why he entitled the story "Homecoming." It didn't matter whether that kind of framing and development was appropriate for a novel. But he was utterly stupefied. On the island, no one pried into another person's background. Even if one found out these secrets, it had long been a custom to keep quiet. Lots of people used false names and lied about their hometowns but no one cared.

Min didn't show any particular interest in the boy's story after he left the island. But he knew about the subsequent events and never said a thing.

Now Sanguk became curious about something. Since the envelope was already open, someone might have read the manuscript before him. He wanted to know who put the manuscript on his desk.

"Don't be so sure! I might know more about you than you imagine."

Director Cho's playful glances and puzzling smile came to mind. Sanguk shoved the envelope into the drawer and got up. Then he went to the personnel office and asked about how the manuscript got to him. It was just as he expected.

"Ah, the manuscript! It came with some other parcels a few days ago," explained the old manager at the desk. Sanguk asked him again impatiently.

"What did you do with the manuscript?"

"Well, Han Min is the one who committed suicide, isn't he? The director saw the manuscript and he took it with him saying that he'd like to have a look at it."

"Did he read it?"

"Since he kept it for a couple of days, I'm sure he looked over several pages. Anyway, why are you asking? Is there anything wrong?"

"No, no. I was just curious because someone left the manuscript on my desk…"

"The director must have had someone put it there, asking you to take care of it."

"I see." There wasn't any more he needed to ask. He left the office.

12

Director Cho's determination to create a soccer team was far stronger than Sanguk had expected. As if set on conquering the hearts of the all of the islanders with a soccer ball, he had pursued this plan ever since he had brought it up. He gave soccer balls to every village and created two teams from among the patients who were able to kick a ball; the Presbyterians and the Catholics. The director invited a coach from the outside and had the players live and train together. During the training period, the two teams played friendly matches to improve their skills. After playing dozens of these matches, their skills had visibly improved. Once a team from the outside was invited for a match. The visiting team came from Kohŏng county and they unexpectedly lost, two nil. As the friendlies continued, not only did the patients' skills improve but, even more noticeably, their attitudes changed. The atmosphere of the island changed, too. At first the patients reacted indifferently to the director's half-forced soccer training. They formed no opinions, neither good nor bad, in regards the director's decision. They quietly followed his directions. They selected players, created teams and played soccer as instructed. When they were asked to live and train together in a camp, that's precisely what they did. When they were asked to play the friendlies, they did. They simply followed his orders because they were told to do so. The attitude of the elders' council was the same, as was that of Sanguk, the director's counselor.

But the director didn't yield. As soon as his office work was finished, he would go directly to the training camp and meddle. He was drawn to the soccer everyday. Finally the people began to change their attitude. As the Presbyterian and the Catholic teams had more games with each other, the islanders became noticeably more interested in watching. They cheered enthusiastically and a whole day was devoted to these soccer matches. Most of the patients slowly became drawn into the game and at last they became enthusiastic.

"Don't you think it'll be quite a sight? I've never seen a soccer game with one-legged players. Our director is quite imaginative." Haewŏn spoke sarcastically but after having observed a few games, he rolled up his pants and ran onto the field to play.

After fifty friendlies, the whole island was gripped with soccer fever. The attitude of all the players on the field and the cheering spectators had changed markedly from the indifferent attitude they showed during the director's inauguration. The director just let them play soccer. The autumn passed and winter came. There were many sunny days in the winter in the Southern Sea. The director said he would have them kick the soccer ball for a while and there seemed to be no hidden agenda behind it. There was no indication of him hatching a scheme. He had them practice day in and day out. The spring came.

The director seemed to have gained confidence. When the spring came, he took the team off the island. There was a sports tournament in Kohŏng county to commemorate a special day and so he brought the team there. They unexpectedly won the final match, four to two. It was success far beyond their expectations. The director gained more confidence. He led the soccer team on a second expedition, having submitted a request to be the county representative for the Spring Provincial Soccer Tournament that took place in Kwangju.

In early April the pink clouds of the cherry blossoms completely covered the trees lining the streets of the island. The Sorok Island soccer team got on a truck bound for the soccer tournament, passing under the blossoming trees. Like soldiers heading to battle, Director Cho had his military uniform on and the players wore their red uniforms embroidered with the team symbol of a black, fingerless hand. They felt a mixture of excitement and anxiety.

We've been fighting for generations
The black clouds have rolled away
The sun has risen; let's go to the land…

From the square in front of the clinic all the way down to the ferry, the islanders stood along the cherry blossom covered streets and sang the "Song of Sorok" loudly, seeing the team off. The players on the truck waved their fists and sang along in reply. The islanders didn't stop singing until the truck had passed over the hill leaving a whirlwind of dust in its wake and had driven aboard the ferry headed toward the opposite harbor. The already pinkish hue around their eyes became brighter. The result of this expedition was very satisfactory. The sponsor suggested that they withdraw from the tournament when their participation was known, but the other teams' reservations about playing with the diseased ended up being but a trivial obstacle for the determined island players. The result was all the more satisfying and commendable since the players endured these obstacles and resolutely finished the games. At least for the director, it was a satisfying result that far outstripped his expectations. The team secured the provincial championship and this time it wasn't a matter of whether their technical merits were recognized or not. The point was the director's belief that he could instill in them the notion that they were able to compete like healthy people and win. In fact, winning the trophy was visible proof that they were capable.

On this second expedition, there was a reporter at the tournament who wrote an article about the unusual event. Later, people on the island could read about it again and again so that this particular match remained in their memories for a long time. The article went like this:

It was an unusual game. The unconventional players in their red uniforms marked with a black fingerless hand looking remarkably like a Nazi flag, did not control the ball skillfully. Their teamwork was also awkward. Several players would guard the ball, but then the ball would be taken away and quickly be on the home side of the pitch. They would run together as a pack and would foul absurdly. Whenever they gave the ball a good strong kick, the players on the team with the red uniforms would fall over in pain.

Yes, it sure was an unusual game. When a red uniformed player ran with the ball, rather than tackling him, the rival team players would run the other way to avoid him. So, despite their lack of skill, they had the advantage. As soon as the game started, spectators standing near the Sorok players either left or stood far away from the line. When the players ran to the sideline in pursuit of the ball, the spectators became petrified and ran away. Not even a single spectator cheered the island team. But there was no jeering either. Only one person in a distinguished military uniform paced the side lines to and fro, cheering fanatically. The colonel cheered continuously and there was no sign of him letting up. When the team, cornered by the rival team, hesitated and didn't know what to do, he would take out his gun and threaten them, urging them to be more aggressive.

"They're just the same. They're soccer players just like you. They're not different," he'd yell, trying to encourage them when their fighting spirits were low. Like their fingerless insignia, they filled the space left in their shoes by their toeless feet with cotton balls.

"Haven't I told you many times that not having eyebrows and being lepers are two different things?"

They had no eyebrows. But like the colonel said,

it was far different being a former leper than still being a leper. Players were substituted frequently because either their feet were partially paralyzed or got injured and were sore. One of the players fell down and didn't get up after all the substitute players had been used. The colonel threw down the gun he had in his hand, quickly changed into uniform and ran onto the field. The spectators were surprised. They weren't actually watching the soccer game but watching to see which player endured the tribulations in a more saintly manner than the others. The spectators who had until now been indifferent, applauded and cheered for the red uniformed players. Several female students turned their backs and cried. Why was the colonel's desire that strong? The game was finally over. The colonel borrowed the microphone and thanked the audience.

"I'm Colonel Cho Paeghŏn, director of Sorok Island hospital. I apologize for making your afternoon unpleasant by bringing leprosy patients to this tournament. But please consider this as a show of compassion for the underprivileged. The game is over now. For you this means the end of the game, but for the patients this is only the beginning. That they are capable of playing soccer will encourage the other patients and show them that there is hope. After they accept the fact that there is hope, the changes that will take place in their hearts are beyond imagination. I am very happy and I want to thank you. You are entitled to accept my appreciation as well as that of the rest of the players...."

The spectators who left the stadium after the game felt that what they had seen wasn't simply a soccer match. Rather they felt that they had seen a heroic and moving drama. (Yi Kyut'ae's "Sorok Island's Revolt" October 1966 issue of *Sasanggye*)

The team won again. On the day the players returned, the biggest celebration since the founding of the hospital took place. A pine arch was built by the ferry dock where the players disembarked and the world flags from the church fluttered in the wind.

We've been fighting for generations
The black clouds have rolled away

The players and the islanders became one and sang the "Song of Sorok" until their voices grew hoarse. Even Haewŏn and Miyŏn were in the crowd, forgetting all about the tension between them. Miyŏn consciously kept her distance from Sanguk, perhaps due to his lack of response that night when she had revealed her background to him. Haewŏn continued to pester Miyŏn. However on this day, there was no room for jealousy or distance. Everyone was overwhelmed with excitement and became one and sang. Sanguk, too, was in the crowd and he sang with all his might. He felt tears rolling down his cheeks as he sang.

My hometown is a valley
    where the flowers bloom
Peach blossoms, apricot blossoms, azaleas…

They sang the song endlessly. After they were tired of singing the "Song of Sorok," they began singing "My Hometown of Spring," a song that had almost been forgotten. Then they started singing a popular song that had been very dear to the islanders and the song spread quickly through the crowd like a solemn gospel song.

In this lonely cottage where no one seeks me

The maple leaves are piling up neatly
Abandoned by the world...

With the flow of the song, the sound of sobbing spread. Then Sanguk was startled as if jolted by an electric current streaming through his veins. He saw the director standing tall on top of the truck. Director Cho was still on the truck. He was more pleased than anyone else on the island. But he wasn't singing. Perhaps he wasn't as excited to sing and cry with the rest of the people. Instead of tears in his eyes, Sanguk detected a faint smile. Sanguk felt a chill all over his body when he saw the director smile. He murmured softly in fear as he cautiously gazed at the director, "I think something real is going to happen. How did this happen?"

It was strange. A sports tournament is a device used in forming group identity, overcoming individual differences and trivial confrontations between people. Within the grand scheme of group identity, there is no room for an individual's trivial complaints and personal propensities, likes and dislikes. In order to eliminate these problems and create order, sports tournaments are used as a device. It's natural that sporting events have additional meanings beyond the specific meanings that each particular sport carries. To apply this to the island, the director's aim with the sports tournament was to successfully instill confidence in the patients and to restore human trust across the patients' zone and the personnel zone and between the director and the patients. This is what the director himself had said. No matter what his motivations were, Sanguk felt uneasy.

The people were overly excited. Since when had they become like this? Since Sanguk knew the magical spell sports tournaments held on people, he was suspicious of the director's intentions from the beginning. But even Sanguk himself had fallen under its magical spell. The island no longer was a place of five thousand patients. All five thousand patients had become one. All of them felt the same thing and shared the excitement. No one was on guard against the director any longer. Everyone was filled with a hitherto unknown self-confidence. They trusted him and were grateful to him. In the midst of all the excitement, the director alone smiled. And Sanguk shuddered.

13

Just as Sanguk had expected, Director Cho soon presented his next plan. The following morning, he summoned Sanguk to his office.

"Don't you think the island has recovered its vitality somewhat? I think they've gained enough confidence to start something new, don't you think?" As soon as the director saw Sanguk, he demanded agreement over the success of the previous day's soccer match.

"Well, they were all very excited yesterday. It was worth having them start playing soccer." Sanguk waited for the director's next words. Suddenly the director jumped to his feet.

"Good! If you think so too, everything is set."

"…"

"There's no need to have them play soccer now. Let's get started on the real work."

"What do you mean by 'the real work'?"

"I didn't really ask for your assistance in creating the soccer team but now I need you to participate actively and help me."

"Don't you think I should know what it is you're

talking about first?" asked Sanguk.

"I need you to come with me to Kohŏng today."

The director already had a written script in his mind. He acted according to the scenario he had devised and achieved the results he had expected. Introducing soccer to the island and winning the matches were all part of his bigger scheme. He had gotten the results that were written in his script. What the director wanted to start now was only an extension of his fast materializing scenario. After the ferryboat left the island, the director began to explain his next plan.

His plan was to recover land from the sea. Instead of relying on the government's limited rice rations and waiting their turn to enter dreary Napkol hall, it would be better for the patients to cultivate the land with their own hands, providing a basis for a better and more hopeful future. By having the patients recover the land themselves, he wanted to instill in them hope in place of the vision of the dreary, miserable Napkol hall. He wanted to create a new home for the patients who had lost their hometowns and who had been driven off the mainland. He wanted to surround Tŏknyang bay located south of the Kohŏng peninsulas with dikes. By connecting Toyang's Pongam peninsula with P'ungyang's P'ungnam peninsula using Oma island in the middle as a joining point, he wanted to reclaim twenty-five hundred acres. It was a grand plan. Sanguk was speechless. The plan was recklessly grand.

The director paid no attention to Sanguk's reaction. He already had a minutely detailed map that allowed him to look at any part of the island. On the way back from the tournament the previous day, he had invited a surveyor to come and had him wait at an inn in Noktong. Sanguk wasn't there to be consulted. The plan had already been decided. What mattered at this point was that he would tolerate Sanguk's suggestions on how to implement the plan effectively. All day long Sanguk followed the director and the surveyor and looked at the sites.

Sanguk was confused by the dizzying speed of events and things that had happened during Shū's reign surfaced incessantly in his mind. The director's plan couldn't be criticized. There was nothing wrong with him wanting to create a new hometown for these patients who no longer had hometowns. He wanted to instill hope for a brighter future in them to replace the deathly darkness of waiting and counting the days until it would be their turn to enter Napkol hall. His intentions were admirable and they couldn't be criticized. Even in Shū's days, no one could find fault with his motives. He had justifiable motives and admirable intentions. The problem was precisely this overly perfect justification that made it impossible for anyone to challenge him.

Shū's purpose was of course to create a paradise. In his conception of paradise, a park was a necessity. The construction of a park premised on an unassailable justification was yet another step along the path to Shū's and Satō's betrayal of the island. The year the outer road was completed, Shū went to Japan at the request of the Imperial family. At the time, the empress dowager, who had contributed considerable sums to support building the hospital facilities, commended Shū for his accomplishments. Recognizing his contributions, she bestowed a title on him and Shū returned to the island inspired. She had presented him with a royal verse to take back to the island to comfort and encourage the patients and Shū planned to have a monument built with the verse inscribed on it.

The monument was built immediately. The empress dowager's verse was engraved on a huge granite stone transported from Sipcha peak and placed in front of the public hall: "In my regrettable absence, be friends with each other." The unveiling ceremony for the royal monument was problematic. In order to have such a ceremony, he needed to build a park.

That same year around mid-November, the unveiling ceremony took place and many high-ranking officials along with the Government-General's vice-minister visited the island. After they toured the island, they complimented Shū profusely for his accomplishments. Shū was proud of his paradise. He thought it was time for him to add a final touch to his grandiose paradise project.

The island needed a park for the patients to enjoy their remaining days. He immediately got started with the planning and the construction soon followed. No persuasion was needed. It was all for the patients. Since it was for the patients, no explanations were necessary. Everything he'd accomplished until now had impressed Shū himself as well as the others who had come and toured the island and those who had heard about it. He thought he was always right. In order to return their praise, he needed to make the island look even more beautiful. That year winter came early and was unusually cold, but Shū couldn't postpone his plans. He had even invited a famous landscape architect from Japan. Then he started the construction.

First he decided on a site between Chungang and Tongsaeng villages and then began the reclamation of the muddy ground. In the severe cold, the patients were again dragged out to the construction site. Because of these continuous construction projects, the patients' injured hands and feet had become ulcerated and their symptoms had grown worse. But there was no way of avoiding the harsh labor. Now the patients were nothing but slaves. From the beginning any kind of criticism of the hospital's management had not been tolerated. They had no strength to resist. Like machines, they leveled the hills, reclaimed the muddy ground, cut and transported the trees from the mountains. The patients' whose bodies were brutally lashed by Satō's whip were forced to squeeze out every last ounce of strength. After they had exhausted every last bit of strength, they quietly breathed their last and fell to the ground, beaten by Satō's whip.

Suicide and escape became everyday occurrences. Even after the patrol around the outer road had been reinforced several times, there were many patients who died trying to cross the ocean clinging to pieces of wood. Despite this nearly infinite number of human sacrifices, the construction continued unabated. Various extraordinarily shaped rocks from Changhŏng and Wan Island were placed here and there and, to add a southern exotic flavor, Shū imported tropical plants from Taiwan and planted them throughout the entire park area. The following April, the finishing touches were added; it was now so extravagant that it was comparable to any of the parks in the urban areas.

Shū was extremely pleased. However the patients weren't. As with the previous construction projects, the patients couldn't get excited about the completion of the park. The entire island was moving closer to hell—not paradise—with the construction of each new facility. Even with the construction of the park, the greater the patients' labor and sacrifices the more removed they felt from the notion of paradise. For the patients, they had one more thing to curse and absolutely no feeling of satisfaction. Furthermore, in order to maintain the park in its exquisite condition, extra caution and care were demanded from the patients. Shū prohibited the patients from entering the park without permission since he was afraid of possible damage. Whenever a guest visited the island, Shū never failed to take the guest to the park that was always kept nice and neat, a way to show off the paradise he had created for the patients.

It was one betrayal after another. From the patients who jumped into the ocean risking their lives to avoid building this paradise to those who tried to maintain the park in its pristine condition when it had supposedly been built for them to enjoy. The patients were kept out of the park, and so when visitors came to see it, they complimented it profusely. In reality, the park was not for the patients, it was for Shū's guests. The paradise which Shū claimed to have created for them wasn't for them. It was for the people who visited the island and for Shū. There was no paradise for the patients on Sorok island. As long as the paradise didn't exist for the patients, Sorok island couldn't be called paradise. The paradise existed only in selfish rumors. Justification wasn't something that could be trusted. The islanders already knew that. Even after several decades, the islanders hadn't forgotten. Sanguk knew that as well.

The problem lay in the process. Justification shouldn't be used to cheat the process and it certainly shouldn't call for sacrifices. What exactly is paradise? Paradise wasn't the result; it was something that could be felt inside or attained in the process. A true paradise could be attained only when people sought it out on their own and eagerly volunteered to build it and did not regret having worked for it.

What was the director's plan? His intentions couldn't be criticized. But the question was whether the patients truly accepted and supported these intentions. Could they accept and endure when their physical condition didn't exactly give them the mobility they wished for? There was no guarantee that the director's intentions would not end up betraying them. Behind these grand intentions lurked the shadow of a statue. It was impossible to prove whether the director had a statue in mind or not. Was it possible to trust him entirely? Could he be trusted solely on his good intentions? His recovery plan was grandiose.

On returning to the island that evening, Sanguk visited Elder Hwang. He had to see him. The director's intentions were apparent. Sanguk's own position was clear. It was the unavoidable fate of betrayal. He wanted to listen to Elder Hwang's story. He had a perfect story of betrayal. It was the story of the first murder since the founding of the island hospital. The first murder was evidence of betrayal on the part of the patients who had participated. And, as for Shū, his tragedy began after his long-standing dream of having a statue built had been realized. Elder Hwang always told this story of betrayal. Whenever Sanguk found himself and island life unbearable, he went to Elder Hwang for the dreadful story.

Not once had Elder Hwang refrained from telling the story to Sanguk. Sanguk knew the old man well. He also knew why he spent his life immersed in this story and why he never avoided telling it. The old man too knew Sanguk very well.

He knew exactly why Sanguk always came to see him to hear the dreadful story again and again. But the two were lying to each other. Sanguk pretended not to know about the old man and so did the old man. Sanguk simply visited the old man for the story and the old man told it. On this day just like all the others, Sanguk went to see Elder Hwang. He wanted to hear the story of betrayal once again. Without it, he couldn't endure the hospital work and the director. He couldn't tolerate himself. As usual the old man didn't refuse.

"In those days anybody could have done the same thing. Anybody." While Sanguk sat across from him, Elder Hwang stroked his dry cheek with a fingerless hand. Elder Hwang's vacant staring at the empty sky soon pierced through the wall of the past.

In those days anybody could have done the same thing. Anybody—

The old man began the story from the other side of the wall.

"Everyone was busy trying to please his superiors because of the constant demands of hard labor and mistreatment. I mean the people on the advisory council. The work was extremely hard, the food supply was short, their sick bodies were sore from the labor, so you can't blame the people who tried to curry favor with their superiors. When things came to this, that's when judgment day came."

Shū had secretly wished to add a finishing touch to his paradise by erecting his statue. It was the final betrayal. There was no way to find out whether this grand tragic scheme was part of his scenario. The final betrayal was a collaborative effort between the director and the islanders. The old man's story continued. At the time, numerous meetings were held by the council members to discuss more effective ways of mobilizing the labor force and cooperating with the hospital management in the patients' zone. At the meetings, representatives from each village and the chief nurse Satō were present to keep an eye on things. The council members had no room to look after the welfare of their fellow patients. They were only thinking of themselves, trying to figure out a way to get out of the forced labor. They wished to enjoy a little of the freedom and power that came with being council members. They avoided making any remarks that would irritate Satō or the hospital management. Whenever possible, they wanted to prove their loyalty to the hospital.

One day Sungu proposed an excellent idea. Sungu was the one who had been involved in the "deer hunting" incident. He was one of the most trusted representatives of the village. He wanted to show his loyalty to the hospital by volunteering his labor and hard work. His idea was to erect a statue of Shū to commemorate his achievements on the island so that people would remember him eternally. No one raised any objections. Indeed, instead of objecting, they regretted not having come up with the idea themselves. That very day they formed a "booster committee" and rushed through all the necessary decisions. The most important part of this was how to collect the money to pay for the statue. They decided to ask for the money from the patients as a "donation." They deducted a certain amount as a remittance from those who received small allowances from home, and they extorted three months pay from those who earned wages. For the patients who couldn't work and had no way to make a remittance, their rations of food and clothing were reduced considerably.

Soon the fundraising started. Shū kept silent. When he heard the news about the decision to build a statue and that compulsory fundraising had begun, he said nothing. He neither declined the offer nor did he try to stop the fundraising. He was absolutely indifferent to what was going on. Satō took care of everything on his behalf. Sungu who had suggested the idea was the most active in collecting money. Villages that contributed only small amounts were pressured and threatened. Finally forty-seven thousand wŏn was raised and the building of the statue soon began. Shū kept his silence.

The patients' labor had to be mobilized once again. The small hilltop in front of the park was chosen as the site for the statue, and the patients again were forced to work. They built an eighteen-foot granite pedestal on the front of which was engraved "Statue of Director Shū Masahide." On the back of the pedestal, a three foot wide copper plate was added with the names Satō, Yi Sungu and those of the booster committee. The work continued without delay. That year on August twentieth the statue was finally completed and the unveiling ceremony was held. Once again a grand celebration took place on the island. It was an impressive ceremony attended by over one hundred well-wishers including delegates sent by the Imperial household, representatives of various religious organizations, and other influential people from all over Korea. One of Shū's young children timidly pulled the string that hung on the platform, revealing the statue of Shū, which had been draped with a soft white silk cloth. An immensely imposing Shū appeared, his dark shape overpowering the assembled crowd. With the accompaniment of music, they sang a song that was composed especially for this particular event.

> Dedicated his life
> To improve this country
> Let us honor this statue
> Dear director, our pride
> Built on the hill of grace
> Today is the day to celebrate…

Sungu received an award on behalf of the rest of the patients for his excellent service in erecting the statue. An entire day was set aside for the celebration. However, the tragic farce of betrayal surrounding the statue didn't end there.

After the statue was built, the patients struggled with another burden. The hospital designated the twentieth of each month as a "Day of Thanksgiving" and the patients, regardless of their physical condition, were forced to gather in the park and pay tribute to both the real Shū and his statue. Everyone had to gather around the statue and pay their respects and listen to a speech given by Shū.

It happened on one of these days of thanksgiving, twenty-five years after the founding of the hospital. It was an early summer day when the heat was intense. On that day the first murder was committed on the island. The streets in the patients' zone were completely deserted because the patients were all at the park for the regular monthly service paying tribute to the statue and listening to Shū's speech. There was only person who hadn't left the village. It was Sungu. For some reason Sungu, feeling sick, skipped the monthly "thanksgiving" assembly. He stayed in his room, resting quietly. Not everyone was granted an exemption from attending the gathering simply because he or she wasn't feeling well.

It was a privilege that he could enjoy since he was regarded as a faithful subject in the eyes of his superiors. He had even received the distinguished award for his contributions to erecting the statute. But Sungu wasn't the only person who wasn't there at the thanksgiving assembly.

It was just at the time when everyone prayed solemnly at the park, the sweat rolling down their necks. Sungu was about to fall asleep in the hazy silence of the summer afternoon when a man opened the sliding door of his room. It was his next door neighbor Yi Kilyong. Kilyong was a fingerless leper. Sungu was so taken aback by Kilyong's sudden entrance he had no time to defend himself. He couldn't even resist. There was a knife tied to his fingerless hand. Even before Sungu could sit up, the knife penetrated his chest.

"Everybody said the island was a paradise for the lepers," said Kilyong.

Elder Hwang's story was coming to a close. No smoke came out of his pipe.

"They had good reason to think so." After he sucked on his smokeless pipe a few more times, he slowly ended the story.

"I guess that young man, Kilyong, didn't agree. After he turned himself in, he said he wanted the outside world to know about the island, what was really going on here. Well, he wasn't completely successful. A little later, he killed himself in prison. Only the dirty lepers grieved his death. I guess Kilyong wasn't the only person who didn't believe this island was their paradise. Later even more appalling things happened. As you already know, what the lepers did to Shū was proof that they could no longer endure their paradise..."

Elder Hwang was referring to Shū who was murdered at the hands of his patients. It happened a year after Sungu's death, on the twentieth of June, yet another thanksgiving assembly in front of the statue. As was the custom, all the patients had left their villages early in the morning to gather in front of the statue and waited for the real live Shū to appear. After a while, Shū together with his staff slowly walked toward the statue. Just as he was passing the columns of Chungang villagers a man suddenly jumped out in front of Shū screaming. He had a concealed knife. The knife pierced Shū's heart and he fell down dead on the spot.

It happened so quickly that by the time the patients in line heard the commotion and raised their heads, Shū had already fallen. The young man brandishing the blood stained weapon yelled out like a mad person, searching for his second mark: "Satō! Come out Satō!" Shū's staff couldn't do anything. It was an act of revenge on the part of the young man; he was known for his outgoing personality and bravery. He was from Sŏngju and his name was Yi Ch'unsŏng. Shū died like that. Like any other statue of a living person, after Shū died, the statue was torn down. In its place Kura tower was built.

But Elder Hwang didn't go into detail regarding Shū's final days. Sanguk knew the details since he had heard the story before. Today he was more interested in the other aspects of the story. Elder Hwang had already figured that out.

"In those days anybody could have betrayed anybody. Anybody." He omitted the last part of the story and repeated what he had said earlier. Sanguk's mouth was parched. As if pleading, he asked,

"Are you saying you forgive Sungu because anybody could have done the same thing?" Elder Hwang looked at him for a while with strangely compassionate eyes and said, "I imagine so. Sungu, Shū, or anybody else could have done the same thing in that situation."

"Isn't there a rumor that Shū knew about the plan in advance, not because he was driven to it by circumstance. There's a rumor that Satō was the one who gave Sungu the idea for the statue."

Elder Hwang looked at Sanguk for a while and finally, as if he had reached a decision, started to talk again.

"That's a lie. Does it make any difference whether Satō told him or not? Does it matter whether Shū told Satō about wanting to have a statue or whether he accepted the statue when the patients wanted to build it for him? In any case, he betrayed the island. Even Sungu's betrayal, whether Satō told him to do it or he did it on his own. In their situation, whether it was Sungu or Shū, they had no choice but to do what they did. If it's necessary for us to look back, we need only concern ourselves with not creating the same conditions..." Elder Hwang made an obtuse statement and stopped talking. Sanguk kept silent, too. He had heard everything he wanted to hear. He had heard the story of betrayal from the old man reconfirming what he already thought.

Sanguk felt that Elder Hwang had forgiven Sungu too easily. But the old man didn't forgive everything that people had done. Although he forgave Sungu his betrayal, he didn't forgive everyone on the island and the island itself. He didn't forgive them for their basic human nature that made them act in the same way when the circumstances drove them to it. Looking at it that way, the old man didn't really forgive Sungu. All of those things had been confusing Sanguk, but now he was able to focus his thoughts on one point. He wasn't seeking the old man's forgiveness for Sungu's crime. He wanted to understand the man's betrayal precisely. He wanted only to witness the old man's curse.

"By the way..."

There was no point waiting for the old man's story. Wrapped in his own thoughts, Sanguk got up abruptly. The old man didn't stop him. As he was leaving, the old man, having thought of something else, called out to him.

"Is something bothering you? Since you came to hear the story again, something must be troubling you," the old man said, unlike previous times. Sanguk with his back half turned stood awkwardly and replied,

"No. Nothing like that. I just wanted to come see you and hear the story again." Sanguk tried to hide his surprise. The old man had sensed something but he soon nodded his head.

"I'm sure there isn't anything wrong. You never talked openly about yourself."

"There isn't much to tell." He was apologetic and gave excuses, but no matter what he said he already knew Sanguk well.

"Sure. I don't really want to listen to your story anyway. But we need to help each other out. The important thing is that no more horrible things like that should ever happen on this island again."

14

Director Cho revealed his real plans after the islanders had gained some confidence, having experienced the sweet taste of victory that came with winning the soccer matches. But their response was far from what he had expected. There were many more obstacles to overcome in order for him to accomplish his long cherished plans, the most critical one being the distrust of the five thousand islanders. The patients receded once again back into their silence. When he disclosed his new plans, the confidence and vitality that had come with the soccer victories vanished.

"It's about time you leave this island. It's too small for you to make a home here for you and your children..."

One quiet spring afternoon after the cherry blossoms had disappeared, he gathered the village elders in the assembly hall and explained the project.

"I understand quite well that this project will require hard work and will take a long time--longer than any of the previous projects--and the benefits are far from immediate. Even if it's something you dearly want and pray for, it won't materialize at once. Also, I can't guarantee that you'll be better off even after the project is finished."

The director hung a map on the wall, explained the significance of the land recovery plan and then began pleading with the elders. They remained silent. In fact, the moment he mentioned the land recovery plan their faces froze. Despite his unrelenting attempts at persuasion, they were unmoved. The director felt every ounce of energy being sapped from his body. Everything he had achieved in the past year seemed meaningless and he felt as though he was once again standing before the audience in the suffocating silence of his inauguration. But he couldn't back down now.

"We have to do this! Even if you won't reap the rewards, your children will, and their children. For the sake of your children and grandchildren, you have to do this project. I know some of you don't agree. Even one of my closest friends doesn't approve of this plan. But just because there are a few who oppose it, we can't ignore our mission on this island. It's the will of God. Yes, I dare invoke God's name. I call it God's will. And that's right. I know that this is truly one of the most valuable missions God has bestowed on us."

In his attempts to get them to talk he went so far as to invoke God's name. But still the elders didn't respond. It was as if they couldn't hear a word of what he was saying. They didn't even flinch. Instead, they observed him silently as if they were watching an interesting spectacle. No one even cleared his throat. The director saw hatred in their eyes. And then he heard their silent jeers. Summoning all his strength, he continued.

"You have to leave the island. If you don't, at least your children should be given the opportunity to do so. I know that you wish for this more than I do. So who or what is going to make this possible? Your prayers? Your relatives on the mainland? They don't want you to leave this island. You know that better than I. You have to make this happen yourselves. Even if you're unable to leave the island right this minute, you have to pave the way for you and your children to leave in the future. That's all I wanted to say to you today. Now I want to hear your thoughts." After he was done, Director Cho observed their expressions for a while. No one spoke. They stared at his face in the heavy silence.

"You're here representing all five thousand islanders and you and I have to make a very important decision. Tell me what you think," he asked again.

At last, one of the elders slowly rose from his seat. It was Elder Hwang of Chungang village. Everyone's gaze was riveted on him. He turned to face the director and moved his lips slightly as if he had something important to say.

"Please speak," Director Cho pressed him. But the old man did not say a word. Instead, the hint of a strange, chilling sneer appeared around his lips. After gazing at the director for a while, he turned his back slowly. Then he quietly walked toward the door, ignoring the director's pleas. The rest of the elders, who had remained silent, rose from their seats. Wearing that same chilling sneer, they quietly followed Elder Hwang.

"Speak! Speak! Why don't you speak?!" The director screamed holding his gun in his hand. But the elders left the assembly hall, not once turning their heads.

This was the first obstacle and the director's disappointment was beyond description. He was back at the starting point. Moreover, he was flustered that Sanguk had done nothing to help him. He knew from early on that the most influential one among the elders was Elder Hwang. People trusted and respected him. It wasn't hard to figure out that Sanguk secretly sought him out for consultation on matters pertaining to the island. From Elder Hwang's reaction, the director understood Sanguk's stance. Rather than successfully persuading Elder Hwang to cooperate, Sanguk was interfering with the director's plan, subtly threatening him.

He couldn't lose any more time since he anticipated strong resistance from the islanders once the plan was revealed. The director also knew that he could not count on Sanguk to take the lead. From what he knew of him, Sanguk would hesitate until the last minute. He was suspicious of everything that had happened and would happen on the island. His dark past and the things he had experienced on the island had made him a cynical person. His entire thinking was grounded in the island's unfortunate history. He often unearthed parts of the island's history and made all decisions based simply on that. His own unpleasant experiences and the island's history weighed heavily on him and so he always wore a somber and spiritless face. He didn't trust people. He did nothing to try to change things or to accomplish things. The first person to be saved from the island was Sanguk. But he did not give up hope. Through this project, he would be able to experience something new, not only in his mind but in reality. Saving Sanguk meant saving all of the islanders from their nightmare of betrayal and distrust. The director understood Sanguk's deeply rooted distrust which had bonded him permanently to the island. This bond was incontrovertible proof that he could never betray the islanders. It didn't matter if the decision was delayed for the time being. But once the decision was made, he would never attempt to betray the islanders.

The director hastily prepared to launch his project with or without Sanguk or the islanders' approval. He visited sites of large-scale land recovery projects in progress in Yŏngam and Changhŏng to get a broader perspective on the problem. He invited experienced civil engineers to make detailed plans and solidified his construction plans little by little. He spent several days running back and forth between the authorities in central and local governments to get the approval for the project and to secure financial assistance. When the paperwork was almost ready, he had light bulbs installed along the surface of the water where the embankments would be. The light bulbs stretched from the southern edge of the Kohŏng peninsula to two smaller peninsulas, connecting them together. From the P'ungnam peninsula to Odong island to Oma island to the Pongam peninsula, hundreds of lights formed the boundaries for where nearly two thousand five hundred acres of land would be reclaimed from the sea. Among the five small, uninhabited islands in the bay inside the border, four would either be connected to the embankments or demolished. Manjae island, located outside the boundaries of the proposed project, would be used as a source of rock and stones for the embankments. At high tide the depth of the water was about eight meters deep. Although it was an outrageous dream to envision this as fertile land in the future, the director had to show the islanders something in physical form and so he marked off the boundaries with the lights. He wanted to encourage them by having these physical markers and so he did it quickly. Once the construction was underway, the work had to be carried out at or near high tide regardless of whether it was day or night. And so for the night work the lights would also be a necessity.

After this, the director gathered the elders once again. The islanders had remained absolutely quiet during this preparatory work. Even Sanguk who had accompanied him and helped him with the work had said nothing of what the future might hold in store. Far from trying to understand the director's intentions, Sanguk didn't even show the slightest sign of curiosity. The director silently carried out his plans in the midst of the islanders' indifference. He thought he had waited long enough and so, for the last time, he decided to try to persuade the elders.

There was no need for a speech this time. He had a boat ready and took the elders to Changhŏng to show them the large-scale land recovery project that was well underway in Taedŏk town. On one side they were still in the process of pumping the water out but on the other side, they were already clearing the enormous area of reclaimed mud turning it into arable land. Some parts were already being used for transplanting rice seedlings. Director Cho had planned to bring the elders to this site when he first had visited it.

On the boat to the reclaimed area, the director remained silent. The elders kept quiet, too. They followed the director to the boat and when they arrived at Changhŏng they silently disembarked. No words were exchanged between the elders and the director. Sanguk acted as a mediator and spoke to the elders on behalf of the director. Under the early summer heat, the director led the elders to the reclaimed field and the elders walked behind him. The newly reclaimed rice field land was vast—more than five miles wide. Some parts were covered with early seedlings and there were people scattered about here and there busily transplanting rice seedlings on another part of the field. In the midst of this continuous, heavy, intense silence, they walked along the rim of the entire field, not even pausing for lunch. They came back to the boat in the late afternoon and got onboard. The director was extremely hungry and utterly exhausted, but he'd endured it. The tour wasn't over yet. He took them to the site of his proposed project, reaching the designated site after nearly three hours. When they arrived, the shadow of evening was slowly covering the ocean. And, as they'd been instructed beforehand, the workers turned on the lights. The lights that stretched along the dark sea glimmered and drew closer as if the passengers on the boat were going toward a bright path. Enclosed by the lights, the sea that day remained unusually calm.

There was no need to go any closer to the lights because there really was nothing to see beyond that. He stopped the boat in the middle of the sea. For a while he stared at the sea encircled by the lights.

"Watch!" he said. "There's nothing but lights now, but the day will come when you'll sow seeds and reap a harvest from the part of the sea that's surrounded by those lights. I know it's difficult to believe. Perhaps you don't want to believe. But it doesn't matter. I didn't spend an entire day walking around back there and then bring you here to seek your consent. It doesn't matter anymore whether I have your approval or not. Because from the beginning this project has been meant for you, not for me. The reason why I brought you here to look at this is to give you my pledge. Whether or not you approve of it, this sea will be reclaimed. It will be done with or without your sweat. In the end, the sea will be held back by dikes at the expense of other people's hard work and the day will come when this land will turn into fertile land and then it will be presented to you. Even without your help, the sea will be pushed back—I'll make sure it happens. I can always hire workers from the outside. If you don't like this, just watch. After the project is finished and the land has been given to you, you can sow seeds and reap your harvest. That's all you need to do."

The elders remained quiet. No one tried to speak up. The director looked around the boat for a while and continued.

"There is one more thing I want to say. Don't get too caught up in the past. Your past is not something to be proud of. What is your past? Memories of shame, despair and betrayal. As long as you hold on to your dark past, you'll forever remain lepers—like you were in the past, so you'll be now, and in the future. An unwillingness to free yourself from your past is nothing but a stubborn desire to remain miserable. Your children—who haven't suffered from the disease—will be forever bound by the island, unable to leave.

Since you are cured, you no longer want to think of yourselves as lepers. Of course, your children have nothing to do with leprosy. It's time for you to wash away the unpleasant nightmares of yesterday and live for the future. You have to leave the island. What have you done to leave the island? What have you done to prevent your children from becoming lepers? As you already know, I don't believe in God. But I know what your prayers are. If God decided to listen to someone's prayers, I firmly believe that it would be your prayers. I understand very well that your situation merits empathy. You deserve to be comforted by God, but that can't be your prerogative. Don't expect to be comforted. If you don't try to change your situation, your God will not be there to lend a hand. I only wish that you would find solace in the words, 'God helps only those who help themselves'." After he was finished, he looked up into the dark night sky as if it didn't matter whether the elders responded or not. Then, at last, he turned the boat toward the island as if his work was done.

15

The elders began to react the following day. As usual Director Cho got up early in the morning even though he had not completely recovered from the fatigue of the previous day. He had to go over to the construction site before daybreak to supervise the workers from the mainland. When he came out of the room, there was an envelope on the *maru* floor next to the pillar. A small rock was placed on top of the envelope to keep it from blowing away.

The director intuitively knew what it was. Someone from the patients' zone must have secretly snuck up to the official residence to deliver the letter. Since whoever had done it had secretly entered the personnel area, he had no choice but to leave the letter outside. As if handling something precious, he carefully picked up the letter and started reading. It was a letter from Elder Hwang. From the very first sentence, it was filled with criticism.

I don't know why you're doing this to us. We've watched you and you've watched us for a year. You know us very well. When you condemned us and said we had done absolutely nothing to free our children from being called lepers, you were wrong. For several decades we've struggled to leave the island as normal human beings. But we were always being deceived. You are also aware of this. Behind our hopes and efforts to leave the island was nothing but betrayal. Administrators deceived us. Directors deceived us. The hospital staff deceived us. Benefactors deceived us. Pharmaceutical companies on the mainland deceived us. Even our own family members and church members deceived us, turning their backs on us. In the end, the lepers themselves deceived themselves and betrayed each other.

We don't resent all the things that happened. We don't even want to dig up our past and glorify it. In retrospect, it has been a valuable ordeal helping move us closer to God. In the end, a benevolent God saved us from years and years of trial and tribulation. We live within God's compassion. We live on this island within God's care, trusting Him. Our ordeals have ended. God was the only one who didn't betray us. He'll never betray us. You know this as well as we do.

That's why I don't understand why you are doing this.

Elder Hwang was ruthless in his criticism. As a witness to a half-century of the island's disgraceful history, this would be his last chance to make it right. Reading the letter through his bloodshot eyes, the director's face started to lighten.

Elder Hwang's tone suddenly quickened.

Perhaps our ordeals were insufficient.

God had sent us another director in order to end our ordeal. I'm sorry we caused you grief because of our disgraceful past. As much as we want to trust you, you have to trust us. If you want to do this, we'll follow you. We know well that we need to take the initiative if this project is to be our ticket to leaving the island. Moreover, this will determine the future of our innocent children, so we can't entrust our children's future entirely to you. I'm only concerned about God's true will. I'm not certain whether this truly is God's will or not. If this indeed is God's will, He'll give us strength to undertake this project.

I have a favor to ask of you. You explained your plan in the name of God to us yesterday. You criticized us in the name of our children. I want you to promise to us once again in the name of God that we'll be free to leave the island once the reclamation project is successful. If this project ends up being yet another ordeal, you'll be the lowest of human beings for having disgraced God and our children. Please don't forget. God will never betray us.

I will wait for your answer.

After the director read the letter, he sighed in relief. There was nothing to stop him now and there was no reason not to make a pledge. He decided to declare his promise publicly. So he sent someone to

Elder Hwang to explain his decision. Immediately after he got to the hospital, he called Sanguk in to discuss the procedures and prepare for an oath taking ceremony.

As it got closer to noon, the director, leading the entire hospital staff, went to the Chungang assembly hall where he would take the oath. At the hall, two hundred people, including the elders and representatives from all the villages and schools in the patients' zone had already gathered. In the center of the hall an altar had been prepared. The priest who would perform the oath-taking ceremony was present, waiting for the director's arrival. As soon as the director and his staff arrived, the ceremony began.

"Let's begin," the director said, and strode toward the priest who stood in front of the platform. The priest held the Bible out in front of him. The director placed his right hand on the Bible as the priest instructed and waited.

"The director will take an oath." After the priest looked around, he began to ask him questions.

"Do you promise before God and everyone present here that, in carrying out this project, you will not take even a sip of water in your own interest?"

"Yes, I do."

"Do you promise before God and everyone present here that in carrying out this project you will not seek fame, expect rewards or build a statue?

"Yes, I do."

The hall was completely silent. The voices of the priest doing the asking and the director doing the answering were low but assertive, heightening the solemnity that pervaded the hall.

"The director has taken an oath," the priest said to the witnesses. Then he asked the witnesses, "Is there anybody who wants him to take another oath?"

"Yes, here." One of the witnesses stood up. It was Elder Hwang. The atmosphere was once again somber.

"Ask him to take another oath in the name of our poor children. And I'd like you to ask him if, once the project fails, he can before God entrust his life to the five thousand lepers."

"I understand."

After Elder Hwang sat down, the priest turned to Director Cho again and asked, "Do you promise again following the will of the witnesses present?"

"Yes, I do." Director Cho said it more forcefully.

"Do you promise as you have in the name of God, in the name of these witnesses and the children?"

"Yes, I do. And..."

The director answered. Then even before the priest had a chance to pose the next question he jumped in, proceeding to the next step.

Whether in private or in public, the director wore his green uniform with its army colonel insignia. At his right waist hung his gun that had become part of his body. Unexpectedly, he took the gun off and placed it on the altar. With his right hand on the Bible and his left hand on his gun—and in front of the priest—he continued with yet another oath.

"If you'd like, I'll repeat my oath on this gun. If I betray your trust, my life belongs to you. This gun ensures that I keep my oath I made before you and God. Before you and God, this gun will condemn me if I betray you."

The hall had been quiet up to that point but now began to stir at the director's unexpected act. Some heaved sighs of relief while others were frightened by his decisive and forceful action. Amidst the commotion, he stepped down from the altar and finished the oath. The priest waited for the witnesses to settle down as if he was preparing to give a blessing.

Elder Hwang rose again.

"It's not only the director who can betray us. We all know very well that the ugliest and worst betrayal is the betrayal that happens among us. Since the director has taken his oath, it's our turn to do so. We must make an oath."

Elder Hwang walked slowly toward the altar with a somber expression on his face. Again, complete silence hung over the hall. Breaking through the silence, Elder Hwang walked to the altar and placed his hand on the same Bible on which the director had just had his hand and began swearing an oath.

"Our benevolent God, we thank you for sending us an honorable man who's going to provide us with new land. As You have sent him to us, please allow us five thousand islanders the courage and wisdom to endure and overcome any hardship together. If this indeed is Your will, please make this our last trial. We pray that none of us will stray from your path. Please allow your weak followers to witness Your glory. Our bodies are not ours but belong to You. Our souls, too, are not ours but belong to You. Use our bodies as You will. Please guide us feeble souls to stay away from committing the slightest betrayal. In the name of our countless brothers who are already with You and in the name of our children who are not yet born, we make this oath. Amen."

16

After Director Cho had taken the oath, everything went smoothly for a while. Once the groundbreaking was set for the tenth of July, the full preparations for the project were begun. The director obtained the necessary construction permits which, along with relief funds, had been promised to him during his numerous trips back and forth to Seoul. He held periodic meetings with the elders to discuss procedure and concerns over the islanders' well-being during the construction. If everything went as planned, they would reclaim two thousand five hundred acres, more than twice the current size of the island. According to the director's estimates, this would support the households of one thousand former patients—approximately two thousand five hundred people. They could relocate another one thousand poor and impoverished farmer households onto the reclaimed land, allotting each person about four acres. This would mean that a family of five would get twenty acres of land. Because of the former patients' physical condition, he planned to encourage them to engage in vegetable and grain farming and entrust rice farming to the other resettled farmers. Apart from vegetables and miscellaneous grains, he estimated the yearly yield to be 153,000 bushels of rice and 102,000 bushels of barley.

But this would only be possible after the project was completed. In the meantime, the workers' daily maintenance had to be addressed. With its goal of seventy percent completion, the first phase of the project was budgeted at fifty million *wŏn*. While construction was underway, the hospital agreed to pay a wage of thirty to thirty-five *wŏn* a day to patients working at the construction site on top of their usual two cups of rice and two cups of barley. In addition, the director secured separate relief supplies which would be an important resource during the project.

From out of the two thousand former patients who were physically capable of labor he organized two working groups. He planned to alternate between these two groups each month. Of the island population of five thousand, sixty-five percent were former patients, giving a total of three thousand three hundred. Of that number, two thousand five hundred could be mobilized for physical labor and so forming the two work groups posed no problem. The director created the "Oma Recovery Corps" combining the two work forces. He named himself project chief and made Elder Hwang second-in-command, representing all of the islanders.

The director asked the elders' council as well as the volunteers from the patients' zone to organize themselves into the two work forces and to dispatch themselves to the construction site. He spent days visiting the reclamation projects in the Changhŏng and Yŏngam areas, negotiating with the engineers and buying the necessary tools and equipment. Those who finished working the first shift were asked to help build the transportation floats for the rock fill out of pine logs. He passed many a busy day. The preparations were almost complete by the time the start date drew near. The necessary equipment had been purchased and the supplemental workers from off the island were waiting. Finally, the director built a headquarters office near the center of Oma island and hoisted the banner of the Sorok soccer team—the fingerless hand—as the Oma recovery project flag. At the base of the flagpole where their standard fluttered in the ocean wind, he placed a plaque inscribed with the poem "Oma Island," by the leper poet Han Haun:

Lepers' resentment for
Being expelled from the land
Hope to live on the land
Acquiring land which
They never had before
To be unleashed from the oppression
By reclaiming the land
And living on the land
At last

Finally, the tenth of July—groundbreaking

day—came. The island played host to all sorts of festivities. High-ranking officials, including the provincial governor and a cabinet minister, were in attendance. The churches rang their bells in prayer for the success of the project. A celebratory soccer game, with the entire island split into two teams, was played on the field in Chungang village while, at the elementary school, they held a children's song and dance festival.

Following the suggestion of the workers, they did not forget to offer a pig's head at the site of the groundbreaking ceremony. With three pig heads for the three embankments, they appealed to the spirits of earth and sea. During the night, all of the construction lights were turned on, bathing the entire island in a light so bright it seemed like it was day. Under the flames of these glittering lights, the director drank together with the patients late into the night and gazed down at the sea imagining the future fertile land.

But after the groundbreaking, an ordeal awaited the director. He knew this would happen and so he had anticipated it. Persuading the islanders had been the first trial. Now the second trial would come from the outside. He had been secretly worried about this. But he had not expected it to come so soon. It was the morning after the ceremony and the director had returned to his official residence drunk. He had just finished washing his face when a worker who had stayed overnight at the construction site on Oma island burst through the gate, out of breath. He said a large gang of mainlanders living near Oma island had come to destroy the construction site. When the director heard this, he rushed to the site.

The director and his staff reached the headquarters after the riotous rush had swept over the island. When he got off the boat, he found two surveyors lying on the mud shore unconscious. Their equipment and tools had been smashed to pieces and were utterly ruined. The Oma flag that had been raised in front of the headquarters was in tatters, thrown to the ground. The poem-inscribed plaque—Expelled from the land, to live on the land—was trampled, crushed to splinters, even before the work had begun.

Inside, the office was a complete mess. Broken desks and chairs were scattered everywhere. Not a single window was intact. One worker, jammed under a desk, was still moaning, bleeding from his forehead. From the moment he got off the boat and as he walked up to the office, the director trembled with fury. The attackers had left the island before he had arrived. Although it was uncertain how many boats there had been, he could still see them floating in small groups out on the ocean. If they had ransacked the office this badly, the situation at the embankments would be worse. Glaring at the boats carrying the invaders, he touched his gun several times. But he was calm and did not act recklessly. He told himself that he needed to remain calm. First he decided to check on the wounded and then he told the project officers what needed to be done.

"Take them to the hospital immediately. No matter what, these damaged things have to be replaced today. Make sure things return to what they were like before. We can't let them think we're afraid of them or that we've been defeated by this violence...We have to show them we're determined to get through this under any circumstances. Keep this in mind and make sure things return to normal by today."

He gave his instructions and then took out a small boat, following those of the intruders. He knew this was something that he would need to go through at least once. He understood the feelings of the nearby mainlanders. Since they lived in close proximity to the leper island, they had a particularly strong fear of the disease. Even if a proper understanding of the disease was common, they continued to suffer financially, losing money on the seaweed they harvested around the shore. It was always sold cheaper than the market price because of the fear of contamination. Due to the reclamation project, the ocean would be blocked and that would mean the disappearance of their livelihoods—the seaweed and shellfish beds. If the land recovery was successful, the patients would become their neighbors. The threat of the loss of their livelihood and their primal fear of the disease had driven them to these lengths. The director was certain. Confrontation with them was inevitable.

Since the damage was done, he was determined to get to the bottom of things. Disregarding the others' suggestions that it might be dangerous to go by himself, he got on a boat with only the driver and headed toward the mainland village. The invaders' boats were gathered near the shore of the P'ungnam peninsula where the first embankment would be, and they were still ransacking the area. Some of the attackers had gotten off their boat and they were hacking at the equipment and at the warehouse. Others were throwing light bulbs into the water. When the director's boat reached the shore, the attackers stopped what they were doing and stared at him.

The tall director with the uniform and a gun slung at his waist. With his hand on the gun, he stood at the bow of the boat. The mainlanders seemed a bit fearful seeing him. When the boat reached the beach, he quickly got off and stood in front of the crowd. The mainlanders neither moved away nor drew closer. They just watched him, standing where they were. They remained silent, watching him cautiously. The director stood in the middle of this crowd, surrounded by them.

"Who started this? Who?" the director shouted, looking around once. They remained silent.

"This is an insurrection!" Waiting for their response, he shouted again, threatening them. Even then, no one from the attackers' side spoke. They stared silently at the director and waited for his next move.

"You know that you're under military rule—the military took control after the revolution. As a soldier on active duty and a director, in order to protect the lives and property of the five thousand people of Sorok island and to maintain order and safety, I have the authority and right to settle this insurrection," the director continued. He wanted to threaten them first and then persuade them.

"I understand your situation well. I know that you'll suffer directly and indirectly due to this reclamation project. I've been thinking about it, too."

As the director continued speaking, the mainlanders who had watched silently approached him. He became more confident.

"Let's talk. This problem won't be solved by just smashing and breaking things. No matter how many times you ransack the place, this project will continue. And, we'll complete it. Because those five thousand islanders have survived and endured worse ordeals and misfortunes than you have. They undertook this work as God's will and as a covenant between themselves and God. They won't give up. Violence won't make them quit. So, let's talk. Let's find a way so that we can reach a compromise. Who can talk as your representative? Please step forward."

"We don't have a representative. All of us are representatives!" somebody in the crowd yelled out cynically. Since the director had not been forceful enough, they began to be less fearful of him. As if on cue, people began to chime in from every direction, attacking the director.

"That's right! We don't have a representative. If you want to talk, don't try to do it behind our backs. You have to talk to all of us right here."

"What's there to talk about? The only thing we can say is to stop what you're doing. If you're trying to persuade us, it's better to shoot us with that gun."

"Before that, why don't you talk first. You said you understand our situation well, so tell us what you know."

It was impossible to have a talk with a representative. It was clear that they could not choose one person but they were ready to have a group discussion.

"All right. I had no intention of discussing this matter secretly. I'll talk first. If you have questions or requests, ask them one by one in an orderly manner." After the director calmed everyone down, he continued. A strange public meeting had been called to order on that pebbly beach at high tide.

The director admitted he knew of the potential financial loss to the nearby mainlanders because of the construction. Then he explained how he would compensate them for their losses. He acknowledged that living with lepers as neighbors caused direct and indirect harm, especially the threat of losing the seaweed beds and the like. He even expressed his sympathy and understanding of their fear and anxiety about contagion. But he explained that the people who would be coming there were either former patients or unaffected people who had parents who were affected. They were completely recovered and as healthy as the mainlanders. As long as they knew that they would meet the same refusals, denials and persecution if they tried to acquire land on their own as they had before, they had decided they would rather endure and continue fighting here where the process had already been started. He asked for their understanding.

"Since you've been near them for so long, you know their situation better than anyone else. We can't persecute them. It's not their fault. You already know that they can't be condemned for being affected with disease. Even if leprosy is a proof of their sin, only God can judge them. We can't do that. Since you know their situation well, you can't possibly judge them. Please don't try to drive them out of here."

The director promised the mainlanders that if they allowed the islanders to settle here, he would allocate a portion of the recovered land for rice farming. He even expressed his willingness to compensate those who could not possibly live with lepers as neighbors and wanted to leave. Despite the director's promises, the people could not accept his proposition.

"You're trying to threaten us into leaving!"

"You want lepers to come here and you want us to leave, hunh?"

"Don't even listen! He thinks he's God because he has a gun. He's telling us not to judge but look at him. Isn't he God since he's the one who decides whom to bring in and whom to expel?"

The jeering continued from all directions. The director could ignore these since they were emotional outbursts. After he finished talking, he realized that his attempts at persuasion were futile. When the director asked them to speak, a man in his forties in the crowd gestured toward the director. The man had a calm look.

"Now can we ask you a question?" the man asked.

"Certainly, go ahead." the director answered, looking him straight in the face. But the man's question was unexpected.

"Are you a doctor or a charity worker?" the man asked slowly but in a clear voice. From his behavior, it was clear that the man had gone through a lot. He could be one of the instigators of the insurrection.

His question was brazen. The director knew what he was getting at. This question posed a dilemma for him. Even though he tried very hard, he could not find an answer. The gap between his position as a physician who considered treatment, contagion, relapse, and hospitalization and his position as a hospital director who understood the unfair treatment they received was enormous. But the director was not the type who would waste his time hesitating. His determination and actions always preceded his thoughts. He contemplated the answers to difficult questions after he had taken action.

But the director couldn't answer the man's unexpected question. They pushed him further into a corner.

"We can't figure out whether you're a doctor who is trying to cure them and trying to stop further contagion, or a charity worker who is trying to persuade us of their situation because you feel sorry for them."

"He said he's a soldier who puts down insurrections," someone shouted from the crowd. The man's intention in asking the question seemed to have a deeper meaning. He continued.

"I guess you don't want to answer. It doesn't matter. We don't really want to hear your answer anyway. Whether you're a doctor, or a charity worker, or a soldier trying to stop an insurrection, one thing is clear. Like us, you were never affected with the disease and as much as we fear the disease, so do you. We are certain of that fact and that's all we wanted to say."

"..."

"Don't condemn us because we don't want to listen to you. To be honest, we don't take this matter as seriously as you think. It'll become evident as time passes. But we don't believe this project will succeed. The only thing that we are worried about is that the lepers might cause a terrible commotion once the project fails. I'm telling you this not for our sake but for your own safety. We know them better than you do. We've watched them for a long time. Do you know how many murders they've committed? You don't understand their true nature. When this project fails...we'll have to witness another horrible murder. Like you said, if we truly care about our neighbors, we need to stop this now..."

The director was speechless. The man firmly believed that the project was doomed to fail so he wasn't worried about having to leave the island or the threat of losing his livelihood. He spoke as if he was really concerned and wanted to advise the director—at least to help him as a fellow healthy person.

Conversely the director was being persuaded.

The director knew the man's shrewd ulterior motives. The man wanted to get him on their side by using their shared status as healthy people as a pretext. He was trying to persuade the director, even threaten him.

"What about you others? Is there anyone else who wants to speak?"

The director looked around waiting for someone else to speak, but after the man finished talking, the rest remained silent as if they all agreed with him.

"If you don't have a questionable medical history, you'd better listen to what's been said now." A man whose face was hidden behind a fellow invader advised him cynically, then laugher quickly spread through the crowd. They had no intention of compromising or trying to understand the situation. Director Cho felt completely black. There was no point in talking to them. It was impossible to persuade them with words. He needed to persuade them with actions. He decided to return to the island but, before he returned, he needed to express his determination once again.

"I must have a leper in my family in the past. So

there's nothing more to talk about. On top of what I said earlier, there is one more thing. Whether you think of me as a doctor, or a charity worker, or a soldier going around to subdue insurrections, I won't tolerate this ever again. Once is enough."

17

Ironically, the unfortunate attack turned into a blessing for the project. The news of the neighbors' raid became a catalyst, inspiring the patients and instilling in them a fervent desire to succeed, reawakening their attachment to the land. When the wounded were carried onto the Tongsaeng village pier, all of the patients gathered around as if they had come to greet heroes returning from war. They prepared to leave for the first project site immediately. When the director returned to the island, the boat carrying the first group of workers was ready to shove off. The patients had already divided themselves into groups and had begun leaving in an orderly manner. As the boat left the pier, the departing group sang the "Song of Sorok," their voices carrying over the sea. The islanders standing on the pier to send them off cheered loudly. It was a solemn scene. After half a century, their dream of leaving Sorok island was at last close to being realized.

Director Cho turned his boat around to head out to the Oma island construction site.

"Long live, Director Cho!"

Recognizing the director's boat, the workers cheered in unison from their boats. The director was overcome with joy and wept. He recalled what had happened that morning.

"God, please don't let their long cherished wish come to naught. Please give them the courage to triumph over any obstacles and in Your mercy allow them to achieve what they have set out to do." The director was not Christian but he found himself repeating these words over and over again.

After the boat arrived at the construction site, he sent it back to get the rest of the workers. Then he began to instruct them. Before sunset, the entire first group had arrived at the site. From the one thousand workers, the director chose three hundred and set them to build the first embankment between P'ungnam peninsula and Odong island. He selected six hundred for the third embankment from Pongam peninsula to Oma island. The supplementary workers from the outside had already been assigned to build the second embankment between Oma island and Odong island. From the one thousand workers, he selected about a hundred people who were not physically strong and assigned them to supervise the distribution of materials and to record work progress at the second embankment site. By sunset, a huge tent village had appeared at the head of the embankment on the P'ungnam and Pongam peninsulas. The director alerted everyone about the possibility of a second raid by the neighbors.

The real work began the next morning. The first thing they started working on was quarrying stones and dumping them into the sea. To build the first embankment they leveled the mountain top near the tip of P'ungnam peninsula and for the third embankment they began tearing down Manjae island in the middle of the bay. The workers carried the stones from the island and the mountain on their backs to the boats, then dumped them along the line of light bulbs. The nature of the work was simple. They used primitive methods, but it was extremely risky. They would dump stone upon stone into the sea until they appeared above the water line. The stones needed to reach more than eight meters down and stretch for more than thirteen miles before any sign of them would appear at the surface. It was a long process and there was no guarantee when the embankments would start to show. The only thing the director could count on was the workers' faith and their patience.

Fortunately the workers' enthusiasm surpassed the director's expectations. Because of their high spirits and ambition, the morale at the construction site could not have been any better. From morning until night, the sound of exploding dynamite echoed through the two quarries. A long procession of workers carrying stones on their backs to the boats covered the hills and sea like ants. At night when all the lights were on, the sea would shimmer. Trying to work around high tide, the movements of the workers became quicker.

They poured all their strength into the project so

that after a week they were exhausted to the point where they could no longer continue. The plan to change shifts after a month had to be modified. The time between shift changes was shortened to fifteen days. But there were no complaints from the patients. No one tried to avoid work and no one complained. Neither the director's encouragement nor his interference was needed. The order of the construction site, the living facilities, the guards, the management of workers were all competently taken care of by the elders' council and the workers themselves. Therefore, the director, as chief of the Oma recovery project, did not have much to do. This was largely due to the help of Elder Hwang, his second-in-command, and the elders' council. But it would not have been possible without the workers' unrelenting will and dedication. The director was extremely satisfied.

The progress made by the patients on the first and third embankments was far greater than that of the healthy workers from the outside on the second embankment. One of the director's great pleasures was his frequent meetings with Elder Hwang at the construction site. After Elder Hwang had been appointed second-in-command, he was always at the construction site. Although he would wander idly around the site, he could read solemn devotion and prayer on his face.

"In the past decades people have done so many things on this island that you couldn't possibly imagine anyone would do. Now, something else that's humanly impossible is about to take place. Perhaps among humanly impossible works, this will be the last of the mysteries. This must be the will of our benevolent God!"

Every time Elder Hwang saw the director, he would gaze at the ant-like procession of workers, and he would subtly compliment the director's decision to undertake this project. The director could not help but be elated that at last a sprout of warm humanly affection and faith was growing inside the frozen hearts of the islanders. In Elder Hwang, the director unexpectedly found a source of comfort and encouragement. Another person who equally encouraged the director at the construction site was none other than Haewŏn. The director took particular interest in Haewŏn after hearing things about him after he had come to the island. Even after segregated instruction had ended—and healthy and uninfected children were moved to the regular elementary school—he remained at the preschool and took care of the children. Miyŏn, whom Haewŏn had dearly wished to drive off the island, remained at the preschool as well and continued to aggravate him. According to island rumor, Haewŏn was having a difficult time with Miyŏn, unlike with other women. As Sanguk had expected, Haewŏn had at last confessed his love to Miyŏn but even with this, his last secret method, he could not make Miyŏn give up and leave the island. Rumor had it that this was a subtle way on her part of punishing Sanguk.

Because Miyŏn was willing to accept Haewŏn's love, he began to keep his distance from her. It was apparent that his love for Miyŏn was not genuine and that is why he could not confidently confront her. Like an addict in withdrawal, Haewŏn had been keeping to himself since then, struggling in his misery.

—For Haewŏn, his disease was like a medicine that made him continue to live. His disease made him hate and curse the world and that in turn gave him the strength to live. His madness and mania for pink was his way of supporting himself, I think.

Sanguk, who usually kept his distance and liked to complicate things, was strangely interested in the relationship of Miyŏn and Haewŏn and had said this once to the director.

—Haewŏn lost his object of hatred. Miyŏn shattered his world when she accepted his love. Haewŏn had been deprived of his object of hatred, the very thing he had been holding on to. After such a painful loss, he began to experience a new despair. He made so many false confessions of love to so many young women but failed to realize that deep down he had a strong desire really to love them. Miyŏn awakened in him an honest desire to love her and forced him to realize the extent of his self-deception.

—For Haewŏn, it might have been better if Miyŏn had flatly rejected him. When the dream that he had hidden from even himself seemed suddenly about to come true—that he truly wanted to love a healthy woman—and it was now possible to realize his dream, it was a shock to him. He knew it would be more painful and difficult to love her than to hate her. It was inevitable that he'd fallen deeply into despair.

The director smiled secretly as he sensed a jealous note in Sanguk's attitude toward Haewŏn. He heard through the rumors that Miyŏn's action was partly a way for her to punish Sanguk so he guessed that there was a conflict between the two. If Miyŏn had created a subtle conflict between Haewŏn and Sanguk, he expected that Haewŏn's less subtle actions would solve it one way or another, since Sanguk's perpetual intellectualization and passivity could only prolong the situation. He remembered Haewŏn's poem in the Kura journal, written for his sister who was still in the patients' zone. The poem was not so much about his empathy for his sister—instead he used his sister's misery as a pretext to express his own self-realization. The director continued to examine the serious look on Sanguk's face and wished to see the resolution of the conflict within Haewŏn's despair. Haewŏn's poem in the Kura journal went like this.

The beautiful pink dappled your face
Nobody calls them flowers
Nor can we
For your beautiful color
If the tears we shed became flowers

Sister, we would be walking on a road of flowers.

One day Director Cho found Haewŏn carrying stones among the procession of stone carriers at the first embankment.

"My sister is still in the patients' zone. I came here because of her. I don't have any strength to work for anyone but her," Haewŏn stammered when he saw the director, leaving these words as he passed him. Watching him return to the procession with the stones on his back, Director Cho nodded. It did not matter for whom Haewŏn volunteered to work. Whether he had written a poem for his bedridden sister, or in order to overcome his despair regarding Miyŏn, as long as everyone on the island became one both in body and mind, it made no difference. Once again, the director had regained his conviction about the project.

But what made the director most content—and shocked too—was neither Elder Hwang nor Haewŏn but rather when one of the soccer players who had escaped returned to the island and showed up at the construction site. It was Yu Kilsang whose will and ball handling skills were so much better than the others that he stood out. The director had taken a special interest in him. But about the critical time of the reclamation project, he deserted the soccer team and left the island. He was a traitor. Unexpectedly, he showed up at the construction site with Sanguk and visited the director at the headquarters office. The director found out that he had been working for a few days. He was overwhelmingly pleased. He knew why he had come back to the island without asking him. There was no need to say anything to him.

"Well, now that you've returned I'm not going to question you, but if it happens again, that's it." The director said it unpleasantly, but he was very grateful.

There was still one person who remained a mystery—Sanguk. As the director's confidant, Sanguk was always close by. But he still questioned the director's motives and was skeptical of the work. He carried out the director's directions faithfully, but was always distant. He never once put his heart into the work, was never enthusiastic and never added his own suggestions to the director's ideas or plans.

"Well, you never know. There is no guarantee that no one will desert the island from now on. It all depends on whether this project turns out as planned."

It was Sanguk who brought Kilsang and pleased the director. But it was also Sanguk who inadvertently threatened him with his indifferent reaction to the director's concern that the escapes should never happen again for the sake of the patients' morale. Apart from Sanguk, everyone worked hard. But then since Sanguk carried out his own work faithfully, he worked hard in his own way. In fact, even though the project was only in its initial phases, Director Cho was the only person who was already anxious about the result. The eager workers carried the stones on their backs with beads of sweat on their foreheads morning, noon and night. During high tide, they busily rowed the stone-laden boats beneath the strings of lights.

Boom, crash.

The sound of land crashing here and there, the sound of stones being thrown into the sea, the sound of the workers carrying stones and singing to forget their exhaustion, the busy and chaotic construction site, the workers' forgetting the change of day and night, their hands and feet scarred and their faces and shoulders turning black as coal.

18

Two weeks later, however, Director Cho had to change the first group half way through their scheduled shift. Patients started to get injured or sick due to their enthusiasm and eagerness. After ten days, the progress at the site declined rapidly. It was impossible to continue working for a month straight. At last the director decided to relieve the first shift.

On the director's orders, the one thousand workers of the first group returned to Sorok Island after two weeks. At the Tongsaeng village pier the second shift of one thousand were waiting and left for the construction site. The pier was once again filled with people coming and going, some offering welcoming arms and others waving good-bye. It was getting dark but around the pier, with all the torches, it was bright as daylight. The welcomers were as excited as if they were greeting long-lost lovers they had not seen for ten years. And those who were seeing others off—friends and relatives—did what they could to hide their tears, unable to turn their backs easily. For people who lived in a place where hardly anybody who left ever returned, partings and reunions were the most precious human experiences they had ever known.

After another two weeks there was another shift change and again the pier was crowded with people coming and going. Two months passed. The progress seemed to taper off but after the shift changes the enthusiasm returned. The work progressed without much difficulty or change. July and August came and went. When September came turning the sea gray and cold, the director started to feel anxious. No matter how many stones had been thrown into the sea, there was no sign of the embankments emerging. He did not expect to see the embankments after a month or two, but working with no visible progress whatsoever—just waiting patiently—was difficult to endure. He was afraid that the stones were being washed away as soon as they were thrown in and nothing was left below. Divers were sent in to check and they assured him that the stones were still there. But he grew more and more impatient and worried. He became fearful of the workers who continued to move the stones without complaint. He also became fearful of the sea. Only white bubbles surfaced after the stones were thrown in and he was fearful of that sea. And, he began to be afraid of himself as well.

One afternoon, the director heard an ominous rumor. It was the first one since the project had begun. It was something he had not imagined at all. He heard it through an unexpected person. As usual, he was looking down from Oma island headquarters at the shore where there was still no sign of the embankments. He was suffering from a hallucination that the long procession of workers would run toward him in anger at any moment. Then he saw a group of them running toward the hilltop where the headquarters office stood.

He felt tense and waited for them to reach the office. Soon he realized that these people were not patients but outside workers from the second embankment. It was strange. Among the angry crowd, there was one short, frail looking fellow, being dragged along. They were coming toward the director. There was a patient who had been chosen as the record keeper of the daily progress at the second embankment. The director wondered if there had been an accident. Fortunately it was not an accident.

"Director, you need to interrogate this guy. There's something fishy about him," said the patient who was working as the record keeper, pushing the guy toward the director. The director had no idea what was going on so he decided to ask why they had brought the man to him.

"He's not a day laborer. He didn't come here to make money like the rest of the outside workers. If you interrogate him, you'll find out the real reason why he came." The patient started to explain, shoving the man toward the director. Among the outside workers, there was one person who seemed inexperienced in this kind of work. The way he carried the stones on his back and the way he carried himself. His speech was different from the rest of the workers. When asked where he had worked before, he could not answer confidently and clearly. After observing him for a few days, together with several other workers, the record keeper tried to interrogate him and he would not open up. Since he refused to speak, they became more suspicious of him. And that's why they decided to bring him to the director.

While listening to the explanation, the director closely examined the man they had brought. He was rather short but had broad and firm shoulders. Behind his thick black-rimmed glasses, his innocent, innocuous yet sharp eyes stared back at him.

His jacket was stained with sweat and mud, which showed that he had been working for some time. But even the director could sense that he did not really belong in this kind of work place.

"Look at his hands. Just by looking at his hands, you can tell he's not a day laborer," a worker standing next to him said, shaking his fist, ready to strike him.

The director examined his hands. Although scratched and blistered, the man's hands proved he had never done this kind of work before.

"Why are you here?" The director asked bluntly. Realizing that he could no longer keep silent, the man spoke.

"To tell you the truth, I'm a reporter from the C Daily News." It was just as the director had expected.

"Can I see your ID?"

"I planned to leave because I realized that I wasn't going to get much of a story this way but…" said the man, with an embarrassed smile, as he took out his ID from the inner pocket of his muddy jacket.

"I didn't know there were any interesting stories to get here," the director said in a low voice, as he alternately looked at the man's face and his photo ID.

It was later that evening that the director heard an unpleasant rumor from the C Daily News reporter. No matter how he had come to the island, the director was thankful that he had taken an interest in the project and invited him to his place. In order to relieve the tension that had been building, he asked him to have a drink with him.

The reporter introduced himself as Yi Chŏngt'ae. The director discovered that he had already gathered an enormous amount of information. From the history of the island to the details of the recovery project and its progress, he had completed gathering information. He was interested in learning about the actual conditions at the construction site, the atmosphere at the work site as well as the patients' morale.

"You know Elder Hwang, the second-in-command of the Oma Recovery Corps?" Yi Chŏngt'ae asked abruptly. "Have you ever heard the story of how he came to the island?"

"Well…I've heard bits and pieces about him. I wasn't too keen on finding out about his past. Why? Is there a story behind his coming to the island?" The director had no idea what Chŏngt'ae wanted to say, so he asked him. Chŏngt'ae nodded twice as if he knew that the director did not know and went on.

"Yes, there's a horrible story behind it. Actually his past doesn't really matter. Everyone who has come to the island has a horrible story like Elder Hwang. What I'm trying to say is that sooner or later the time will come when Elder Hwang himself will reveal his past to you."

"I have no idea what you are trying to say."

"Okay. I'll get to the point. Everyone on the island who knows Elder Hwang believes that when the old man tells his past to someone, something ghastly happens. That's the way it's been until now. He doesn't like to talk about his past but when he does it serves as a signal that something horrific and tragic will happen on the island. It happened during the Japanese occupation and after Liberation. Every time the old man recalls his past, he carries out an act of retribution."

"..."

"The embankments. When do you think they will appear? Unless the embankments surface soon, you might hear Elder Hwang's story before the project gets finished. If that's the case, you will..."

"I see." The director quickly interrupted Chŏngt'ae. "You don't seem to expect that we will succeed."

He thought he had met another tough troublemaker. Chŏngt'ae had carried stones on his back together with the workers until his skin had peeled off. He even refused to leave as the director suggested, insisting that he wanted to spend a few more days with the workers. The director was determined to carry out this work but he felt himself weakening in the face of Chongt'ae's strong counsel. Hiding his weak self, he said resolutely, "But before I ask you, there is something I want to say. I already know what's going to happen if the embankments don't appear. Before I started the project, I pledged an oath in front of Elder Hwang. But I'm not worried. Elder Hwang is not the impatient person you might think."

"Even when there is no sign of the embankments appearing?"

"The embankments will eventually surface. I'm waiting for that day."

"Do you think Elder Hwang will wait forever?"

"Sure. Not only Elder Hwang but all of the islanders are waiting patiently for that day. They can wait much longer than what you'd expect. You've seen them at the construction site. Their enthusiasm hasn't subsided a bit."

"Do you really think so?" Chŏngt'ae asked seriously. He gulped down his drink and continued cautiously. "Don't believe what's visible to your eyes. I met someone who's ready to hear Elder Hwang's story again. You said that their morale is still high but there is a visible difference between when I first came and now. It's only a matter of days. Some are saying 'Isn't it time Elder Hwang told his story again?' The number of people who want to hear his story is increasing by the day. Surprisingly, Elder Hwang knows this all too well even though he doesn't hear it directly from them."

"..."

The director was at a loss for words. He felt that what he had dreaded had finally come to pass. Suddenly he remembered Sanguk's smiling face, that cold smile. Chŏngt'ae was telling him the truth about what he had heard and seen. The director could not possibly change the situation simply with his own conviction and determination. Moreover, he could not criticize Elder Hwang or the rest of the islanders. But he could not throw away his hope and faith in Elder Hwang and the islanders. He continued to listen calmly to Chŏngt'ae, hiding his agitation. Chŏngt'ae seemed to want to shatter the root of the director's faith.

"I don't think there is any reason for me to tell you about Elder Hwang's past. It's not a pleasant story, plus my telling you doesn't mean anything. I just hope that you don't ever have to hear the story, not from me or others, but especially from Elder Hwang." Similar to the advice he got from the people who had ransacked Oma island, Chŏngt'ae was subtly warning him as a fellow healthy person.

"..."

"Anyway, don't expect to wait forever. There is no way to know how much longer they will wait."

This was a truly ominous warning that the director could not easily accept.

19

Another month passed and there was still no sign of the embankments. Work efficiency fell day by day but there was nothing Director Cho could do. He could not come up with an idea of how to raise their morale. He could only wait. Instead of carrying stones on their backs to where they could dump them into the sea, he decided to bring in hopper cars to increase their efficiency. And he waited for a sign of the embankments. A day seemed like ten years. It was unbearably long and painful.

The director was himself exhausted, tired of waiting now that half of Manjae island had been scraped into the sea. Soon winter would be on them. Morning and night, the cold wind bit through the workers' clothes and slowed them down. There were some who began to avoid the night shift. Given their condition it would be impossible for them to keep working once winter came. It would have been ideal if the embankments surfaced now, but since there was no sign of that happening, he might have to stop the work until the following spring. He needed to make a decision fast.

The director was afraid of running into Elder Hwang. He didn't know when he would start talking about his past. Although he was afraid of the old man, he was actually waiting anxiously to hear the story. He could not quite make up his mind whether he really wanted to hear the story or not. Around this time, while he was vacillating, another accident occurred. A patient was hurt by falling rocks at the stone quarry for the third embankment in Pongam village. This was only the beginning.

When the director reached the accident site, the fellow patients had already pulled the injured man from under the rocks. He was completely covered with blood but fortunately his life was not in danger. The director treated the man after having him carried to a nearby medical tent. He had the man rest in the tent while they waited for the boat that would carry him to the hospital for further treatment. Then he went outside to order everyone back to work. This kind of thing happened often. Some workers had been buried under rocks before but fortunately no one had lost his life yet. At any construction site, this kind of accident was bound to happen.

Some suffered concussions after falling while carrying stones and others had nearly drowned when their boats capsized. After the weather turned cold, the accidents happened more frequently. Today's accident was one of those usual ones.

The real accident was still waiting to happen. But today's crisis triggered something far more serious. After the director had ordered them all to go back to work, he made a safety inspection of the site. Suddenly he heard a woman screaming. When he turned around, Elder Hwang, who had been standing next to him, was already running toward the area from where the woman's shriek had come. The director felt that something terrible was about to happen. The woman's scream came from the other side of the hill in a little gorge behind the medical tent.

All around the construction site there were women selling things to the workers. During rest time, the workers would often buy rice cakes and bread from these women. Some even invited the women to sit and have drinks with them. The director prayed that nothing had happened and followed Elder Hwang. As they had expected, a man covered with blood was on top of one of the vendors, trying to crush the very life out of her. It was the man who had just been injured and had been lying inside the medical tent. Like a snake coiled around a frog, trying to swallow it, the man held the woman, violently squeezing her small body. Her clothes had been torn off, revealing her breasts and thighs. They were smeared with blood, possibly his, possibly hers. The woman lay trembling under his weight, as if she no longer had the strength to cry out. Dumbfounded, the director stood there motionless.

He felt every ounce of his strength drain away, as if he was the one pinned under the man. He closed his eyes for a moment, trying to collect himself. His legs shook. Elder Hwang rushed to the man. Grabbing onto the man's hair, he was finally able to pull him off the woman. The man did not care whether someone came or not.

"Let go of me! Leave me alone!" he screamed, not wanting to let her go. He clung to her even harder. In a burst of superhuman strength, Elder Hwang managed to separate the two and the man glared sharply at Elder Hwang. The man's eyes were bloodshot. Suddenly, he slapped Elder Hwang on the cheek several times and then sank to the ground.

"Why don't you leave me alone? For once this leper wants to be human, so why won't you let him? If you had left me alone, I would have thrown my rotten body into the sea—instead of those rocks—to make the embankments appear. Why can't you just leave me alone?" The man wailed, covering his face with his hands. Even though the man had slapped him, Elder Hwang looked down at him quietly and sympathetically. The director still didn't budge, his feet seemingly glued to the ground. He just gazed at the wailing man. Ten or so patients gathered around but they too were speechless when confronted by this atrocious spectacle. The woman vendor staggered away, unable to cover herself properly with her tattered clothes. But no one paid any attention to her. The man kept on raving, unable to calm down.

"If you want to dam up the sea, go ahead! If that's what the director or Elder Hwang want, go ahead. But don't tell me to carry any more stones. Why don't you have us throw our useless bodies into the water for the embankments rather than see us die smashed under the rocks. You must know this already, Elder Hwang. Why are you keeping quiet? What kind of lunacy is this, trying to dam up the ocean!"

The next day Elder Hwang finally spoke about his terrible past. That afternoon, on the day following the incident, the director sat alone on the hillside near the Oma island headquarters, staring down at the gray ocean that kept getting darker and darker. He looked forlorn like a winter crow perched on a branch. There was a bleak solitude that had enveloped him. He was tired and lonely. Last night's incident could not simply be forgotten. He had needed to perform surgery on the man that night. Performing surgery on a leper was extremely difficult. He did not have time to think about how difficult it was nor how tired he was. He performed the surgery by himself. It had lasted two hours. He had nothing on his mind other than his determination to save the man. His desperation to save the man under any circumstances had made him push himself to perform.

But successfully finishing the surgery was not

the end of it. After he returned to his room, he took out a bottle to help him forget his exhaustion. He was completely worn out but there were some neighbors from the mainland who had come to see him. It was the same group of people who had ransacked the construction site on the first day of the project.

"Don't worry. We didn't come to ask you to stop the project," one man said.

"Believe it or not, now we wish that the embankments would appear soon too." They said that they were also praying for the ocean to turn into land so that they could have their share of the land and live harmoniously together with the director and the patients. They were trying to make the director understand their plans to drive the lepers back to Sorok island once the embankments appeared. After the initial work was done, they would take over the reclaimed land. It was their way of mocking him.

"Anyway, everything depends on the appearance of the embankments. I hope it'll be soon."

This was their way of saying that they pitied him. They were certain that the embankments would never appear. Even if they did eventually appear, they felt that the patients would not wait that long. The mainlanders no longer needed to fear that the project might succeed. What had happened that afternoon made them feel stronger about their beliefs and made them feel that they had the upper hand. Since they had come all the way out here at night, they were not going to leave easily.

"But you know what? There's something you have to take responsibility for." One of the men was finally getting to the main point of their visit.

"It's about today's unfortunate incident. One of your patients raped one of our village women. Like I said before, we're not here to stop you. I hope your project succeeds. But our positions are different. We can't let our women be raped by those lepers just because of your work. We can't just let it go. What do you think about this?"

The director was ready for this. He was not going to let this matter slide. He apologized sincerely to them for what had happened earlier. He promised them that this kind of incident would never happen again and that he would prohibit the women vendors from entering the construction site. As for what had happened, the man would be punished accordingly and the victim would be compensated. The director's apologies and promises were not readily accepted. The visitors said they could not be satisfied with the lawful punishment the man would receive. They insisted that the man would have to endure what the woman had suffered. They wanted to take the matter into their own hands and punish the victimizer. Unless the director conceded to this, they could not accept his word that this would not happen again. If he refused, they would not be able to believe in him at all.

They argued until late into the night. When they realized that the director was on the verge of collapse, they started to get up to leave.

"Don't think we're cruel. The time will come when you will understand us. Are you going to be able to protect your family who are here suffering with you, when their true nature surfaces? Of course, we hope the embankments appear soon. But it's not as easy as it seems, is it?" Before leaving, one man shot these last words at him.

It was a dirty threat. Even if the embankments appeared the patients would not be able to farm the land peacefully. But the project would fail even before it reached that point. There was no way out. The director had no place to turn for help. He didn't have the strength to go down to the construction site. He sat on the lawn in front of the headquarters and gazed down the hill. He was afraid of the patients who looked like ants scurrying about hauling the rocks. He had a vision that they would come up at any minute to attack him. He shuddered at his own imagination. He stayed like that for a while. Then he heard someone so he turned around. Elder Hwang had his back to him and was staring down at the ocean just like the director. He had no idea when the old man had come up.

"People usually have one or two secret stories about things that they have endured that they could not possibly overcome." Realizing that the director had noticed his presence, Elder Hwang started to speak.

"Having stories like these allows a person to endure even more difficult ordeals. Looking at you like this, I'm compelled to tell you something." Elder Hwang had something to say. The director was not sure exactly what was on the old man's mind. He remained quiet and waited for him to continue.

"I'm sure you are like that, too. You must have felt this kind of compulsion. Seeing you in this state, I want to tell you a story. Perhaps I'm getting too old..."

The director finally realized that it was time. The old man was trying to talk about his past. That was the reason why the old man had come to see him. The director's lips felt like they were frozen shut. He looked at Elder Hwang, petrified, and remained silent. Elder Hwang slowly turned to look the director in the face.

"What are you afraid of?" Elder Hwang reprimanded him. "You already know that if you are afraid of lepers they get nastier...I guess I can't hold back on the story now." Elder Hwang turned slowly and squatted down. Then he lit his pipe and kept quiet for a while, staring at the ocean again. The director felt suffocated, unable to utter a word. He felt paralyzed and helpless. He could only watch the movements of the old man.

"No one knew where they came from and where they were going. They were like drifters, wandering in flocks. Those who rushed down from the North during the famine of 1912." The old man began to speak of the past. It did not matter any more whether the director wanted to hear or not. Elder Hwang ignored the director's gaze and began to unfold his memory of the past.

"I'm sure you've heard about the famine of 1912, haven't you? It was the most horrible thing."

During the famine, Elder Hwang had lived with his mother and grandfather in a remote village near the Myohyang mountains in P'yŏngan province. His grandfather worked as a tinkerer and he had helped him with his work. Every day during the famine, from the autumn through the winter, hundreds of refugees streamed by their hut in droves en route to the south. For the young boy it was just another source of fun seeing the throngs of people moving by. Then one day, he and his grandfather returned to their hut from the village only to discover that the boy's mother had been brutally murdered. She was naked from the waist down and was covered in blood. Her eyes were wide open, her gaze fixed on the ceiling as if she was still waiting for the boy. It must have been the vagabonds who had passed the hut on their way south. It was that same night that he and his grandfather left the hut to go south as well with the waves of migrants. They left his dead mother in the hut. They wore all the clothes they had and wrapped some barley and salt in a piece of straw matting. They had no place to go. With no destination in mind, the boy and the grandfather kept walking south with the crowds of migrants. At night they would spread their straw mat by the roadside and sleep. Come morning there would always be someone who had died of hunger or from cold and turned into a corpse. The boy and the old man slept clinging to each other so they could endure the cold at least for a little while. But this lasted only for a few days after they had left the hut. The warmth of the weak and tired old man and the little boy was not enough. One morning, when the boy woke up, his grandfather was dead. His grandfather held onto the boy tightly as if to give him the last ounce of his body heat. The boy released himself from the old man's stiff grip, took the handful of barley and trudged on alone.

Elder Hwang stopped for a minute and coughed dryly as if he was thirsty. With a strangely unpleasant smile, he continued, "So it was then that I met a kind woman while I was plodding along alone like that."

As the boy trudged along, a woman who was

about his mother's age approached him and asked him in a kind voice to accompany her. Elder Hwang said he felt fortunate at the time that he had met the woman. The woman shared her food, a mixture of boiled barley and wheat. But he had to pay for his fortune. That night they spread the straw mat on the roadside and instead of his bony grandfather, he shared the same mat with the woman's warmth. He felt warm. The woman brought the boy's hand to her breasts, which were much bigger and softer than his mother's whom he had left in the hut. While caressing the woman's warm breasts, he watched the movement of the stars. But the woman suddenly robbed him of the constellation's glow. She covered his face with her skirt.

The next day, the boy again accompanied her, sharing her boiled barley. At night they again slept on the same straw mat. The woman was even more unreserved the second night. The boy knew what she wanted. He sucked her breasts and pushed his head under her skirt to rub the spot that would tickle her. The woman giggled and enjoyed being tickled. Sometimes she would whine and moan, tightening her plump thighs around his head. It became a routine every night and the boy did not get enough sleep. But he could not stop. He could not leave the woman because he was getting handfuls of boiled barley and the warmth of her flesh. Walking alone would be boring and at the same time scary for the boy. The only way to keep the woman was to continue with that every night.

After spending several nights like that, the boy lost his chance to repay the woman's kindness. As she walked along, she was always on the lookout for someone. Sometimes she would wait for the beggars to pass by and she would look carefully. One night she took up with a group of beggars in Ch'ungch'ŏng province. That night as if she had finally found the person she had been looking for, she followed the beggars. The woman and the boy spread out the straw mat among the beggars but for some reason she would not turn her ticklish spot to him. She was entangled with one of the beggars, rolling and tossing with him all night long. He was just thankful that the woman and the beggars did not try to expel him from the gang. From then on, the boy stayed with them. The beggars did not insist on going south and they did not even rush. Not only did the woman not drive the boy away but she continued to share the boiled barley with him. From time to time the woman would give the boy a bowl of warm porridge or soup she got from the beggars.

There was nothing the boy could do for the woman to repay her kindness. He needed to find something else. The beggars gave him a new job to do. The boy could not refuse. Whether he liked it or not, he had to do what he was told. He had no intention of leaving the beggars. Even if he thought of escaping from them, he could not possibly do it because they were violent and strong. Every night he snuck into the other camps and stole the barley or wheat hidden under the straw mats. Sometimes he took hair ornaments from the women's hair knots and the clothes the mothers used to cover their babies. He even killed a starving dog with a stone and carried it back. When he found a dead woman on the street, the boy would tell the beggars where the corpse was. Then they would come and strip off her skirt and would take turns playing strange games with her. While they were playing, the boy had to hold her cold and stiff legs apart for their convenience. After they were done playing with her and had left spitting, he would rush over and cut off her hair. One time as he tried to pull off every single strand from the corpse's skull to get the longer ones, he almost got separated from the beggars.

But eventually he left the group because he learned that they were a group of lepers whom he had heard about from his grandfather. But he did not leave simply because they were lepers. By the time he found out, some red spots had already appeared on his own body. He was not scared that he had become infected. It was like that time when he left his dead mother alone in the hut, like that time he left his grandfather stone cold on the road, he was not sad or scared.

"Well, this is nothing." The boy felt a strange courage and strength. He felt confident enough to live alone. One night, he secretly left the woman and the beggars and went the opposite direction. He walked all night. The following morning, he found himself in Ponghwa in Kyŏngsang province.

Elder Hwang's story was getting more and more horrific.

For two or three years, he was an errand boy in a tavern in Ponghwa. Since the red spots were not too obvious, the owner did not suspect that he was a leper. The owner was extremely conniving and deceitful. He had a woman who worked during the daytime at the tavern as a hostess and at nighttime she would sleep with him. When a guest wanted to spend the night at the tavern, the owner would introduce him to the hostess. Then he would steal things from the guest. When the boy learned about this, the owner entrusted him with the thefts. When something went wrong, the owner would appear furiously and accuse the guests of playing around with his wife. The guests would not even think of retrieving their things but run away immediately for having fooled around with someone else's wife.

The boy did not have to bother the owner very much. He had nothing to lose. He would recruit guests and fix them up with the woman himself. He was able to take care of everything by himself. When he got caught stealing, he would simply smirk and casually take a kitchen knife out of his jacket. The drunken guests did not dare challenge him. They could not do anything. The boy was ready to slice anyone who challenged him. His menacing smile and face reeked murder. After doing this for a few years, he got bored. He thought of leaving the tavern. Around this time the red spots on his body were getting noticeable.

One late autumn day, the owner left for a nearby town to get food and he was left alone with the woman. He usually returned in the evening but late into the night there was still no sign of him. And there were no guests that night. The woman could not keep her legs together at night. She needed a man whether the owner or a guest. She was bored and offered him her breasts. If the owner did not return, she would even let him sleep with her. He was not too enthusiastic about the offer. He remembered the woman whom he had met on the road. Then he thought he'd have a little fun with her. He told her that he was a leper and he kept it a secret. The hostess thought that he was joking. He smirked then showed her the red spots under his clothes. She ran away frightened.

But he did not stop there. He chased after her with the kitchen knife in hand. The woman wanted to believe that he was simply playing around but when he caught her, he stripped her and slashed out her ticklish part.

"Leaving the tavern that night I thought of my mother whom I had left in the hut. I didn't mean to, but maybe because I had seen another woman who had died with her eyes open," Elder Hwang sighed deeply as he turned toward the director. His story seemed to be coming to a close. But the director still did not dare open his mouth. Once in a while he felt a chill that made him shudder, but he kept quiet. The director struggled to maintain himself within the heavy silence and Elder Hwang's voice grew soft.

The director wanted to know what the old man wanted to do and why he was telling him his terrible past. He was screaming inside, "Tell me! Tell me what you want! Do you want to stop this work? Are you planning another terrible retribution?" But he could not say this aloud.

"You know that this story is not only mine, don't you?" The director did not understand what he was getting at.

"It's the story of everyone on this island. I'm sure particular circumstances vary, but every leper has the same story. We're all like that. We all went through horrible experiences before coming to the island. And even after we came to the island we experienced even more horrible things and survived. Then you suggested that we do this. But you knew the situation very well, right?"

"What is it that you want to say?" The director could no longer endure the silence so he challenged him. Elder Hwang looked at him quietly for a while and continued, "I think you misunderstand something. You seem afraid of me. That's the problem. If you are afraid, everything will go wrong. Like I said before, we lepers become even nastier and more violent when we see that people are afraid of us. That tavern woman. Looking back I realized that if she hadn't been frightened of me, I wouldn't have killed her. When I saw her frightened I became violent. Lepers don't get frightened of each other. We know." Elder Hwang was saying things that were far from what the director was waiting to hear. He thought that Elder Hwang was trying to make sure he was on the right track. The director understood his story as such but he was leading the story in a different direction. The director thought Elder Hwang was hiding something from him.

"What do you want me to do now?" The director

asked, extremely annoyed.

"What do I want you to do? You can't possibly ask me that." Elder Hwang responded in a scolding tone. "It's simple. What you need to do is continue to order us and to work us hard. That's all you have to do. I told you my past, thinking that it would help you."

"…"

"Don't be afraid to order us around. We've been through a lot, so once we set our minds to it we can do anything until it's done. You have a perfectly justifiable purpose, so there's no reason for you to hesitate. You have a justification to make us work because this is as worth enduring as anything we've been through. But if you show that you're afraid, that's the end of everything. They could even throw their own bodies into the water to make the embankments appear. If you show them you're frightened, their willingness to sacrifice their lives will turn to malice and revenge…"

"…"

"The bitter cold of winter is approaching. There is no sign of the embankments. I'm sure you're anxious and worried. But you can't just stop here. You have to be strong. There is no need to worry about the cold weather now. Few of them have ever known what it's like to have proper shelter during winter, so winter won't be a problem for them. Even if they throw themselves into the sea to make the embankments appear, we can't blame you."

Elder Hwang rose slowly as if he had nothing more to say. The director was still at a loss for words. He now understood what Elder Hwang was getting at. He was deeply grateful for his considerate advice. He wanted to grab his hands and express his thanks. But he had become more afraid of him. Elder Hwang concealed his true feelings. There were more things he desperately tried to hide than what he had revealed.

The director knew Elder Hwang well. Elder Hwang was trying even harder to maintain himself even though he was crumbling miserably inside. He could understand that the patients would throw themselves into the water because they were spiteful. But that same spite and revenge could well turn into malice. The problem for the director was toward whom the spite and vengeance would be directed. He was afraid of Elder Hwang precisely because his spite and vengeance were ready to turn into malice. But he also sensed that Elder Hwang was wavering. The old man was just as anxious as the director about the embankments. Despite his promise that he would not tolerate another betrayal, he realized that the malice from the past had been reawakened within him. He could not help himself now that he sensed that the director was afraid. He had to wrestle with himself not to let his disappointment become malicious. The old man continued to suppress it. He wanted to be patient and wait until the embankments surfaced. The director could not completely ignore the possibility that he might become malicious. Elder Hwang was wavering now. By telling the director his past, he was trying to learn from his own past mistakes. But he did not reveal his anxiety at all.

The director knew him well. To a certain degree, the situation had come to its worst point. There was nothing he could say. Elder Hwang had started to go down the hill but stopped and turned again toward the director. "I haven't said all this just to make you feel better. When I said you could do whatever you wish with us, it's not that you can just make us work. In case you have misunderstood, let me say one more thing. We have learned two things in our lives that have seeped into our bones."

"..."

"The first is that nobody who is not a leper himself really works for the sake of lepers. The second is that we lepers don't work for others either. This means we don't believe when people say they are working for us and we don't work for them. This goes for you, too. We don't believe you are doing this for us. So don't think we are doing this for you."

"I don't think I'm doing this for you or because somebody is expecting me to do this," the director said, looking straight into Elder Hwang's face.

"Good! I'm glad you think that way. Then you'll also believe that we won't blame you or hold a grudge against you." Elder Hwang tilted his head a little. He was criticizing him again. "But I'm sure that's not all. Until now it was clear that you misunderstood the whole thing. You thought you were working for our sake and we for yours...Otherwise, why would you be so afraid now?"

"If I looked that afraid of something, it might be correct to say that I was afraid of myself or of the ocean. But do you really think I don't have to worry about a possible disappointment that might overwhelm the patients?"

"Of course you can't let that happen. Our talk today was about how we can prevent them from being disappointed. Even if they get disappointed, there's no reason for you to be afraid now. You shouldn't be. If you are, the lepers can easily read your mind. The fact that you think you are working for our sake would be laughable. And it would be even more ridiculous if you thought we were doing this for you. We would be disappointed in you. Lepers don't work for others."

20

The work continued in spite of the bitter cold. It became a struggle against the winter and a cruel sea that refused to tolerate human encroachment. Ultimately, it was a long and dangerous battle, one that pitted human tenacity and will against nature, testing the patience of both.

For Director Cho, the battle against the humans

was more difficult than either the battle against the sea or the battle against the bitter cold. He had to fight against the patients and Elder Hwang who in turn fought against him. Both sides showed a tremendous amount of patience as if trying to see who could endure the longest. In the end, it was not a battle against the sea or the bitter cold. It was a battle of wills.

But the long and painful battle was coming to an end. Early the following year, near the end of February, the gray and cold South Sea slowly began changing its somber color. The director walked out of the headquarters and saw something different. Along the first embankment between the P'ungnam peninsula and Odong island he saw a long white streak which he had never seen before. All of a sudden he realized something and quickly descended the hill. He ran so fast that he almost rolled down the hill. When he got to the bottom, he took out a boat and went toward Odong island. Once he was on the water, the white line disappeared.

Was it a hallucination?

It certainly wasn't. He realized it immediately. It was around high tide. Both the ebb and flood tides were extreme at this time of the year. And so at the peak of the ebb tide, the sea was shallower than usual while the flood tide was higher than usual. The streak of white he saw on the water was an outline of the embankments left in the wake of the outgoing tide.

The white line was not exactly the embankment. It was a string of white bubbles just under the surface right above the embankments. The white bubbles could only be seen from high up. From the boat he could only see one wave after another. He moved quickly forward like a madman. When his boat passed Odong island and entered the first embankment project site, he saw another stretch of white like the one he had seen from the hill by the headquarters. There really was an embankment! He thought his heart was going to burst. He could not control his excitement so he closed his eyes and waited a little while. He was afraid that the white band would disappear while he had his eyes shut so he hurriedly opened them again. The white line remained, long and straight under the endless procession of waves crashing against it.

The director did not see the embankment as

simply a mass of rocks. He felt he was seeing the most beautiful thing he had ever seen. The white line, though vague and insubstantial, was beautiful and extraordinary. It was not just a pile of stones but a beautiful thing embued with life and breathing with a soul. He floated cautiously along the embankment, as if in a dream.

While his boat moved along the embankments toward the peak of P'ungnam peninsula, there was an unexpected procession of other boats. Two boats carrying stones followed him after he passed Odong island. Soon those two were joined by others, forming a long procession. The long trail of boats looked as if it stretched across the entire ocean.

"Long live Director Cho!"

"Hurray Sorok Island!"

"Hurray Oma Recovery Corps!"

The patients in the boats were cheering like fanatics. The people on the P'ungnam side also began to gather on the beach realizing what was going on. As soon as someone started singing the "Song of Sorok," everybody on the shore and in the boats joined in.

We've been fighting for generations...

People were swarming into the waves from the peninsula, feeling the embankment beneath them, waving the Oma flag with the hand with the missing fingers. Those on the boats joined them quickly, jumping out into the water before they had quite reached the dike. Everybody was singing and dancing with feverish excitement. They shouted hurray as they surrounded Director Cho. Then still walking on the embankment they started to rush toward the middle of the sea. They could not feel the frosty cold water of the early spring. They jumped into the water with excitement. Even in this disorder and chaos there was one person who did not lose his composure. Elder Hwang walked slowly toward the director and said, "I don't think they can wait." His voice was calm and low, but the director noticed it was trembling. "Let's walk across now. Why don't you lead us?" It was a strange suggestion. Elder Hwang wanted to walk across the frigid sea. But the director soon realized that it was not so strange.

"Sure, I'll lead the way. Who could refuse to walk on the water between P'ungnam and Odong on a happy occasion like this?" The director's voice was trembling, too.

"Let the director walk first." Elder Hwang yelled at the patients who were already starting to cross. Everyone stepped aside to let him through. The director did not hesitate. He didn't even bother to roll up his pants or take off his shoes. Instead, he stepped right into the water and got a foothold on the embankment. In the meantime, the tide had ebbed further and the water reached only to his knees. He strode like a giant kicking the waves far below with confidence. Elder Hwang followed four steps behind. And behind the old man, the rest of the patients followed.

The singing never stopped during the crossing. Parts of the procession stopped as some of them danced in the middle. Nobody seemed to care about the ice cold water. The director never turned around to look at the procession behind him, not because he could not endure the freezing cold water that made his ankles numb and made him want to cross as fast as he could, but because he was the winning general in a war against the sea. It was a triumphal procession of five thousand lepers ascending from a hopelessness and despair deeper than the ocean itself. He could not help it—tears ran down his cheeks. He was weeping. Since he did not want the patients to see him cry he could not turn around.

The procession over the ice cold ocean was certainly a bizarre scene. But those who participated in it thought it neither strange nor reckless. It was an earnest and inspirational scene. But they couldn't be satisfied with this one inspirational and dramatic procession—the second and third embankments still remained. After the patients made that trek to Odong island, their wavering morale soared and the construction site was full of life and renewed hope. Work efficiency reached new heights and they worked harder than ever. Manjae island, which was used as the quarry for the third embankment, quickly got smaller.

One month after they had walked on the first embankment, Director Cho and the patients could do the same along the second embankment. When the second embankment surfaced, even Sanguk joined in and walked with the director. When the first embankment had appeared and the patients had been excited to the point of madness, Sanguk had been calm. He was strangely fearful of the situation. When everyone joined in the procession the first time, he was not willing to join. But when the second embankment appeared, he quietly followed the director. Only the third embankment was left.

Manjae island got smaller and smaller. After April and May had passed, Manjae island sank under the sea. The third embankment would take more time to emerge, not only because it was the longest of the three but also because it needed to be much thicker. When it was completed, the three dikes would be connected and the tide would be blocked, exposing the seabed. Since the current outside the third embankment was very rapid and powerful, they had to make sure that it was particularly strong. More stones needed to be thrown in to finish the third embankment. By the end of May, Manjae island was left looking like a capsized boat, having sunk completely under the water with only the pillar left to mark its location.

The director stopped the quarrying on Manjae island. He decided to leave the stone pillar as a vestige of the island, in order to let those who inquired about the history of the island know that this was the symbol both of a people who had been expelled from the land and of their will to cultivate the land for their children—they had used that island to build the land for their children.

It was at the end of May that the director and the patients walked the whole one thousand six hundred yards of the third embankment connecting Oma island and Pongam village. But even after they walked over the third embankment, the director instructed them to continue dumping stones. After doing this for a while, the seabed slowly surfaced. It became wider and wider everyday. Even at high tide, the waves could no longer cover it. The waves that chased each other toward the embankments tried hard to get in but ebbed away in failure.

Their Canaan was in front of their eyes. When the dikes were thick enough that the sea bottom had completely exposed itself, the director threw a celebration party on the hill of Oma island at the headquarters office. Looking down from the top, he and the patients were awed by the miracle they had created. Where the sea had been was now a vast land. This land of twenty-five hundred acres appeared gloriously before their eyes. The small islands that had dotted the surface were now only little hills crouching on the former seabed. The sea spread out far away to where their eyes could not even reach. A single streak of water had found its way through and wandered around the seabed like a pilgrim. Looking at the empty space outside the embankment where Manjae island had been was refreshing. Only the thin stone column glimmered faintly. This was the second Creation. If using the word Creation was a blasphemy, then it was the most solemn and beautiful piece of art that humans could achieve in God's power and benevolence.

Looking down at the lonely stone column shimmering hazily in the bright afternoon sun, he felt assaulted by a strange terror. And he remembered what was to be carved on the stone column he wanted to leave as the last vestige of the island for their descendents:

> For the lepers who aspire to be humans
> Provided them with land
> For those worn-out souls
> Making the great mountain the sea, the sea into land
> The Providence of God!

21

After they'd thrown more stones into the water, the next step was to raise the level of the ground up to the top of the embankments. Hopper cars were the most convenient way to transport the soil and so they purchased as many as they could afford. The hopper cars, filled with dirt, shuttled busily back and forth. Those who were not busy pushing hopper cars carried sacks of dirt on their backs. This work was much more exciting than throwing stones into the void of the bottomless sea. The embankments were getting thicker by and by and were able to endure the powerful ocean waves. As the embankment walls grew thicker, the length of the rail got longer.

Since the results of their work soon became visible, the patients' morale was high and the work progressed quickly. By early July when the work of raising the ground was well under way, there was only one serious concern. Typhoon season would begin soon. Director Cho had been worried about the typhoons for some time. In the meantime, on the fifteenth of August, the change over from the former military government to a new civilian government had occurred, and it was expected on the island that the director's position would be taken over by a civilian doctor. But the director gave up his twenty-year military career and became a civilian in order to remain on the island. He discarded his uniform but he kept the gun upon which he had sworn the oath before the Oma island project began as a reminder of his military service. He spent every day at the construction site, and was so busy he didn't even have time to reminisce about—or even miss—the military. If the typhoons came before the embankments were strong enough to withstand the severe pounding, all their efforts would disappear overnight.

The director was extremely concerned but there was nothing he could do except rush to make the embankments as strong as possible. Fortunately this year there were no warnings of strong storms throughout the summer. They thought that God was protecting the island so there might not be the threat of a typhoon hitting this year. Early in September, however, when they had begun to think that they were almost safe from the threat of typhoons, news came of an approaching typhoon. The embankments were still not strong enough to endure one. The director paced back and forth, unable to calm down. He could not express his concern openly because he was worried that the patients might become agitated. All day long, he listened to the weather forecast on the radio, praying that the typhoon would change course. However, by late afternoon white waves covered Tŏknyang bay. Clouds moved low and unbelievably fast on the gray horizon. The director stopped the work and ordered all the equipment and material to be stowed away for safety. The hopper cars were stowed as well.

After dinner, he organized a night watch and remained himself at the Oma island headquarters to listen to the radio. The typhoon was dashing north from southern Cheju island and was expected to arrive at Oma island by daybreak. The forecast stressed repeatedly that the storm's center would probably cause severe damage. The director didn't get a wink of sleep as he listened for the approaching footsteps of doom.

"Please don't let the typhoon hit. Even if it

means that ocean and land change place, please don't, not here..."

In spite of his prayers, soon after midnight a strong wind and pounding rain began to lash at the windows. The director could not just sit inside the office and repeat his prayers. Suddenly he got up. Taking his raincoat, he went down the hill. When he reached the embankments, the patients were there as well. The patients sat with straw mats over their heads in the rainy darkness, as if they were out in the market place getting soaked. Seeing their silent prayers to be saved from danger, the director again felt a lump in his throat. But in the face of nature's power, the humans' prayers were futile. Since dawn, strong winds had pounded the embankments relentlessly, as if they wouldn't let up until the embankments were smashed. Even prayers were useless. The violent wind was strong enough to blow away the embankments. For three days and nights, the sky, the sea and the land were entwined in a chaotic fury.

The patients did not sleep for those three days, watching the raging waves destroy the embankments. They covered themselves with straw mats and prayed for the typhoon to go away. But the powerful waves pounded the embankments continuously, making the walls thinner and thinner. After two nights of watching the dikes being devoured, the director could no longer just stand around and watch. On the third night, he went up to the headquarter office alone. That night he sat in the dark office and listened to several roars that sounded as if the entire seabed was splitting in half.

Around dawn on the fourth day, the storm finally abated. The storm was gone but only after it had completely destroyed the embankments. There was nothing more left to destroy. The embankments had sunk back into the ocean without a trace and the vast reclaimed field of two thousand five hundred acres had returned to the boundless ocean. The sun that rose after the storm shone brightly and a few seabirds circled over the water. It was the beginning of a long and dangerous betrayal.

The patients remained silent. They wouldn't eat or sleep. With the straw mats over their heads they loafed around here and there. This was a truly an appalling sight. The director was utterly dejected.

Having witnessed nature's unbelievable betrayal, he could not even think about cursing. He spent a few days enveloped by utter emptiness. After that, he began to realize the terrible despair of the five thousand patients. Their despair as the time passed turned into resentment and bitterness. It was clear who would become the object of their resentment and hatred. They could not possibly find a proper target. Of course the object of their hatred should have been nature that brought on this disaster, but they needed a more immediate target. The director had to be the object of their hatred. Like the patients, he couldn't blame nature. He had no choice but to blame himself.

The director was burning with desire to take revenge. When Elder Hwang said that the lepers didn't work for others, he had truly meant it. The director's promise to himself that he would not think so to avoid becoming the laughing stock of the patients must not have been entirely true. But this time for sure the director was firm in his decision. As Elder Hwang said, he no longer wanted to start the project again from the beginning for the patients. He decided to start over in order to take revenge on nature and to overcome his despair. Eventually he would triumph. After he made the decision, he went over to the Oma island headquarters.

But he realized that he could not start with only his decision. The patients were still lolling about like animals on their straw mats. He could not predict what would happen if he tried to make them go back to the construction site. Even Elder Hwang wouldn't say anything. The director needed to find something to motivate them, so that they could overcome their despair. He could not expect them to find an incentive on their own; he needed to find one for them. Even for the director, this was not an easy task. He didn't think that he could find an opportunity on the island. He had to find it off the island.

He left the island quietly and, like a wanderer, visited other reclamation projects. He visited Changhŏng and Yŏngam again. As the last place on his journey, after visiting small and large reclamation sites all over the west coast, he went to Tŏkchŏk island where three brothers had fought against nature for eight years to reclaim a small plot of twelve acres. After visiting other reclamation sites, he realized that what they had done at Oma island was not all in vain. He realized that even without the storm, the embankments would have been destroyed. It was inevitable. The rocks that were thrown into the sea would have sunk away at certain intervals. In order for the embankments to stand on solid enough ground to prevent them from collapsing, they needed to repeat this process several more times. He learned various technical things but more than anything he learned an important lesson at the three brothers' reclamation site at Tŏkchŏk island.

On the shore of Tŏkchŏk island, three brothers in their thirties had built a one hundred and sixty yard long embankment to reclaim their twelve acres. They spent eight years, throwing rocks into the sea. They used only hammers and prybars to break the rocks. Even after eight years of watching the embankment sink over and over, they kept on working. They were extremely tenacious. It was not about reclaiming twelve acres of land. It was a fight against the sea and they sacrificed their youth to it.

"The sinking finally stopped. But the reason we stayed here wasn't to reclaim twelve acres of land. We needed to triumph over the sea. With our strong determination to succeed, we simply couldn't leave."

What was left in the three brothers after eight years of the embankment's constant sinking was an endless hatred toward the sea and their strong will to overcome it. The sinking stopped but if they had to repeat it again ten times or twenty times, they would continue to throw rocks in on top of the sunken embankment. The director could not waste any more time wandering around. He returned to Oma island. There was one problem he still needed to find an answer to.

"How can I encourage these patients who have been thrown into the abyss of despair?"

He still didn't have a concrete plan to make them start working. He could explain the reasons for why the sinking had occurred but simply explaining the plain facts would not get them back to work. Their despair and wounds were too deep. Even the story of the three brothers on Tŏkchŏk island could not make them start working again. Eight years of experiencing this sinking was a lonely, endless struggle. It was an extremely moving story but he couldn't expect the patients to be moved by it. Even if the story could move them, it would only lead them to the realization that they had to endure endless sacrifice and despair. The director was doubtful whether they had the strength to endure like the three brothers. The real possibility of failure would only bring fear.

He needed to find an incentive elsewhere. As it turned out, the director found an incentive in an unexpected place and from unexpected people. When he stopped by Kohŏng on his way back to the island, he heard a strange rumor: before long the present director of the island hospital would leave. Even though this rumor was related to him, he had no idea about it. After listening to the explanation, he could guess why this kind of rumor spread. The target of the rumor was not the director. The object of the rumor was the Oma island reclamation project. A rape had occurred near the construction site and the young men from the nearby villages had come to the director to protest and left with the following words:

"Don't worry. We didn't come here to ask you to stop the work. Believe it or not, we pray that the embankments will appear soon."

The director was certain that they said it because there was no way the embankments would appear, so they were sneering. But he conjectured that it was true that they were hoping to see the land surface from the sea because they wanted to get a share of it. They wore a strange, mischievous expression, saying that it was possible to use the lepers until the embankments surfaced. After this was done, they could drive the patients off the island and keep the reclaimed land for themselves. What they wanted to do was take the land away from the patients.

The mainlanders saw the possibility of the ocean being transformed into land. It was common sense for them that the embankments would sink once or twice. This current incident could be their one and only chance to take the project away from the islanders. The mainlanders were saying things such as,

"After the dikes collapse, there is nothing else you can do, Cho Paeghŏn. Even if you accept it as nature's doing, the lepers won't."

The mainlanders were plotting to take the land away from them. In fact, they were already working on a petition to take over the reclamation project.

The villagers welcomed this idea and supported them. They could not take over the land after the construction was completed; they wouldn't have any standing to do so. Now that the patients were faced with difficulties was a perfect time to do it. The authorities were troubled by the friction between the patients and nearby mainlanders, so they thought this would also be a perfect chance to settle the matter. The director would be the biggest hindrance for the mainlanders in carrying out their plan, and so they spread a rumor hoping to drive him off the island.

"Since you failed miserably, it's time for you to wash your hands of the matter."

"We'll take over from here. If you insist on interfering, we'll make you leave."

They were capable of doing this. The incentive the director couldn't find himself, he finally got from the outside. He returned to the island immediately.

There was no way to verify how the rumor had started, but as long as it circulated and provoked the patients to start working again, that was all that mattered. Even if it meant deceiving them, he could not think that far ahead if he wanted to get them back to the construction site. In the best interest of the five thousand patients, he had to make such decisions. After he returned to the island he called a meeting of the elders' council and explained the technical faults and the reasons for the sinking of the embankments. He gave examples of other reclamation projects and stressed his hope that this one event would not make them give up on the project altogether. As expected, the elders were indifferent, showing no interest. The director told the story of the three brothers of Tŏkchŏk island. In order to gain twelve acres of land, they had continued to fight even after their embankments sank eight times. Their willingness to struggle without regret seemed to move the patients. But that was about it and nothing more.

When he said they needed to start working again not to acquire thousands of acres but as human beings who had an obligation to improve their own lives, the elders kept silent. Even the story of the three brothers couldn't instill strength in the patients who had buckled with fatigue. He had no choice but to use his trump card. Finally he told them about the people who wanted to take the project away from them.

"There are people on the mainland who are dying to see you give up on this project. I'm sure you can guess who they are even though I won't spell it out. Even if you don't give up, it's possible that they can get what they want. They are plotting to drive you back to the island so that they can take over the project themselves. Do you think they want to do something you couldn't accomplish? Do you really think they'd do this if they expected to fail? Why are they so eager? They know that this won't end in failure. They want to take over what you've done so far for free."

He tried all kinds of arguments, threats and exaggerations. He tried to awaken the hatred and resentment toward the mainlanders that was buried deep inside them by reminding them of their past persecution. He exaggerated their fears in order to draw out their instinct to survive.

"You know well what kind of people they are. You know how they persecuted you and how they judged you. Have you forgotten how they drove you to this island and how you had to make this small island your home? I'm sure you can't forget what difficulties you went through. You must not forget. But how is the situation now? Is it any different now? If you desert this island and go to the mainland, do you think you will be accepted and live there freely as you choose? Has their bias toward you changed that much? No, it hasn't. It's still the same. You have to fight them the same as before. But you can't retreat after losing a battle. That failure would mean the loss of your last privilege as living human beings. Waging this fight means your right to live. So you can't just step back and give up now." The director's exaggeration almost turned into a lecture.

"The longer we stay this way, the more time we give them to make excuses to take away what we've achieved. They're even plotting to drive me away because I'm a nuisance to them. They hope—and perhaps some of you think this as well—that if I leave and all of you return to the island, everything will be settled. But it isn't that simple. You can't go back as easily as you came here. Someone once said this to me. Rather than throwing in rocks, make the embankments appear by throwing in their bodies. This really was right. For the past year, you weren't just throwing rocks into the sea but you were also throwing your bodies in. The embankments under the sea are not just rocks but also part of you. Even if you return to the island, the part of your body that is lying under the sea will remain there forever to protect the embankments. And the people waiting impatiently for you to leave will reap the fruits from the land you reclaimed with your bodies for generation upon generation..."

22

The patients were motivated to start again because of the mainlanders who hoped they'd give up. The construction site was filled once again with the sounds of exploding dynamite and clattering hopper cars. People lugging rocks on their backs went back and forth. Even though the embankments were under water, their faint outlines made it easier to throw in the stones. After three months passed, the embankments reappeared. But they vanished again after ten days. But the patients didn't really care whether the embankments appeared or not. Even after the embankments peeked above the surface, they continued throwing in the rocks. When they saw the embankments disappear overnight, they showed no signs of disappointment like they had before. Silently, persistently, as if there was no end to the work, as if it was their fate, they threw stones and more stones into the sea.

The patients' incredible perseverance troubled the mainlanders who were hoping to take over the project. As the work progressed, the rumors about the director and the construction became more widespread. The rumor that the director would soon be dismissed from his post flowed onto the construction site. The newspapers reported on the friction between the lepers at the Oma island construction site and the nearby mainlanders. The director's superiors asked him directly about the circumstances of the conflict. The situation was not pleasant. He could not pretend nothing was going on. He could not be driven away from the island like this.

The director had to do something. First he induced the council of elders to come up with a new rumor. He knew he was deceiving the patients but for the future of the island, it was necessary. What was important was the result, not the means. If it produced good results, the means used to get to that point shouldn't matter. It wasn't that difficult. Now the elders' council was on the director's side. They understood the importance of the project and the patients could not suppress their anger.

Soon a petition condemning any unreasonable outside interference regarding the Oma island land recovery project was drawn up. All of the patients signed another petition opposing the director's transfer until after the project's completion. Their enthusiasm made both the rumors and the underlying mainland conspiracy weak and ineffective. In the meantime, the dumping of the rocks continued. It took another three months before the embankments appeared. They stayed for only a few days and then they sank again.

The fight continued. When the embankments disappeared, the patients made them appear again, then they'd sink back. The three embankments took turns appearing and disappearing, as if playing hide and seek. When ten meters of the first submerged embankment was rebuilt, twenty meters of the second embankment disappeared. When this was done, thirty meters of the third embankment sank. Like the director, the patients also began to develop a certain tenacity. The reclaimed land was no longer their object of interest. They were fighting against the forces of nature. They weren't trying to reclaim land any longer. It was their determination to defeat this thing that made them throw in the stones endlessly. The embankments were no longer an object which would give them unlimited control over nature—they had become a dangerous living organism that continued to fight back against their insurmountable human will.

But if this fight were to continue endlessly, the people were bound to be the first to get exhausted. And, when people get exhausted psychologically, they reach out their hands out for help from anywhere. When summer approached, more accidents began to happen. One time, a mound of dirt collapsed, burying ten workers. Fortunately nine of them were saved but one died, buried under the dirt. Another time, a boat carrying rocks capsized and one person drowned. That time, the director halted all work to find the body, spending three whole days on the search. Morale plummeted at the construction site as did efficiency. Finally the patients' attitude toward the director changed. Among the fatigued patients, rumors and superstitions began to circulate.

"We started something that was impossible from the beginning. The earth and ocean spirits obviously don't like what we're doing."

"As long as the spirits meddle, even if we work for several more years, the only result will be more deaths."

They refused to follow orders or listen to any of the director's explanations. He thought he needed to appease the islanders first. In order to comfort them, he decided to hold another *kosa.* He prayed to the spirits to pacify their anger by sacrificing a pig's head on each embankment. But the prayers had no effect. Even after the kosa, the sinking continued and the patients' fear of the spirits' fury intensified. He realized that sacrificing mere pig's heads would not pacify their fury. Finally, the identity of the invisible wrath behind the rumor's circulating among the patients emerged.

One night a little past midnight, Sanguk unexpectedly visited the director, who was spending the night at the headquarters office. He dragged in three patients clad in mud, their clothes torn, as if they were prisoners. One of the three who was limping badly was the one who had been seriously injured when the dirt had collapsed. The atmosphere surrounding the four was ominous and the director felt uncomfortable. He shivered when he saw Sanguk's cold, frozen face.

"These men tried to commit murder tonight," Sanguk said in a cold, matter-of-fact way. Sanguk could not fall asleep so he had decided to take a look around the embankments. He had walked toward the embankments and when he approached the submerged point of the embankment where puddles formed, he heard a sudden scream from the darkness. He ran and found two patients strangling a third person, trying to push him down into the water. The third person resisted with all his might trying not to fall into the water, but he slowly lost his strength and was unable to resist the two who were pushing him. As he lost his ability to resist, his screams grew faint. Sanguk explained that the two were the assailants and the one who had the limp had almost become a water spirit.

"Why did you try to kill him?" the director finally asked after listening to the explanation, staring at them angrily. All three hung their heads and none of them spoke.

"They said what's the point of living now that he's a cripple. Being a leper is already bad enough. It's best to die for the sake of the other patients." Sanguk replied, his voice dripping with sarcasm.

"That's murder! What kind of person tries to kill their fellow neighbor! What do you mean, it's best to die for the sake of the other patients?" the director shouted angrily. But Sanguk was calm. He continued with his explanation in a low and calm voice as if he were trying to reproach him for shouting.

"It's because you don't understand them well. They don't think that the sinking is simply a natural phenomenon. According to them, it's caused by the five Oma islands. The spirits of the five islands want five human sacrifices. If five human sacrifices are not made, their fury won't be appeased and the sinking will continue. Two people have been sacrificed, one drowning and one buried under collapsed dirt. Now they want to sacrifice three more people..."

The director kept silent.

"Today I was able to stop this because I was at the right place at the right time. But to prevent similar incidents, you'll need to have a concrete plan. As long as the sinking continues, the patients will believe that the islands want a human sacrifice. If you don't stop them from believing this superstition, they'll grab every opportunity to sacrifice someone."

The director could say nothing. He was appalled at what he had just heard but he could not figure out what he could do. He felt shivers running down his spine and his knees felt weak.

"Get out! Get the hell out of my sight!" the director screamed as if he was insane. Frightened by his screaming, the three men stepped back and hid behind Sanguk. Unlike the director, Sanguk was calm and collected, and watched him like a spectator.

It was only after Sanguk and the three men left the office that the director realized Sanguk's intentions in reporting the incident this late. It was not to seek a solution or to ask the director to mete out punishment. Using the incident as a pretext, Sanguk wanted to convey what he had wanted to say to the director. The man who had almost been sacrificed was calmly resigned to this and wore a look on his face that suggested the inevitability of this tragedy. It was a murder that even the victim agreed with. It was proof that they were ready to start killing each other to put an end to this terrible agony. Murderous despair was in the air. Certainly Sanguk had wanted to show this to the director.

"As long as the sinking continues, the patients will desire another human sacrifice..."

This was Sanguk's true warning. He also knew the patients did not really want their fellow patients to be human sacrifices. Rather they wanted the director himself. He understood well that he ought to be the one. Perhaps that was what Sanguk wanted to say. If that was so...the director felt that he had hit an impasse. He could not fall asleep. He stayed up all night trying to find a solution. Of course he could follow Sanguk's advice, using "concrete preventatives" and "wise methods." With his calm, clear tone, Sanguk was implying that halting the construction was the best thing to do. But he couldn't do that. He thought of discussing this matter with Elder Hwang but recently even Elder Hwang seemed to have lost confidence. He remembered the agony and hesitation he had seen in Elder Hwang's eyes which he hadn't detected before. Because of this, the director often avoided his gaze.

He needed to overcome this by himself. There was only one way. By dawn, he knew what had to be done.

"If what they want is to sacrifice me, then I'll have to let them do as they please."

As long as he was certain he could give himself to them, he could also demand something from them in exchange. If the patients wanted his life and he was willing to sacrifice himself, then he had the privilege of demanding the price of his life. Staking his life as collateral, he decided to ask them one last thing. He still had a justifiable purpose which Sanguk once feared. Now that he was willing to sacrifice himself, he could use that justification.

Immediately he generated a new work schedule. And in order to get the patients to follow it, he posted a list of instructions at the entrance to the construction site. The instructions and regulations that he posted on the bulletin board were intimidating and strict, laced with threat, as if a declaration of war. The instructions were as follows:

1. The deadline for the completion of the three embankments is December 31 at the latest. We must complete the work by the deadline.
2. In order to complete the work as scheduled, any counter-productive behavior that can hinder the progress of the work will not be tolerated. From today on those who violate the rules will be severely punished.

"Prohibitions"

a. Demoralizing others by objecting to or criticizing the project deadline.
b. Evoking fear in others, disrupting the order of the construction site by spreading groundless superstitions or similar rumors about the Oma island spirits.
c. Physically or spiritually assaulting fellow patients and initiating, leading, and cooperating with such violence.
d. Holding any kind of unnecessary assembly that is not required for the progress of the work.
e. Those who cause any kind of hindrance to the completion of the project will also be considered offenders.

23

After Director Cho's strict and intimidating regulations were posted, the atmosphere around the construction site settled down. However, the sinking of the embankments didn't stop. The patients quietly shuttled the dirt to the site without complaint. Even when another accident took place, there was no change in the expressions they wore on their faces. Two weeks after the director posted the new work schedule, the dirt collapsed again and two people died. If the Oma island spirits truly wanted human sacrifices these two would make four. Now there was only one sacrifice left.

Strangely, after witnessing this horrible sight, the patients remained indifferent as if the accident was something that happened routinely at the construction site. The bodies were removed and all was again quiet. The director knew well the meaning behind their silence. He saw the shadow of approaching death in their ominous silence. Finally, the curtain was slowly lifting on the second betrayal. This followed the first betrayal of nature's destruction. That night he returned to his residence and he pledged his last ounce of determination.

Then, he quietly closed his eyes and waited.

When a member of the hospital staff rushed into his house, he was not surprised. He already guessed what was going to happen.

"Please leave immediately." The staff member told him that the patients from Oma island had left the construction site and were heading toward his residence. In order to prevent him from escaping, they had already sealed off the island.

"I don't know where you can go but you have to leave here now. It doesn't look good. They're a mob. I'm sure they'll try to harm you." Even before he finished talking, the director could hear the song the patients were singing.

We've been fighting for generations
The black clouds have rolled away…

The song was coming closer and closer, wafting angrily over the sea. The director sat with his eyes closed. He listened to the song, not stirring at all. He had no intention of leaving. He looked as if he was not even paying attention to the staff member who was rushing him to leave. He felt fortunate that he had no one to take care of now, ever since his wife, who had tired of island life, had returned to the mainland. The staff member, amazed at his extraordinary composure, hastily left the residence by himself.

The song was close now. It no longer sounded like a song. It sounded more like screaming and roaring. The island had been plunged into chaos. At last the director got up from his chair. He could see clear to the bottom from his residence which sat atop a hill. The sea and hillside were covered with torches. Each patient had a torch and the boats carrying them looked as if they were engulfed in flames. They came closer and closer to the shore as if it were a battleground. The lead party was walking toward the residence and the rest of the patients followed. The director went back into his room and took out his gun. After he had retired from active military service and become a reservist, he kept the gun in a drawer. He took out one bullet and loaded it cautiously. He loaded only one bullet. After he finished loading it, he continued to fiddle with the gun, waiting for the patients to come closer.

"Come out, director!" As the torchlight flickered

in the window, he could hear the patients' screaming voices mixed with singing.

"Cho Paeghŏn. Come out, you bastard! We came to get you because the Oma island spirits are hungry for your blood!"

"Don't drive the lepers to death by themselves. We'll help you see the bottom of the embankment. Drown and see for yourself."

Their screaming voices lapsed into the "Song of Sorok;" wrapped in layers of revenge, spite, and resignation. They resumed the abuse after singing the song.

"Listen, Cho Paeghŏn! If you don't come out, we'll come in and get you!" Finally some of them broke the door down and entered. The director slowly walked out of the room and appeared before the patients, who had already surrounded the house two or three layers deep. When he calmly walked out to the yard, they were completely silent. Only the crackling of the torches stirred the silence of the night air. Besides torches, every patient tightly held a hammer or pickaxe, cutting off any possibility of escape. Facing the thousands of angry and disfigured faces wavering behind the torch flames, he felt as suffocated as the time when he first came to the island and stood before their silence during his inaugural speech. He didn't recognize anyone from among the wavering faces. But this time the silence did not last long.

"The bastard has a gun!" Somebody screamed, breaking the silence. As if on cue, the torches began to move rapidly and dangerously.

"Kill the bastard!"

"Kill him! He tried to buy fame and honor with lepers' blood!"

"We have to avenge the deaths of our fellow lepers." But the screaming did not last long. One torch moved quickly toward the director. When the torch drew near, everyone abruptly stopped yelling. Perhaps this might be their last time seeing each other so they quietly gazed at the two people facing each other. The one who stepped closer to the director was none other than Elder Hwang. He stood five steps back from him. This "five-step" regulation had long been abolished on the island but as if wanting to remind the director of the past, Elder Hwang maintained this distance. He lowered his torch and held it to his side. Then, as if he had come to share a joke with him, he started speaking slowly in a relaxed voice.

"Director Cho! I think the problem is that you lacked the ability to determine what lepers could and couldn't do..." Elder Hwang spoke as if he didn't care how the director would react. He circled around him and continued.

"When was it? When the mainlanders said they wanted to take you away, we should've let you go if we knew things would lead to this. We should've let you go then. We shouldn't have stopped you. But who knew...It's too late. The reason we didn't expect this beforehand was because we've been blind to God's true will. Even after we knew what God's will was, we hesitated to follow his will." Relaxed, he continued to circle around him.

"It's strange. It's always the pathetic and powerless lepers who belatedly understand the will of God, realizing what humans can or cannot do. All the directors in the past refused to recognize this. That's the problem. Twenty years have passed but that Director Shū, he was like that too..."

The torches were now several layers deep and the patients watched intensely like cannibals witnessing their chief performing a last sacrificial ceremony. Only the sound of flames shooting out of the torches into the dark sky could be heard.

"Director Shū assured us he would build us a paradise at the time. At first we were so grateful that we shed tears of joy and excitement. But that wasn't the will of God. From the beginning, God tried to stop us. 'Lepers' paradise…it's nonsense.' But Shū wouldn't give up. You already know but look what happened…it was horrible. The lepers thrust a knife into their master whom they had feared and obeyed as if he were God. They made him pay with his own blood for the countless lepers who bled…But I don't think Shū was the kind of person who got pleasure from seeing lepers bleed. Perhaps he thought that the sacrifice of their blood in building their paradise was not a betrayal. The problem was that he didn't recognize God's will even up to the very last minute. He was the only one who didn't see it. That's how I see it. But who knew you were like him too. It's strange, but every director who came to the island couldn't differentiate what humans are capable of and not. They were always late in realizing this when the lepers already knew it. That's why things have come to this..."

"Stop it!" The director shouted suddenly, unable to stand it anymore. He felt suffocated by this talk that seemed to circle around closer and closer as if it came from a wild animal trying to disorient its prey. He heard that whenever horrible things were about to happen, it was Elder Hwang's habit to bring up the past and slowly tell the story. He couldn't endure it. It was as if the old man's ominous tone of voice was a sticky spider web that slowly immobilized its prey. Elder Hwang was the venomous spider waiting for the right moment to inject his poison, numbing the director's spirit and robbing him of his physical strength.

"I'm sure it's not your intention to make me realize this. Get to the point. What do you want? What is that you want to do with me?" he asked, trying hard to suppress his impatience.

Elder Hwang circled around him as if he was intoxicated by his own story. Suddenly he stopped circling. Then he stared into the director's face for a long time apparently troubled by what had happened. Then, like one who just remembered what he needed to do, he looked at the director's tense expression, smirked and continued.

"Of course. You must be curious. But there's no need to rush. These people didn't come here to harm you. They only want..."

"They, they...don't say they. Be honest. Why don't you say we? So, you only want...what?"

"Ok, let's say we. Everybody here is a leper except you. And..." Elder Hwang did not try to rush to get to the point. But his expression and tone of voice, in contrast to the director's, was unbelievably calm and clear.

"You might not believe it even if we tell you we didn't come to harm you. Far from it. We won't hurt you. We came to see how you plan to keep your promise..."

"..."

"You still have your gun. I'm sure you haven't forgotten what you swore when we first started the project. You swore in the name of our benevolent God and the children of the five thousand patients that there wouldn't be any kind of betrayal between us. You said if there was any kind of betrayal, your life would be ours. But we're not trying to collect on what you promised then. Like I said before, we weren't working for you. We're nothing but the most pitiful and ugliest servants of God, incapable of judging others. We can't possibly judge you. But the problem is the second oath you made. The proof is the gun you're holding right now. We couldn't forget the vow you made on that gun. You truly surprised us. So, today…it's a nasty curiosity, but we came to see how that promise would be carried out. That's all. It's your misunderstanding if you think we came to hurt you." After he finished, Elder Hwang moved back a few steps, as if his mission had now been accomplished.

The director now understood perfectly what the old man wanted. No matter how he put it, what they wanted to see was his blood. He knew that they wouldn't return quietly even if he told them he wouldn't do it. What the old man had done was issue an ultimatum shrouded in treachery. But The director wouldn't accept defeat.

"It wasn't only me who took an oath. You people made it with me, too," he shouted, pursuing Elder Hwang who had stepped back.

"Of course we did. We swore an oath together with you," said Elder Hwang, giving him a look that seemed to say there was no one more pathetic than him, and continued slowly, as if trying to make him understand. "I think you still misunderstand one point. When we started the project, there was no betrayal. The betrayal began after it became clear that God was trying to stop us. We tried to obey God's will but you insisted and that's when the betrayal began. Even when the will of God became apparent, you disobeyed Him and made us bleed to death…Is it because it wasn't your own blood?…Because it was the dirty lepers' blood?…That's when the betrayal began, when you let us bleed to death…"

It was a strange way of juggling words. Both sides had made a vow not to betray each other when they started the project. Talk about betrayal. The director felt as betrayed as the patients. Perhaps it was Elder Hwang and the rest of the patients who needed to pay for their betrayal. But what Elder Hwang said was exactly the opposite. God was only on their side and the director was the only person who ought to be punished for betraying them. Perhaps it was because he wasn't a leper. It was clear from the beginning who had betrayed whom. It was him, non-leper, versus all the islanders.

The director couldn't accept the idea that he had betrayed anyone so for the last time he asked Elder Hwang.

"Then killing me tonight is something humans should do? Is it really God's will for me to bleed before your eyes?"

Elder Hwang's expression suddenly changed and his tone of voice was cold.

"It was you who drew their blood. Although we lepers have shed blood for ourselves, you haven't shed even a drop for yourself. You only asked us to bleed. Even when we told you we don't want to shed any more blood, you insisted on continuing. From that point on, we were shedding blood not for ourselves, but for you. In any case, for whoever it was, God doesn't want us to bleed. But if we could save ten drops of blood in the future by shedding one drop tonight, even God will forgive us. Everyone is agreed on this..."

This was an incredible revenge. The director could no longer contain himself.

"OK. If there was a betrayal, I'll do as promised." He rubbed the barrel of the gun against his chest twice and stepped toward Elder Hwang. Then, he held out the gun to him and said calmly, "Take this gun and have someone here shoot me."

"No, that's not the way," Elder Hwang's tone of voice was extremely aloof but chilling. He wore a bitter smile and said it in a joking tone. "We already told you that we won't judge you...What you promised, you need to carry out yourself. We only need to watch."

"What? You won't judge?" The director's retort was almost reflexive. He thought this might be his last chance to speak his mind so without waiting for the old man's answer, he continued quickly, angrily. "Please save your pathetic excuses! You judged me ten times, a hundred times in your mind. Why does your benevolent God always stand on your side and never on mine? If your God is with me and if I believe that I have never acted against His will, whose name would you use to make sure I carry out my promise?"

Surprised at the director's sudden outburst, Elder Hwang was at a loss for words. He could not step forward to take the gun from him nor could he avoid his attack. And so he stood still, hesitating to answer. Once he started, the director couldn't stop. He didn't need to wait for Elder Hwang's response.

He pressed him hard again.

"You always talk about your God, but if you have your God, I must have mine too. If your God wants to stop the project to prevent shedding more blood because He pities your situation, my God has told me to complete the work to prevent many more lives who might become sea spirits trying to escape from the island by swimming across the sound. In order to put an end to your wandering habits and to put an end to your dangerous attempts at escape to the mainland, the place from where you and your children were driven out. My God's will is to reclaim the land for you and your children, and for you to have a place to live where you can pray and praise your God." There was no sense of fear or hesitation on the part of the director. He was determined to speak his mind. He was trying hard to save a bit of his dignity.

"The reason why I never mentioned my God was because I thought our efforts weren't enough to receive His blessing. In order to accomplish His will, we needed to sacrifice more sweat and blood. If we couldn't prove our faith to each other, we couldn't prove our faith to God."

"..."

"All of you tried to believe in God's will and I wanted to prove first that we have to have faith in each other. But there isn't much difference between the two. I don't know how your God and my God could have such different wills. I wonder if your God truly wills you to return to your former state of despair and your wandering life. I'm not sure if He wants you to continue this life of government rations, grudging charity, and the walk you take one step at a time toward Napkol Hall. Your God doesn't want those who attempt to swim across the ocean and end up being swept away by the waves to become sea spirits."

"..."

"I still don't know why I have to shoot myself. I don't know who betrayed whom. But I have no intention of begging for my life. If you truly believe that killing me would save your lives, then shoot." After he finished, the director threw the gun to Elder Hwang.

"It's loaded with only one bullet, since I'm the only one you want to judge. You'd better not miss."

But Elder Hwang didn't try to pick up the gun.

Standing motionless, he stared at the director. Nobody tried to pick up the gun either. As the flames of the torches grew weak, the atmosphere sank deeper and deeper into heavy silence. Then, at that moment, a shadow from behind the director walked toward the gun. It was Sanguk. He did not have a torch in his hand but, hidden in the darkness, he had watched everything. He calmly picked the gun up from the ground. He looked at Elder Hwang and then slowly at the patients. Suddenly he began to shout like a madman.

"What are you doing? What are you afraid of?!" The patients who kept silent began to stir a little. But this was only temporary. Overwhelmed by Sanguk's excited voice, they kept silent again.

"Your God commanded you to avoid shedding blood but how many lives have been sacrificed because of this man? You've worked hard and shed unnecessary blood for the director, for him to gain fame. That's why you came—to collect reparations for your sweat and blood. Now he's waiting for your judgment. So, why are you hesitating? What are you afraid of?" He screamed at the patients as if he had gone insane. It was an outburst of hatred and despair directed at the patients. It was also an expression of his own hopelessness. His relationship to Miyŏn had come to an end due to the one between Haewŏn and her. Was it because of this that Sanguk's despair was even more violent? It was unclear.

Listening to Sanguk's violent outburst, the director had an ominous feeling that Sanguk was targeting him and not criticizing the patients for hesitating. He sensed that the explosion of Sanguk's hatred would be directed at him.

"Come on! Somebody come out right now and shoot the director. If he dies, then there will be no more bloodshed."

"..."

"No one! There is no one to do it. OK. If you can't judge the director, then it's your turn to be judged. If you created this chaos for nothing, then this one bullet should be used to stop your condemnation of him. If you can't even shoot him, then you have to prove your courage to condemn your own betrayal. Somebody come out and either shoot him or get ready to be judged for your own betrayal. Who? Who will do it?!" Sanguk's face was pale and beads of sweat dotted his forehead. His outburst continued a little longer.

"Why won't anyone step forward? Shoot the director so that you can return to your old leper selves again. If you don't even have the courage to shoot him, then you have to have the courage to be judged for what you've done tonight. You dirty lepers!"

The director remembered what Elder Hwang had told him. "Don't be afraid of lepers." Perhaps he meant in a situation like this. The patients could not detect fear in the director at all.

"Sanguk..." Elder Hwang said finally, stepping forward. What Elder Hwang said after this was beyond anyone's expectations.

"I think it's best to save the bullet. To be fair, there should be two bullets. Since there's only one, let's save it for later." He slowly took the gun from Sanguk's hand and continued while carefully stroking the gun.

"Now it's clearer than ever the value of this one bullet. Good thing that Sanguk made us realize it. I'm relieved to hear that you said all those things for us lepers. Lepers like to hear harsh words like that. We were always either driven away or had to obey like dogs. I'm not saying this to make fun of us or to be sarcastic. I just realized listening to you curse us just now. This bullet...if we couldn't shoot the director, we know very well whom the next target would be. Unfortunately, as you said, we still lack courage. Not enough courage means we haven't experienced enough hardship. We need to save this bullet for now..."

Elder Hwang walked toward the director and placed the gun cautiously on the ground. Then he said, "Don't you agree, director? As you know already, we lepers are cowards. I knew it would end like this. We're pathetic and filled with cowardice. Even myself, from the moment I left my dead mother until tonight, I've only been brave doing things like following gangs who rape starving women or killing that poor woman who worked in the tavern. And I was happy when I found a sack of barley after my grandfather passed away. Whenever I really had to be brave, I made excuses and avoided the situation..."

"..."

"But Director Cho, don't criticize me too harshly because I want to save the bullet a little longer.

Don't think I don't have the courage to shoot myself even after knowing about my own betrayal. I want to save the bullet because I wish to let the lepers overcome these ordeals and finish what they have left undone. If you understand this point, it'll be easier to deal with us."

"..."

"OK. With this gun, drive these lepers back, so that they go back to the Oma island construction site and overcome their lot. Take the gun and drive them back."

After saying this, he turned around slowly. When the old man descended the hill, the rest of the patients quietly followed him. As the old man said, there was nothing else the director could do now. Actually, he had no strength left. That night, Elder Hwang and the rest of the patients went to Oma island. Even Sanguk said nothing further to the director and followed the patients at whom he had been hurling abuse and whom he had chastised maliciously. The director stood alone in the yard until very late, staring down the hill at the torches that brightened the dark sea heading toward Oma island.

24

The construction resumed. Director Cho's original plan to finish the embankments by the end of the year had to be postponed until the following spring. He no longer rushed to get the work done. After that night, the patients worked patiently. Another year came to an end and a new year arrived. It was the third year since they had begun dumping rocks into the sea. The director was determined to complete the project this year. But it was extremely unlikely that the project would be completed as he wished.

One day, several unwelcome guests visited the director at the construction site. The men came to evaluate the progress of the work and to investigate their technological resources. They said they were from the Korean Resettlement Development Company. They explained that the reason for their visit was to survey and evaluate the reclamation project at the invitation of the Provincial office.

"This can't be!"

After meeting with the surveyors, the director could guess the seriousness of the situation. This was the ultimate betrayal. He felt what was inevitable had finally come to pass. He could not suppress the feeling of betrayal and felt that his blood was circulating in the wrong direction. He left the surveyors and quickly went to the provincial office. This could not be happening. He knew that he would have to deal with this some day but he had no idea that their conspiracy had advanced to this point. In short, they were in danger of losing the project. The surveyors had not simply been sent to Oma island to evaluate their progress. There was no way that the provincial office would be generous. They refused to openly say it but the fact that the surveyors had come implied that someone was ready to take over the project. It didn't matter which group, organization or individual was trying to take it over. This was not the problem. The problem was the people who didn't want to leave the project up to the hospital management and up to the patients, conspiring behind the scenes and pressuring certain groups of people and bureaucrats.

Perhaps it had something to do with the elections. Winning and losing was determined by mere numbers; that was the mechanical election process.

The islanders of Sorok did not have the right to vote. Not that they couldn't legally vote but since their identities were uncertain and their legal residence was unclear, it was extremely complicated to have them vote. At the same time, it was a perfect place to garner lots of votes if everyone agreed on an issue. Sorok island was a place where a large number of votes could be had.

One year, a brilliant politician came up with this idea. When election time came, he campaigned for the islanders to exercise their right to vote. He put a great deal of effort into getting them to cast their ballots and as a result he was able to reap his reward. He thanked the patients and the hospital management and promised that he would continue to work for the best interests of the island. In order to prove that his promise was not mere bluster, he continued to show interest. Since then, this politician was not the only one who showed an interest in the patients and the island. Those who were waiting for their chance at election simply couldn't afford to overlook the island. Every candidate wished to become the islanders' "servant." The patients were the largest constituency in the district and the candidates had to win over the patients. They had become a group no politician could ignore.

Yet the situation did not always turn out favorably for the islanders. The district election results were not solely determined by the islanders' vote, because the mainlanders still held the majority. In other words, the mainlanders who wanted to take over the construction project used their votes to exercise their power. When a candidate found the majority trying to influence him, he had no choice but to ignore the minority. Perhaps what was happening now was part of this process. He could guess the situation, without needing to listen to an explanation. Whatever the mainlanders' justification for taking away the construction project or whatever position the people who let the situation come to this held, it really didn't matter much at this point.

The director was surprised when he visited the provincial administrative office and realized that the situation had progressed so far and was far more serious than he had imagined. He had expected that the representatives of the neighboring mainlanders and their supporters had visited the administrative office frequently to petition to take over the project.

But the province had assigned the Korean Resettlement Development Company to assume responsibility for the project. Therefore they would gain control of the project. The surveyors said they had come to evaluate progress but it was only part of the necessary process for a take-over. It gave them a chance to look at what the prospects were before assuming responsibility.

"I think it's best for you to let go of this project. I personally understand your position and how you feel, but there's nothing we can do since the pressure both from above and below is great." This came from one of the officials whom the director often talked to regarding the project. When he said the pressure from below was great he meant the mainlanders' petition had reached the governmental levels, higher than the provincial office. And this intimated that executives from above had already decided to conclude the project this way.

"Of course, to be fair, we should've consulted with you and negotiated with you before anything was done. But if we'd followed the proper procedures, we were afraid that unnecessary troubles would arise...Those both above and below agreed that you wouldn't give up the project voluntarily even if it took several more years."

From his point of view, the official regarded what the director had done as a complete failure. He wanted to say that since the deadline had been extended several times and there was nothing to show for it, it was best to abandon the project and hand it over to others.

"I'm sorry to say this to you but according to the papers we have, not only is the construction progress too slow but the entire blueprint has to be reexamined since the embankments are too narrow. Of course, it really depends on who's looking at it, but I'm afraid you've launched the project too hastily. To be honest, you really don't have any experience in this kind of work. Your enthusiasm made you start the whole thing without covering the basics. Moreover, the patients weren't equipped with the proper tools or skills. In order to increase their morale, only a visible result was required..."

The director wanted to strangle the man but he got up and went to the governor's office. When he met the governor, he started complaining about the unfairness of the change in ownership of the project.

"This is a dirty trick, it's thievery. Lepers beg and

steal. Never before have healthy people stolen from lepers."

The governor knew the director well. No matter how much the director complained and attacked, there was nothing he could do. He only smiled sheepishly.

"People hate it more than anything else when lepers beg. I'm sure you feel the same. I wanted to stop them from begging by successfully carrying out this project. I wanted them to live harmoniously, cultivating the land they'd reclaimed with their own hands, even if it was only a small plot. They've gained confidence and hope. But look what's happened. The insignia on the Oma island project flag is a hand with the missing fingers of a leper. They transported rocks and dirt with fingerless hands under the flag with the missing fingers. They were determined to throw their diseased bodies into the sea to build the embankments. That's the result of the present work. You can't take away the project under the pretext of slow progress and lack of skill. I don't know who made those excuses to take over the project but I can't give it up. Even if they lack skill and equipment, and even if it takes another year or two,

I'm going to finish this work. Those fingerless lepers and I will complete it."

After the director finished his remonstration, the governor tried to calm him down and said, "No matter who completes the project, the right of land allocation belongs to the province..."

He meant to say that since the province has the right of land allocation he would do his best to assure that the patients got a fair portion of the land in return for their hard work. He said this on the premise that the director would let go of the project. The governor could not possibly guess what the director was thinking deep inside.

"Taking away the Oma island project from the patients is not only taking away the land. For them, there is something more valuable and precious wrapped up in Oma island. Their hopes and their confidence that they could take charge of their own lives is worth ten times, a hundred times more than the reclaimed land. Taking Oma island away means depriving them of their will to live. For the first time, let them have hope. At least let them experience the pleasure of living. I can't back down."

After the director met with the governor, he

went straight to Seoul and met with a cabinet minister, but the minister had nothing to say.

"I guess it must be something urgent for you to come up to see me like this," the minister said uncomfortably as if he wanted to avoid the subject. "It's unreasonable to assume all responsibility because one is enthusiastic and stubbornly persistent. Each person has his limits, capabilities and positions." He laughed several times and patted the director's shoulder repeatedly as if he was trying to placate a cranky child. It was obvious that he had been harassed by the problem of changing the ownership of the Oma island project for some time. The director could guess that the minister had more or less agreed to the transfer of ownership. He was in utter despair.

"No matter how you decide on this matter, I can't step aside. Five thousand patients, the hospital management and I will complete this at any cost."

He firmly stated his determination as he left the minister's office but considering the minister's position, the director had hit an impasse. He was completely walled in. His last hope was the islanders. He returned to the island with a heavy heart. When he returned to the island, he quietly asked the surveyors to leave. Then he met with the elders' council. He explained exactly what the situation was. He told them that he had just returned from the provincial office and Seoul and told them what he had learned about the future of the project. He explained that they had misunderstood the whole of the project. They believed it had started with the director's persistence alone, that the whole project was his brainchild and they thought that as soon as he was removed, no one else would interfere in the transfer of ownership. But this project had not been started by one person's enthusiasm nor could it have been. He further stated that he firmly believed that simply by forcing him to give up wouldn't enable them to appropriate the project.

He added things beyond what he had learned to arouse their anger and to incite them to finish the project as soon as possible. He thought the only effective way to maintain the project was to eliminate any and all justifications or excuses that could interfere with it. If they could complete the project before the official change of ownership, they couldn't take away the land. In any case, they needed to rush to finish. No one knew when the order would be delivered to hand over the management of the project. They could not afford to leave any room for them to take over the project. He repeated that they needed to finish the project with their own hands and that he wanted to see them complete it...He pleaded with them.

The elders listened to the director with unchanging expressions. When he finished speaking, they left quietly without any words of encouragement. They were completely expressionless and indifferent. But the director's plea was not a complete waste of time. Before daybreak there was a commotion. It was a good thing that he had quietly asked the surveyors to leave the island. That night several workers secretly went over to the resettlement development office in Pongam village and broke into their residence. But they were able to dodge this attack since the director had made them leave the island beforehand. Even when the patients found the residence empty they refused to give up just like that. After they realized that the surveyors had left the island, they searched all around the residence. Some went to the Noktong area to block all escape routes in case one or two of them were still left on the island. They staked out the residence until morning.

The news about the definite measures to turn over the ownership of the project to a different organization had obviously had a shocking effect. They couldn't find a visible target for revenge and their burning anger had changed to an incredible enthusiasm for work. Their zeal not to have the project taken away was transformed into great enthusiasm. It was beyond the director's imagination.

At the construction site, there was no day and no night. They continued working even in the biting cold days of snow and strong wind. There was not a single person who doubted the result or concerned himself much about the project's success or failure. They were working to avenge themselves against those who wanted to rob them of their project. Even when they worked in the biting cold, not a single person suffered frostbite or injury. The director was very satisfied. Witnessing their sincerity, he vowed once again that he would not let others rob them of Oma island.

He gained confidence that this was possible by their strength alone. Their enthusiasm and high spirits alone could sweep away all the excuses, pretexts and justifications of those who wanted to rob them. Even the sinking of the embankments seemed to have stopped. If they kept up the work at this pace, before long all the embankments would be connected and the ceremony could finally take place. After the connecting ceremony, nobody would be able to find a proper justification to take the reclaimed land away from them. The most important thing was the patients' enthusiasm. Even if the order came down before the connecting ceremony, given the present atmosphere, the patients would not let go of Oma island without putting up a fight.

"If there is someone who wants to take the land away from them, come now and see. They are consumed by an unbreakable attachment toward the island. Who can possibly take the island away from them? No matter how brilliant the justification or excuse, they couldn't possibly take over the project seeing how attached they are to the island. Who could endure their curses and their revenge if they forcibly took the land?..."

The director believed in the patients, and he hoped that the embankments would be completed before the situation took a turn for the worse. There was no other preventive measure. However, there was one thing even the director didn't know. The people plotting to take over the project, rather than being ensnared in this trap, were far ahead of them, plotting their next step. The director only wanted more time to finish the embankments and had no idea that they were already plotting to deprive him of even his ability to conspire.

One day the director realized the truth in a particularly excruciating way. He received transfer orders for a sanatorium in Masan. Obviously, those planning to assume control of the project were trying to get rid of him first because, with him around, it would greatly inconvenience their job. From the beginning they wanted him off the island. "It's unreasonable to assume all responsibility because one is enthusiastic and stubbornly persistent. Each person has his limits, capabilities and positions." He remembered what the minister had said, and it became clear what he meant. He heard rumors that if he continued not to cooperate they would dismiss him from his post. Not that the director had never entertained the possibility, but he didn't think that they would stoop this low to achieve their goals. But it happened as they had planned, just as the rumor said it would. It happened unexpectedly.

The director felt a darkness descending over him. The only comforting thought was that the transfer order came a month before the expected date of the take-over, perhaps because it would require a great deal of preparation for the hospital work as well as the reclamation project. His new post was a national sanatorium in Masan and the transfer date was set for the seventh of March. He still had about a month's time. There was no discussion of his transfer nor did his superiors call him. There was only a short official memorandum. Even after he received the memorandum, he heard nothing from his superiors.

The director was compelled to go to Seoul immediately. Worried that this might cause a disturbance among the patients, he asked the hospital staff who knew about his transfer orders to keep silent. He even canceled making rounds at the construction site and shut himself up in his office for a few days, trying to think how best to deal with this unexpected situation.

25

After mulling it over for a couple of days, Director Cho decided that before he left for his next post they'd need to speed up the project. Since he wanted to see the "connecting ceremony" before he left, he'd need to rush to get the Oma island's future settled. After reaching this decision, he went out to the construction site and delivered a new work schedule.

First he went to the headquarters and asked for Elder Hwang. While intimating that he was going to leave the island soon, he expressed how important it now was to finish the embankments as soon as possible.

"I have to leave by the seventh of next month at the latest. But I can't leave unless we finish the recovery project. I have to prove that the patients can finish it with their own hands. I'm asking you to please hurry and finish up before I have to leave. I'll have to leave right after the ceremony."

The director spoke resolutely, implying he'd stay on the island until the ceremony took place. In fact, he might even give up his new post. Since he was no longer a soldier at the mercy of his superiors, he had this privilege. That was one advantage to being a civilian—he could resign if he wanted to and stay on the island. But that was not the best choice. Without the directorship he would only be able to prove his devotion. The people who were trying to drive him out wouldn't support him just because he had decided to stay. He needed to think about this some more.

Elder Hwang listened with indifference as usual, staring pensively out over the ocean. His blank gaze shifted to the trucks that rumbled up and down the hills hauling dirt. When his gaze finally returned to the director, who was standing next to him, he had a mischievous look about him.

"I've heard that people with the family name Ch'oe are very stubborn, but I've never known a Cho to be headstrong. You're the first." Elder Hwang said it as if he was joking. "We've already said we're not working for others so we can't let you ruin your life for the sake of a bunch of lepers. You're ready to risk your career for the connecting ceremony? We can't let that happen. We'll hurry up so that at least you can see the ceremony. When would be good?" Since the director was clearly determined to stay until he saw the ceremony, Elder Hwang decided to rush it.

The director understood what Elder Hwang was getting at. The director's confidence in him would not be shaken, regardless of whether Elder Hwang meant to tell him to leave by the deadline or not. Elder Hwang decided to rush the ceremony since he knew there was nothing else that could be done neither for the director nor for the islanders.

"Let's say the sixth of March. That's the last possible day that I can stay here as director."

The ceremony date had finally been set. And since the date was set for the sixth, the new deadline for the completion of the embankments had also been set—they had to be finished before then.

Both the increasing threat that the project would be taken away from them and the news of the director's impending transfer led to an unexpected change in morale at the construction site. The new deadline was announced—the ceremony had to take place before the director left the island. If the deadline wasn't met, the director was determined to stay on the island even if that meant resigning. His determination and his willingness to protect the project at any cost became widely known and so the patients once again regained their enthusiasm to finish the embankments before the deadline. The news of the director's impending transfer was the spark that ignited this enthusiasm.

One evening after the director had returned to his home after checking the progress at the construction site, Sanguk came to see him. The director felt a bit uneasy with this unexpected visit. The two often saw each other at the construction site but Sanguk never talked about anything other than business. Last year, when the director was attacked by the islanders, Sanguk was the only one who had come forward to help him out. But he never mentioned the incident again. The director felt uncomfortable that he wouldn't talk about it. The few times Sanguk did talk about things other than business, it was unpleasant, just like that night, and Sanguk would be sarcastic and defensive the whole time.

Even after he'd led Sanguk into the room, the director felt uncomfortable with his visit. Sanguk would not be this calm if there'd been an accident at the construction site. He had come to talk to him about something else. Sanguk was not the type to beat around the bush once he had decided to do something.

"There's something that only you can do, so I've come to ask for your help." He began to explain why he had come. He said that the islanders, led by the elders' council, had launched a petition drive to stop the director's transfer. Sanguk wanted the director to stop it.

"At this point, there's no use in trying to stop them and there's no one else who could. I don't think there's anyone who would volunteer either. Even if there was someone, he or she wouldn't do it, for fear of being labeled a traitor. You're the only one who can stop it."

Sanguk implied that if the director didn't stop it, there was a definite possibility that the island would be filled with real traitors.

The director knew nothing about the petition drive. Something similar had happened once before. At the time, he had expected it, so he knew the situation well. Actually he had hoped for it. But this time, he hadn't had an inkling of it. Sanguk was under the impression that the director was playing innocent, pretending not to know.

"Those bastards! What are they doing? Why are they wasting their energy on something that useless? Why didn't you stop them?" The director was enormously offended that Sanguk had come to see him about this. He ensured Sanguk that he would stop the petition drive the very next day. Even after he had made sure that Sanguk needn't worry, he still wasn't sure why he was so sensitive about this, and he was offended by what he seemed to be saying.

To ask him to stop the petition drive meant that he wanted him to leave. If opposing the petition drive meant betrayal, accepting it meant betrayal as well. If he didn't try to stop it, he'd be labeled a traitor. He simply couldn't understand Sanguk's intentions. If the islanders wanted him to stay a little longer and he himself thought this would be best for the project, why would this make him a traitor? He didn't understand.

He thought Sanguk was being quite insulting. But Sanguk was not someone who would back down, even in the face of the director's strength.

"Which side are you on, Manager Yi? Are you simply asking me to stop their petition drive or are you asking me to leave the island immediately as ordered? I can't quite make out which side you're on. I know I'm indebted to you and I'm sure you aren't holding a grudge against me—or are you?" the director asked jokingly.

"Isn't it your decision whether you leave?" snapped Sanguk, ignoring his tone. When Sanguk said he didn't care whether he left or not, it meant he wanted him to leave.

"I'm disappointed. Even if everybody on the island wanted me to leave, I thought you'd be the one to stop me...I know that you were the one who distrusted me the most, but I thought you might have changed your mind by now. I thought you'd grown to trust me now that we've worked together for a while...But..." The director continued in a joking tone to cover his uneasiness. The reason for Sanguk's visit had become apparent.

"It would've been the same with anybody else. I also didn't think that the Oma island project should be yours alone." Sanguk expressed his thoughts unflinchingly. "I know you're the one who started it but it doesn't have to be you who finishes it. Don't think that you're the only one who can. I'm sorry to say, but I don't see any reason for you to be so adamant about seeing the ceremony."

"In other words, what you're saying is, I shouldn't think this is something that only I can do. It's selfishness for me to want to see the project finished because I was the one who started it..." Without the slightest trace of humor, the director repeated what Sanguk had said, looking straight into his eyes.

"No matter what you think of me, I'm one of the ones who trust you. And because I trust you, I can say this even though I know I'm being rude. Please don't try to see the project through. Leaving the island without seeing the ceremony might be better for the islanders," he said resolutely.

"What you've accomplished on this island is extraordinary and you've become important to the islanders. Regardless of whether the ceremony takes place or if, as you fear, the project gets handed over to someone else against your will and that of the islanders, what you've accomplished on this island won't change. Neither the ceremony nor your departure will make any difference. But still you insist that no one else take credit for it. That's why you want to see the connecting ceremony: then no one else can take the credit you feel you deserve. You're being selfish. You yourself have nothing more to give. You want to see the completion of the project as a reward for what you've done."

"It's that statue again. You're still afraid that I want to erect a statue, right?" the director asked scornfully. But then he smiled confidently as if to reassure Sanguk that the statue was not on his mind at all. But Sanguk was not about to accept his reassurances.

"I know. I know better than anyone else that you never dreamed of building a statue. But even if you don't want it, others might build one for you. That's how it would happen just about anywhere else. I'm not worried about that."

"Then there's no need for you to worry about the petition." Since Sanguk was being aggressive, Director Cho couldn't be polite. "Like you said, if it's common that statues are built by others, regardless of whether the person wants it or not, then it really doesn't matter what I want, right? Since I never wanted to have a statue built for me, shouldn't I be proud of the fact that they want to build one for me?" The director deliberately said things that would annoy Sanguk.

"If it happened somewhere else, it would be something to be proud of. But things are different here. As you already know, there was once a statue of a director. And it wasn't built because the owner of the statue wanted it. He didn't even mention it. But everyone knew that that's what he wanted. Because he wanted it, they had to build it and dedicate it to him before he mentioned it out loud. For the islanders, it was the same whether the director asked them to build it or not."

"So you're saying that even though I don't show it, deep down inside I also want a statue?"

"Like I said, I trust you. But the islanders are ready to build you a statue."

"What? How?"

"You can't blame them. They still don't know what it is that they're going to start in the near future. But it's not difficult to understand if you think how things have changed since you first came. First of all, the escapes that used to take place regularly and caused such a headache have stopped. On top of that, you never backed down in your dealings with the patients. Instead, you always handled them skillfully, explaining things clearly so that they could understand, and you always succeeded. Now they follow you whatever you do. Even though they're dead tired from the construction work, they pretend they're not. They don't complain about the pain and fatigue or even attempt to escape. It's because they follow you willingly. I'm sure you're satisfied with this and I have no intention of criticizing you on this point. But you need to think about the other side of the coin of them not wanting to escape. The fact that no one defies you—that no one wants to or is even able to defy you—you need to think deeply about that. Their wish for you to stay grows stronger and stronger. That means that, unconsciously, they have begun to build your statue, even though it's still invisible. The day will come when they actually erect a statue in your honor..."

"..."

"As you said soon after you came, this was an island of the dead. You woke them to life and now they are living beings. You instill hope and faith in them and you've fostered a new trust between neighbors. I just want to say that the hope and trust you inspired in them must not become another shackle. If another statue is erected, it's not difficult to guess what the result of that will be…"

"…"

"I can't stop them from having the image of your statue in their minds. I think that it's truly valuable that they preserve your image like that. Even so, the statue shouldn't be yours alone—it has to be for all five thousand patients. I'm sure you'd happily agree. As long as you stay here, they won't be able to transform their statue of you into a statue for themselves."

"What is it that you want from me?" the director asked impatiently unable to stay quiet any longer. He'd kept quiet for a quite a while and Sanguk, who had been talking excitedly, seemed to have forgotten his presence. The director's curt tone was not that of someone ready to accept advice but rather that of someone who was resisting.

"No, I already know what you expect from me. Before I can accept your advice, I'd better decide first whether I'm Buddha or Jesus." He sneered sarcastically at Sanguk. But once Sanguk had gotten excited he wouldn't cool down easily. In spite of the director's sarcastic response, Sanguk continued to aggravate him.

"What I'm asking you to do now is not so difficult that your only choices are to do either as Jesus or Buddha would. I'm just trying to explain that, no matter how precious the statue the patients' have grown in their hearts is to you, you can't possibly complete it. Please. Just leave the island. The time has come for you to leave. Let them finish your statue for themselves, not by remaining here, but by leaving. That's the only way to preserve what you've accomplished. You've done everything you possibly could for the island."

26

Even after his conversation with Sanguk, Director Cho still had no intention of changing his plans about meeting the new deadline or participating in the connecting ceremony. He didn't understand why Sanguk was so adamant about him leaving. Whatever his intentions, Sanguk had made one thing clear, and the director now realized that he could no longer stay. There was no need for him to stay. Sanguk had repeated his demand that he leave over and over. But despite Sanguk's pleas, he wouldn't change his plans to leave until after the ceremony. He intended to complete the project as scheduled and disregard Sanguk's request.

He had to reconsider his decision a few days later. Maybe Sanguk still had things to say to him or maybe it was his way of reminding him of their long conversation. Whatever the reason, Sanguk left the island suddenly. In so doing, he became even more of a cipher to the director than he had been before.

Sanguk had in fact escaped. Just as people had done in the past, he risked his life by leaving from the Tolburi shore, jumping into the cold water and swimming across the sea. But Sanguk wasn't a patient—he was a member of the hospital staff—and so it was entirely unnecessary for him to "escape" like this. If he had wanted to, he could have simply gotten on the ferry and left. But he chose to leave from the Tolburi shore and swim across. He didn't just leave, he escaped. It was another "escape incident."

It wasn't clear whether he had made it safely across or not. He had left several pieces of evidence on the shore to prove he had escaped: he'd taken his clothes and shoes off before he jumped into the water and they remained there on the beach. Even before he went to the beach, he had gone to the main hospital office and met with the staff, making sure that they could reconstruct his last hours on the island. Then he deliberately created this commotion. The director could only guess at the message he was trying to send. To a certain degree, he could speculate as to his reasons for resorting to this dangerous adventure and what he meant to say by it. It was his final attempt to pressure the director and to make it impossible for him to stay. It was a shrewd and wicked act that would compel the director to leave.

Whatever Sanguk's motives were, the incident certainly left a bitter aftertaste. The director thought he could forgive Sanguk his rudeness when he had insisted that it was best for him and the islanders that he left. He thought he should respect Sanguk's deep concern for the island. But he couldn't forgive him for "escaping," especially from that wretched place, the Tolburi shore. Sanguk had attempted to revive the sense of betrayal deeply embedded within the patients by causing this disturbance. He was deliberately trying to provoke them.

The problem was that most of the patients still weren't aware of Sanguk's past. His personal history and his connection to the island had never been revealed. Sanguk chose to escape not because he couldn't endure the island like the other escapees, but because he wanted to provoke the patients.

—There's nothing the director can do now.

—Why would someone like him stay here when he was better off on the mainland?

—Watch, the director will try to avoid taking any responsibility.

After the director had stopped the petition drive against his transfer, the patients began to view him with a critical eye and morale at the construction site plummeted. The patients gave up on the idea that healthy people truly cared about the island and now the same lack of concern seemed to be true for the director. Surely Sanguk had guessed this would happen and that was why he had left without revealing his past. He knew well what kind of effect his escape would have on the patients and he knew that it would jeopardize the director's position as well. Sanguk had betrayed the island and the patients as a healthy person and that troubled the director the most.

The patients' reaction to Sanguk's "escape" was just what the director expected.

—If Sanguk wanted to escape like that, there's nothing more to say.

—There'll be plenty who will be busy running away, just like him…

The patients began to change after Sanguk's escape. Instead of rushing to finish the embankments, they dawdled. It was an uncomfortable and dangerous rebellion.

There was one person who openly harassed the director—Yun Haewŏn, Mr. Pink Mania, who had had a peculiar relationship with Sanguk concerning Miyŏn. In order to forget the pain that Miyŏn had caused him and to engage in an introspective self-evaluation, Haewŏn had begun carrying rocks at the construction site. He said he did it because of his sister in the patients' zone. He had begun to accept the jealousy he felt over Miyŏn. Late one evening, Haewŏn, dead drunk, went to see the director at the headquarters on Oma island.

"That guy pretended that he understood lepers so well, but he couldn't deceive himself any longer," Haewŏn slurred his words.

Despite all the problems they had had, Haewŏn and Miyŏn's relationship was about to bear fruit. They had even decided to have a simple wedding ceremony on the day of the connecting ceremony. Their wedding was big news all over the island.

"He couldn't give his blessing to our marriage because he didn't like the idea of a leper marrying a healthy woman. This escape is his way of expressing how disgusted he was."

Haewŏn, too, had no idea that Sanguk was born on the island as an unaffected child, though Sanguk had never told this to the director either. Given the seemingly irrefutable fact that Sanguk was a healthy person, Haewŏn's competing desire for Miyŏn had driven him to complete despair. They overcame that hurdle. For him, Sanguk left—just as a healthy person could—right at the time the wedding was about to take place, as a way to denounce the wedding and to deliberately flaunt the healthy man's right to leave.

Sanguk's escape was more destructive to Haewŏn than one would have imagined. Haewŏn tried to find an underlying motive for his actions and the director could understand why. As Haewŏn guessed, Sanguk's escape could well be attributed to his opposition to Haewŏn and Miyŏn's relationship. It was possible that Sanguk wanted to provoke rebellion on the part of Haewŏn by staging his escape. The fact that Sanguk kept his background a secret might be proof of that. Sanguk also knew that his status as a healthy person competing for Miyŏn's affections had been unbearable torture for Haewŏn. Even so, he didn't reveal his background to Haewŏn. Perhaps it was to impede him. Haewŏn conjectured that perhaps Sanguk wanted to destroy his relationship with Miyŏn and that was why he left. He knew that this would provoke a violent reaction and send Haewŏn spiraling back down into another bout of despair.

A few days later, Miyŏn also visited the director and explained the situation. She said that after Sanguk's escape Haewŏn's attitude had changed and she asked for his help. Their relationship had worsened ever since the evening that Haewŏn had gotten drunk and gone to see the director. She said that

Haewŏn's jealousy toward the healthy was exploding. He had become jealous of Sanguk, all the other healthy people, even her. He had become as obsessed with pink as he had been before. He had completely reverted to the person he was before he started working at the construction site. Their plan to have the wedding ceremony on the day of the connecting ceremony had been shattered and their dreams of a life together had evaporated.

What was more surprising was that Sanguk had not revealed his secret to Miyŏn. Despite the fact that Miyŏn had told Sanguk her background, Sanguk had never indicated that he wanted to reveal his background. It was not a coincidence that he kept his background a secret even from her. Perhaps he didn't want to seek her love as someone who had the same background. But if he truly had wanted her or if he could sincerely accept Haewŏn and Miyŏn's relationship, he should have told her. But he had no intention of doing so. He was certainly aware that Haewŏn was jealous of his health. He also knew that his health prevented the two from getting closer and so he consciously let this happen. When their relationship reached a decisive point, he had rejected it aggressively by escaping. It wasn't clear whether he did it because he truly couldn't accept their union, or whether he wanted to bring a disastrous end to all three of them, including himself. But by keeping silent about his background and by escaping as a healthy person, he was the one who had forced the break in their wedding plans.

The director could do nothing for Miyŏn. That Sanguk had been born as an unaffected child on the island meant nothing to Miyŏn at this point. He suggested that she reveal her secret to Haewŏn now and thereby pacify his jealousy of healthy people. By doing this, they might still be able to hold their wedding. But Miyŏn said that it was useless.

"The reason I haven't told him that I was born on this island—even though I know he's both tormented and intimidated by healthy people—isn't that I want to flaunt my status as a healthy person. I didn't tell him because I really hoped he'd conquer his fears and overcome his jealousy of healthy people by himself. I didn't want him to think that lepers could only marry other lepers. I wanted him to develop some self-respect. I wanted him to gain the confidence that he too could marry a healthy woman who had nothing to do with leprosy. I wanted him to forget his own history of being diseased and to make him realize that marrying a healthy woman really is nothing, it's not that difficult. I won't give up until he realizes this. I won't reveal my secret until then. There's no reason to rush to get married. My lips will be sealed until he overcomes this pain and agony. I'll wait." This was Miyŏn's answer to the director's suggestion. There was nothing more he could say, seeing that she was determined to wait. In any case, Sanguk's leaving had had a serious impact.

His reasons for leaving were still unclear. But whatever they were, his escape had renewed the spirit of rebellion and distrust among the islanders. It was destructive in a dangerous way. There was nothing the director could do. He couldn't go around asking the patients to speed up the work. But then again he couldn't just sit there in his office, waiting for the day of his transfer. Since it had come to this, he could not resign his post and stay on the island. That would be seen as another trick. Maybe he could just leave the island instead of waiting for the day of his transfer. But he couldn't even do that.

27

Director Cho was up against a wall. Then something happened that made his position even more tenuous.

He received a telegram from his superiors instructing him to complete all of the paperwork for the hand-over before the new director's arrival. He was also supposed to facilitate the work of an evaluation team who were to arrive soon. The meaning of these orders was quite clear. It would be the new director who would officially sign over the project. And the land reclamation would be taken over later by whatever group had commissioned the survey.

The director was in no position to do anything about this. He certainly could confront his superiors even if it meant losing his job but the survey team would eventually come to the island—he'd be responsible for their safety while they were on the island. Although he was treading on thin ice, he would have to plead with the patients to stay calm when the surveyors came out to the construction site for their inspections.

"A group of surveyors will arrive to inspect our progress on the project. Since we're working on a new deadline, there's no need for us to be hostile. Please leave them alone to do their job. We need to concentrate on our own jobs if we're going to reach our goal. Ignore what they do and what they say about us."

When the surveyors—it was the same team from the resettlement development company who'd been there before—came to Oma island, the patients were indifferent. The director was absolutely amazed at their utter unresponsiveness. Before, they had been ready to kill the surveyors in order to protect the island. Now, when the surveyors returned, the islanders showed no interest whatsoever. It was the same as saying they didn't care whether the island was taken away from them or not. Their indifference meant they were willing to leave its future up to the surveyors. This, too, was a dangerous form of rebellion. The director didn't quite know how to interpret their silence, their expressionless faces, their passive and unquestioning obedience. He felt shivers running down his spine. But what was even more shocking than the patients' silence and their chilling indifference was the surveyors' inappropriate behavior.

The director intended to complete as much of the work as he could before he left. If the Oma island reclamation project was handed over to the resettlement development company, he needed to have all the necessary paperwork finished before he left for his new post. There were only two weeks now before the new director's arrival. Even if it got to the point where he ended up staying, he couldn't just sit around and watch the project be handed over to the resettlement development company. He needed to settle the matter in the best interests of both the patients and the hospital administration for the sake of the new director. Since a detailed survey and progress appraisal were being done, it no longer mattered whether the connecting ceremony took place or not.

The director asked the managers of each department in the hospital to have their operation reports ready while he spent most of his time on the Oma reclamation project, trying to conclude it in a way that would provide the most benefit to the islanders. He asked the survey team to finish its inspection before the end of February and he initiated an inspection of his own with a survey team comprised of hospital workers. While he accompanied the hospital survey team on their inspections, he wrote various other memos and prepared as best he could.

Finally at the end of February, the two survey teams met to compare notes.

The differences between the two teams' results were staggering. While the director's team evaluated the project as being eighty-three percent complete as of the twenty-fifth of February, the official survey team evaluated it as forty percent complete. Eighty-three percent versus forty percent. The director was stunned. He had expected some differences since each side had their own vested interests, but this was beyond comprehension. The director was particularly interested in the degree of completion because, even if the project was transferred into the resettlement company's control, the patients' efforts would be recognized and they would get fair compensation for the work they had done. Even if the hospital management changed, the right to the land distribution would remain with the provincial office. And irrespective of the results of the evaluation, the provincial office had promised that the patients would be fairly compensated for their work.

Even so, he felt strongly that it was absolutely necessary that the patients' contribution be evaluated as significant for the sake of their morale. If possible, he wanted to get a higher appraisal than the present state. Conversely, it was in the best interest of the resettlement development company to have as low an appraisal as possible. That was their job.

The director could not accept their appraisal. He demanded an explanation of the survey team's methods and the standards that they had used to reach their forty percent. Then he had his own survey team closely audit what they presented. The director, with the knowledge he had gained from his experiences, enthusiastically explained the results of his own survey team's evaluation. He even suggested that they bring in a third team with no vested interest in the project. But it was useless. From the very beginning the two side's interests clashed, and so it was impossible to find a solution that would be fair to both. Neither theoretical explanations nor persuasion had a chance now.

The official surveyors insisted that the project had numerous technical flaws stretching back to the very beginning. Therefore they could not evaluate the project based solely on what was visible. Their point was that supplementing construction deficiencies and amending partial construction would greatly decrease the visible results of the present construction. For example, the embankments were too narrow and needed to be widened. Moreover, their angle had not been carefully calculated to account for the pressure of the tides, which varied according to the depth of the water and the current, and so this also needed to be corrected.

The director's team had their own arguments. But considering the clash of interests, the resettlement development team didn't even try to compromise and so no resolution could be reached. As long as they were unwilling to listen to each other, there was nothing more the director could do.

The director fought on, tormented by a profound sense of betrayal. The patients' indifference made him feel even emptier, that everything he had done was in vain. They still showed no particular interest in the island. They showed no interest in whether he would be leaving or not, they didn't even seem interested in whether the connecting ceremony that was scheduled to take place in a few days would actually happen. They didn't seem to care at all. After the appraisal came in at forty percent, the director tried to raise it—even a little bit—and so he went from place to place, trying to find something. But the patients themselves, who should have been the most interested party of all, didn't seem to care.

The director had become used to their silence and indifference but this time he was extremely disappointed. Over the past several years he had dedicated himself to the island and the patients, but now he felt that all his efforts had been in vain, that they had vanished without a trace. The patients' indifference to the unfair appraisal was a sign that they had been exhausted by their dreams of reclaimed land. Perhaps it was the start of their betrayal. They finally realized that their dreams had been in vain and so they were plunged into a deep emotional void.

Day by day, an overpowering emptiness began to take hold of the director. He felt miserable.

28

One day early in March, Director Cho finally realized that his departure was right around the corner. He hadn't decided for certain that he'd leave but now he felt that it was inevitable. He dragged himself to the Oma headquarters to collect his thoughts and to confirm his intuition. He gazed with mixed feelings at the seabed for a while, feeling like a commander who, exhausted from fighting, was forced to leave before the battle was over.

In the distance, cold waves struggled to climb the thick new embankments, covering them with white salt flowers. The thin white stone pillar stood glimmering in the soft twilight where Manjae island had once been.

—Here, for the lepers who longed to become humans and to shelter their weary spirits, the Providence of God, the mountains became ocean and ocean became land!

Suddenly those words echoed in his head. This was not the first time he had heard them. They were the words he kept inside. He repeated them again and again, hoping that the whole of Oma island would indeed turn into the promised land for the lepers, for those who had dedicated their lives to the island and for all of their children and their children's children who would protect it. The words would stay behind on the stone pillar that would still be there long after the disappearance of Manjae island. He repeated the words. He couldn't carve them into the pillar yet. Some day. But now he wasn't even in a position to wait for that day to come.

"If only I had known that they couldn't own this land, that I'd be forced to leave and that no one would miss me!"

The director's heart ached with deep regret and profound bitterness. His biggest regret was that he couldn't carve the words he long had cherished onto the pillar. Regardless of who finally took possession of the land, these words should have been carved there. And no matter who it was who ultimately reclaimed the land, the words needed to be carved there. The words would bear witness to just how much this land meant to the patients and that, in the end, they were able to realize their dreams. In order to make the prayers and efforts of the islanders known, the words had to be left behind…

And so there he was, wrapped in regret as if it already was too late, trying to forget.

"You've changed a lot."

A voice from behind suddenly broke the silence. It was not a hallucination. It was a real person's voice. When the director turned around, he found Elder Hwang standing a few steps away with his hands clasped behind his back, half turned the other way. The director had no idea that someone was standing behind him. Just like the time when there was no sign of the embankments ever emerging, even after days and days of dumping stone upon stone into the sea. Then as now he had been in utter despair, consumed by his fear of failure. Elder Hwang had encouraged him at the time, when he'd gazed at him expressionless.

"What does he have in mind…?"

The director had tensed up at Elder Hwang's unexpected appearance.

"What do you mean by I've changed? How have I changed?" he asked. Their conversations had always been like this. Elder Hwang always tossed out a comment from left field and then feigned indifference as if he had forgotten what he had just said.

While the director waited for him to reply, Elder Hwang lowered his eyes and slowly looked out at the seabed. Then as if he had finally realized the director's presence, he answered slowly.

"When you first came, it was late evening, wasn't it? You made a fuss and embarrassed those who were at the pier to greet you, right? I'm sure you remember. When I heard about it, I was surprised. That's why I still remember it." As usual, he was beating around the bush. This was his way of having a conversation. Before he actually got to the point, he would always talk about other things. The director needed to wait patiently until the old man revealed his main point.

"Yes, I remember...I'm impressed that you still remember."

"Of course I do. That's the image I have of you. Do you understand what I'm saying? When you first came, you were a simple and modest person." He was slowly getting to the main point. It was clear that Elder Hwang hadn't come up the hill to encourage him.

"But I'm not like that now?"

"No. You've changed. Yes, you've changed. And

you're going to change even more."

"..."

"Now that you're leaving, you have too many things on your mind. I'm saying you want to leave this island in glory. You've changed." Elder Hwang was talking as if his departure was inevitable. The old man was perfectly capable of thinking like that. The director couldn't care about that now. He was surprised at what Elder Hwang was getting at. What does he mean by, I want to leave in glory? When did I ever dream of such a thing? Since when do I look like that to Elder Hwang and the rest of the islanders?

"This is what you mean by I've changed?" He was annoyed. But he realized that there was no point in getting upset now, so he asked him cautiously. But Elder Hwang's tone was both deeply solemn and very stubborn.

"I'm sure you'll deny it. That's because you haven't realized it yourself yet. But I can see it clearly. You can't fool me. Do you want me to give you proof that you're secretly harboring this wish?" Elder Hwang moved a few steps closer as if he had some sort of evidence that could force him to confess. And then he sat down quietly. Suddenly the director remembered the words he wanted to carve on the stone pillar on Manjae island. He was startled.

—Perhaps I can't deny what he said about wanting to leave the island in glory.

But Elder Hwang wasn't thinking about the verse that the director had hidden deep within his heart.

"I often saw you arguing with the surveyors from the resettlement development company about the appraisal. Of course we're very grateful that you're trying to get them to give us more credit. I think it's in your nature." He stopped for a minute and took out a cigarette. After he lit the cigarette, he spoke slowly, staring off into space.

Just as he had suspected, Elder Hwang was not thinking about his wish to carve the words into the pillar. It was something Elder Hwang and the rest of the patients feared; it was the statue. That was why Elder Hwang had come to see him in the headquarters.

"I'm grateful for what you're trying to do but there's something you don't know."

"I'm sure you think that what I'm doing is all

about my own personal gratification or for personal glory. That I want to be recognized for my accomplishments so when I finally leave I'll be getting on the ferry surrounded by the patients, all of whom are grateful for what I've done. You're talking as if you're not at all interested in winning even one more inch of Oma land."

"Perhaps I didn't hear right but hasn't it already been decided how much land will be given to us for farming regardless of how much we've accomplished?"

"That's true. But like you said, things don't have to be done as promised. Do you honestly believe the results of the appraisal won't be taken into account when the time comes for them to divide the land?"

"Even if that's true, we can't do anything about it."

"Is that really true? Is that how you really feel?"

"Probably. We did our job and it's up to them whether to give us more land or less land. Even if they decide not to give us any land—not even the smallest plot possible—that's entirely up to them too."

"Do you really think that five thousand patients all think like you? Are they as unconcerned as you are about this?"

"Even if they aren't, that's fine. You know them well, don't you? That's how they've lived. They're used to it."

"…"

"But there's no need to feel sorry for them. I told you before that lepers don't work for others, so when they started the project, they were already enjoying their share of the benefit. They've worked hard for the past few years to acquire more farmland so they could become self-sufficient. In their own way, they dreamed of their paradise. That in itself is a great blessing. There's no need to feel sorry for them. There may be something you haven't learned yet. Because you don't understand this, you're continuing these useless arguments with the resettlement development company. I can't blame you for wanting to leave the island after the matter's been settled to your satisfaction, but to my eyes it could be that…"

"It could be that I want to have all the credit for myself, not to mention a statue." The director smiled bitterly after he'd said what was on his mind. Could what Elder Hwang was saying be even slightly true? "Leaving in glory" meant dreaming of a statue. Perhaps this was something he couldn't deny; he had unconsciously harbored this dream. The director couldn't express his feelings openly now. A mysterious smile crossed his lips and he said to himself, "Sure. Even after I'd decided to leave, I couldn't let go of my desire to leave in glory. Since this is clear, it might be better to leave as soon as possible, even tomorrow morning."

The old man continued speaking, after staring at the director for a while, slowly changing the tone of his voice, trying to comfort him. "Sanguk said…Oh, I think I forgot to mention that he came to see me the night before he left and explained why he was leaving. I should've told you this before. Sanguk explained to me why he had to leave, and after hearing his explanation, I couldn't stop him. Among the things he talked about was the statue. Sanguk said it was an invisible statue of the director. He said that we lepers would probably fail to see your statue in us and become its slaves. Maybe he was right. Please don't feel bad because of what I'm saying. I just don't want any misunderstandings. Maybe it's time I speak my mind...we won't have many more chances to talk now that you've decided to leave."

"..."

"To be frank, Director Cho, I must thank you more than anything. Do you know why? You haven't yet demolished the statue I keep in my own mind. It's the only statue I have in my mind."

The director was surprised. The old man was contradicting everything he'd been saying until now.

—What? Elder Hwang had a statue in his mind? He's thankful that I haven't demolished it yet?

"Statue? Didn't you just tell me not to dream of statues? Whose statue do you keep in your mind?" The director was confused. Unlike the director, Elder Hwang's voice grew lower and slower and was filled with confidence and faith.

"Yes, it's true that I told you earlier that you shouldn't even dream of having your statue built. But that's what I mean by 'misunderstandings.' Before I said it as an ugly leper. I wanted it to be easy for you to leave. But it was just the opposite when I said it as a normal healthy person. Think about it.

Maybe you know this all too well. It's only natural that every person dreams of having a statue in his likeness. There's nothing wrong with that. The problem is how you go about getting it. Your methods were good. You allowed the patients to overcome their horrible experiences. Whether you wanted it or not, you made all the lepers on the island forge your likeness inside of them. Do you know how you did it? Do you know how you alone were able to get them to keep an image of your statue inside them of their own accord? I know you want to say you went through many tribulations and from time to time you had to hide your true feelings. But in my opinion, it was because you alone could put up with the statue to the very end. You tried so hard not to have your statue built by others that that made them keep your statue in their minds. Sanguk couldn't accept this. He said this was the quickest path for them to become slaves to you and your statue. I know how Sanguk felt but I'm too old. My days may be few. I'm not afraid of your statue anymore..."

The director noticed that the old man's voice was trembling so he turned around. He was weeping silently, faint tears flowing down his face. Elder

Hwang, the one who had neither felt sad nor scared when he witnessed his mother's death, the one who had happily tripped along the road all by himself having found a sack of barley after he had woken up next to the frozen body of his grandfather, the tinkerer, the one who cared little even after he realized that he'd contracted leprosy, was crying like a child. Seeing him like this, the director felt strange. He was unable to trace his face back to his old self. Tears streamed down his terribly disfigured face as if all his hatred and the agony of a lifetime had finally found an exodus. Seemingly unaware of the tears that streaked his face, Elder Hwang simply gazed down at the ocean. Seeing Elder Hwang in this miserable state, the director felt that he was finally seeing the face of a true person. A tantalizingly opaque veil had finally been lifted and the director saw the face of a human being, not a leper. He now understood clearly what the old man had been saying.

He still had one more question he wanted to ask him, not because he had finally seen his true face and he understood everything. The fact that Sanguk visited Elder Hwang before he left the island did not surprise him, and he wasn't at all curious about their conversation. What puzzled him was why the old man and the rest of the patients could not accept him. He was no longer afraid of the director but why was it that nothing could be accomplished on the island? Why was he feigning ignorance even though the director was leaving without having finished anything?

"I understand what you're saying. But I don't understand why I should leave the island. Why do I have to leave having accomplished nothing and without having gotten their forgiveness?" The director said what was on his mind. The old man seemed to ignore him as he watched the far horizon. Realizing that he could not completely ignore his question, he said finally, "It's because we lepers don't believe in faith."

"If you didn't act in the name of faith, how did you perform the island's work?" the director asked. There were no traces of tears on the old man's face now.

"Well, if we didn't act in the name of faith, that means we didn't believe in love…if we had neither faith nor love, that means we had only hatred and distrust…"

"Why only hatred and distrust? Aren't you and the rest of the patients believers in God?"

"Yes, I've been thinking about that, too. Why is it that the believers in God have more hatred and distrust than those who aren't? And where did those feelings come from? I thought this was our true nature. We invoked God's name, His faith and love, but in actuality we didn't carry out His teachings. Sanguk told me this when he came to see me, before he left the island. He said this was 'freedom.' He said what we have done on this island we did in the name of freedom. In order for us lepers not to become slaves, we need to assert ourselves in the name of freedom. On this island, freedom is a way and that is how it's been done. He left the island because he only believed in freedom. Sanguk guarded himself continuously against both your statue and the islanders' statue but in the end he left the island because of 'freedom'."

Elder Hwang talked about Sanguk thinking that the director already knew Sanguk's secret. There was nothing strange about Elder Hwang knowing Sanguk's past before anyone else. The director asked him another question.

"If what you're saying is true, is there any connection between the patients' inability to forgive me and their tendency to act in the name of freedom?

Are you saying that acting in the name of freedom is somehow improper?"

"Of course, at least on this island. That's my conclusion after many days of contemplation. Don't you know why freedom is a mistake on this island?"

"..."

"There's something more valuable than freedom. That's love. We needed to act in the name of love before freedom."

"..."

"Freedom—sure, it's good to have. With it, you can go wherever you want and live however you want. What more could anyone want, especially us lepers? But, as you know, we've never enjoyed this freedom. We fought endlessly. But we only fostered distrust and resentment. Of course if you think about it, that's only natural. Freedom is not something that you wait around to be offered. It's something you have to fight for. But in the midst of this struggle, it's only natural to discover resentment and distrust. Sanguk, too, wanted to act only in the name of freedom, but he didn't realize all the ugly things such as resentment and distrust that came with it. He didn't know how to forgive. It's freedom's fault that the patients escaped every chance they got, and that we lepers could neither trust you nor be grateful to you for everything you'd done. The only things that came from believing in freedom were distrust, resentment, and jealousy. In every fight there's a winner and a loser. We've developed a particular brazenness, like when I told you to leave the island. If you think about it, trust should come before freedom. Without this trust, we probably shouldn't have acted as recklessly as we did. Since we lacked trust, our persistence in pushing for freedom just made the distrust and hatred more intense."

"Are you saying that from now on you'll abandon the notion of freedom? If you relinquish freedom, in the name of what do you plan to carry on? How will you decide which path is the right one?"

The director now understood what the old man wanted to say. Even so, he was curious about one point. Had Elder Hwang truly abandoned the notion of freedom? If so, how would the island change? Would the dangerous, useless escapes finally stop for good?

Elder Hwang already had a good answer to the director's queries.

"It's love. Now that we know that freedom is insufficient, we couldn't possibly continue to hold onto it. Freedom is something you have to fight for, so there's a winner and a loser. Love is giving so there's no winner or loser. Everyone wins. This doesn't mean that we will forsake all those things that we need to do in the name of freedom. I'm saying we need to place love before freedom. There's no need to separate the two if love and freedom can coexist. Given what happened on this island, there was the possibility that freedom could reside within love but not the other way around. When the day comes when this island is full of love and true freedom exists within that love, things will change drastically."

Then, as if he had said everything he wanted to say, he rose slowly and walked down the hill toward the construction site. Although it was March in the South Sea, the biting ocean wind cut through one's clothes and seeped into the skin. The director was ready to get up. Then, Elder Hwang, who had walked several paces down the hill, stopped. He turned around and muttered to himself.

"You know, it sure is a strange fate," Elder Hwang said, not expecting a reply from the director.

"Those who need to act in the name of love don't know how to, and we end up learning from a person whom we've been praying for to learn love...what kind of strange fate is this..."

This wasn't something the director could answer. Elder Hwang's last words were what he had really wanted to say. They were meant as a lesson that he wanted to instill in the director.

"You've done your best. Everything you've done on this island you've done out of love. Us dirty, narrow-minded lepers couldn't accept you because we couldn't love. We wanted everything done in the name of freedom and so we couldn't accept you. Everything was done backwards and upside down. What you've done for the island could never be in vain. You at least tried to give us love."

Almost in a daze, Elder Hwang continued to talk to himself even as he walked away. "It is to this love that we will build our statue. It will be invisible, but it'll be the first one we have wanted for ourselves, and nobody can force us to pull it down. As long as this island remains an island of lepers, only this one statue of love should be left..."

29

Seven years had passed since Director Cho had left the island. Even though seven years ought to have brought changes, the island remained pretty much the same. The only thing that had changed was the people. Three different directors had come and gone. One stayed only half a year and left before he had become familiar with the patients' treatment and the island's situation.

Not only had the directors changed, but the patients had changed as well. They changed constantly. Many of those who were elderly when the director left had died and been laid to rest in Mallyŏng hall. One autumn day, Elder Hwang, the director's last friend, also found a place of eternal rest and had so left the island. But more new lives had been born and they continued to grow. These people were the ones who had changed.

But, except for them, the island had not changed during these seven years. The Oma reclamation project remained unfinished—nothing more had been done after the embankments were connected. For the past few years, only the white salt flowers covered the two thousand five hundred acres. The provincial authorities who owned the rights to the land had still not agreed on an owner.

The lives of the islanders were reverting to the way they were before the reclamation project. More than anything, the escapes continued. People escaped for no particular reason, creating a tumult on the island. Perhaps it is not correct to say that the only thing that had changed was the people. In fact, the people on the island had not really changed either. Their physical appearance and their names were different, but they were the same inside. Even their daily routines remained the same.

The island stayed the same. And that was precisely the reason for the frequent turnover in directors. Of course, the position wasn't exactly sought after, and no one willingly accepted it. If asked to go, most hesitated. But if three directors had come and gone, the responsibility for their leaving lay not only with them. Of course one of the reasons that the island never changed was the fact that the directors were always changing.

In order for change to take place on the island, the Oma reclamation project would have to be completed. As had been promised at the project's outset, the patients should have had the pleasure of getting their fair share of the land for all the hard work they had put in at the construction site. They should have farmed the land and reaped its bounty. Only a resolution of the Oma reclamation project could have changed the lives of the islanders. And only the Oma project could have revived their quickly disappearing faith. It was the only way to change the unproductive lives they were accustomed to.

But no director could accomplish this. No one could find a fair solution to the problems of the land distribution. Every new director hoped to solve the Oma island problem. Instead, they ended up leaving the island in a hurry, in no small part because of their powerlessness to resolve the problem. It could not be resolved easily.

One sunny spring day toward the end of March, just when the island would soon be bathed in cherry blossoms, a familiar face appeared on the island. It was Yi Chŏngt'ae, the reporter from the C Daily

News. He got off the ferry that now carried both patients and healthy people traveling from Noktong over to Sorok island.

Chŏngt'ae had first come to the island to report on the project six months after it had started, when there was still no sign of the embankments no matter how many stones had been thrown into the sea. He had even carried stones to help out. Then he left the island with an ominous warning to the director:

—Director! Please don't wait forever. There are no assurances as to how long they will wait patiently.

Now he had come back to the island. It was because of some bizarre wedding preparations that were taking place, preparations that people on the mainland could not easily overlook. A wedding was to take place between a healthy woman and a former patient. It was to be an unusual and rarely seen wedding.

He had come to the island to report on the wedding. Besides the wedding, he had another reason for visiting. He wanted to meet the person who had acted as matchmaker and had successfully brought the two together. Chŏngt'ae knew from before that the bride and groom were Miyŏn and Haewŏn. He was interested in their relationship and was sympathetic to them; he also understood well what their wedding symbolized for the island and the islanders. The person who brought the two together and arranged the wedding was Cho Paeghŏn, the former director.

One evening in early March seven years ago, Director Cho had left the island without any formal ceremony, two days before the connecting ceremony. He had quietly crossed the pier, with only Elder Hwang and the Manager of Personnel seeing him off. For the director, returning to the island had been like fate. Even after he had left the island, he could not forget it. He continued to hear news of the island: he heard that Oma island had disappointed the patients; he heard that new directors had come and gone. When he heard news like this, he became so anxious that he couldn't do his own work at his new hospital. He knew what he had to do and, because he knew, the work at Masan hospital was no longer a good fit for him.

He wanted to return to the island. He had to return to the island. Every time he had an opportunity to meet with an executive who was responsible for assignments, he expressed his wish to be reassigned to the island. Unfortunately his requests fell on deaf ears. It was obvious that his requests were rejected because his superiors didn't wish to add more problems to the existing distribution problem confronting the Oma island project.

He thought of resigning several times, but he didn't have the courage to do so. This lack of courage was not because his request had been rejected, but instead because he couldn't find a good reason within himself for wanting to return. He still wasn't prepared to answer to Elder Hwang and San-guk who had made him leave the island. They said that because the island desired to be free they couldn't forgive him. Elder Hwang explained that the islanders had acted in the name of freedom while the director had acted in the name of love. And he understood this, expressing gratitude but he refused to acknowledge his way of acting in the name of love. He couldn't accept it. Elder Hwang didn't want to believe freedom existed within love now that freedom could be attained in the name of love. He only talked about what love symbolized but he could neither feel it nor actually believe in it. In the end, Elder Hwang drove him from the island. The director still could not understand that the island's freedom and his love had to be exclusive. He still could not understand why his method of love could not be accepted by the islanders and why it could not exist in concert with their freedom. Unless he understood this clearly, even if he were to be reassigned, he couldn't return. Returning would be meaningless.

He waited for five years. He waited for a revelation of how the island's freedom and his love could be reconciled, and he waited for an answer to the riddle of why the islanders' desires and his methods could not be accepted. Then one day, the director received a letter. It was from Sanguk who had left the island before him. With that one letter, the director understood everything. Finally he resigned from the Masan hospital. Then he returned to the island. But this time, he came not as the hospital director, but as an individual who wanted to do something for the island.

It had been two years since he had returned to the island. The islanders continued to call him Director Cho. After two years, he still couldn't find a solution to the problem of Oma island. He carried on a seemingly endless battle with his invisible opponents. Now he wasn't even director. When he set foot on the island again, he thought that would be the best way to resolve the invisible tension between him and the islanders. He thought his position as an ordinary person would help bring together their idea of freedom and his idea of love. But in reality, that was not the case. It turned out to be another failure.

Chŏngt'ae did not know all of these details. He neither guessed nor had he heard how the director had come to the island in the first place. He also didn't know the circumstances that had led him to decide to return. But he had a particular interest in the fate of the island and the islanders, as well as in the director's persistence. Even after the director left the island, Chongt'ae continued to be interested in the things that were taking place there.

One day, he heard that Director Cho had returned to the island and so Chŏngt'ae decided to pay him a visit. He wanted to hear why he had left the island, why he had resigned his position in

Masan, and the circumstances leading up to his return. Even in Chongt'ae's eyes, the Oma island project was a complete failure. He had a feeling that if he met the director, he could hear directly from him his thoughts on why the project had failed. For the past few years, he had wanted to visit the island and meet him, but he simply hadn't found the right opportunity to do so.

Finally the opportunity came. He heard that an unusual wedding would take place that April when the cherry blossoms covered the entire island. The one who had brought about this union was none other than Cho Paeghŏn himself.

—Was he up to something again?

Chŏngt'ae decided to visit the island. At the end of March, on a warm Sunday morning, he got on the ferry.

When he finally reached Director Cho's place after spending the night at an inn in Noktong village it was ten in the morning. The director had rented one of the official residences in the personnel zone. He was living a lonely life without a family, with one young woman, a former patient, looking after him. Although Chŏngt'ae went on a Sunday morning, the director wasn't home. Because it was Sunday morning, the streets were empty, the patients all having gone to church services. The director wasn't a Catholic, so he couldn't have gone to church. Instead, the young woman told Chŏngt'ae that he had gone up into the mountains to gather wood. She trudged off and came back with him a little while later.

"Look who's here! Aren't you the reporter Yi Chŏngt'ae?" The director still remembered him. Not only did he remember him but he actually appeared happy to see him.

"What a pleasant surprise! What brings you here again?"

He had returned hurriedly and there wasn't even a single weed in his basket. When he entered the gate, he handed his shovel and hoe to the young helper and walked toward Chongt'ae with arms wide open as if he were going to hug him. He looked delighted to see him, as if he had been yearning for company for a long time. He grabbed his hands even before dusting off his own. Without asking why he had come, he pulled him inside the house. He made him sit alone on a *tatami* in a waiting room and scurried about trying to prepare something for his guest. He washed his hands, changed his clothes and then he told the young helper to bring various things from the store.

"If Chŏngsun is around in the waiting room, ask her to bring in something to drink. I have a guest."

"I'm not going to meet anyone today so bring some liquor and some side dishes."

"And later, go down to the Kura Inn and ask Old Ch'oe to prepare a room for our guest."

Without asking Chŏngt'ae what his plans were, he instructed her to do this and that, deciding everything himself, as if he knew why Chŏngt'ae was visiting the island. In any case, Chŏngt'ae would need to spend one or two days on the island to cover the wedding. The director finally sat down to talk to him. They could drink to their hearts' content.

"Let's drink. I know you've come to see the wedding but since the date is set for the first of April, you still have a few more days. The cherry blossoms have to be in full bloom. We can drink plenty before then, don't you think?"

30

Soon after the tea had been brought in, some liquor was brought in. The two of them emptied their cups as if they had not had a drink in a long time. After a little while, Chŏngt'ae came to a realization. Director Cho had not been a good-natured person. He had been serious. And rather than magnanimous, he had been honest to a fault. Yet the man Chŏngt'ae saw before him was now unbelievably jovial, boisterous even. As he got more and more drunk, his boisterousness became cloaked in an aura of madness of which he was apparently unaware.

But Chŏngt'ae knew. The director had not really become a jovial and good-natured person. Chŏngt'ae perceived a secret agony in his loud and boisterous laugh; he felt both his loneliness and his hope. He knew that bottled up in this silence were so many things he had endured that he wanted to talk about. Chongt'ae himself knew how difficult and lonely it was to endure these kinds of things in silence. He sensed how desperately the director wanted to talk to someone to share his anguish.

"I want to show you something. Can you tell me what that is?"

After the director had become a little drunk, he relaxed so much that he began using familiar terms of address. After they had finished the first bottle and a second one had been brought in, he suddenly pointed at something in a corner of the room as if he had just remembered it.

"I thought you would have asked me...what does it look like to you? That thing in the corner there."

He pointed to something that looked like the stump of a large tree. The bark had been peeled off so it was white, and there were some black spots here and there as if it had been scorched by a flame.

"That? Isn't it a tree stump?"

Chŏngt'ae didn't quite know why he had asked. But that wasn't what the director meant.

"You're right. It's a tree stump with the bark peeled off. But that's not what I asked you."

"What is it that you asked then?"

"I wanted to know whether you could call that a work of art. You must know since you've been to exhibits in the city. Have you seen anything like it at those exhibits?"

"You mean to tell me you trimmed that stump to be some sort of a sculpture?"

"No. I only dug it out of the ground and stripped the bark off. Then I trimmed it. And then it began to look kind of like a sculpture. Isn't it beautiful? So..."

When the director's young helper said he had gone up the mountain to get some wood, she meant that he had gone in search of dead tree stumps. He hadn't started this yesterday since there were lots of stumps all over the house.

"If you think it's beautiful, isn't that enough for it to be a work of art?" He was cautious with his answer.

The director wasn't quite satisfied with his answer.

"No. I'm not looking for that kind of answer. I want certainty. What I mean is, I want others to be convinced, too. Not just me, I want others to think of this as a work of art. Can others see and appreciate the beauty in this tree stump?"

"..."

Rather unexpectedly, the director was talking about the nature of art. Indeed he was inquiring about the dialogue between a creator and his creation—the rapport and spiritual communion between an artist and his material. This was one aspect of his madness. Chŏngt'ae sat in silence, at a loss for words.

"I often think that there are many beautiful and precious things on this earth as long as you try to see them. But unless you look for them, these things don't easily reveal their beauty. You can't possibly see them. So many beautiful things are hidden from us, they disappear without ever really being seen by anyone."

When Chŏngt'ae didn't say anything, the director continued enthusiastically. His eyes glittered and he spoke as if he was being pressed.

"That stump is a good example. When you go up the mountain, there are lots of those stumps hidden under ground. If you left them alone, they'd all rot and disappear. But when I go up the mountain and dig them out of the ground and find their roots, their beauty returns and starts talking to me. People these days, in an attempt to find the essence of reality, break windows with their bare hands. Some even try to tie ropes here and there. But this stump doesn't require that much effort. No need to embellish it. It has its own natural beauty. One needs only to find its hidden beauty. One needs only to find the roots that are left buried in the ground to rot. Can this be art? Why can't you call this art?"

"But it looks like you did more than just dig it out of the ground. What are these scorched spots? Didn't you do that on purpose? The stumps were not enough by themselves, so maybe you tried to create some sort of effect to realize your vision..." Chŏngt'ae paid more attention to the spots. The director's answer was sincere and clear.

"Ah, those! They're the traces of my conversations with the stumps."

"Traces of your conversations?"

"When you're worn out from fighting, you need to talk to yourself. You probably know that there are only so many battles you can fight. The Oma island reclamation project, the patients' invisible rebellion...Because of a shortage of physicians, I sometimes help out with the operations, but the tension and anxiety during an amputation...Waiting endlessly is an unendurable struggle, too. But then there isn't a visible opponent to struggle with; no neighbors to talk to. I had to talk, even to myself. Of course there are many ways to talk to oneself. Drinking, going up to the mountain to dig out stumps…If that wasn't enough, I would heat up a poker and jab them, scorching them like that. It felt as though I was burning my own skin. After that I would feel less burdened and frustrated. Those black wounds are the traces of my conversations with the stumps. That was the only way to survive. I didn't do it to create art."

Does a sculptor truly have a conversation with his material every time he creates something new? Can the spiritual communion between a person and the piece of work be this fierce?—Listening to the director, Chŏngt'ae thought that his stumps could well be precious works of art. If the director helped revive the beauty within these stumps by digging them out of the ground, had conversations with them and, by having this spiritual communion, he felt comforted, then these stumps possessed the true meaning of art. As the director said, if both the beauty of the stumps and the spiritual communion between the stumps and the director could be expressed to others, these stumps should be considered art. At least Chŏngt'ae certainly understood it.

The stumps with their scorched black spots began to turn into living things, transformed into beautiful saviors that expressed the director's words and spirit. It wasn't clear whether he was aware of this. Perhaps they symbolized the fierce relationship and the unresolved issues between the director and the islanders. This was another manifestation of his madness. At times, the director looked as if he was full of confidence but at other times he looked like a powerless middle-aged man. Regardless of whether he wore a look of confidence or fatigue, Chŏngt'ae could sense his insanity and felt the waves of anxiety that undulated with terrible emotions.

"You've been on the island so long you've gone crazy."

He couldn't help but spit out what was on his mind. He really thought that the director was going crazy. But he didn't think he was in any danger. As for Chŏngt'ae he was glad to have found the director like this. When he recognized the director's insanity, he felt the burden of wanting to visit the island again that he had carried inside for so long had been lifted.

"You think I'm crazy? Do I look crazy to you?" Surprised by Chŏngt'ae's words, he stared at him. But Chŏngt'ae knew the director was not angry with him. There was no need for either of them to get angry. The director knew this too.

"Well, I guess you can say that. In fact, I hear it from the islanders from time to time. I know," the director said, a bit weakened.

"But I'm not embarrassed. If I hadn't gone crazy like this, I wouldn't be able to endure life on this island. I needed to go crazy to endure it. Don't you get it? You can't stay on this island without going crazy!"

"I'm not trying to put you down." Chŏngt'ae's voice was calm now. He really believed that the director could not sustain himself without going crazy.

"I'm not trying to pass judgment on the fact that you're going crazy. Personally, I feel fortunate to see you this way."

"Fortunate?" the director stared at Chŏngt'ae with a puzzled expression.

"Actually I have a reason for coming to the island. I didn't come here to drink with you."

"Of course. I'm sure you have a reason for coming. The wedding will take place the day after tomorrow."

"Yes, I have to see the wedding ceremony. But there's something even more important."

"What's more important than that?"

"I guess you could call it the dismantling of a giant idol?"

"..."

"Actually I'm indebted both to the island and to you in a strange way. I guess it's something of a question I need to settle..."

"..."

"When the Oma island reclamation project began, I wrote an article for a magazine about you and the islanders. I guess it was about a month after I left the island, after I worked for a week at the construction site. The article I wrote ended up leaving a question unanswered for me. I remember warning you before I left that if you kept waiting, the patients would betray you. But after I'd left, I actually wrote something that was the exact opposite. I said that the Oma island project would eventually succeed. I insisted that, with your iron will and tenacity, the project would succeed."

"Are you saying that your own article remains an embarrassment for you?"

"Yes. You were depicted as the greatest of heroes in my article. But what was the result? The construction was completed but the results were far from what you had imagined in the beginning, right? There's no sign of the problem having being solved and you're still waiting. I'm certain you'll agree on this point."

"I guess you consider the reclamation project a complete failure."

"At this point in time, there's no other way to see it."

"Since you created a false hero, you feel responsible now for what you wrote..."

"I'm glad you follow me. Yes. If I have to be responsible for creating a false hero, don't you think I should correct the mistake and write an accurate account of that hero now?"

"Just write that the former hero was an impostor."

"It's not that easy. Let's say that you resolve the problem of Oma island in favor of the islanders—

you could still be a hero. But the problem is not as simple as being excused for the article by your settling the Oma problem."

"..."

"I didn't depict you as a hero for your sake, I created a hero for the entire island. Now that the situation is as it is, I wonder if it was really necessary to create such a hero. I'm beginning to have my doubts. I heard that the patients continued their escapes. There's not a single person who dreams of finding their paradise on the island. Because of the problems with Oma island, the patients' lack of trust has intensified...The hero failed in the end. The hero's failure is more painful and lonely. It was an unendurable misfortune, even for the island. I had to rewrite the article. Why did the hero fail? Why did the island become more miserable under the hero? Did the island really need a hero? Where could the islanders find true happiness...?

"..."

"I'm sorry to say this, but all of my answers were unfavorable to you. The article I need to write is extremely unflattering."

"Then, simply write that Cho Paeghŏn was a

wretched impostor. Why are you carrying this as if it were a great burden?"

"It's not that simple. Even if you failed, I still believe in your sacrifice and your good intentions. The relationship between the ruler and the ruled needed to be understood in the context of these two things. It doesn't work just with one-sided good intentions and enthusiasm. You failed not because you didn't have enthusiasm or good intentions, but because of the poor relationship between you and the patients. So even if I write an unfavorable article, I don't want to betray your good intentions. That would be an unbearable torture for you as well. I wanted to salvage you as a person. But in my article, I couldn't find a way to do this. I guess it was because I didn't know you well enough. But meeting you today..."

"Now you know how?"

"I think so."

"How?"

"Looking at you going crazy...I think you found a way to save yourself from the island. If I write about your craziness, I can save you as a person."

"Thanks. I'm grateful that you've been thinking

about redeeming me for so long, but…" The director looked into Chŏngt'ae's face as if to say thank you. But Ch'ŏngt'ae didn't know if the director was truly grateful or not.

"Since you seriously thought about salvaging me, I have the burden of explaining my failure. Now that you've figured out a way to save me, what you need to do next is to find answers to why this island failed." He said it in a way that seemed to say that Chŏngt'ae could ask whatever questions he might have about the island. Even though he said it like this, Chŏngt'ae saw in his eyes that the director didn't really want to acknowledge his failure.

"Well, let's have a look around the island then. I think it's better to judge after seeing it for yourself, rather than listening to me. I know you're already familiar with the island, but things have changed since…" The director meant that Chŏngt'ae needed to see with his own eyes the changes on the island to judge whether it had failed and, if it had, what had caused that. The director stood up as if he intended to show Chŏngt'ae around the island himself.

31

Director Cho had his reasons for wanting Chŏngt'ae to see the island and judge for himself what had gone wrong. As Chŏngt'ae followed the director around the island, he noticed there were many new things. The cherry trees bordering the roads were already covered with their pink blossoms. When they were in full bloom, the trees would be like flower clouds—screaming and yelling with riotous color. Some of the branches that reached southward had already blossomed but this was just the prelude to a chorus. In the fields below the tree-lined streets, the spring breeze combed through the rows of barley as if through a woman's silken hair.

The island was more peaceful and pleasant than what he had imagined. It hadn't changed much; what had changed were the people and their daily routine. As he looked around the island, Chŏngt'ae realized that lots of things had changed. After the director had come to the island, the barbed wire dividing the two zones had been taken down. The prohibition against patients crossing over into the personnel zone had also been lifted and now everyone could come and go as they pleased. Next to the main office in the personnel zone was a break room set up like a tearoom and the girls working there were all former patients who only had slight blemishes. Director Cho's helper was also one of these former patients who now had free access to the personnel zone. Chŏngt'ae remembered that on the ferryboat there had been both healthy people and patients.

"We try to encourage the cured to work, not only to give them independence and confidence, but also to increase understanding of the disease among their families and the staff as a way of eliminating bias. This is not my doing but that of the present director. I only made a few suggestions here and there," the director explained. The families and staff were dissatisfied with the director's decision at first, but after a while, they began to overcome their prejudices. They were able to walk into the break room and treat even the girls with the blemishes normally.

Former patients were also working at Kura inn. There were lots of visitors from the mainland who came both to encourage the patients and to gain a better understanding of them. There had been no accommodations for visitors before. If someone had to spend the night, they were either housed in the director's residence or they had to cross back over to Noktong and spend the night there. They would return to the island the following morning. It was inconvenient and so Kura inn was built to provide rooms for those who came from far away. It was like a regular inn and was located between the hospital and the director's residence. Originally it had been managed by healthy people but, after the new director came, he changed the staffing. He arranged for former patients with minor blemishes to manage it. The director had made a reservation for Chŏngt'ae there.

"The people who visit are particularly sympathetic and are supposed to come away from their visit with a better understanding of the disease. So, it's fitting that the patients manage the inn. In reality, though, many unfortunate things happen. The guests refuse to eat anything that the patients have prepared. Some think it is a regular inn but once they see the former patients working there, they don't even want to use the linen. To save face, they can't flatly say no and so they usually end up spending a fitful night before leaving early the next morning. I guess that's only natural." Director Cho smiled sardonically and added that even those who came with the intention of improving the patients' living conditions and help eradicate the unfairness of anti-leper prejudice couldn't entirely accept them.

In any case, the island was changing. The preschool that had separated healthy children from their diseased parents had been closed and the children now lived with their parents. Few children had developed symptoms since then. Anybody could take the ferry to the mainland. There were several new recreational facilities for the patients, such as a park, a monument based on a poem ("Barley Pipe"), and a deer zoo. Moreover, for the young people, a book club had been started and people had become active both reading and writing. In each village, choirs and music appreciation clubs, mostly comprised of students, young men and women, in particular, had been organized. Every village now had a chapel and had become a place for spiritual cleansing. With the Oma island reclamation project and the soccer team as starting points, the unruly lives of the islanders had seemingly gained some stability.

For many years, the island had been governed by a director as its absolute ruler. The director was the king and the island his kingdom. It was evident that this island was now dreaming of a new form of rule, based not on restrictions but on harmony. In a way, reading, writing, taking walks in the park, singing, and going to church to pray reinforced the patients' emotional stability. But these things were also the result of their increasing self-confidence and their burgeoning independence as distinct individuals. Before, the island and the patients had existed really only as a group. But this transformation from group to individual symbolized their newfound freedom from the former absolute rule.

The island was changing, being liberated bit by bit from the oppressive bonds of numerous regulations and restrictions. Chŏngt'ae was not entirely sure but he felt pleased to see the changes. And, in just a few days, a miraculous event would take place. Haewŏn and Miyŏn's wedding was quite meaningful to Chŏngt'ae.

There had been wedding ceremonies on the island before, but castration of the lepers was against the divine will. One of the peculiar characteristics of leprosy was that even the most severely infected patients could still reproduce. Even though the rest of their body might rot and decay, not so their reproductive organs. This could not simply be a coincidence, it was the will of the Creator. And the patients would not disobey divine will. They formed a family among themselves. Rather than having elaborate wedding ceremonies, the majority of them resorted to simple church ceremonies and their neighbors' blessings to unite as one.

But this time it was different. It was not a marriage between patients; it was between a healthy woman and a former patient. Even though Haewŏn was cured, he still counted himself as one of the diseased and Miyŏn knew the situation well. It was truly to be an eventful day.

"When I came back from Masan," the director explained, "they were still not married. The wedding was originally scheduled for the day of the connecting ceremony, but all of a sudden Sanguk left the island so they broke off their wedding. Haewŏn's long-standing hatred toward healthy people flared up again when he witnessed Sanguk leaving the island at a difficult time. All of Miyŏn's efforts were for naught. Haewŏn's jealousy toward Sanguk turned once again into a hatred of women. He was incorrigible in that way. But what made it worse was that his sister, who lived in the patients' zone, committed suicide. He came to the island and got sick because of his unusual attachment to his sister. When I came back to the island he turned into an alcoholic and Miyŏn was waiting for him. It was incredible that they both got transferred to an elementary school in Chungang village together, after the preschool was closed. So, I decided to act as a go-between...Of course, I had my reasons for doing so." The director explained the circumstances leading up to the wedding. In any case, the wedding ceremony was going to happen and the preparations were in full swing.

The reception was arranged with the support of the present director. He had built a house for Haewŏn and Miyŏn in the buffer zone between the patients' zone and the personnel zone where the barbed wire once stood. It was to show that there was no need for the healthy and the diseased to live apart. Director Cho's intention was to increase the number of houses where both healthy people and patients lived together and transform entire villages into places where segregation no longer existed. And this was not all. To add to the festive mood, he planned to hold one of the long forsaken soccer matches. He also set the wedding date early in April and announced it to the nearby villages so that the many visitors rushing to the island to see the cherry blossoms would also know about the wedding. He asked the minister at the Chungang village church to conduct the ceremony and entrusted the decoration of the church to the teachers in the patients' zone.

Many things had changed, more than what Chŏngt'ae had thought on the ferry. There were a few strange things. He saw no excitement on the faces of patients who should have been elated with the wedding preparations. They worked silently with no outward signs of joy. He couldn't understand this. What was more bizarre was that even after getting rid of the oppressive regulations, the escapes continued. When just enough time had passed that they had been forgotten, they started up once again. Now that he had looked around the island, he could perhaps change his mind about it. But he couldn't be certain. The expression on the director's face and his words made him hesitate. He thought that he still didn't have a clear understanding of the island. In terms of what he had seen so far, the island had certainly changed. He couldn't say that they had only repeated their failures. It could be that only the director had failed, not the island. The reason for the continued escapes could be attributed to Director Cho's obsessive perfectionism and his inability to resolve the Oma island project. It was understandable that the director's personal failure was exaggerated as the entire island's failure.

Chŏngt'ae wasn't sure. Ignoring his hesitance, the director hurried him from one place to the next that might pique his interest. On their way to a special patients' ward that had been a critical failure next to the church in Chungang village, the director revealed a problem that was completely different from what they had been discussing up to then.

"There is one problem," the director said abruptly with a concerned look as if he had just remembered something.

"Haewŏn…is asking for something…Since you'll hear about it soon enough, I'll tell you now. He insists on having that dammed castration before the wedding." Haewŏn threatened that he would cancel the wedding if he didn't have the surgery.

"What's his reason? I mean, he decided to go through with the wedding." The director smiled sardonically at Chŏngt'ae's question.

"Castration was the island custom most resented by the patients. Even now the hospital encourages it. Just like the young women you often see on this island who get eyebrow tattoos when they want to get married, for the young men, it's castration. Opposition to it is intense as well. The fact that Haewŏn wants it done and the hospital's refusal to consent has created a lot of tension. The hospital is in an awkward position."

"Why not?" Even though Chŏngt'ae could vaguely guess the reason, he asked.

"It's because his demand isn't a simple expression of rebellion. It comes from a deep mistrust and profound disappointment."

"In what way?"

"He says that the island has been ruled by selling out the lepers' children. The present has been governed in the name of the future of the islanders' children. But the island failed, and so the present has been deceived in the name of future; but on this island the present is more important than the future. Because of this, the rebellion continues. The rebellion is fundamentally based on failures of the present and not on a rejection of the future. The lepers have continued their rebellion to avoid being deceived once again. Not wanting to have children is Haewŏn's way of emphasizing the failures of the present. So, the hospital has a dilemma. Carrying out the operation means acknowledging this failure of the present."

"Does the bride agree?"

"Well, Haewŏn claims she does, which is not surprising since Miyŏn herself is rash and daring. She is well aware of the island's situation…"

"So does that mean that both of them see the island as a complete failure?"

"Well, I'm not the one to judge whether they do or not, but since they don't want any children, they apparently only want to think about themselves. I understand that the present moment should be valued more…" The director said nothing after that. But when they entered the special wards situated next to the Chungang church, Chŏngt'ae saw the tragic reality of the hospital that could not otherwise be easily seen.

The first ward the director took Chŏngt'ae into was full of elderly patients missing fingers, toes and, in the worst cases, arms and legs. Young patients who could move around freely attended to their needs. These young patients were all volunteers and came from the patients' zone. Most of the elderly patients either read the Bible or listened as their aids read to them. They listened quietly or closed their eyes and prayed. Since most of them were not able to move, they needed help with eating and going to the toilet. The next ward was full of patients who not only had lost limbs but important sensory organs, like their eyes, their ears or their noses. If they were able to see, they couldn't hear, if they could hear, they didn't have eyes or noses. They relied either on their vision, their hearing or their sense of smell. Again the young volunteers attended to their needs. The wretchedness of the situation could not be expressed in words.

The director quietly guided Chŏngt'ae to the last ward. The patients there were the most seriously afflicted. They had lost all of their sensory organs, except for their warped mouths. They had no limbs and their ears, noses, and eyes had dissolved into oblivion. They were nothing but lumps of flesh swaddled in gauze. They had lost their sight and hearing long ago. Even large parts of their mouths had been erased from their faces. When they tried to talk, only strange sounds came out. There were well over three hundred patients in the special ward.

"They live only to pray and to praise God. And they are grateful because they feel filled with God's blessings. They can't see, hear, or speak but God gladly listens to their prayers. We can't understand what they say, but God can. Nowhere else could human prayer be more sincere." He added a few more words as he left the ward. After that, he kept quiet for a while. He could only show him the truth, but he could no longer explain it. Following behind the director, Chŏngt'ae thought the same.

—How can they live like that? How can they pray and feel grateful....

This was a shocking experience, unlike any that Chŏngt'ae had ever had before. It was a strange feeling. He no longer needed to hear the director's explanations.

"I can't judge whether they see it as a failure or not. But I agree that the present should be given priority..."

The director's words rang in his ears once more. This was a part of the island that couldn't be related to the future. What the present could offer the patients was more important than anything the future could offer. Chŏngt'ae could now begin to see the vague outlines of what had been hidden from view and the underlying cause for the director's strange insanity. His long fight for the Oma reclamation project, the pressure of the islanders' silent rebellion, the doubts that constantly weighed on him, the prejudice of the mainlanders, his sincere hopes for the islanders—all of this was too much for any one man to endure. In this sense, all of the islanders were just as insane as the director. And that also symbolized a failure on the part of all the islanders.

32

Chŏngt'ae spent the night at Kura inn. Director Cho offered to let him stay with him if he didn't feel comfortable at the inn. But, under the pretext of making it back in time for dinner, Chŏngt'ae returned immediately to the inn after he'd left the patients' zone. He remembered what the director had said about visitors quickly leaving the following morning after spending a night there. Since he had worked at the Oma island construction site with the patients, the thought of spending the night at Kura inn didn't bother him.

But he still felt a little uncomfortable when he got back to his room. Despite the size of the inn, there was virtually no trace of staff or other guests. Chŏngt'ae seemed to be the only guest and an old man with a fingerless hand guided him to his room. Then he was left alone. There seemed to be no one else there. Around dinner time he heard a girl outside calling to him, "Sir, here's your dinner. Please put the dishes outside your door after you're done." When he opened the door to accept the dinner tray, the girl had already disappeared. After he was done eating, he put the tray outside the door. He didn't hear any sounds of someone coming to take it away. He didn't want to wait any longer for someone to come so he opened the door, but the tray was still there. After a little while, he opened the door again and it was gone. He hadn't heard any footsteps but some one had come to get it. Everything at the inn was done in this manner.

After he finished dinner, he got ready to go out but as he was leaving his room, the director suddenly showed up.

"I didn't think you'd be staying quietly in your room so I came by. You're on your way to see the bride and groom, aren't you?" The director said this decisively—as if he couldn't permit it—and pushed Chŏngt'ae back into the room.

It was true. Chŏngt'ae was about to go see Haewŏn and Miyŏn. He had to meet with them sooner or later and he felt compelled to hear from them the circumstances leading up to the wedding and how they felt now. After spending half a day with the director touring the island, he wanted to see them alone. That's why he had returned so quickly to the inn. Telling the director he needed to return to make it in time for dinner was simply an excuse to get away so that he could go see the couple.

"Yes, you guessed right! After all, I did come to write about their wedding."

"If you rush it, you'll ruin everything. You must understand that everything has its time. Sure, it's not a bad thing to hear that they're confident about their decision and that they're determined to show that a former patient and a healthy person can get married and live happily. But your unusual interest in their wedding already reveals your bias: you think patients and healthy people are different. Even though they're both determined and confident, they're still treading a fine line. I know that you want to meet them no matter what, but if you're really wishing for their happiness and for the happiness of the island, don't rush it. Wait until after the castration issue gets resolved. It won't be too late to talk to them after the wedding. I'll show you something interesting instead."

As soon as they had sat down, the director handed Chŏngt'ae an envelope.

"I'm not sure if you remember Yi Sanguk. He used to work here as head of the Hygiene Division but he left abruptly. It's from him. I got this letter when I was in Masan. If you read it, you'll get an idea of why the island was destined to fail. Didn't you say your main goal was to figure this out? You said that after you'd found a way to save me as a person, your next endeavor was to find an answer to why the island was doomed to failure."

Chŏngt'ae had to give up on his idea of seeing Haewŏn and Miyŏn for the time being. What the director had said was true. Even his generosity didn't seem coincidental.

"Can I read it now?" Chongt'ae asked, and the director said to go ahead. Then he called out in a loud voice toward the quiet hall outside the door.

"Is anyone there?...Bring something to drink. We have an important guest. We can't just let him go to bed like this. I want to take advantage of this myself and get drunk..."

Chŏngt'ae started to read the letter, showing no interest in drinking. The director explained that, five years after Sanguk had left the island, he had written a long letter that read something like a confession to him. The director had left the island by that time as well. As he read the letter, Chŏngt'ae understood why the director had come to visit him.

Inside the envelope Chŏngt'ae found two letters, both from Sanguk. One was addressed to the director when he was at Masan Hospital, which was five years after he had left the island; and the other seemed to have been written seven years earlier, just before Sanguk left the island. Apparently he had been carrying it around with him. Chŏngt'ae read the letter Sanguk had sent while the director was at Masan first.

Dear Director Cho:

It's quite embarrassing to write a letter…I'm sure you must be quite surprised to hear from me after all these years. But I've always wanted to write to you to express my belated gratitude and apologies after I left the island like that. I also wanted to explain why I had to flee the island as I did, even when I knew you'd be disappointed.

But I waited until today because I wasn't sure whether my reasons were truly justifiable. You already know my story so I'll be frank. I wasn't confident enough to explain why the islanders, including me, couldn't accept you and why I had to betray you by leaving the island. Even if I had excuses or reasons for doing so, I wasn't sure if it was something that I could easily explain.

At the time, I thought I was justified so I thought about explaining it in writing. But I never sent that letter. Instead, I went to see you one night and said all the wrong things. Then I left the island. It was because I had no confidence in my reasons even if they were sincere and truthful for both me and the islanders, I wasn't sure what would become of the island if we disavowed what we had accomplished together with you. Until today, I didn't have the confidence to explain why. That's why I kept the letter and read it from time to time after I left. Every time I read the letter, I asked myself about my own actions, your fate and that of the island. Then I waited.

But I couldn't find an answer. One thing that was clear to me was that I was always grateful to you for your devotion, your efforts and your sincere interest in the island. I couldn't completely accept your notion of a paradise even though I was thankful to you. At the time, I had no choice but to leave the island. Circumstances drove me to it.

You must think my reasons for leaving had to do with Haewŏn and Miyŏn. After I left, I heard a rumor that I was trying to break them up. You must have guessed the relationship between me, Haewŏn and Miyŏn. To be frank, yes, I was a little disturbed by them. I can't deny that, at the time, deep down, I was hoping for the island's destruction. One of my main reasons for running away was to show the islanders that a healthy man had the privilege to leave the island as he pleased. I heard later that you were particularly concerned about this. I apologize for bringing back unpleasant memories.

No matter how painful it is to think about, it's necessary to explain in detail why we couldn't accept the paradise you offered us. I waited so long to send you this letter and still don't have a satisfactory answer. Since you have a special interest in the island even now, I can only express my frustration at not having found an answer. If I were to find an answer, I would've sent you a letter long ago and returned to the island. If I were to talk only about my reasons for leaving and why, even to the end, the island couldn't accept your paradise, then I'd be able to give you some answers. I have told you this before in my other letter: it's because you and the islanders' walk a different path. No matter how much you sacrificed yourself in the interest of the islanders, you couldn't live like them. That's the reason why the paradise you tried to create couldn't be their paradise. You called it their paradise and they yours.

I realized how deep the gap was between each individual's fate after I left the island. Many different things have happened since then. Through my work, I tried to live harmoniously with people on the mainland. But I couldn't adapt to their lifestyle and their everyday consciousness. I couldn't forget the island. The people on the mainland made me think of the island and myself. It was impossible to live among them like I'd never lived on the island. Even when I tried so hard to become like them, it was nothing but hiding my true self. It was difficult to live with a self that had no courage and patience. I'm trying very hard to endure until the feeling that I'm living in hiding vanishes.

In any case, the reason why you couldn't reach a mutual understanding with the islanders was because of your different lives. The islanders had to exercise the particular type of freedom that their fate had taught them and they had to live in the name of that freedom. I know you understand that the repeated escapes were premised on this freedom. But something was wrong. Their purpose wasn't to create friction. Escaping wasn't their sole purpose, either. There was nothing other than friction and escape. Nothing could be accomplished on the island and nothing was accomplished. Even this wasn't their goal. The patients' didn't want to see the island fail. Somehow so many things went wrong.

I still don't understand why things went wrong, where the mistakes came from, why they were repeated, and what needed to be done to correct them. I understood finally that I couldn't share my life with the people on the mainland. Even though I was away from the island, I was fated to spend my life on the island. I knew I had to return some day. You left the island too. Five years have passed since you left. But you know what's happening on the island. I also believe you now have a deeper understanding of the island. I hope to learn much from you when I see you. I can ask you this because you're off the island.

I know it's late but before I close I want to thank you again for all your sincere efforts to create something on the island. Although nothing was accomplished despite your hard work, I pray that your efforts will remain in the minds of the islanders forever.

Sanguk's first letter ended there. In the postscript he added that he was also enclosing a letter he had written at the time he left the island. Whether it really was that letter or not was unclear. It was an apology to the director for the anguish he had caused him.

"So, the letter that he enclosed was written five years ago. I received both letters two years ago when I was still working at the hospital in Masan." After keeping quiet for a while, the director spoke. He was sitting in front of a little table with drinks on it.

Chŏngt'ae took out the second letter and started to read it, not paying much attention to him. The second letter was longer and biting.

Dear Director Cho:

I'm not sure whether I will actually send this letter to you. Even now I am not convinced that the decision I have made is right. I still don't have an explanation or even a justification for what I'm doing. I have to leave the island. I have no choice but to do this. It's clear that I have to leave and I'm about to leave now. Nothing can be done to stop me.

Even though I cannot explain my motives nor justify my actions, I have to leave. Since I'm about to leave, I want to take this opportunity to say some things that I've been holding back. I feel that this is the least I can do. If I do mail this, by the time you read it, I'll be gone. I may be a coward, but at least this way I can be more honest with you.

First, I'd like to say that it's time you left the island. My desire for you to leave didn't start yesterday. As you know, the day you came, I didn't trust you. I doubted your intentions and had my guard up. I had hoped you'd leave without regret when the time came. Now is the time.

Perhaps you still don't understand why I had my guard up and why I wanted you to leave. If I may, I will explain some fundamental misunderstandings you have of the island. Your biggest mistake was when you planned to build a paradise on this island—a paradise for lepers. You certainly promised the patients that you'd make this island their paradise and you really believed that, with sincere effort, the island could be transformed into a hometown that five thousand lepers could be proud of. You believed in yourself. So you worked hard for several years to make this a better place and I can't deny that you deserve to be commended for what you've done so far.

But to tell you the truth, your paradise was flawed from the very beginning. I'm not trying to bring up Director Shū's paradise again this time. I don't intend to point out your mistakes by evoking the ghost of Shū's statue. Thanks to all your efforts the islanders' long distrust that originated with Shū's statue has by now dissipated. You suppressed your personal desires, endured the shadow of the statue and proved your true intentions to those who constantly doubted you. I don't worry about you wanting to build your statue anymore. What I've been concerned with and what worries me even now is not your reasons for wanting to build a paradise. Despite your sincerity, you are the embodiment of that paradise.

Who are you building this paradise for? Whose paradise is it? I know you wanted to build it for the five thousand poor and wretched patients and you still believe it to be so. But I have evidence that you aren't entirely confident when you say that the paradise you are building right now will actually be their paradise. Your paradise is built with a high barbed wire fence. A barbed wire paradise can be no one's true paradise.

I know you want to retort, "what barbed wire?" You destroyed the barbed wire that separated the personnel and the patient zones. But you can't really believe that taking down the physical barbed wire also meant destroying the imaginary wall. You must have guessed that this invisible fence—much more than the visible one—was the one that really governed the patients. Perhaps by taking down the actual barbed wire, you secretly built a stronger and thicker enclosure around the island.

I said to you once that we don't live the present as a finality. Even if the present moment is satisfying, if there's no possibility that the present can be enriched in the future, there can be no paradise.

Paradise with neither choice nor change is an unendurable hell. So what is your paradise? What kind of paradise are you creating? To be honest, the paradise you're creating was yours long before it could truly be theirs. Perhaps it's a paradise only for you. You want to create a paradise where the patients can enjoy their lives to the end. You believe it should be a paradise where they can enjoy themselves, not a place where one can change or where one can abandon tomorrow. You want to create a paradise that can't be spurned.

But if it is a true paradise, the choice should be given first to the patients and they should be able to abandon that paradise if it means a betterment of their lives. A true paradise depends not so much on its design and how great it may appear, but more on the degree to which choices are allowed. Paradise without choice can't be a paradise forever. You and the others had hoped that the patients would believe it to be so. When the mainlanders saw it as the patients' paradise it only became their paradise, not the patients'. And when they tried to make this a perfect paradise, it became a suffocating hell for the patients. Ultimately you were building a new kind of barbed wire fence. Invisible yet higher and crueler.

This is not the only proof that your paradise is enclosed by an invisible wall. The real reason that your paradise could never be their paradise is your prejudice—prejudice as an outsider. You weren't trying to create a paradise for everyone, it was a paradise for the abused lepers who had been chased off the mainland. This is precisely the reason your paradise is surrounded by barbed wire. You want this paradise to be their hometown where they can live in peace and harmony. Taking their sad history and customs into consideration, you created special regulations that were only appropriate for lepers. Of course, these new regulations and customs couldn't be accepted by the healthy people and they couldn't get used to them. You wanted the lepers to stay in this paradise with no one wanting to leave. "Your paradise is here in front of your eyes." You called the patients who tried to escape from the island traitors.

A paradise for lepers—here is where another invisible wall was built. Even though they're afflicted with disease, they also share the basic human desire to realize their dreams. Just because they lead a different kind of life doesn't mean that their dreams should be different. Even if they've forgotten that, we can't. We have to make sure that we constantly remind them that their dreams shouldn't be different.

You're not trying to build a paradise for humans but for lepers. From the very beginning, your paradise was one that made sure that all the lepers stayed in one place and were prevented from leaving. Your plan to create a paradise on the island was, in many ways, identical to the other policies that threatened the patients, telling them that once they left the island, they would be unable to avoid abuse and retaliation. Yours was different in form but in the end it had the same effect. You only tried to understand them as lepers, people who could be accepted under special conditions with certain compromises. You didn't try to understand them as normal people. In that way, you made them build your leper paradise.

For the poor, paradise is where wealth is abundant, and for the sick, where health can be regained. For the ones who really lack, they can certainly call this their paradise. But it can never be a paradise for everyone. "You poor souls have never been accepted by anyone off the island. Your past is painful and is full of terrible wounds." So the "paradise" you have designed is nothing more than a temporary respite for the indigent and a hospital for the ailing. As long as they have hopes and the desire to live as normal people, your paradise is a form of terrorism, constantly violating their hope.

An enclosed paradise cannot be a true paradise. You've never given a thought to the wall and even now you refuse to acknowledge it. The faith you had in your paradise was strong and unchanging. Then you wondered why the patients couldn't accept it. You wanted to say there was no reason for them to reject your paradise since your choices aligned perfectly with theirs. Perhaps they could have accepted your kindness on faith, but faith was precisely the problem. Unfortunately the patients are unable to have unconditional faith. Because they couldn't trust you unconditionally, they couldn't fully accept your choices and your paradise.

It's not entirely your fault that they couldn't completely trust you. From the beginning, you've been leading different lives. For the patients, the island had to be their eternal paradise whereas for you, it didn't have to be. Your paradise wasn't for the rest of your life. Actually it wasn't even for you. You didn't deny the fact that some day you would leave the island. Regardless of your reasons, the circumstances that led to your departure proved this. You could never share your entire life with the patients and that's why there couldn't be complete trust. Because one can't truly experience someone else's fate. You can't have absolute trust between people living with different destinies. And to them your love and concern could only be seen as narcissistic, self-indulgent pity. They couldn't possibly have accepted a paradise from someone whom they couldn't trust. Perhaps it's not entirely your fault. You and the patients have different destinies. The problem still remains. Paradise for lepers has its limitations. It's that invisible enclosure, the barbed wire. Without realizing it, you gradually built it higher and higher on this island paradise for lepers. Whether you did it intentionally or not, you managed to govern quite well within the enclosure.

I'm not writing this letter to go over what you did wrong. I'm interested in how this enclosed paradise you built has changed and how it will change in the future. To get to the point, I need to tell you about the escapes and what they symbolize. Because the escapes you so despised were the ultimate betrayal of your paradise.

The escapes started when they could no longer endure the abuse and hard labor. Despite the promises, the endless labor and oppression turned this island into an unendurable hell. From then on, one by one, they started to escape from the island. Some escaped to see their families and some left because they heard rumors that on the mainland there was medicine that could cure the disease. But you said that there was no need for the escapes because there was neither cruel labor on the island nor truth to the mainland rumors. The regulation that once they set foot on the island they could not leave had long been abolished. If they wanted, they could simply leave without attempting a dangerous escape from the Tolburi shore. There was a time when those who regained their health were encouraged to leave since there were so many patients. There was no need for them to attempt escape.

But what was really going on? The escapes continued for a while. When you came, they caused a major headache. Why was that? I think it was immediately after you came that I took you to the Tolburi shore and explained their reasons for escaping. "The hospital no longer keeps the patients against their will. We're doing our best to encourage them to leave. Even those who aren't completely cured can request a leave for a certain period of time. They can leave and come back. But no one has taken advantage of this. Whenever they get a chance, they risk their lives and try to escape from the Tolburi shore."

At the time you didn't understand that those who refused to leave the island when given the chance and those who risked their lives to escape were one and the same. You couldn't solve this conundrum. I remember explaining it to you in terms of "patient" and "human." Now I can explain their contradictory actions, which you had a difficult time understanding, as "patient" and "human." As I mentioned before, those who couldn't leave even if they wanted to were the "patients." They were driven to this island because they were afflicted with the disease. Once they got here, the hospital staff filled them with fear, hatred and the sense of a curse as a way to keep them from getting the courage up to leave. "You came to the island after being mistreated on the mainland. There is no other place than this island where you can live comfortably. You have to live with others with the same disease. If you leave, abuse and cruelty await you and in the end will strike you down. Even before the hospital gets the chance to punish you severely, outsiders won't tolerate escape from here. They will take vengeance on you. As a diseased person, your life on the mainland would be hell..." This is the same thing you were saying with the Oma island project—you said it clearly when you took the elders to the site for the sake of the patients and not for your own sake. You tried to use the same reasoning when the embankments didn't appear even after they had dumped countless stones into the sea. When the embankments that finally surfaced were destroyed by the typhoon, you tried to encourage them by reminding them of the hostility they had experienced on the mainland.

In fact, you tried to threaten them in the same way that others have done in the past. You tried to instill in them fear and spite, turning them into nothing more than "patients" who would not—or could not—dare to leave. So, even when the hospital management told them they could leave, they became perfect patients. The fear that had been instilled in them couldn't be shaken off so easily. They could no longer leave the island. It was like being exiled to the land of the cursed.

Still, once in a while, they dream of liberation from their existence as "patients." They are human beings before they are "patients." Since they're human beings, they want to leave the island and seek a normal life. They want to rid themselves of their identity as "diseased" persons.

Of course, their hope was a betrayal of the island as well as of the hospital. When it started, they were in the process of becoming human, and were no longer simply patients. They were living dual lives—one as "patients" whose lives were different from those of the mainlanders and one as "humans" harboring their own cherished dreams. When they were forced to accept their lives as "patients," they were driven to a point where they wanted to escape, even if it meant risking their lives. That's why they chose to escape—to be free of this fear of the mainland, which had long been implanted in their minds. Eager to conquer these terrible fears of the outside world, they chose to escape, not as a road to banishment but rather as part of nurturing their hopes and having confidence in their choices.

Irrespective of where their motives lay and regardless of their success or failure, the escapes were an expression of their desperate struggle to break the shackles of bondage to the island. This was a successful form of revenge on a ruler who had been forcing this meaningless paradise on them against their will. They were fated to wait defenselessly for their time to be with God, so it was a worthwhile attempt on their part to take charge once and for all of their own lives. Their escapes were the last proof that they were still alive. It was also proof that this island wasn't a grave for sad spirits but that it could also be a place for living humans. As long as the escapes continued, there was still a thread of hope that it could be a place for the living. So, for the islanders the escapes meant supreme virtue.

But since you came, the escapes stopped. What did that mean? And what happened after they stopped? You probably think it was because the island was becoming a true paradise, with no barbed wire to jump over. Perhaps you want to say that they had woken up from the nightmare of escape and that the island had become a model place where all patients worked together to create a better place.

But is that really true? Is that why the escapes stopped? Proof that there was no longer any barbed wire? Was the island really becoming a paradise of hope?

No! I still don't believe this. Despite all your assurances, I can't help but doubt it. It's because the barbed wire didn't completely disappear from the island. Like all the previous directors, you had one thing you demanded. You wanted to make them perfect patients. And you accomplished this. The patients really did become "perfect" patients. They didn't try to leave the island. Not only did you not threaten them like the other directors had, but you also encouraged them to create the island themselves so that they would have no desire to leave it. You were able to instill in them dignity as patients. You didn't make them fear the visible wall, but you built an even higher one that couldn't be seen.

The more perfect as patients they became and the more proud they were of their paradise, the fewer there were who tried to jump over the wall. There is no wall safer, higher and stronger than a wall no one wants to jump over.

But what kind of paradise were you creating? It could only be a paradise for the patients. It existed only as a paradise after they had accepted their misfortune. The reason that your paradise could be their paradise was they had become accustomed to having their dreams restricted. The secret here was that the ruled became comfortable with being ruled just as a bridled beast soon gets comfortable being bridled. If that was enough for the patients, they would soon forget about escape and get used to your paradise.

Director, what's become of your paradise that escapes no longer happen? It's turning into an island of the dead. As the island gets closer and closer to your ideal paradise, it's becoming more and more like an island of dead souls who are shackled by your ideas. It is fast becoming an island of dead souls where it is impossible to find individuality. If you wanted to, you could easily turn the island into such a thing. Given what you've done, it wouldn't be difficult to persuade the islanders to do as you wish.

You probably don't like my saying that you can control them as you wish, but it's the truth. From my experience, the nature of a society surrounded by a wall depends not upon its inhabitants, but upon a handful of leaders. The directors on this island have demonstrated that, and you're no exception. Yes, you asked for as many people's opinions as possible, and you pretended to listen. You created the elders' council and always asked for their approval and their suggestions. But you have to admit the elders' council was nothing more than a puppet show. It was only a formality. They never proposed anything on their own, they only provided you with the necessary appearances. They helped make sure that your plans could be carried out smoothly. I'm not trying to rebuke the elders. They knew the situation and what was best for the islanders.

I was curious to what degree order would be established between the ruled and the ruler. Since you came, I've learned to what degree the rule of law is arrived at by a ruler and to what degree by the ruled. I realized that it was a useless fantasy. The barrier between the ruler and the ruled can't be torn down without the courage to sacrifice or become martyred. Regardless of the good intentions of the ruler and regardless of where the privilege to rule originates from, as long as the power to rule exists, the ruled have no choice but to give in, unable to endure. My sad conclusion is that irrespective of the hopes and prayers of the masses, only the ruler has the absolute power to change things. Everything is determined by the power of the sole ruler in this kind of miserable society.

The elders can't be blamed. You insisted on your paradise. By explaining clearly to the islanders that, once they left the island, they would be abused and cursed by the people on the mainland, the wall got higher and higher. By reminding them of the situation within that walled paradise, you could control them and the elders as you wished.

During the last couple of years, seeing the relationship between you and the patients, I've only managed to see how easily a ruler can subjugate his people. I haven't seen the birth of a brilliant order where the ruler and the ruled coexist as equals. Even if, within this enclosure, the ruler had only had good intentions to begin with and the ruled had properly guarded themselves against the ruler, if they didn't awaken to a proper understanding of this enclosure, the ruler would end up manipulating them, subjugating them. And so, in the end, the ruled would end up subjugated by the ruler, bending to his every wish.

As long as the wall exists, you are capable of this kind of maneuver. You certainly can create that kind of paradise on the island. But as I said earlier, this could never be the patients' paradise. They'd exist as slaves, maintaining the paradise. They would neither enjoy it nor benefit from it.

Director, now I will tell you my final reason for writing this letter. Don't try to complete your paradise. Don't leave the island after perfecting it. Your intention to leave the island after seeing the ceremony is wrong. Don't despair because you are leaving without seeing your paradise perfected. For the poor souls of the patients as well as for your own poor self, leaving now would be the wisest decision. If you insist on your paradise, the moment your dream is realized, a new type of betrayal and vengeance will emerge.

It may sound strange, but the patients were already enjoying the blessings of the paradise even before its completion. You already know this. In order to appease and persuade the islanders whom you managed, the blessings of the paradise had to be paid in advance. Even before the paradise had been attained, you made them adopt the dream of a future paradise. It was an easy way to control them. You made them pay today for tomorrow's dreams. For the patients, their present situation was unendurable so it was an effective way to rule. Whether you were conscious of this or not, for the past few years, you've been using the same tricks. You can't deny this. When their dreams of paradise are realized what will they gain from that paradise? They've already experienced the blessings in advance. Paradise can offer them nothing. A paradise where there are no blessings is no more than a suffocating enclosure that restricts them.

They'll start taking revenge. Treachery and betrayal will rear their ugly heads. It's because they already know that they've received their future paradise as an advance. And the betrayal will take place in the form of escapes. In the end, your paradise can never be and should never be realized. Even if the farms at Oma island become their new homes, they will never be a path for leaving Sorok Island. It'll be another perfect enclosure they can't leave. Please leave the island without any regrets. Don't threaten them by saying that another director will come and do the same thing to realize your dream. Even if another person comes with the same intentions, it has nothing to do with you. If you really want a paradise for them, you have to give them a chance to challenge themselves.

Your thinking that the island can't do without you, your arrogant declarations that your intentions are sincere and that you think of nothing but the welfare of the patients, only make the island into a miserable concentration camp. You can't share your life with the patients. For the last time, I want to express my deepest wish. To prove my sincerity, I will leave the island tonight. There's nothing more you or I can do for the island. The only thing left for me to do is to make you realize that there's nothing more you can do. I still remember the old way that the islanders proved themselves to be human—by escaping. An escape reminds those who live on the island and who will continue to live on it that this is not an island of the dead, but one for the living.

Director, please don't ignore my plea. I hope that merciful God will convey all of the meaning I couldn't express in this letter and I pray that God will convey everything my human words lack.

33

Yi Chŏngt'ae was quiet for a while after finishing the letters. "What a vicious attack!" he said finally, slowly lifting his head to look at Director Cho.

"I don't quite get why he had to attack you like this. Just like Sanguk said in the letter, it isn't clear why nothing worked out, why things happened the way they did."

The director's face was red from the alcohol he'd been drinking by himself while he waited for Chŏngt'ae to finish the letters. He filled a cup and handed it to Chŏngt'ae and smiled meaningfully.

"Well, it's natural that you don't understand. Sanguk himself wasn't sure why he felt compelled to criticize me like that, nor why he had to leave the island, nor why nothing we tried on the island worked. The answer was simple. You remember Elder Hwang, the second-in-command of the Oma reclamation project, don't you? He managed to explain it to me one day."

"What did he say?" Chŏngt'ae asked as he quickly emptied the cup. As he filled the cup again, the director continued slowly:

"Sanguk mentioned it in his letter, too. But according to Elder Hwang it was because everything was done in the name of freedom. You get freedom by fighting, so naturally conflict and distrust arise. Sanguk, too, talked about the island's freedom and acted in the name of that freedom but as he hinted at in the letter, he didn't fully understand its essence like Elder Hwang did. He didn't know how to explain the phenomena that emerged in the name of freedom. He couldn't figure out why the island changed as it did, why he had to abandon the island, and why he had to attack me like that. In his first letter, he wanted to ask me for answers. In the letter he wrote later he hinted at it, but he still hadn't found a satisfactory answer. Since the island couldn't accept me, he had no choice but to betray the island and me—just like the island's fated freedom. It was because he acted only in the name of freedom and was only concerned about that freedom."

"'By acting in the name of freedom, conflict and distrust are born. As a result, it was impossible for peaceful harmony...' Does this mean that Elder Hwang rejected the sort of freedom that was sought for on the island?" Chŏngt'ae asked.

Now they filled each other's cups. They were exchanging them in a seemingly endless parade, back and forth across the table.

"No. In the context of the island's long history and the islanders' experiences, freedom was the only thing they considered worthy of their effort. It was natural for them to act that way. What Elder Hwang was trying to say was that if the island failed because they only tried to act in the name of freedom, then there was something better than freedom that the islanders had to find."

"Did Elder Hwang know what that was?" Chŏngt'ae asked.

"He called it love. Unlike freedom that you struggle to gain, love comes from giving. Instead of producing hatred and resentment, which comes in the course of fighting for freedom, love teaches forgiveness. He said that I at least tried to love. The patients who should have acted in the name of love really acted only in the name of freedom. But I don't think he tried to distinguish between love and freedom. How can I put it? It was useless unless love and freedom could coexist. Acting in the name of love which includes freedom or vice versa produces the same result. It ultimately means that living by love and living by freedom are one and the same thing."

"If he knew that, why couldn't he live by love within that freedom? If you learned this from him, why weren't you able to live by freedom within that love? Elder Hwang talked about this, yet he made you leave the island, didn't he?"

"Looking back, I think it was because there was no mutual trust. Elder Hwang said that, without mutual trust, freedom couldn't exist and because we acted without trust, only conflict, hatred, and suspicion were left. No trust meant no love. Therefore love without trust was the same as not giving love. In this sense, love and trust were equal. But later when I thought about it, it was slightly different. It all depended on where one stood."

"What do you mean by that?"

"You see, the patients who were being ruled were in the position of acting in the name of freedom and I, who was the ruler, naturally had to act in the name of love. The ruler had to act in the name of love and those ruled in the name of freedom. In that way, the love of the ruler had to be accepted by the ruled and the freedom of the ruled had to be accepted by the ruler, both agreeing on the same harmonious path. In this way, the ruler and the ruled stood in different positions. I, the director, had to act in the name of love and the patients had to act in the name of freedom."

"Since both you and the patients weren't successful, does that mean there wasn't any mutual trust?" Chŏngt'ae kept asking questions. And Director Cho kept answering them, showing no sign of getting tired. Instead, he explained everything enthusiastically as if these explanations were his raison d'être.

"That's right. Because I couldn't gain their trust, I had to leave. At the time, I was confused. After explaining what I needed to do, Elder Hwang still didn't seem to want to seek that trust. I thought that he didn't have the answer to that problem. Freedom—freedom without trust—and distrust were part of the island's fate and Elder Hwang could do nothing about it. Elder Hwang explained it, hoping that I would leave the island. He had no intention of seeking mutual trust, making the patients learn to love. From the beginning, he had no faith in me. Later I learned the reason why he and I couldn't develop mutual trust. I learned this when I got Sanguk's letters five years after I'd left."

"You mean the ones I just read?"

"Yes. Only after I read his letters did it dawn on me. I understood why Elder Hwang gave up seeking my trust. It was natural that he did what he did. After the long awaited riddle was solved, I came back to the island. It's ironic that Sanguk's first letter drove me off the island and the second letter made me return."

"I want to hear those answers."

"Sure. I was about to tell you. It was nothing other than what Sanguk said in his letters—'common fate.' Despite the fact that we pursued our common fate in the name of freedom and the island's freedom, the lack of success was related to the gradual remission of the disease among the islanders. He didn't quite make the connection and wanted to ask me for an answer. But the answer was already there, inside his question. I realized that absolute trust was only possible between people in a similar position. It's easier to understand if you think about what he said about paradise. The reason for his refusal to accept my paradise—not accepting my motives—and his evaluation of my sincerity and concern as self-indulgent pity was because, ultimately, I wasn't going to share my life with the patients to the very end. Even after he left the island, Sanguk shared the same fate as the rest of the islanders. True love doesn't rescue just one side. It was only possible after accepting it in the name of common interest. That means even after the paradise was created, I couldn't leave it. Leaving after it had been created would mean that there could be no trust. Perhaps Elder Hwang knew this and that's why he didn't try to seek my trust. In any case, I realized this after I read his letters. That's why I was able to return to the island, with the determination to spend the rest of my life here. And to earn their trust..."

The wind that slid down through the pinewoods along the slope of Sipcha peak gently rattled the windows. The director remained quiet for a while as if he had reached a conclusion. He examined Chŏngt'ae's expression carefully. The dim light bulb made their red faces look strangely sad. Finally, Chŏngt'ae broke the silence. "Have you been able to earn their trust since you've come back? Since you began to share your life with them, have you been able to act both in the name of love and freedom within this greater idea of trust?"

As Chŏngt'ae expected, the director slowly shook his head and said, "No, it was another failure. As you saw today, those patients in the special wards...if true freedom and love existed on this island, the tragedy of those patients should've already disappeared. If it couldn't disappear completely, at least we should've done something to help them with their faith. But we're doing nothing for them. Haewŏn is another example. If true freedom and love existed on the island, he wouldn't have asked to be castrated before the wedding. We need to find a way to resolve this problem. Right now, the hospital is at a complete loss as to what to do. Haewŏn's request for the surgery and the hospital's inability to consent is not an expression of acting either in the name of love or in the name of freedom. It is another fierce battle. The rest of the patients are quietly waiting to see how this problem will be resolved. No matter what the outcome is, this is another failure. The Oma island project is still left hanging, and patients still risk their lives, attempting to escape by swimming across the strait."

"..."

"Perhaps Sanguk thinks differently. He always thought that all of this was my own personal failure, not the island's. By attributing everything to me as my personal failure, he tried to interpret this as the island and the islanders' victory. He said he would eventually return to the island but he hasn't. There's no sign of him so it's clear that he still can't accept me. The answer to what he wanted to ask me ended up being my return to the island. But his refusal to show up means he still can't accept me. His wish to make me fail has in fact succeeded perfectly. In his success, my ultimate failure was predetermined. In any case, the result is that the island's productivity is almost at a standstill."

"I don't understand. You returned to the island, earned their trust and shared their lives, but even after that you couldn't achieve anything in the name of freedom and love. Why is that?"

"I'm sure you're curious to know. Actually there's a very simple reason. I realized it soon after I returned to the island. I'm no longer director of the hospital. I came back as just another island resident."

"Does that make that much of a difference?"

"Of course. There was a big difference between love and freedom. After earning their trust, I was able to share their lives and together with them, act in the name of love and freedom. However, in either case—love or freedom—there has to be power first. Without power, love and freedom are nothing but empty words. You can't get love and freedom unless they're accompanied by power. Even if power is not the underlying principle of either love or freedom, it has to be the basis of both their practice and their realization. Based on the exercise of power, love and freedom can finally be valued equally. In short, what I'm saying is that sharing the same fate and earning each other's trust leads to this consciousness of common trust and faith. With that consciousness, freedom and love can assume their proper places in a powerful system of practice and, for the first time, be properly valued."

"So you're saying that you failed because you didn't return as director of the island? Since you could no longer rule with the power of the director, you were doomed to fail again?"

"Yes. As long as we don't share our lives, the strong force of order only produces an idol of power. Since I was determined to share my life with them, I needed the power to control. Freedom and love should have been practiced within this frank and open system on the island. But I was no longer the director."

"Then what about the present director? If he has this understanding of the island's fate and if he knew the secrets of your failure, couldn't he use his power to act in the name of love and freedom in the right manner and make it work?" Chŏngt'ae asked. He even forgot to empty his cup even though he would occasionally bring it to his lips during pauses in the conversation. The Director Cho had another negative answer.

"That's true. I often consult with the present director regarding the welfare of the island. He is very concerned and understands the island better than anyone else. But it's difficult for him—or for anybody for that matter—to share the lot of the islanders. Even if the present director is determined, it would be difficult. Elder Hwang and Sanguk knew that well. One can't simply choose to share another's future and become one with that person. One's fate is self-generating, it can't be added to simply because one wants it to be. That's why I'm doubtful if I can ever truly be one of them." The director now spoke in a mournful tone, frustrated with the situation. Chŏngt'ae shared a similar frustration.

"Then, are you saying that this island can never change, under any circumstances? There's nothing anyone can do about the island?" he asked accusingly, as if no longer able to bear it. But to Chŏngt'ae, the director seemed not to care. He accepted the accusations and the criticism. He spoke in a deep voice as if all his beliefs and past experiences had converged and now weighed heavily upon him.

"If destiny is self-generating, then the basis of power should be part of it. The director's power and position is bound to be considered one-sided regardless of the patients' fate and their choices..."

"Do you mean to say that the director should be chosen by the islanders from among themselves?"

"Of course. If not, it'll only make for selfish justification. Justifications were always covered by the pretext of serving power and authority. That was the primary reason why the island failed."

"Do you think that day will come?"

"I'm not sure whether it will come or not but it has to eventually. No matter how long it takes...perhaps it will take longer than anyone can imagine." The director took the cup again and drank. Chŏngt'ae was scared of him now and suddenly became frightened for the future of the island. He waited silently for the director to empty the cup and fill the empty one that sat in front of him. When he had, the director asked a question.

"Well, now do you understand why I had to repeat the failures one after another?" He seemed relieved now that he had explained everything. There was the hint of a strange smile about his lips.

"I think so. To a certain degree..." Chŏngt'ae nodded slowly without realizing it. Then, once again he asked cautiously, "Are you going to try to endure this and wait some more? Do you still have a reason to remain on the island after your repeated failures? Like you said, sharing a destiny is not as simple as one thinks." The director continued to smile a smile that revealed the desperation and determination of one who has failed repeatedly.

"Of course. I have to wait. Even if it's impossible for me to live as if I were one of them, I have at least earned a seed of their trust. I can't trample the seedling of their trust by leaving the island. I can wait as long as I have their trust and faith. No matter how small or insignificant this trust may be, I will wait until it grows to become as strong as a common fate...However long it takes, as long as we can accomplish something on the island, I can wait. Trust is the beginning of everything on this island."

"But you can't go on waiting forever!"

"Of course. I'm not simply going to wait. With their trust, there are many things to do here. However small and insignificant, we can all get together to make things happen. That's the way one expands trust. It's important to start from something that isn't visible. Something small that isn't visible for example is the union between a former patient and a healthy person."

"You mean Haewŏn and Miyŏn's marriage?"

"Since it's the first union of a former patient and a non-patient on the island, it's the first true link between healthy people and the patients. That's why I tried so hard to bring them together. The island needs a new beginning. It's possible to begin anew. That's the most important thing."

"..."

"From that point on, the patients will learn to become strong, to truly love and to enjoy freedom. I'm waiting patiently for the day when they'll be able to choose their own lives. I believe you'll be able to help accomplish this in the future..."

34

Finally it was the first of April, the day of Haewŏn and Miyŏn's wedding. It was a typically warm and sunny southern spring day as expected. The ochre roads that swirled around the mountains were festooned with cherry blossoms that had bloomed overnight like the first bars of a splendid symphony. The green of the barley fields celebrated the vitality of life, and the clouds floating above Sipcha peak were for once far higher than the pines on the summit. The emerald waters of Tŏknyang bay glistened under the glorious sun, as if the dark and gloom of the winter days had been lifted away.

The wedding was scheduled for noon. The church had been decorated to perfection the day before and the new couple's house had been cleaned and furnished. Just as the newlyweds wished, the honeymoon was to be replaced by a short visit to the Oma island reclamation site. Everything was in order and just as planned.

It had been especially fortunate that Director Cho had been able to persuade Haewŏn to give up being castrated, doubtlessly the result of the director and the islanders' attempt to work together as one. If Haewŏn had insisted on having the surgery it would have been yet more proof of the director's failure. The evening after Chŏngt'ae had arrived, the director had gone to see Haewŏn and had settled the matter.

"I promised him that the hospital would never

force anyone to be castrated again. The present director had already agreed to this. The hospital had trouble dealing with the unaffected children so they continued to recommend the surgery."

The director promised Haewŏn that the hospital would no longer make this recommendation and, in return, he couldn't request to have it again. He had asked to have the surgery in order to avoid selling the island out in the name of the lepers' children. It was somewhat of a contradiction that Haewŏn had exchanged his request for the complete abolition of the surgery. But, being familiar with the island's peculiar paradoxes, it was not difficult for the director to understand this. The present director knew well that the abolition of the surgery was a difficult and sensitive issue.

The custom of castration caused extreme anguish and grief among the patients. Was it in complete defiance of custom? Or was it his way of testing Miyŏn's faith? Even to this day, he thinks that Miyŏn is a normal healthy person, unaware that her parents were lepers. He, too, has a desire to have children. Perhaps he wanted to have his children in a better place...

The director told Chŏngt'ae that he and Miyŏn had agreed to keep her past a secret in order for Haewŏn to overcome his belief that only patients were able to live together. It was necessary if he was to gain more self-confidence. Then the director asked Chŏngt'ae to wish them happiness and encourage them in their proud union.

"By the way, I know it's your job to pry into other people's business. I'm going to tell you this now but please keep quiet about it. I don't want you to cause any trouble. Miyŏn was born and grew up on the island as an unaffected child. Please remember that nobody on this island, except Miyŏn and I know this. Neither Haewŏn nor any of the islanders know her secret. Please let Haewŏn and the islanders think this marriage is between a former patient and a non-patient."

With the director's understanding and his resoluteness, the wedding could take place. But because of the complications, the director didn't want Chŏngt'ae to meet the bride and the groom before the wedding.

On the wedding day, it was more peaceful and bright than the director and Chŏngt'ae had imagined possible. Everyone was busy getting ready for the ceremony. Nobody seemed to care at all about the stories about the wedding that had been whispered back and forth. It was a beautiful day and everyone's expression was unusually bright. From ten in the morning on, the streets from the personnel zone to Chungang village were crowded with hospital staff, patients accompanied by their families and mainlanders who had come for both the cherry blossoms and the wedding. There was a rumor that some provincial and district employees had come to the island as well. At the Kura inn, Chŏngt'ae met a couple of sports officials who were on the island as observers and several former leper patients who now held important positions. Among those who started out early were Miyŏn's foster parents. They didn't mention to anyone that Miyŏn was their adopted daughter. They looked like they were the proud parents of a daughter whom they loved very much. They left the inn early to lead the bride in.

Around eleven, Chŏngt'ae also began to get ready to leave the inn. There was no sign that the director had already left his house so he waited for a while for him to show up. Still there was no sign of him coming from the personnel zone. Those who came up from Chungang village had not seen him. There was no trace of the director among the group headed toward the church that included the present director.

Chŏngt'ae thought that was strange. He thought of heading to the church by himself but he decided to go over to the director's house. He should have been the first person to run to the church, so it was strange that he didn't show himself even as the time drew near.

When he passed the director's house, he was struck by a strange sight. A man was standing beside the wooden platform outside the director's room eavesdropping on what was happening inside. When he saw Chŏngt'ae walk into the yard, he gestured to him to be quiet, putting his finger to his lips. Chŏngt'ae thought at first that the man had come from the church to fetch the director, so he kept quiet. But he felt that he had seen him before. He thought very hard and realized that it was Yi Sanguk. He had returned to the island. Chŏngt'ae was perplexed by the fact that Sanguk had returned.

He was equally perplexed by the director's voice that he could hear coming from inside.

"...Lastly, as one of the islanders, I have a favor to ask of this newlywed couple." He said it as if he was giving a speech to a large audience. He was alone in his room.

"But before I ask it, I must confess that this wedding has a special, and quite wonderful, personal significance for me. I think most of you here still remember the day of the connecting ceremony for the Oma island reclamation project. I assume you thought then that the terribly long, hard work was over when we joined the ends of the embankments."

He was apparently practicing a congratulatory address he would give at the wedding. Sanguk who had gone to the director's house as soon as he set foot on the island, had listened to him practice his speech from outside and was drawn to it. The speech didn't seem like it would end any time soon. Sanguk listened with great interest and his expression was solemn and intense. It was a bizarre sight but Chŏngt'ae couldn't interfere since the director's speech was getting more and more passionate. He was also curious about it—as well as Sanguk's eavesdropping—so he decided to stay and listen. Indeed, he had no choice but to listen and wait. The director came to what seemed to be the main point of the speech. Both Chŏngt'ae and Sanguk listened quietly, like shameless intruders.

"As you may recall, I couldn't be here with you on the day of the connecting ceremony. I had to leave the island. The ceremony took place after I had left. I had longed to see the ceremony but I was extremely unfortunate. But my long-cherished dream has come true today with the marriage of Yun Haewŏn and Yi Miyŏn. Now another connecting ceremony is about to take place before my eyes. Perhaps one could say that a true connecting ceremony never took place. Even after the connecting ceremony took place, there was still no true connection. And because it wasn't really connected, Oma island couldn't function as had been intended. Now it's been abandoned and has no true owner."

He paused a while as if he was waiting for the reaction of his imaginary audience. Unable to predict what the director was going to say next, Sanguk's face froze. He stared through the door with such intensity that it seemed he was trying to pierce him straight through the heart. Unconscious of his actual audience of Sanguk and Chŏngt'ae, the director continued unhurriedly.

"The embankments of Oma island remained 'unconnected.' Why is that? The muddy embankments are connected, but the hearts of the people who need to walk over them remain unconnected. There is no point in talking about whose hearts aren't connected and whose fault it is that they remain unconnected. Let's not talk about failures. But we cannot deny that it remains unfinished. Looking at this situation, we might come to the conclusion that a union of hearts is much more important than the material connection of muddy embankments. In that sense, the marriage of Yun Haewŏn and Yi Miyŏn is a meaningful union of two people from two very different stations in life. The embankments, which were built by rock and soil and only exist as physical entities, are only today being truly connected before our eyes. Especially since I missed the earlier ceremony, I feel quite fortunate and thankful..."

Sanguk's face, which had been tense, began to

relax and he wore a faint smile. Yet Chŏngt'ae could not read the meaning behind his smile. Either he had been moved by the director's direct and pure thinking or he was jeering at his pathetic ambition. Unaware of the reaction outside, the director cleared his throat. He raised his voice once again and slowly continued his speech frankly and resolutely.

He talked about how it was unnecessary to prohibit talking about this unusual marriage between a former patient and a healthy person as if it were taboo. He expressed his sincere gratitude to the bride and groom for their courage, building strong embankments with their marriage. Then he raised his voice.

"Still, the bridge these two people have built before our eyes is only the beginning. It's too fragile to stand against the tremendous waves of prejudice and convention that surround us. It's our duty to make this stronger so that it won't get swept away by these ugly waves. Whether present here today or not, whether healthy or diseased, we all need to assume the same responsibility: accept the will of God. As you did with the Oma island project, you must make this embankment thicker and stronger little by little by giving to it of all your hearts. Only then will the abandoned, reclaimed land become completely ours. Whether or not our dream can be realized on Oma island or not, whether you can be owners of the land or not, we can fully enjoy the new path inside our hearts that's been laid before us. It's said that God only helps those who help themselves. Only after we've built a strong community can we wait for others to join us and only then will we be able to witness the comings and goings of our new neighbors."

The wedding must have already started, but there was no sign that the director was finishing his rehearsal. Sanguk, unbudging, still wore that mysterious smile. Perhaps there would be many latecomers. People from the mainland who had come to see the wedding were still passing through the cherry blossom trees in droves heading toward the church in Chungang village. They were late for the wedding too.

The director was so caught up in his own speech that he completely forgot about being late.

"Now I ask of you two this favor," and he began

to talk about the favor he wanted to ask of Haewŏn and Miyŏn.

"I want to ask you to preserve and maintain the embankments you have joined with your courage and love. There are still so many bridges of love and faith that need to be built, and walls to be torn down. There are many places where two different villages need to become one, creating a peaceful and harmonious place to live. The reason for situating your new house between the patients' zone and the personnel zone was so that the two areas could be linked as one. I hope that with your house as a starting point the two areas will soon be linked. I pray that your place will turn into a new village, making this island one, without borders separating the patients and the healthy. You have made this new bridge possible, opening a new path so that now your neighbors will travel across it freely. These neighbors will help maintain it and buttress it to keep and broaden the path..."

GREEN INTEGER
Pataphysics and Pedantry

Douglas Messerli, *Publisher*

Essays, Manifestos, Statements, Speeches, Maxims, Epistles, Diaristic Notes, Narratives, Natural Histories, Poems, Plays, Performances, Ramblings, Revelations and all such ephemera as may appear necessary to bring society into a slight tremolo of confusion and fright at least.

MASTERWORKS OF FICTION

Masterworks of Fiction is a program of Green Integer to reprint important works of fiction from all centuries. We make no claim to any superiority of these fictions over others in either form or subject, but rather we contend that these works are highly enjoyable to read and, more importantly, have challenged the ideas and language of the times in which they were published, establishing themselves over the years as among the outstanding works of their period. By republishing both well known and lesser recognized titles in this series we hope to continue our mission bringing our society into a slight tremolo of confusion and fright at least.

BOOKS IN THIS SERIES

José Donoso *Hell Has No Limits* (1966)
Knut Hamsun *A Wanderer Plays on Muted Strings* (1909)
Raymond Federman *The Twofold Vibration* (1982)
Gertrude Stein *To Do: A Book of Alphabets and Birthdays* (1957)
Gérard de Nerval *Aurélia* (1855)
Tereza Albues *Pedra Canga* (1987)

Arno Schmidt *The School for Atheists: A Novella= Comedy in 6 Acts* (1972)
Sigurd Hoel *Meeting at the Milestone* (1947)
Leslie Scalapino *Defoe* (1994)
Charles Dickens *A Christmas Carol* (1843)
Anthony Powell *O, How the Wheel Becomes It!* (1983)
Ole Sarvig *The Sea Below My Window* (1960)
Michael Disend *Stomping the Goyim* (1969)
Anthony Powell *Venusberg* (1932)
Jean Frémon *Island of the Dead* (1994)
Arthur Schnitzler *Lieutenant Gustl* (1900)
Andreas Embiricos *Amour Amour* (1960)
Toby Olson *Utah* (1987)
Knut Hamsun *The Last Joy* (1912)
Arthur Schnitzler *Dream Story* (1926)
Mohammed Dib *LA Trip* (2002)
Gertrude Stein *Three Lives* (1909)
William Carlos Williams *The Great American Novel* (1923)
Yi Ch'ŏngjun *Your Paradise* (1976)

*

Green Integer Books

1 Gertrude Stein *History, or Messages from History* ISBN: 1-55713-354-9 $5.95
2 Robert Bresson *Notes on the Cinematographer* ISBN: 1-55713-365-4 $8.95
3 Oscar Wilde *The Critic As Artist* ISBN: 1-55713-368-9 $9.95
4 Henri Michaux *Tent Posts* ISBN: 1-55713-328-X $10.95
5 Edgar Allan Poe *Eureka: A Prose Poem* ISBN: 1-55713-329-8 $10.95
6 Jean Renoir *An Interview* ISBN: 1-55713-330-1 $9.95
7 Marcel Cohen *Mirrors* ISBN: 1-55713-313-1 $12.95

8 Christopher Spranger *The Effort to Fall* ISBN: 1-892295-00-8 $8.95
9 Arno Schmidt *Radio Dialogs I* ISBN: 1-892295-01-6 $12.95
10 Hans Christian Andersen *Travels* ISBN: 1-55713-344-1 $12.95
11 Christopher Middleton *In the Mirror of the Eighth King*
ISBN: 1-55713-331-X $9.95
12 James Joyce *On Ibsen* ISBN: 1-55713-372-7 $8.95
13 Knut Hamsun *A Wanderer Plays on Muted Strings*
ISBN: 1-892295-73-3 $10.95
14 Henri Bergson *Laughter: An Essay on the Meaning of the Comic*
ISBN: 1-892295-02-4 $11.95
15 Michel Leiris *Operratics* ISBN: 1-892295-03-2 $12.95
16 Sergei Paradjanov *Seven Visions* ISBN: 1-892295-04-0 $12.95
17 Hervé Guibert *Ghost Image* ISBN: 1-892295-05-9 $10.95
18 Louis-Ferdinand Céline *Ballets without Music, without Dancers, without Anything* ISBN: 1-892295-06-7 $10.95
19 Gellu Naum *My Tired Father* ISBN: 1-892295-07-5 $8.95
20 Vicente Huidobro *Manifest Manifestos* ISBN: 1-892295-08-3 $12.95
21 Gérard de Nerval *Aurélia* ISBN: 1-892295-46-6 $11.95
22 Knut Hamsun *On Overgrown Paths* ISBN: 1-892295-10-5 $12.95
23 Martha Ronk *Displeasures of the Table* ISBN: 1-892295-44-X $9.95
24 Mark Twain *What Is Man?* ISBN: 1-892295-15-6 $10.95
25 Antonio Porta *Metropolis* ISBN: 1-892295-12-1 $10.95
26 Sappho *Poems* ISBN: 1-892295-13-X $10.95
27 Alexei Kruchenykh *Suicide Circus: Selected Poems*
ISBN: 1-892295-27-X $12.95
28 José Donoso *Hell Has No Limits* ISBN: 1-892295-14-8 $10.95
29 Gertrude Stein *To Do: Alphabets and Birthdays*
ISBN: 1-892295-16-4 $9.95
30 Joshua Haigh [Douglas Messerli] *Letters from Hanusse*
ISBN: 1-892295-30-X $12.95
31 Federico García Lorca *Suites* ISBN: 1-892295-61-X $12.95
32 Tereza Albues *Pedra Canga* ISBN: 1-892295-70-9 $12.95
33 Rae Armantrout *The Pretext* ISBN: 1-892295-39-3 $9.95

34 Nick Piombino *Theoretical Objects* ISBN: 1-892295-23-7 $10.95
35 Yang Lian *Yi* ISBN: 1-892295-68-7 $14.95
36 Olivier Cadiot *Art Poetic'* ISBN: 1-892295-22-9 $12.95
37 Andrée Chedid *Fugitive Suns: Selected Poems*
ISBN: 1-892295-25-3 $11.95
38 Hsi Muren *Across the Darkness of the River*
ISBN: 1-931243-24-7 $9.95
39 Lyn Hejinian *My Life* ISBN: 1-931243-33-6 $10.95
40 Hsu Hui-cheh *Book of Reincarnation* ISBN: 1-931243-32-8 $9.95
41 Henry David Thoreau *Civil Disobedience* ISBN: 1-892295-93-8 $6.95
42 Gertrude Stein *Mexico: A Play* ISBN: 1-892295-36-9 $5.95
43 Lee Breuer *La Divina Caricatura: A Fiction*
ISBN: 1-931243-39-5 $14.95
44 Régis Bonvicino *Sky Eclipse: Selected Poems*
ISBN: 1-892295-34-2 $9.95
45 Raymond Federman *The Twofold Vibration*
ISBN: 1-892295-29-6 $11.95
46 Tom La Farge *Zuntig* ISBN: 1-931243-06-9 $13.95
47 *The Song of Songs: Shir Hashirim* ISBN: 1-931243-05-0 $9.95
48 Rodrigo Toscano *The Disparities* ISBN: 1-931243-25-5 $9.95
49 Else Lasker-Schüler *Selected Poems* ISBN: 1-892295-86-5 $11.95
50 Gertrude Stein *Tender Buttons* ISBN: 1-931243-42-5 $10.95
51 Armand Gatti *Two Plays: The 7 Possibilities for Train 713*
Departing from Auschwitz and *Public Songs*
Before Two Electric Chairs ISBN: 1-931243-28-X $14.95
52 César Vallejo *Aphorisms* ISBN: 1-931243-00-X $9.95
53 Ascher/Straus *ABC Street* ISBN: 1-892295-85-7 $10.95
54 Djuna Barnes *The Antiphon* ISBN: 1-892295-56-3 $12.95
55 Tiziano Rossi *People on the Run* ISBN: 1-931243-37-9 $12.95
56 Michael Disend *Stomping the Goyim* ISBN: 1-931243-10-7 $11.95
57 Hagiwara Sakutarō *Howling at the Moon: Poems and Prose*
ISBN: 1-931243-01-8 $11.95
58 Rainer Maria Rilke *Duino Elegies* ISBN: 1-931243-07-7 $10.95

59 OyamO *The Resurrection of Lady Lester* ISBN: 1-892295-51-2 $8.95
60 Charles Dickens *A Christmas Carol* ISBN: 1-931243-18-2 $8.95
61 Mac Wellman *Crowtet I: Murder of Crow* and *The Hyacinth Macaw*
ISBN: 1-892295-52-0 $11.95
62 Mac Wellman *Crowtet II: Second-hand Smoke* and
The Lesser Magoo ISBN: 1-931243-71-9 $11.95
63 Pedro Pietri *The Masses Are Asses* ISBN: 1-892295-62-8 $8.95
64 Luis Buñuel *The Exterminating Angel* ISBN: 1-931243-36-0 $11.95
65 Paul Snoek *Hercules, Richelieu,* and *Nostradamus*
ISBN: 1-892295-42-3 $10.95
66 Eleanor Antin *The Man without a World: A Screenplay*
ISBN: 1-892295-81-4 $10.95
67 Dennis Phillips *Sand* ISBN: 1-931243-43-3 $10.95
68 María Irene Fornes *Abingdon Square* ISBN: 1-892295-64-4 $9.95
69 Anthony Powell *O, How the Wheel Becomes It!*
ISBN: 1-931243-23-9 $10.95
70 Julio Matas, Carlos Felipe and Virgilio Piñera
Three Masterpieces of Cuban Drama
ISBN: 1-892295-66-0 $12.95
71 Kelly Stuart *Demonology* ISBN: 1-892295-58-x $9.95
72 Ole Sarvig *The Sea Below My Window* ISBN: 1-892295-79-2 $13.95
73 Vítězslav Nezval *Antilyrik and Other Poems*
ISBN: 1-892295-75-x $10.95
74 Sam Eisenstein *Rectification of Eros* ISBN: 1-892295-37-7 $10.95
75 Arno Schmidt *Radio Dialogs* II ISBN: 1-892295-80-6 $13.95
76 Murat Nemat-Nejat *The Peripheral Space of Photography*
ISBN: 1-892295-90-3 $9.95
77 Adonis *If Only the Sea Could Sleep: Love Poems*
ISBN: 1-931243-29-8 $11.95
78 Stephen Ratcliffe *SOUND/(system)* ISBN: 1-931243-35-2 $12.95
79 Dominic Cheung *Drifting* ISBN: 1-892295-71-7 $9.95
80 Gilbert Sorrentino *Gold Fools* ISBN: 1-892295-67-9 $14.95
81 Paul Celan *Romanian Poems* ISBN: 1-892295-41-5 $10.95

82 Elana Greenfield *At the Damascus Gate: Short Hallucinations* ISBN: 1-931243-49-2 $10.95
83 Anthony Powell *Venusberg* ISBN: 1-892295-24-5 $10.95
84 Jean Frémon *Island of the Dead* ISBN: 1-931243-31-X $12.95
85 Arthur Schnitzler *Lieutenant Gustl* ISBN: 1-931243-46-8 $9.95
86 Wilhelm Jenson *Gradiva* Sigmund Freud *Delusion and Dream in Wilhelm Jensen's Gradiva* ISBN: 1-892295-89-X $13.95
87 Andreas Embirikos *Amour, Amour* ISBN: 1-931243-26-3 $11.95
89 Kier Peters *A Dog Tries to Kiss The Sky 7 Short Plays* ISBN: 1-931243-30-1 $12.95
90 Knut Hamsun *The Last Joy* ISBN: 1-931243-19-0 $12.95
91 Paul Verlaine *The Cursed Poets* ISBN: 1-931243-15-8 $11.95
92 Toby Olson *Utah* ISBN: 1-892295-35-0 $12.95
93 Sheila E. Murphy *Letters to Unfinished J.* ISBN: 1-931243-59-X $10.95
94 Arthur Schnitzler *Dream Story* ISBN: 1-931243-48-4 $11.95
95 Henrik Nordbrandt *The Hangman's Lament: Poems* $10.95
96 André Breton *Arcanum 17* ISBN: 1-931243-27-1 $12.95
97 Joseph Conrad *Heart of Darkness* ISBN: 1-892295-49-0 $10.95
98 Mohammed Dib *L.A. Trip: A Novel in Verse* ISBN: 1-931243-54-9 $11.95
99 Mario Luzi *Earthly and Heavenly Journey of Simone Martini* ISBN: 1-931243-53-0 $12.95
101 Jiao Tung *Erotic Recipes: A Complete Menu for Male Potency Enhancement* ISBN: 1-892295-84-9 $8.95
103 Chen I-chi *The Mysterious Hualien* ISBN: 1-931243-14-X $9.95
105 William Carlos Williams *The Great American Novel* ISBN: 1-931243-52-2 $10.95
108 Francis Carco *Streetcorners* ISBN: 1-931243-63-8 $12.95
109 Thomas Mann *Six Early Stories* ISBN: 1-892295-74-1 $10.95
110 Mark Wallace *Temporary Worker Rides a Subway* ISBN: 1-931243-60-3 $9.95

114 Fiona Templeton *Delirium of Interpretations*
ISBN: 1-892295-55-5 $10.95
117 Deborah Meadows *Representing Absence*
ISBN: 1-931243-77-8 $9.95
118 Yi Ch'ŏngjun *Your Paradise* ISBN: 1-931243-69-7 $13.95
126 Ingeborg Bachmann *Letters to Felician* ISBN: 1-931243-16-6 $9.95
129 Norberto Luis Romero *The Arrival of Autumn in Constantinople*
ISBN: 1-892295-91-1 $12.95

Green Integer EL-E-PHANT Books (6 x 9 format)

EL-1 Douglas Messerli, ed. *The PIP Anthology of World Poetry of the 20th Century, Volume 1* ISBN: 1-892295-47-4 $15.95
EL-2 Douglas Messerli, ed. *The PIP Anthology of World Poetry of the 20th Century, Volume 2* ISBN: 1-892295-94-6 $15.95
EL-3 Régis Bonvicino, Michael Palmer, and Nelson Ascher, eds.; revised and reedited by Douglas Messerli *The PIP Anthology of World Poetry of the 20th Century, Volume 3: Nothing the Sun Could Not Explain—20 Contemporary Brazilian Poets* ISBN: 1-931243-04-2 $15.95
EL-4 Douglas Messerli, ed. *The PIP Anthology of World Poetry of the 20th Century, Volume 4* ISBN: 1-892295-87-3 $15.95
EL-51 Larry Eigner *readiness / enough / depends / on*
ISBN: 1-892295-53-9 $12.95
EL-52 Martin Nakell *Two Fields That Face and Mirror Each Other*
ISBN: 1-892295-97-0 $16.95
EL-53 Arno Schmidt *The School for Atheists: A Novella=Comedy in 6 Acts* ISBN: 1-892295-96-2 $16.95
EL-54 Sigurd Hoel *Meeting at the Milestone*
ISBN: 1-892295-31-8 $15.95
EL-55 Leslie Scalapino *Defoe* ISBN: 1-931243-44-1 $14.95
EL-56 Sam Eisenstein *Cosmic Cow* ISBN: 1-931243-45-x $16.95